CATCHING THE LIGHT

Catching the Light

Anna Fox

JANUS PUBLISHING COMPANY LTD
Cambridge, England

First published in Great Britain 2018
by Janus Publishing Company Ltd
The Studio
High Green
Great Shelford
Cambridge CB22 5EG

www.januspublishing.co.uk

Copyright © Anna Fox 2018
British Library Cataloguing-in-Publication Data
A catalogue record for this book is available from the British Library

ISBN 978-1-85756-876-9

Cover Design: Janus Publishing Company Ltd

Cover Image: Painted by Anna Fox

Printed and bound in the UK
by KnowledgePoint Limited, Reading.

Chapter One

'They said *what?*' Patrick lost speed in the overtaking lane. '*Sent to fetch you!* I don't like the look of this.' He regained speed, composed his face and leaned over to touch her hand. 'Not to worry, we'll get to the bottom of it.'

Warm air blew in at her window, and vineyards growing alongside flat fields of new sunflowers spread lavishly for miles – but Patrick was unable to pass on to another subject.

'Look, Rose, I'm sorry about this, and I blame myself entirely: I should never have been late to fetch you, but I'm obviously going to have to pass this on to Sacchetti. Can you bear to go through it again in a bit more – well, you know – detail?' His brows came together again as he flashed a glance at her. 'A white car, you say?'

'Yes. They drove up and got out so quickly, I thought they must be late for their flight.'

Shall I say how strong they smelt? Rose wondered. She smelt powdery and he was dirty, but there was another smell: fear. She recognised it.

'You didn't happen to notice the number plate?'

'There wasn't time, he grabbed my case to put in the boot. The boot was full of greasy old farm machinery.'

'Well, *that's* worth remembering. What did they look like?'

'He was short with bushy eyebrows, incredibly strong, and she was tall and thin and – well, a bit bizarre; she had white gloves and matching sunglasses that came to points – and she wheedled.'

'Wheedled?'

'Well, she was impatient: twisting her body into funny shapes to, sort of, coax me into the car without actually pushing me in. "Il Centra

1

D'Arte sent us to fetch you, signora. Please be so good as to get in.'"
Rose mimicked a rough dialect of southern Italy.

'She called you signora! A young girl like you? How would she know
you were a married woman?' Patrick was caught short; he glanced at her
two or three times to gauge her feelings. 'A widow, in fact.' Again, his
hand came out to touch hers.

It was a small acknowledgement, but it was enough: now she knew
he was thinking of her, and that he understood why she'd come back.

She said, 'Yes, but the woman seemed to know who *you* were. You
drove up when I was trying to stop him shutting my bag in the boot.
Huh! They couldn't get back into the car quick enough. I got my bag
out, though – I wasn't going to let them get away with my bag. They
drove off with the boot open.'

'You did well, Rose, you stood your ground. But now look, I know
why you've come, but I'm determined you should try and live as normal
a life as you can while you're here; the light is marvellously clear, it's
crying out for a paintbrush. Yes, of course we have to take this wretched
business with the white car seriously, but from now on, you're going to
leave the worrying to me.'

Rose allowed herself to relax back into her seat and rest her eyes on
the formal geometry of fields that blended, and finally blurred, into the
distant foothills of Monte Pisano. 'Don't forget to bring your paints,'
Patrick had said in a last-minute call just as she was leaving, and until
that moment she hadn't given it a thought. So, before she set out, she'd
grabbed it: the yellow canvas satchel with all her paints.

Up in the blue a hawk was drifting. Rose watched it in its slow solitary
suspension, the sun hot on its back and warm air pressing up through
its breast feathers; nothing in its brain, she thought, but a picture of
the valley below criss-crossed with swallows. She stayed watching as it
entered the last wide arc that took it back to the hills and out of sight.

Her head fell forward and a dizzy spell unbalanced her. She felt for
the tree and sank against it, where she stayed until the bark against her
forehead made an imprint. The wood was cool but out there the field
had turned into an oven. In the field, on the other hand, everything
was packed – all she had to do was pick it up and go. There was nothing

to stop her. Except that she'd left her hat on the stool which meant walking back over the baking stubble to get it. Worse still, she'd be too hot then to carry her stuff – that heavy stuff – all the way up the track again with only the hat for shade. She pictured her water bottle trickling condensation. She was desperate for it, just to wet her mouth and throat, not too much.

Rose stepped back into a carpet of dry leaves and felt a line of thorns tear across the skin of her leg. As she bent to look she heard a disturbance in the undergrowth: twigs cracked and a bird flew up. She raised her head to listen.

Pressing further into the tree, scanning the oaks and brambles, looking for the sway of a branch or a deflection of light, she waited. Nothing, not a single movement. Even the insects must be resting in the heat. Yet the rustling and splintering was getting closer; it was growing into a steadily advancing commotion. Boar? Armpits and groin were suddenly wet.

Then, in the low brush, isolated quivers caught her eye: Almost certainly a wild pig, several maybe. They seemed to be making a winding furrow towards her. At a few feet distance, when the procession veered round towards the path, she glimpsed what she was looking for: the dark bristles of a boar followed by small streaky bodies nudging and jostling. It must be a sow and her young. The little ones were in rough single file snuffling through brambles and stumbling into gullies, creating a chaotic eddy in the mother's wake.

She knew she was too close to them. Hammers of blood pumped through her ears, cutting out sound. About five feet away from her, the sow stopped at the edge of the track and paused in a camouflage of acacia. Her ears twitched before they stiffened into a forward thrust, and a shaft of sun picked up a vein under the hairs. A cloud of insects she'd thrown up swarmed briefly around her head. She seemed to have her eye on two butterflies, a brilliant blue, darting around a few inches above a puddle in the path. Behind her the little pigs had come to a halt.

Rose jumped as leaves and branches shuddered. The sow launched herself out of the covert and made for the opposite bank. She cantered across the puddle leaving a flurry of cleft prints in the sand, and rushed up into the undulating thicket on the other side. Her family of young tumbled after her splashing and bouncing like a broken necklace in sudden release. The last one barged through the newly forged tunnel, leaving behind one of the butterflies churning in the murky water.

Rose collapsed so heavily onto her stool back in the field, she wondered if she might have cracked it. I'm actually shaking, she said under her breath, and used the skirt of her dress to wipe the sweat from her face. My paints are packed, I must go. But the tepid water from her bottle had made her feel better and the burnished field lay all around her: the barn, the village on the hill, the luminous shadows pitting the ground, all transformed by the new angle of the sinking sun. A coolness spread inwards from the surface of her skin. Heat seemed to have transformed to energy. I can't go now, she told herself. The shadows are changing colour, a miracle is taking place; the light's too good, my head is clear.

Picking up the sketch pad Rose surveyed her two watercolours. Dull. Did she care? Incredibly, not. Instead she looked at the blank paper and felt that age-old slippery panic that always seized her before she made her first brush stroke. The light was changing; she must get going. She poured a little water and selected a brush.

It took her twenty minutes, and then she knew she was finished. The field, the barn, and in the distance, rising like a mirage in the heat, Montecalmo. She had it, and there it was, that papery light surrounding the barn. She could still do it.

A soldier ant ran over her bare toe, in fact there were dozens of them swarming over her apple core, and the blood on her leg was attracting a fly. She wiped it with the back of her hand and licked off the blood. That was a mistake; she should have left it to congeal. And now she was going to have to lug all her painting stuff back up the same stony track she came down on. She didn't mind. A pleasurable itch suffused her muscles and she arched her back and looked at her watch. The minibus from Pisa was due.

Then she froze, not daring to breathe. The family of boar from the wood behind her were feeding so close, she fancied she could smell them: the young ones with their snouts in the earth, the sow cleaning oats off the stems around her. Rose inched up slowly to observe them better, and the water jar tipped over, hitting a stone. She heard a low aborted squeal as the sow's head shot up for a split second to look her in the eye. Instantly the pig was charging back into the woods flanked by her young. Simultaneously, a young boar crashed out of the tall grasses and came to a dead stop directly ahead of her. It confronted her head-on, its bristles stiff and glistening in the sun, animal eyes fixed in wrinkled sockets. Two thick little tusks stuck out like teeth. It hesitated on the brink of resolution, and a trickle of fear ran from Rose's chest and pierced her loins. As she lost sensation in her thighs, a rifle shot seared through the afternoon, and the wild animal fell on its side kicking and squealing. Rose screamed No! with her hands clapped to her ears. A second shot followed, and the boar lay still, a spot of blood below its ear. A young huntsman was striding through the field towards her in high leather boots shouting something.

'Bastard,' she screamed at him.

'Are you mad? It was ready to attack you,' he shouted. 'You are English, you do not belong here.' He gestured towards the hill village, still shouting. 'You stay up there to paint your pictures.'

'You needn't have killed it.' She was hysterical.

'You know nothing, nothing! Look at you! Don't you know you must wear boots down here? There are snakes.'

'*Lasciami.* Piss off.' Rose's legs gave way. She collapsed onto the stool and wiped her drenched cheeks with the paint rag. The huntsman picked up the sketch pad, turned to compare the painting she'd just finished to the landscape behind him and flashed her a look followed by a nod.

After a few moments, she bent to search for her bottle of drinking water, her hand shaking. The bottle weighed a ton, she couldn't lift it.

'I can help you to carry your *pittura*.'

'I'm staying here.' She was barely audible, even to herself.

He shrugged elaborately and replaced her pad on the scrubby grass near her feet. Rose was arrested by his arm. It was familiar. She stared at the mahogany skin, and a half-savoured connection hovered just out of reach. She shuddered and felt her face flood with warmth and with it a rush of strength. She quickly unscrewed the water bottle.

'Look at me!' he demanded.

He was demonstrating to her, stamping his boots into the sparse field. 'When you are walking, you are telling the snake you are coming. You are making a very big noise. You are saying, I am here, okay? Wake up, it's time to go.'

His posturing made her ears buzz. 'I *know* all that,' she said, tipping the water bottle against her lips and drinking. Out of the corner of her eye she saw that he was still standing over her glaring at her sandalled feet and breathing, bull-like.

At last, slowly, he wandered over to the dead boar and nudged it with his boot. Then, as he pushed up his sleeves and unleashed the rope she examined his arms, and still the sight stirred her, but more obscurely than before. She concentrated on the rope. Over and over he wove it in a figure of eight around the dark trotters, taking his time, carefully almost, as if the carcase might feel the knots. The dead animal was rolled and shifted over the prickly grass. She closed her eyes to it and waited.

He was done. He grasped the woven rope and swung the heavy kill onto his shoulders, staggering under the weight. Slowly the boar's head jutted back as he straightened. Drops of blood fell from its open mouth missing the blue checked shirt, but flecking the cotton khakis covering his buttocks. With a slow striving trudge, the stranger made his way across the fields. Rose watched and waited for him to turn back and acknowledge her, but he reached the unmade track without looking back, and then was lost to sight.

II Centro seemed to be deserted but Rose guessed they'd all arrived and were busy unpacking. There was a strong smell of garlic: dinner was under way, they were safely upstairs. Now was the time to do it. She crossed the cool flags and ran halfway up the steps to the telephone. It was fixed in an alcove in the wall, scarcely big enough to squeeze into with her painting satchel and stool. Quickly she dialled, before it was too late to change her mind.

'Mama? It's Rose.'

Silence. Rose had a picture of the slightly bulbous, half-hooded eyes of her mother-in-law. Had Augustina lost much weight since it happened?

'Mama, are you there? Mama, it's alright, please don't be angry, I had to come back.'

She waited.

'Say something to me.'

A scuffling came through the receiver, together with a small metallic tap. And then at last the slow, measured voice of her mother-in-law.

'How long will you stay?'

Rose wiped cold sweat from her face. A volatile swill of nausea chilled the surface of her skin, and now she was swallowing constantly to control the flow of moisture in her mouth. Fear and pity for Augustina rushed in. Day after day following Dodo's death, spent on her knees in prayer till the candles burnt out. Did she have anyone to turn to now? Did she need human sympathy when she had her God?

'Just for a couple of weeks, I'm at Il Centro,' she managed to say.

'Why are you here?'

'Why? Well, to see you. And ... to talk a little more about Dodo.'

This time there was an interminable pause. She clamped her jaw and tried to breathe evenly.

'Tomorrow at eleven? Thank you, Mama. *Ci vediamo domani.*'

The receiver fell from her hand and she leaned over, feeling the sweat from her forehead trickle down her temple. It was all coming back: the numbness, the blinding fright, the lurching stomach. She supported her head against the cubicle wall.

A door slammed upstairs and she heard an explosion of laughter. And now the urge to get herself up to her room was so strong, it almost carried her there; in her haste, she stumbled halfway up the cold stone steps and slammed her satchel against the wall. Slowly, she straightened up as two girls burst down the steps with a clatter. The one in front stopped dead when she saw Rose and the one behind almost fell into her, still laughing.

'Hullo – Oh.' It was the one in front. 'Are you alright?'

'Yes. Fine.' Rose nodded reassuringly.

A spasm of doubt passed across the girl's face before the one behind her ducked sideways to make herself visible.

'We're Phoebe and Dill,' she said, beaming broadly.

'We're looking for a loo,' said the first one with an almost identical smile.

'Who are you?' the other one asked, tucking her hair behind her ear and leaning forward as if she may not catch what Rose said.

'I'm Rose. And – and, it's past the payphone and straight on.'

'What? Oh, thanks.' They both looked disconcerted, but began to make their way, not quite ready to leave. Suddenly one of them threw a wide smile over her shoulder. 'See you at dinner then!' And all at once there was a cascade as sandals clipped the steps like a falling house of cards as they rushed on.

Rose opened her bedroom door and went straight to the tiny window and struggled with the latch; the shutter pushed open and banged against the wall.

And here she was again. She could see for miles around: a panorama of hills stretching away to distant mountains. She leant out, the better to see the patchwork of fields and woods touched by the late afternoon sun. Her throat constricted and tears clouded her vision. Breathing in a long unsteady breath, she wondered how many times she had tried to paint this. She heard a cuckoo down in the valley and noisily, luxuriously, inhaled another mighty breath; then, turning with her back to the window, she examined her room.

Primitive: a paint-smeared table under the window, two kitchen chairs with rush seats, a battered unstained wardrobe tilting forward on sloping floorboards, and an old mirror, densely opaque, above the bed. They'd asked if she wanted her old room back – the one with a luminous green light from the wisteria – far too romantic; quickly she'd asked for a bedroom at the top. Memories would come whether she liked it or not, but she wasn't going to make it easy for them. She sat on the bed, narrow and iron framed, and poked the mattress: horsehair. Everything she wanted: simple, basic, wiped clean of association – except for the view from the window, and that was her solace.

Now she would unpack.

There was a knock on the door. Rose stopped in her tracks as it swung open and an older girl walked in. 'Mind if I have a look?' She paused as she appraised the room 'Oh very Van Gogh!' she said, raising heavily accented eyebrows.

'Isn't your room like this?' Rose asked. She felt her cheeks burning.

'No,' she said, 'I'm afraid it's rather civilised. It's a Bonnard, without the clutter if you know what I mean; there's a bathroom attached.' She fingered the old mirror between the beds with sudden interest.

Rose struggled with a wave of annoyance (was it normal to march in like this?) as she watched this tall person heading for the window, her cropped hair as sleek as the handle of an ebony cane. Sweeping past the proffered chair, she left Rose behind and lifted two elegantly bony arms for support against the window frame, effectively embracing the hills and sky.

Her voice was emphatic and strong. 'I haven't got a view like this, mine overlooks the square.' She stood gazing at the valley for a moment before turning back, arms briskly folded, chin tilting up suddenly.

'Isolda Seagram.' Her name hung like a banner between them.

'Oh,' Rose said, 'hullo. I'm Rose Pazzi.'

There was a sudden stillness in Isolda; everything seemed to stop as she stared at Rose unseeingly. Rose searched for something to say – had her name meant something to her? At last she said, 'Have you met our tutor, Patrick?'

Isolda relaxed, her arms falling at her side, breathing as if she'd just raced upstairs two at a time. She grimaced. 'Bit of an old fogy.'

How could this girl get it so wrong! Patrick! Rose thought of the broad, attractive man who was her mentor, her father-figure; she could hardly believe that she was talking about the same person.

'Well, you have to wonder what sort of a teacher he'll make. It's not going to be "cutting edge" exactly, is it?' Isolda went on.

For once Rose was unable to say a word; surely age and experience counted for something? This woman with her air of authority must have heard of Patrick, even if she hadn't seen his work. An old fogy – it was outrageous. And she couldn't even find the words to defend him; she was helpless, floundering – and now she was fighting to hide her tears. How much did this person, Isolda, know about painting, after all, and what was she expecting? Obviously she wasn't here to learn, nobody wants to learn from an old fogy. Was there a remote possibility that she was some sort of an expert, and was *right* about Patrick? Rose refused to believe it; and yet the horrible suspicion had been planted. There was something wrong.

But Isolda's attention was diverted. Her eye seemed to be caught by something on the terrace below. She stiffened for a moment before turning away from the window, her chest rising and falling.

'Time for a good long soak in the bath, I think,' she said sharply, looking up, then abruptly strode to the door; but as she grasped the handle she turned back as if remembering where she was. Inclining her head with almost oriental politeness, she said, 'You must come and see my room some time,' before closing the door behind her.

Rose heard her footsteps go halfway down the passage, pause, and then come back. The door snapped open.

This time Isolda's attitude was friendly – too friendly, Rose thought, it was peculiar. 'I'm quite willing to exchange my room for yours if you want a closer bathroom, by the way.'

'Oh, no,' Rose replied. 'I mean – it's kind of you, but I like the view!'

And then she was gone.

Rose crumpled onto the bed. She had a picture of the telephone receiver dangling on its cord. Had she put it back? She covered her face with her hands. '*Why are you here?*' She was seeing Augustina tomorrow at 11 o'clock. Nausea threatened to take a hold again, the flesh beneath her skin swarmed. But it didn't do her a bit of good to go back over it again.

She sighed deeply and frowned at her suitcase next to the bed, still not unpacked. She would go and see her mother-in-law tomorrow and pay her respects. She wouldn't stay long, just long enough for Augustina to get used to her, and then, maybe, there would be a little space for some questions. And here Rose stopped short of thinking of anything other than Augustina's sorrowful, empty eyes. She would unpack her bag in her new bedroom. That was all for now.

She bent to haul her suitcase onto the bed and snap open the clasps. A pack of dogs howled out from across the valley. Hunting. It was early evening: boar would be out foraging. Quickly she went to the window.

A few feet below her, the terrace was showing signs of life. Isolda had seemed shocked by something out here, she couldn't think why. If Rose leant over to her right she was able to see the long tables set for dinner beneath a covering of vines, but apart from various terracotta pots spilling over with flowers, she saw only a map spread out on a small table. It was weighted down with a blue throw-away lighter and a packet of Gitanes.

Chapter 2

Dark, whistling swifts in family formation plummeted past the partying crowd on Il Centro's terrace and shot down towards the valley missing by millimetres the vines that cascaded down the ramparts. Shadows lengthened over the fretwork of small fields and vineyards as the distant birds plunged and rose in their ritual quest for insects; and behind a line of pencil-thin cypresses the blue of the Apennine ranges was intensifying.

Patrick paused for a minute with a full bottle of local Chianti in his hand, struck by the arrival of a couple of latecomers. Two tall girls: rather distinctive. Could these be the sisters? They were drifting out onto the terrace in a trance, a state of incredulity, and when they reached the iron balcony they both lifted their faces to catch the scent from the fields. One of them turned back to study the decrepit tiles of the wash house bordering the terrace, and, to his irritation, he was reminded of the leak he'd discovered when the snow melted. (Sunday was a good day to tackle it, Sunday morning.)

This was encouraging. The darker one was pointing out the slope of the roof to her sister: very keen. She was clearly lining up her painter's vantage for the morning. Yes, you see, he told himself, I forget. I forget about the sheer pleasure this place gives them. The loveliest spot on God's earth. Have I really got so used to it? This is how we should come out here: with a fresh eye. Each day with a fresh eye. Ah well, here we go again, the first evening, and a long season ahead.

Patrick went straight over to the two girls. Very attractive – you felt they were on the point of exploding with high spirits. 'I'm Phoebe and this is my sister, Dill.' He decided to introduce them to Kitty, she'd look after them. Now where was she? This was the trouble, she was so tiny, you practically had to go down on your hands and knees to look for her.

He felt a light touch on his elbow.

'I'm here, Patrick dear!'

Kitty! His oldest friend in the village. She was indispensable, she filled the gap. There was absolutely no question she talked the hind legs off a donkey, but he personally found it charming, it helped oil the wheels. Especially on these first nights which were a bit touch and go. And of course, if there were any beans to spill, she'd spill them, she got enormous fun from it. On the other hand, he had to remind himself, there were occasions when her indiscretions had given a number of people quite serious jitters, himself included.

'Oh, my! Two *very* tall girls.'

Kitty almost toppled backwards. He put out a precautionary arm. But then she would insist on wearing these impossible shoes. He looked down. Green high heels with ankle straps, this evening. What age was she? Seventy? Seventy-five?

'We count ourselves very lucky to share this view. We're up there,' Phoebe said, pointing, and they all looked up to a small window adjacent to Rose's room. 'I gather some people overlook the street.'

'Oh, but I love the street.' It was the sister.

'Oh, *of course*!' Phoebe was holding out her tumbler to be refilled. 'In fact we could easily get drunk and disorderly on any one of these views, couldn't we, Dill?'

Kitty opened her palms to them. 'Montecalmo is a piece of heaven, girls. Arcadia. Didn't they tell you?'

Patrick poured the darker sister her second glass of wine. They could knock it back, these newcomers. It was the same every year, demolishing twice as much as any other night. He couldn't possibly hold it against them, look at them all. It did his heart good, they were having a whale of a time.

He wondered if it was time to spread himself about. He leant towards Phoebe and Dill to excuse himself. 'I'm leaving you in the very capable hands of Kitty, who I'm sure will fill you in.' He turned, and was immediately confronted by a forceful girl with a strong voice.

She announced herself. 'Isolda! Is it Patrick? I believe you're going to tell us how to paint all this.' A massive hand at the end of a long, thin arm came towards him. Patrick went to shake it, but the hand extended past him to indicate the landscape. Good heavens, if he'd been a dog, he'd be rolling over on his back paddling his paws. An unmistakable Alpha lady. A top dog. She went on before he could respond. 'I remember reading about your movement a few years ago. The Neo-Barbizon Southerners. It's an odd title, if you don't mind my saying so – for a contemporary group.'

He laughed to give himself a moment to collect his wits. Of course, he met all sorts of unusual people among his students, it was what kept him on his toes. He welcomed their diversity – but this girl was absolutely unexpected. Suddenly he knew he was not going to be able to teach her.

'Ah ha, yes, the title was given to us by one of those fashionable critics. It began with just a few of us in India. We lived close to villages, and painted the farmers going about their work.'

'Hippies!' She was triumphant.

'Y-yes, you could say there was some truth in that. Some of us produced less work than others.' He smiled. The baggage, she was pushing her luck.

A man with his back to him was complaining, but his voice unfortunately was carrying far and wide.

'Spartan, is what I'd call it. Reminds me of conscription – iron-framed bed and a locker for your kit. What's yours like?'

Patrick felt a moment's discomfort. Was this all they could talk about, bedrooms and bathrooms? Well, he could almost guarantee that once they got down to painting, all this wrangling would be a thing of the past. He noticed someone give the military man a nudge. He responded immediately, swivelling on his heel to face Patrick, as straight and well balanced as a toy soldier. 'Hah! The great man himself! Always admired your painting. It's got what I call ...' his head, with its thin moustache, rocked like a metronome as his mind searched for the right word. '*Life!* That's it.'

Well, this was surprising. 'I count that as a real compliment! I'm not guaranteeing I'll remember it, but let me know your name ...'

'Jim. Plain Jim. And I tell you something – I haven't come here to paint Tuscan clichés. Oh no!'

'I would hope not, Jim.' Patrick was doing two things: keeping things going with Jim, while trying to catch what Kitty was saying to the two sisters. He had a suspicion she was about to launch into the Pazzi story. He should have warned her to avoid it.

'Ah yes. That's Rose.' Her soft Scottish lilt had dropped a semitone, but he could hear her clearly. 'She married a local boy who was …' she hesitated, 'the poor lad was killed three months ago.'

In the pause that followed his heart sank. He had a quick look round to see if Rose had come out to join them. He had warned her not to come back to Montecalmo. In fact he'd practically insisted. It was too soon for her to face the world again – but she'd been adamant. This was going to be difficult.

Kitty went on relentlessly. 'It happened just outside the village. It was a terrible shock to everybody, he was such a nice friendly boy. Good family too.'

'A car accident?' It was Phoebe's voice.

'Well, no. He was – it wasn't a car accident.'

Patrick fixed a blind but steady eye on Jim's moustache. Oh Kitty, stop there! You're going to have to stop there, or I shall have to barge in.

'Thank goodness she's joined you lot on the course, it will do her a world of good. But, what am I thinking of? This is a happy occasion. Cheers, girls!' Patrick heard a clink of glass, and now she was dispensing her usual hospitality. 'I have a studio in the castle in Via del Pozza which I hope you will have time to visit while you're here.'

And then he saw her. He saw Rose hovering beside the French windows. A wraith in a white dress. He went straight over.

'Rose, my dear, what's happened.' He spoke softly.

'I don't think I can do this, Patrick.' Her eyes stared from dark holes.

He touched her arm and was reminded of the febrile heat of a wild animal. Shocked, he turned and guided her back inside. They'd created a stir, it was the last thing he wanted. 'You don't have to; we can get your supper up to you on a tray.' They were safe at last inside the empty winter dining room.

'She didn't want to see me.' Rose subsided onto a wooden chair, her voice faint.

Patrick guessed she'd been on the phone to the Pazzi family. His thoughts were in a turmoil. What could he say to her? A young girl, fresh to the family name, daring to approach a matriarch who was bound to be in very heavy mourning for her only son. It was a reckless gesture, born, he supposed, of despair. Oh, the poor girl! It was too soon, it was still too soon. He was deeply affected himself, they all were. It was a tragedy that few people in the village could understand, or even accept. She should have waited, in all conscience, she should have waited. Patrick sat in the chair next to her, and had to lean close in to piece together what she was saying; her speech was hopelessly disjointed.

'I had to come. This is my home now until I find out what … why…'

He held her hands to steady her. Dear God, what a change in her. Not a trace of the feisty girl he knew. The doors into the kitchen swung open, startling them both. Jason appeared in his white apron supporting three bowls of salad, one in the crick of his arm.

He called out, 'Nearly ready to go, guvnor,' as he headed for the terrace.

Rose stood up with the look of someone on the brink with a parachute strapped to her back. 'I'm going to join you.'

'*That's* my girl! Just give your face a splash, and then come out and sit at my table where I can keep an eye on you. I'll wait.'

He watched her straight back receding all the way over to the far corner of the room. At the door she turned to look back at him. Her usual lopsided grin had all the aspiration and hopelessness of a clown. He nodded and smiled encouragement. Had Alfredo's uncle, Tancredi, fobbed her off with some excuse on the telephone? he wondered. It would have seemed like a deliberate snub in her shaky frame of mind. Tancredi, strangely secretive, until he decided to hold one of his semi-public gatherings – which were always too exclusive to include him, he noticed. He'd finally received an invitation to the Villa Pazzi because Rose made sure he was at her wedding in the family chapel. It was easy to see how all the dark rumours had sprung up around this second son, Tancredi. In Montecalmo he'd acquired the status of either a medieval prince or a Mafia godfather, depending on who you were talking to – either way, he was unapproachable. Immaculately observing all the usual social rites at his nephew's wedding, but only as a duty, he felt: the man's mind was elsewhere. He himself, surprisingly, received a very civil welcome. But, dear God, he wouldn't like to be a newcomer into that family. And she was such a lovely, spirited girl, far too good for Alfredo Pazzi, in his view. Dodo, she'd called him – as feckless as his father who was charm itself but a complete wastrel, a hopeless gambler.

That day the boy had squealed to a stop outside Il Centro in his Alfa Romeo Giulietta Spider – superb car, he thought with a pang, but excessively noisy. And to thump on his horn like that! For Christ's sake, he was trying to conduct a class out here on the terrace. They'd all dashed to the edge to look down at the road to see what was going on – palettes abandoned, water spilt, pastels going in all directions – his entire class finished for the day. None of them knew who he was, although any local, of course, would know him for the Pazzi boy from the sound of his car – there was barely a day when he wasn't roaring round the countryside when he was at home. And there he was, pulling at the handbrake and waving up at them – '*Ciao!*' – and they all waved back. 'I am calling for Rose,' he'd shouted. There was an almighty clatter when Rose's stool fell over as she came over to join the rest of them crowding over the balcony. Well, then of course she saw him and something marvellous happened to her – she became weightless. And that, he supposed, was the nub of it. Callow youth that he was, she was mad for him, and he for her, no doubt. Well, they'd had a few weeks' happiness together before the poor boy was wiped from the face of the earth.

Slowly he stepped out onto the terrace, staying close to the French windows. The levels of energy out here were almost deafening. Could she really cope? He was filled with doubt.

Jason had placed the salad bowls in the centre of the tables under the vines, and now he was lighting a long line of candles. His credentials were exciting: a recent graduate of the revered kitchen of Bertrand Blanco-White. He must remember to let the name slip out casually. The news would spread like wildfire, especially with this lot. They were all of them talking fit to bust, exuberance about to hit the ceiling. But of course there was no ceiling! Patrick squinted through a stray tendril of wisteria at one or two stars. The moon would be up soon.

This evening was expectant; he felt it, somewhere in his solar plexus. And furthermore, he was sure it wasn't going to be all about Rose having a breakdown. It was not inevitable, she was pretty steely underneath. Look at the way she'd dealt with those two characters in the white car. No, that was not something he wanted to think about this evening. He had a duty to his new students, all of them, not just Rose. Patrick found the bottle he'd put down and was about to pour himself another glass just as Rose appeared by his side. She was still pale – fresher, but impossible to fathom. He put his arm lightly round her shoulders, and inclined his head to speak. 'Later – in the next couple of days perhaps – only when you're ready, my dear, it would be a good idea, I think, to drop round to the *Policia* just to – you know, keep them up to date. Sacchetti. He's your man.'

'I will,' she said, and to Patrick, seeing her bright, blanked face, it seemed she was happily agreeing to pop in to the *alimentari* to buy the morning paper.

Jason caught his eye and nodded. Patrick obligingly rang the brass bell hanging just above his head producing a sudden lull. Jason tossed a winsome head. 'Dinner is served, ladies and gentlemen.'

The meal was unexpectedly delicious: oval earthenware platters of some roasted endive dish with, bubbling inside it, additions of something cheesy, something tomatoey, and covered by, Patrick guessed, a layer of – could it be yoghurt? He was not by any means *au fait* with the culinary scene but the effect was both intensely piquant and also refreshing. Levels of wine in the decanters had certainly dwindled, barely a few drops left at his end of the table. It didn't matter, spirits soared of their own volition, and compliments for the meal were pouring in. Besides which, he was regaining his spirits. In all good faith, he was going to allow this pleasurable turbulence to run its course. He winked at Rose at the other end of the table and had another drink, at the same chastising himself for it. He couldn't afford to get carried away, but really, was there any reason not to relax and try and enjoy himself like everyone else? He did feel as if he'd come through a bit of a crisis.

Apart from his extraordinary extravagance with chocolate, up to now Jason hadn't put a foot wrong. A touch temperamental, but wasn't that what these lads were supposed to be? A first-class meal, and now they were all peeling fruit and pouring coffee, pissed as newts. He could guarantee there wouldn't be so much *vino* tomorrow, but then they wouldn't expect it. They were a lively lot, although possibly no more than usual. Time would tell.

Patrick observed them with a practised eye from his position at the head of the table. It was odd that the numerical balance was invariably in favour of women. Men were mostly more trouble, it was true, wearyingly determined to make their mark in various ways, but he would actually like to see a few more of them. The forceful girl who'd questioned his credentials (what was her name?) might almost be a man, incredibly thin. What in hell would she look like if you took her clothes off? All muscle and sinew, difficult to muster an erection. Bright girl, though; whatever she was saying they were all busting themselves laughing. Good God, her hands were enormous, extraordinary, worthy of Michelangelo's David: massive double-jointed thumbs, tipped-back fingers with fleshy pads; and look at the way she offered her upturned palm in place of the blunt gesture you might expect: a tentative plea for – what exactly? Understanding? Acceptance?

Oh, blast, that was the third time the empty carafe had been picked up and put down, he'd better summon Sandy and ask her if they could spare another one. He scanned the rows of heads for his long-term helper and second in command – never difficult to find: hair, a glorious setting sun with a dark mist rising. There she was! Oh, no, definitely not, absolutely out of the question. She had that volatile, tight-lipped look about her. She'd wipe the floor with him. She was *right*! This was a business he was running, for Christ's sake, he couldn't afford to get carried away. Thank God for her, thank God for Sandy. He dreaded the day she gave in her notice or decided to get married or whatever it was young girls did now. An absolute tartar, but where would he be without her? He'd had a rather frightening chat with her yesterday when she said she was getting too old for the job. The preparation for this first intake had taken it out of her, she'd said, as pale as a sheet. And then she'd listed it all on her fingers: the cleaning, the decorating, the sheets, the towels, the plumbing, the generator that packed up, and all those bloody hot water bottles she'd had to get in because it snowed last week.

Alright, she wasn't *actually* scrubbing the floor or making the beds, but in fact, it was true, she was the first one they all turned to. 'Ask Sandy, she'll know.' It was always like this and he had to admit to being the prime offender. Why did she do it? She had initially come to help out when Brigid left him, and then, she'd just stayed on, become part of the establishment every season.

Rose was leaving her place at the table with a strange expression on her face. Patrick half rose from his seat. An image of her running to the parapet and leaping off flashed into his mind: her gathered skirt flying, arm outstretched, like a Chagall with the moon behind her. He sat down. It was alright, she was on her way back to the winter dining room. He had a feeling he'd have to remind her again to drop into the *Policia* on the hill. Not a pleasant prospect for a young girl to have to face an interrogation all over again, but if she really thought she was going to get to the bottom of what happened to that poor boy, she wasn't finished with the police yet.

Funny about the strangely myopic young man who'd joined the course yesterday, bloody persistent. He couldn't possibly have squeezed him into II Centro, Sandy would never have forgiven him. Well, he was in the *pensione* in the village now, willing to pay the full whack just for tuition and a few meals. Patrick had a sudden yearning for a cigarette as he saw the new recruit light up one of his Gitanes. He watched him take his first few puffs, and had an uncanny feeling the man knew he was under scrutiny. Rankine, that was his name. Somewhat damp and hairless, with a rather bland smile as if he wanted to discourage contact. Impossible to tell what he was thinking. The only certain thing about him was his tenacity, judging from the way he'd insisted on a place on the course. Who did he remind Patrick of? A literary character. Graham Greene sprang to mind. One of those chaps with panama hats – combing the souks of Port au Prince. And was there any talent? he wondered. You just couldn't tell about talent, and by that, he meant the real thing, the inner eye, whatever you cared to call it: suddenly it was there to take you off guard and you couldn't for the life of you see the connection between this unlikely person and their gift – quite random.

The twin aromas of Gitanes smoke and espresso coffee had banished the scent of honeysuckle, and now pools of light along the tables outshone the pink fading over the hills. The swifts had gone, replaced by bats streaking by with ghostly speed.

Rose had come back. He watched her gazing at the candle in front of her, her head slightly tilted, those eyes, flickering now over the terrace. Tracing the bats, of course. Extravagant, multi-talented, but deeply emotional, even before all this happened. What on earth was he to do with the poor child? She wouldn't get any joy from the boy's family, and furthermore she was almost certainly in danger here. He would suggest she go back to England and paint portraits of Corporate Man and his house – and then he realised it wouldn't matter what he said, she was wholly dedicated to finding the truth out here. He was reluctant to admit it to himself but there was no other way to describe that extraordinary incident: it was an attempted abduction. After what had happened to the Pazzi boy, it couldn't be more serious. Almost as soon as he started to tell Sacchetti about it, he'd had to restrain the man from calling in Rose for questioning; he'd had to insist she be left alone for a couple of days. Patrick rubbed his forehead. Had he done the right thing? Was it enough just to advise her to stick around Montecalmo? He had a distinct feeling she'd been out painting near the old barn earlier today. How on earth was he going to warn her of the risks of going too far afield without alarming her? At the moment, she was completely indifferent to personal danger. But God dammit, they'd almost got clean away with a brazen abduction in broad daylight. Pisa airport! It couldn't have been more public. He was unable to bring himself to think about what they might have done to her; still less, to reason the motives for Dodo's death in the first place. He had not used the word 'murder' since the day it happened; that day when the world became unsafe for all of them here – and in the most blessed part of Italy he knew: a terrible, brutal killing. And why? Somebody knew. And the thing that really worried him was that this was the very girl who was determined to find out.

Getting slowly to his feet, Patrick tapped his glass with a fork for attention, and for a split second as all the faces in the crowd turned to rest on him, he caught a terrific blast of energy. Not entirely benign, he couldn't help thinking. He stammered slightly, but recovered when somebody laughed and banged on the table for silence. *That* had knocked him sideways. He sincerely hoped he was going to be able to handle this lot. Extraordinarily, the sensation vanished as if it had never been there, and once again he was overwhelmed by the usual levels of generosity. It positively beamed from the rows of shiny faces. 'I'd just like to say how very nice it is to see you all, and welcome everybody, and I hope you've all settled in as best you can, and are going to have a very happy and, of course, hard-working time here ...'

Chapter 3

As always, only one shutter had been opened in the heat. A blinding shaft of sun pierced the cavernous entrance hall of her mother-in-law's villa illuminating the white cotton of her dress. Rose tried to smooth her hair for about the tenth time that morning and glanced nervously at the swirling allegorical frescoes surrounding her. It was the smell, the faint blend of beeswax and old clay, that got to her; she thought she'd braced herself for this moment, but the familiar smell had caught her out.

Tendrils of something clammy seem to be gumming up her lungs. She heard Giselli, on her way back from the usual obligatory announcement to the family, and stepped closer to the window. Quickly, she breathed in the sweet air from the garden as if it were her last remaining source of life. Giselli's bow legs carried her painfully across the darkened hall towards her; she watched her progress – her dear old friend who had welcomed her at the door with her butterfly opening and shutting of hands and sighs of pleasure.

She felt the cool dry hand on her arm. '*Prego, prego.*'

'*Grazie* Giselli,' Rose whispered. She leant towards her. 'How is Rodolfo?'

Rose never failed to be touched by the conflict of overwhelming love and worry that gripped Giselli when her simpleton son was mentioned. 'He is coming home to see me,' she shyly smiled and nodded. There had always been room in the house for Rodolfo's visits, together with a kind of benign tolerance – amusement even from Tancredi who said he was useful for running errands. Dodo used to say he'd taught him how to backward somersault until one day he'd fallen on his head and Augustina put a stop to it.

Rose allowed herself to be led over the worn tiles of terracotta into the next long hall of frescoes: images of mountains and lakes and spindly acacia lit by the white blaze of light from an open shutter at the end. They were coming to the double doors of the smaller drawing room, where she knew Augustina liked to sit. And by now it was too late to turn and run.

She heard a harsh shriek behind her. A parrot flew through the hall and out of the window at the end into the garden. The sight of the parrot gliding past the vegetation of the fresco struck her as being perfectly natural; at the same time, its presence appalled her. A desecration almost, in this hushed house. She looked at Giselli who appeared not to notice, which surprised her. Instead, smiling and nodding, she pushed the doors open and stood aside to let her through.

And here was her mother-in-law, half lit from the opened shutter behind her. Signora Augustina Pazzi, in mourning for her son. Rose paused and caught her breath. Oh, Mama, poor Mama. She was sitting in a tall-backed chair with the kind of slumped stillness that comes with exhaustion. She did not show her teeth to smile. Instead her upper lip expanded slightly as she put down a small book of prayer. Rose had seen her teeth only once when, through a crack in the door of her private room hung with icons, Augustina's bowed head had lifted towards the bright candles, her braced mouth a shocking mask of grief. But that was shortly after Dodo's death when everything seemed unreal and no memory could be trusted.

'*Buongiorno*, Rose, *come sta?*' The formal greeting was spoken extremely slowly. She inclined a pallid cheek to be kissed.

'Oh, Mama!'

Rose sank to her knees and kissed her mother-in-law's hand which was immediately withdrawn. Augustina made some low clucking noises and turned to give a short instruction to Giselli, who nodded and left the room.

'Yes, yes, I know, but we cannot allow our feelings to be the queen. Please, you will sit over here.'

Again, Rose grabbed her hand and pressed it to her cheek, her words rushing out. 'I know it has been difficult for you, Mama, you've suffered, you have suffered so much.'

The small box of sugared almonds she had found for Augustina fell to the floor as her mother-in-law writhed violently, struggling to free her hand. Rose scrambled up awkwardly and laid the gift in her lap.

'Dodo used to say you liked sugared almonds.' It came out in a whisper, it was still hard to breathe.

She was waved to the chair on the far side of the table next to her, a solid marble-topped table, against the wall. And now, with at least four feet between them, Augustina relaxed visibly, unaware of a sudden blustery movement of leaves through the open window next to her. It was the old magnolia that grew up against the house. Rose could just see its reflection through the pitted glass of an old mirror opposite.

'How is your father?' Augustina asked.

'My father is well now, thank you. His knee is almost better.'

'And the weather in Ireland?'

'The weather in Ireland was rather wet.'

'I think it rains too much in Ireland.'

'Has it rained over here in Tuscany, Mama? At Easter, perhaps?'

'Yes, we had some rain at Easter.'

'How is Tancredi? Is he well?' Rose observed no change at all in her expression. Perhaps she had learned to live with her brother-in-law all those years ago when he'd moved in. And maybe that was all she wanted: someone to run things smoothly for her.

'Apart from some small trouble with his shoulder, he is well.'

'Did he enjoy his holiday in Budapest?'

'I believe the weather was not very good. But, he does not allow these things to trouble him.'

In the mirror, the old magnolia outside swayed. Rose wondered if a squirrel or a pigeon were disturbing the branches and stared in fascination as a human hand grasped the gnarled wood fixed to the wall. The reflection was sepia and muddy but it looked as if a man, coal black, was climbing to the top of the tree with great deftness and ease, and as he passed by he showed no interest in the room where they sat.

Sweat prickled the surface of Rose's skin. She did not want to alarm her mother-in-law who had no idea what was taking place so close to her.

'Do you have a new gardener, Mama?'

'New? No.'

'A man here to cut some trees, maybe?'

Augustina turned to Rose with heavy lidded eyes. 'You have seen a man?'

'I think I have seen a man climbing the tree outside the window.'

'Impossible.'

A passing giddiness caught at Rose as she laid her arm on the cold marble table top. Had she actually seen someone? She had an image of the parrot in the hall: the parrot was real, she had heard the parrot, it had squawked, it had startled her. She looked again at the blurred, refracted light in the ancient mirror. The magnolia was barely visible. The surface of her nose was very wet; she wiped it on the back of her hand, and tried to remind herself why she'd come here.

'Mama, I have not been so well since the spring.'

She dared not mention Dodo's name, but Augustina knew.

'I am sorry to hear that.'

'I feel so far away, and I still don't know what really happened, why it happened.'

The sheer understatement of her appeal shocked her. She bit her lip. Was there no other way to express the full weight of her desperation?

'It might be that it was a mistake,' Augustina said.

'A mistake?' Her flesh turned cold.

'Maybe.'

A *mistake*. The concept ballooned dangerously in her head.

'Are you saying, the bullet was meant for someone else?'

Augustina slowly raised her head as she dropped her eyes in affirmation.

'And he needn't have died?' She knew she was beginning to sound hysterical.

Augustina was alarmed, she fidgeted with her box of almonds.

'I know nothing, they tell me nothing,' she said, waving her hands as if to protect her face, and the almonds fell to the floor again.

'Oh, Mama, I'm sorry, I'm sorry.'

Rose was already half out of her chair and was being waved back frantically.

'I am not strong. I must not think about my son in this way.'

'Of course not, Mama, I didn't mean to upset you, *mi dispiace.*'

'I must be ... quiet ...'

Augustina was running out of breath, her lips were working, she was making small noises in her throat.

'But, you know, Mama, sometimes, I can't bear it either. Sometimes I have to talk to somebody. You see, nobody will tell me what happened, *why* it happened, Mama.'

'You knew him for one or two weeks, he was *my son* ...' Augustina's voice was breaking into a harsh wail.

'I was his *wife* for two weeks. I knew him for three months.'

Augustina rose from her chair, balancing precariously on her feet.

Rose felt the trapped pain of fear in her groin.

'My son had *the world* to choose a wife. *Why* was it you?' She stumbled and caught the table for support. Then, still clutching the table, she raised the other hand and pointed a finger at Rose, her breath rasping.

'You put the Evil Eye on my family.'

As in a dream, Rose watched Tancredi slip in, dressed immaculately in freshly laundered clothes. His normally lazy eyes sharpened as he cut across the floor to grasp Augustina's arm, to deflect it by force, making her turn into him. She surrendered with ugly, cawing cries as all the while he soothed her with low words.

Eventually she quietened and allowed herself to be guided towards the door. The two of them almost collided with Giselli coming in with a tray of aromatic coffee and three glasses of water. Giselli placed the tray on a table near the door and took Tancredi's place, tenderly offering her arms to Augustina. Slowly the two women moved out of the room together.

'Relax, please, I'm not going to shoot you.'

Rose flinched as she met the eyes of the man who was Dodo's uncle. Tancredi was crossing the floor towards her. He placed the tray on the marble table and offered her one of the tiny cups. She took it obediently but did not drink, her attention being caught by his methodical arrangement of himself onto the arm of a chair as he held aloft his coffee cup. When her own tiny cup and saucer smashed onto the marble, she gasped for breath. Coffee spread over the shiny surface.

Tancredi removed a folded handkerchief from his pocket. He walked over slowly and dropped it in the dark brown puddle, and then stood for a minute holding the sodden linen between his finger and thumb. Finally, he left it on the tray, and placed the broken china next to it.

Events were taking place outside her control. She felt she must get some words out or she'd be lost, floating in limbo again. She wanted to go home to her father, she needed him, but she was here. Why did she come? She couldn't remember. She came because she was compelled to come, but they didn't want her. She searched for the threads.

'Mama tells me ...'

A puff of annoyance crossed Tancredi's brow; he held up his hand.

'My sister-in-law,' he began, 'Augustina ...'

He checked his irritation abruptly as Rose turned to him with the full force of her distress thinly in check. He began again, speaking softly.

'You must try to forgive her. She is taking medicine, she is not so strong.'

The spectre of Augustina pointing at her reappeared briefly, but as in a pantomime behind thick glass. Rose hung on to Tancredi's words as if they offered a lifeline.

'You know, perhaps it is a little soon to come here. Maybe later, when Augustina has had some rest you will come again and we will take some tea together, maybe if it is not too hot, in the garden. You must bring your friends. You know, the fountain in the water garden has been mended, it works well now.'

Rose felt weightless, as if she may float up and over Tancredi's head. She heard her husky voice come from somewhere else.

'Thank you.'

'It has been very bad for you. You have had much to suffer.'

Rose waited in the silence of the shuttered room, for a few minutes or it might have been longer, she didn't know. Her eye was deflected from Tancredi by yet another commotion in the old mirror on the opposite wall. This time it was a pigeon flying into the magnolia and noisily settling onto a branch. Then Tancredi seemed to be criss-crossing the floor. First to the bell tassel hanging by the door which he fingered uncertainly before going back to the tray to replace his empty cup. Then after a few moments in rapt contemplation over the English sugar tongs, he strolled to the open shutter to gaze out over the garden. Here, a momentary thought distracted him before a decisive swivel on his heel propelled him onto the fireplace. Standing with his back to it, he stared intently at the worn rug beneath his feet, and absent-mindedly released the top button of his jacket. Arrested by the scent from his body, he took a long, savouring sniff and twitched his lips.

Suddenly Tancredi smiled. Rose blinked rapidly and wondered if this was a signal that her visit was at an end. A parrot screech from the garden was followed by a shout which was answered by another shout. Then, somebody ran scrunching over a gritty path.

Tancredi glanced at the open window and stepped forward.

'Please, forgive me, but very soon Augustina will need me to ...' he gestured to the bell tassel.

Rose floated out of her chair, judging her approximate position.

'Of course.'

Tancredi held out his arm.

'You are staying at II Centra D'Arte? Then I know where to find you. You will visit us again I hope. And please, bring your friends, they are welcome. For tea maybe, and cucumber sandwiches.' Rose was being ushered without resistance into the anteroom and out into the passage towards the hall. 'You will wait here for a minute while the fellow comes to drive you back.'

'Thank you.'

Tancredi stopped and drew a long envelope from his inside pocket.

'Oh, yes, yes, while I think about it – some business following Alfredo's death – I must ask for a signature.' He unfolded the document and smoothed it out on the table by the door. 'Of course, if you are feeling unwell ...' He lifted his shoulders and opened his palms to appeal to the nearest fresco.

'Oh, no ...' Rose took the pen she was given. The document was dense with legal jargon. She noticed there was a space for her to sign below the two signatures of Tancredi and Augustina. 'What am I signing for, Tancredi?'

'It is quite simple – to say that there is no change with the arrangement regarding our house. Villa Pazzi will remain in our care – Augustina's and mine.'

Why did he need her signature? she wondered.

But Tancredi was staring into the middle distance. He cleared his throat with an absent-minded air.

Slowly Rose signed her name and laid down the pen.

'Of course, we will not talk of this again to Augustina. I am sure you know, she is not ready for questions and must stay in her rooms.'

Rose nodded and took her straw boater from Dodo's uncle as he opened the heavy front doors. She felt his hand in the centre of her back propelling her onto the portico. To her surprise, Iacopo was already waiting with the car. He smiled up at her and immediately she felt better. She walked down the curved staircase towards him without looking back.

The comfortable back seat felt even safer. She sat forward.

'Just drive, Iacopo. I'll tell you where to go.'

As the car turned, she felt a sudden constriction in her throat. She couldn't do it. Her fingers tightened into fists as the car made inexorable progress down the avenue of cypress towards the gates. It had to be done, this was something she had to do. It was why she had made herself come all the way back to Italy. Her mind went blank suddenly. For a moment she had no idea why she was in the car driving along. They were pulling out of Villa Pazzi, that was certain. Iacopo was driving.

It was while she was watching the familiar gates swing slowly apart that she became overwhelmingly convinced that she was doing the wrong thing. She was heading for something, somewhere, and it was almost too late to stop it.

'Stop the car!'

Iacopo pulled into the verge outside the gates. Rose stepped out and stood in the shadow of an oak tree for a few moments. She looked out across the stretching valley with distant vineyards, freshly leafed, and it was during those few seconds that present reality returned to her in small fragments. Before she went anywhere near that place, she told herself, she would need to be prepared to remember something that frightened her so much that she trembled uncontrollably rather than think about it.

Rose reminded herself to breathe. Instantly, exhaustion permeated her limbs. She would build up her strength. She would go in the end, she had to go, but not now. Later, she would ask Iacopo to take her. The moment would come.

She climbed back in the car and leant forward to touch his shoulder. 'Il Centro please, Iacopo. Il Centra D'Arte.' And straight away she knew what she would do. Those two sisters she'd met clattering down the steps on her way up to her room – they would be the guests she would invite to tea. Didn't Tancredi suggest she bring some friends with her? She would ask them both if they'd like to come; she liked them; Augustina would like them; Tancredi would approve of them. Basking in the light-hearted aura of Phoebe and Dill she'd be less of a nuisance to them. It would give her some breathing space before she tried again – because she would try again, whether they liked it or not.

Chapter 4

Phoebe pushed open her bedroom window and leant out. The sky was a pale cerulean blue. A swallow fluttered up, up, up, arched over and descended earthwards. On a nearby hill, etched against the early-morning mists, the little church of San Cristofero sheltered behind its line of cypresses, and, punctuating the strident birdsong in the valleys, a cuckoo called.

Phoebe sighed with the utmost satisfaction. God was in his heaven and this was his world, his beautiful, fragile world. She blinked as sky and landscape swam together in hot tears. How was she going to paint it? Well, she couldn't. It needed a Monet for this, and a Monet she was not. But *she could try*, she could try. She made her first exploratory move and imagined the landscape as a painting: her own painting with its characteristic deep shadows and vigorous brush strokes cunningly employed to deflect attention from her tenuous grasp of form. But where were the shadows? There were no shadows, the landscape was bathed in suffused light. Phoebe edged herself further out from the window in an attempt to emulate the swallow's concord with nature, knowing, in the confusion of her aspiration, that she must relive her first sublime impression. But the wings of inspiration were heavy. Ah, Monet, where are you now? How long would it take you to make a start on this? An hour? Less, before the light changed. Then you'd set aside the canvas to dry and select the next one, partly painted. And, without taking breath, you'd carry on with yesterday's. And there you would sit and arrest the climbing sun. Did you steal a kip in the middle of the day I wonder, when the light was not so captivating? A little break from that tireless quest to get it right? She pursed her lips. This was not helpful.

Just a minute! What about the ladder! She had noticed a home-made ladder propped up against an olive tree on her walk last night. Much better to get a pat on the back for a nice ladder leaning up against an olive tree than chilling ranks of raised eyebrows for San Cristofero and the cypresses. At last, a ray of hope. For the time being, she'd leave suffused light for another day.

Behind her, Dill stirred. There was a noisy intake of breath and her arm, pink from the sun, emerged from beneath the sheets to describe a quarter-circle before coming to rest on her hip. Beautiful Dill. All pale silky hair and pinkness. Why couldn't she look like Dill, be like her? Phoebe slumped into the wooden chair with feelings of failure on all fronts.

It was true she made up for it in other ways. She was more alert to nuance than her sister, saw the funny side. And she never took people on face value. Dill did. It fascinated her that Dill happily accepted whatever she was presented with. It got her through life with enviable ease – until she was let down. But what did that matter? Her tolerance was endlessly elastic, she'd forgive anyone practically anything. And to cap it all, she'd got herself married to a duke. And of all the dukes in England, it had to be Edward.

Admittedly he had his head screwed on which was more than she could say for the rest of that blimpish band of brothers; and now, of course, everyone said Dill was born to the role, or rather, had restored to the role all those old-fashioned niceties one felt ought to belong to a duchess: visiting the tenants to play with their children, counselling the head gardener on his difficult marriage, reorganising the zoo to give the animals more privacy (never mind if they were hidden from public view). It never seemed to strike Dill that all this unsolicited charity took her away from those members of her family who might actually need her. Her own sister, for instance. Yes, alright, Edward had let Dill come with her to Italy, but she knew she was going to have to pay for it sooner or later in some devious way. She sighed. This was the trouble! Everyone who knew Dill felt bereft when she wasn't there.

Phoebe wondered if it was the last word in meanness to squeeze two cups of tea from one bag: she knew she hadn't brought enough for both of them. There was a short, sharp blast from a miniature trumpet: Dill's fart, she would have recognised anywhere.

'Oh, come on, Dill, I know you're awake.'

She heard a series of squeaks, followed by a clean intake of breath and then a pause. 'Is it breakfast?'

'Breakfast! It's half past six.'

'Why are we awake, exactly?' Dill was caught by a yawn.

'Because we woke up,' said Phoebe. She was in need of comfort, she didn't know why.

Dill struggled to sit up in bed, both eyes tight shut. 'Have you got up early to paint?'

'Don't, don't!' Phoebe turned her face away. 'I don't know why I'm here, I can't paint.'

Dill was shocked.

'Darling, you're good. Far better than me. It only needs for you to go out there and make a start. Look at the sunshine!'

'I can't tackle the big subject, Dill. I know I'm going to go off and paint something I can do standing on my head.'

'Why not? It'll give you confidence to go on to something else.'

Dill sat there draping her knees with her shapely arms, blue eyes blinking. Was it fair to dump her troubles on her sister like everyone else?

'Did you sleep well?' Phoebe inquired.

'Like a log.'

'Bed comfortable?'

'Well, actually I wondered if I might have been lying on a bump, but then I went straight off to sleep so it didn't matter.'

What a heel Phoebe was. She'd spotted the lump and quickly swopped beds; her sister deserved better from her. She'd make them a decent strong cup of tea in that kitchen place overlooking the square.

A few minutes later, as she watched the kettle come to a boil, Phoebe began to warm to the ladder in the orchard. Dill was right, it was better to start with something she knew.

After all, as she told herself on the way out to sketch her ladder half an hour later, subject dictated style, just as style must suit subject; and the subject she'd first singled out was clearly suited to her style. Phoebe stopped dead as she pushed against the iron gates that opened onto the path outside. Was this pure self-justification? She had a lightning image of Van Gogh's sunflowers: not so much flowers as coiled, writhing creatures about to devour each other. He must have had a good idea how they'd turn out, but he didn't say: I can't paint flowers, I'll leave that to Redon. Perish the thought, *that is how he saw them.* Phoebe pictured his blazing eyes in that half-starved face fixed on the pot of sunflowers. Van Gogh would draw energy from a brick, let alone a flower. And furthermore, who could look at a sunflower now without seeing all that clotted yellow paint? Sunflowers had been transformed forever. And now, she realised with the lightning spread of irritability, her comfortable theory had been turned on its head. She stood poised, suspended over the step for a full five seconds. Either way, how on earth did this help her with suffused light? Too much! The whole thing was beyond her. She closed the gate behind her and swung off down the track to the olive grove dismissing comparisons as odious.

Phoebe was wearing the old shorts she'd taken out of her suitcase almost as many times as she'd packed them in, and at that moment felt as free as a bird; as the cuckoo, in fact. There it went, abandoning its progeny in neat little foster homes dotted all over the valley. She stopped. The ladder had gone.

Without thinking she jumped over the wall into the olive grove, landed on the dewy grass and saw that the ladder had simply been moved. It was propped up against another tree. The farmer, with his back to her, was pruning the new olive shoots with a knife.

It was now blindingly obvious to Phoebe that the ladder must be preserved for posterity – exhibited on the Tate Gallery's ground floor perhaps – suspended from the ceiling even. For a few indulgent seconds Phoebe allowed herself to picture three or four discerning art historians gazing up at her extraordinary *objet trouvé*. This was ridiculous. It was, of course, custom-made for the orchard, and here, naturally, she was going to paint it. She'd ask the farmer if he'd mind.

For the tenth time since arriving in the country she regretted her ignorance of the language. What if he mistook her for a tourist? This evoked such distaste she blushed and had to restrain herself from ducking out of sight. Then she remembered, there was no law of trespass in this part of Italy, so really no reason to think he'd bat an eyelid. Nevertheless, what was she to do with herself, now she was here?

Certainly she wasn't going to skulk back over the wall like a child stealing apples; the thought made her cringe. She'd mime it: flourish her sketch book, paint the air with an imaginary brush. 'Centro D'Arte!' she'd say, and point up to the village. Perfect.

Phoebe held out her arm to hail the farmer, and as she stepped forward her foot caught in a gully and she smacked down like a ninepin. Rolling onto her back, she opened her eyes and looked up into an old acacia jutting over the path. 'Shit!' She spat the word. Her ankle was painful. She lifted her leg and slowly, very slowly, rotated her foot. It wasn't broken. But would it see her back over the wall?

The acacia's frilly branches extended into bare corkscrew arms, the withered arms of a witch doctor. She wanted that witch doctor here – now, to lay his parchment hand on her ankle and say a spell to end this horrible pain. Trying not to cry, she fixed on the underside of the tree, and wondered if anyone had ever been able to paint lying on their back. She imagined being hailed as the first horizontal painter ever. She was able to see Il Centro itself if she turned her head; all those tiny windows cut into the massive walls. Somebody was leaning out of an upper window with binoculars. Surely it was Porky-pies who smoked those vile cigarettes! Was he bird-watching? Surely not from inside, and wearing his panama. No, she was ready to swear the binoculars were being trained on her, she sensed a connection. Struggling onto her elbows Phoebe beckoned to the distant figure. He promptly lifted the binoculars to focus on the sky. She slumped back onto the grass.

Mortification turned to waves of anger that swept her recumbent body, and tears trickled into the inner channels of her ears. How dare that pimply myopic ignore her desperate summons? Couldn't he see that she was in trouble? *He* didn't want to be seen and that was for sure, the oily bastard. He must have watched the whole wretched pantomime.

A cooling vision of Dill stroking her hand became almost material, it was so yearned for. Help is on the way, darling, her sister was saying. A shadow fell over Phoebe and she blinked and held out her arms.

'At last you've come,' she choked.

The farmer stood over her with the pruning knife in his hand. For a long time, they beheld each other in mutual incomprehension.

'*Buongiorno*,' Phoebe said finally, dropping her arms, 'I've cricked my ankle.'

'Delacroix said, "I begin with a broom and finish with a needle."'

Patrick had set up a big easel in the studio for his students and had dashed off the bare outlines of a house set against a vast landscape. Positioned by the door of the house and drawn in elaborate detail, a pot of geraniums was benefiting from his very special attention. Bent over at a somewhat uncomfortable angle, Patrick was carefully filling in every leaf. It was his first tutorial and he was feeling his way with the new class.

His students sat on stools and canvas chairs, everywhere but in the hot sun. It streamed in through arched windows, striking the stone floor and reflecting onto lime-washed walls of mottled creams. In shadowy corners of the adjoining studio behind Patrick, painting boards and folding stools were neatly stacked. And from the wide ceramic sinks in the printing and cutting room, a wettish, faintly chemical smell excited unaccustomed nostrils.

'I'm drawing in all the leaves,' Patrick called out as if he were a small boy reassuring his mother, 'and I won't forget the petals.'

There was a respectful silence behind him as the class followed his every move. He sighed. Delacroix had obviously fallen on deaf ears. With an air of martyrdom he scratched away at the leaves praying that for someone, the penny would drop. Gradually, with his back now giving him all kinds of hell, he sensed a difference in the breathing, an easing-up; and he realised that at last, he was probably getting somewhere. Well, at least they were enjoying the crude sketch – *but could they see he was beginning at the end?*

Patrick called out, the obedient child again, 'I'm counting them!'

An American girl said suddenly, 'Are you picking on me?'

Laughter spread round the class and Patrick stood up beaming.

The American girl was grinning round. 'He's taking the piss, it's not fair. I mean, how did he know about me?'

Patrick said, 'We all do it don't we? We go for the detail. And it won't do. See the big shapes first.' This was better, he was getting to know them.

He caught sight of Rose curled up on the chest against the wall. Her stillness was striking, and a picture she looked. It surprised him to see her there at all: his first tutorial. She doubtless knew as much about the core of his lecture as he did, yet here she was joining in, backing him up. It warmed him. She didn't look too well. No wonder! She'd had a meeting with the Pazzi family. He made a note to ask her about it.

There was a kind of rushing shuffling disturbance behind him. He turned to see the two tall sisters coming in clutching notebooks and pencils. One of them had a crepe bandage round her foot and was draped around her sister's shoulders.

'So sorry. Dill had to find a chemist,' Phoebe said.

'Phoebe has hurt her ankle quite badly,' Dill announced to the class, and then shot an anxious look at Patrick.

Immediately, almost the entire class jumped up to offer their chairs. It was pandemonium with people flying in all directions; Patrick felt his authority slipping away. Really, this kind of disruption could not have come at a worst time. The appalling pasting he'd had from Sandy that morning had almost finished him off. And the worrying thing was, he had no idea why she'd flown off the handle. He was sure it wasn't the pre-menstrual whatsits, they'd all just about survived that particular minefield last week. Besides, there was usually about three days' warning before all hell broke loose. She'd get a very particular evil look in her eye and they'd all know to batten down. There was no warning this time. The bolt, when it came, was out of the blue. 'If you think I'm going to carry up the groceries, settle your dispute with the *enoteca*, fix the generator *and clear up the bloody cat shit – think again, buddy*! I'm off!' All guns firing, broadside on. Of course, he was down on his knees mopping up the cat shit almost before she'd finished, but it was no use. She'd slammed out into the town, arms going like windmills. God knows where she'd gone, she hadn't come back. It was the *buddy* that hurt him. *Buddy*. It was impersonal, cold; he couldn't think where she'd got it from. And she came down on the word like a hammer. He felt a distinct chill, as he thought of *buddy* being the final nail in his coffin. Was this blow-up with the cat shit going to be the last straw? Given the polarity of her emotions, either by now she would be back in the kitchen shelling beans, or her rage had already propelled her onto the next flight home from Pisa.

Rose was sending him that fragile, enquiring signal.

'I think we've settled down now, Patrick.' An elusive smile flickered across her face and he felt extravagant gratitude. She'd come to his class when she might have been occupying her time more creatively; she was a lovely girl. He needed all the friends he could get in these volatile times.

The class was facing him now with expectant faces: paper masks strung across the room like a Greek chorus. Now where was he? Delacroix or Ruskin? He felt frazzled and wondered if Margheretta was still away visiting her mother.

'Now, you're all here to paint the landscape. It would be quite natural, indeed, entirely normal to take a look out there and be daunted. Fear not, help is at hand.' Big grins all round, poor sods, as if he had the secret formula up his sleeve. He continued, 'First of all, forget the details. Begin by thinking of it in blocks – and if it helps, you can find a nearby tree to use as an anchor.'

'What about the light?' came the appallingly non-specific question.

It was the student with the bandaged foot. Wasn't it Sandy who'd told them she had a grand title? Or was that the extraordinary sister who looked like Leonardo's study for Saint Anna?

'Suffused light, I'm talking about,' Phoebe said.

'Ah! When the air itself is alight. Moisture that blurs the lines and hides the source. Let me tell you a story.'

Patrick wondered how on earth he was going to make a meaningful story out of a student with an irritating habit. And, more significantly, why? *What the hell was he doing* going out on a limb like this? A whiff of armpits came to him. Did he remember to change his shirt that morning? He crossed his arms and clamped his hands over his biceps. He'd started now. Bash on.

'A couple of years ago we had a student who kept scraping out her paintings just as fast as she painted them. Every day, she'd be out there on the terrace painting the same pocket of landscape; and every day, she'd scrub out her work. When I got round to her, the day's work had gone, I never got to see it. The canvas was getting threadbare – threadbare, but stained in *pastel* colours, I noticed. "What are you after?" I said. "The light," she said.'

The girl with the injured ankle was leaning forward as if her life depended on it. He was going to let her down, he knew it. She was going to be the second one to abandon him in a single morning. He must concentrate, concentrate.

'Well, all this time people were producing paintings all around her. It didn't seem to worry her. She was learning, she said. But not from me, you notice!' He liked that. This was leading somewhere after all. 'Because, as we all know, the only way you really learn, is from your mistakes.'

Rose was smiling, bless her. She'd been here herself two years ago, she might have remembered the student. He released his arms from their straight jacket and sniffed bracingly. No armpits. Good.

'Well,' he continued, 'time was getting on. The last day arrived and still nothing to show for it. So I sent her out into the field to paint a tree, and this time – *starting with the dark*. To all our surprise, she came back with a finished painting.'

Phoebe was transfixed. 'What was it like?'

'Very fine indeed,' Patrick replied.

'But what about the light? She didn't learn about the light!'

'She knew more about it than when she started.'

The girl looked thunderstruck. She'd put her bandaged ankle onto a stool and scowled at it.

'Just paint what you see, keep at it.' He raised his eyebrows at Phoebe. 'Alright?'

She nodded, heavily. Patrick thought, she cares so much. I'm lucky to have her. He leaned down and addressed himself directly to her. 'Study Turner,' he said softly. Then, to the class he said, 'And, even when it works, remember, it's only paint.' A vision of Vermeer's *Girl with a Red Hat* came to him. Did Vermeer use paint? It was difficult to believe.

'Look. It's simple, but not easy,' he said, treading cautiously. 'It usually takes a lifetime. And the fear never leaves you.'

The thin girl with the cropped hair pricked up her ears. Good Lord, she was going to say something, folding her huge hands together.

'Can you expand on that? Fear. Fear because you happen to be a fearful type? Or, do all painters have a predisposition towards fear? Is fear a recognised component of the creative act, anyway?' Isolda tilted her head queerly to one side.

39

Patrick was stunned. He was a modest practitioner handing on his skills, and that was more or less it. Surely she'd felt a certain amount of apprehension herself? It was his fault. He had to stop telling stories. She'd got the wrong end of the stick.

Rankine spoke. 'We know from his letters that Vincent Van Gogh was f-fearful before he puh-painted a picture. How f-far that is attributable to his m-mental state is open to conjecture.' How very curious; the man had no trouble with his stammer when he got to pronouncing Van Gogh. Impeccable Dutch.

Isolda cleared her throat. 'I think we're being asked to consider the mental state of Fahnsohn Ffahn Hohhh, more generally known as Van Gogh.'

There was an explosion of rudely unsuppressed laughter and Patrick felt a clean flame of anger that, to his relief, died in the instant. His class was being taken over by pseudo intellectuals. Somehow, he had to steer them all back to sanity.

He said gruffly, 'I think we've all felt something of Van Gogh's fearfulness.' The girl was incredibly bony, her knees were like a grasshopper's – no woman had a right to be so thin. She held one upturned hand in the palm of the other like booty, her casual cruelty behind her.

'When I'm faced with an empty canvas,' he went on firmly, 'I don't mind telling you, I'm scared. Well, it's a step into the unknown, isn't it? Where's the journey going to take me? Suppose, at the end of it, I know I can't do it?' He smiled. 'Jump in. It's an act of faith.'

The two sisters were having a quick whisper. Had he come up with the right formula? They looked brighter. He had a sudden need for Margheretta. Ah, Margheretta, her softness and yielding flesh. He'd nip round after and see if she was back. She'd be missing him, too.

Quickly, Patrick looked up to address the class before the thin girl had a chance to strike again. He directed the announcement towards the sister with the bandaged ankle. 'Tomorrow I'm going to be talking about colour. And I'll be able to give you a few practical hints on how to achieve what you want.'

* * *

Sandy was back on her perch on the kitchen stool. Patrick had to restrain himself from rushing over to hug her. She was shelling broad beans, good girl. He glanced at her mouth darkly set in a deathly pale face, and reined himself in; whatever happened he must avoid taking her for granted. Jason, he noticed, was at the other end of the table leafing through a book of recipes.

'It's good to see you back.' An understatement if ever there was one.

'Is it?'

'Well, yes, I thought you'd be on the plane for London.'

'There wasn't a spare seat. I've booked for next Thursday.'

'You mean you're leaving us on Thursday? Which Thursday?'

'Next week. I've arranged for Caroline to take over till you find someone else.'

Jason picked up his book of recipes and strolled past them, rolling his eyes at the ceiling.

Patrick said, 'What have I done, Sandy?'

'Done? Nothing!' she flashed a look at him. 'I've had enough. I'm going to find myself a life. As they say on TV.'

Patrick bowed his head and stared at the spotless stone flags. His eyes roved over the marble surfaces and up to a gleaming bunch of copper pans suspended from hooks. It was true she didn't actually do the scrubbing and the polishing, but she was responsible for it, and if one of the girls was ill, she did it.

'You work yourself to the bone,' he said. 'We expect too much of you.'

Patrick jumped as the paring knife was jammed into the wooden table. Sandy's fist was still tightly clenched round the handle as her shoulders heaved with long drawn breaths.

'Yes, you expect too much of me. Yes, I work myself to the bone. But, for what? *For What?*' Her eyes bored into his, wildly.

This was too much for him. He began walking towards the door muttering something about discussing it later.

'Going to see Margheretta?'

The question followed him like a showman's dagger. He froze. Years earlier, his young daughter had listened to him talking soppy nonsense to the dog and ticked him off for liking the dog more than he liked her.

At the time, he was charmed by her childish bid for more attention. He turned to look at Sandy and she blushed and looked down.

So that was it: a demand for attention. What a child she still was. Weariness overcame him. He nodded, 'Yes. Margheretta is expecting me. I'll be back for lunch.'

The sun was blinding when he stepped out into the square. He walked to the parapet to collect himself and breathe some air. Halfway down the hillside old Giovanni was out with his two oxen – the tiny weather-beaten figure staggering over the stony earth tugging his creamy white beasts behind him. It didn't surprise him to see the barmy old fellow out with the plough at the wrong time of year, what puzzled him was that Lucia had not put a stop to it. Automatically, Patrick reached for his sketch book and pencil. He watched Giovanni's trilby fall off and heavy cloven hoofs trample it into the earth. Slowly, so slowly, he could almost feel his own joints crack, Giovanni bent to search under the two beasts; and after a long time, with nothing to see but the two bullocks and their plough against the landscape, Patrick began to sketch. After a minute or two the old man crawled out again from under their flanks, thrashing the dust from the hat against his trouser leg. His dear, demented old friend. How long had he known him, twenty years? Haranguing the olive trees now, as if they were responsible for all the misfortune in the world. At last he replaced his hat, and with it, his self-respect.

This was a rare sight, what luck he'd happened on it. Tomorrow he'd come out here and paint it. With the pencil covering the surface of the paper like lightning, in his mind's eye Patrick saw an Etruscan farmer ploughing the same patch of burnt umber two thousand years ago. There would have been little difference. Hard lives like this had survived their term in the same strenuous way for thousands of years. People had lived and loved and gone to join their ancestors, smelling the same smells and looking out over the same landscape in the evening before turning in. He folded away the sketch book and slipped the pencil into his pocket. The image had calmed him. It put his own paltry plight in perspective. Worse things had happened to him; his wife, Brigid, had left him all those years ago. He was alright, more than alright. He had his work, he lived in the most beautiful spot on God's earth. But for a woman … well yes, life was obviously tough for a woman here, and from his ex-wife's point of view, extremely lonely in the winter. Sandy, undoubtedly the best manager he'd had, was away for most of the winter earning her living elsewhere, but it was non-stop once she was here.

Margheretta's apartment was next to the *gelateria* in the main street. The door was easily overlooked, being of a nondescript colour and set flush to the wall.

Normally it was left slightly ajar so that the residents, mostly elderly, wouldn't have to worry about forgetting their keys.

Once inside the small Renaissance courtyard, Patrick paused to sniff the damp air from the broad-leafed vegetation round the well. He crossed to an alabaster basin jutting from the wall where fresh water trickled from a spout, and drank deeply, splashing his face.

'Patrick!' The voice hailed him from above. It was Margheretta. He loved the way she spoke his name with the first syllable on a downward cadence. He looked up and saw her smiling down at him from the third floor, her long hair framing her face in dark curls.

'I have just returned this minute,' she said. 'Come.'

Patrick bounded up the stone steps two at a time and ran along the square boundary of short balconies till he reached the last set of steps where Margheretta was waiting at the top with her hands outstretched. He wound his arms around her body, impatient to smell her neck and hair. She shrieked and gasped and tried to push herself away, holding her finger against her lips to remind them both to be discreet.

'Bring them in,' she said, pointing to her suitcase and a carrier bag containing a new pair of shoes standing outside her door. While she fumbled with the key in the lock he closed his hand over hers to turn the key, and picked up the luggage. Breathlessly she turned to face him as the suitcase and carrier bag shot through first, landing with a bang on the tiled floor behind her. He lifted her clear of the floor and her scanty shoes slipped off one after the other. Once inside, with his foot he nudged the door shut behind them.

Chapter 5

The police station was once a small villa standing halfway up the hill leading up to the South Gate of Montecalmo. It was attached to a garden of olive trees transformed to blossom since Rose was last here. All so pretty and ordinary. She slowed almost to a standstill and fixed her eyes on a mark on the pavement. That age-old hint of nausea that dissuaded her from breathing spread to the lining of her mouth. She stopped to wait for it to subside. It wasn't Sacchetti – she could deal with Sacchetti whoever he was: the white car would be easy to describe. No, it was the other, the unthinkable, the terrible danger of recall: of seeing that sharply delineated scene with wide-open eyes, when up to now she'd allowed herself only a lightning glimpse. This numbness was what she wanted; she had hugged it to her for three months, she couldn't afford to let it go. It was a terrible danger she was heading for, and yet there was nothing to do but risk it.

They were outside examining one of their cars parked in the road. One of the policemen was hidden beneath the bonnet, the other paced the sidewalk, with his hands clasped behind him. Rose approached them in a state of trance-like determination.

She stopped by the car.

'*Buongiorno, signorina.*' The more senior officer greeted her formally.

'*Buongiorno.* My name is *Signora* Pazzi, and—'

His detachment fell away. He bowed.

'Signora Pazzi. Come this way please.'

She followed him into the hall, with her eyes on the patterned tiles. The familiar blend of polish and hot electrical equipment rushed into her nostrils and now she was seized with dread. For a few moments she stood with her hand on the banister to steady herself. This was crazy, she couldn't face it.

'Signora?' He stood a few steps above her.

She paused.

'I'm coming,' she told him, and prayed her Italian was good enough for all the details she would have to understand later.

He had shown her into Cornero's private office, which was familiar to her but slightly different from last time. Still the ornate furniture she found so oppressive, but now, instead of stuffy oil paintings, swords criss-crossed the wall and fancy pistols hung beneath. She sat on the crackling leather chaise longue and took a quick look at the family photos on the table behind her: strange faces.

The policeman stood sideways behind his desk looking at her. He looks like a jackal, she thought. Any minute he's going to trot round the desk and round me up. Instead, he turned to face her and gave a short bow. 'May I introduce myself. My name is Maresciallo Sacchetti, I am from Sicily – and I would like to say I am very glad to see you, signora. I believe you have some information for us.' He sat and reached for a pad and ballpoint pen. 'Our friend, Signore Patrick, tells me there was an attempt by two people in a white car to take you from Pisa Airport – shall we say "against your will".'

As Rose talked through her experience she couldn't help but notice the avidness in his thin face for especially small details. 'Do other women smell of powder to you, signora?'

'Well, yes, some do.'

'But, this time, the smell of powder was – unusual? Very strong?'

'You see, she was wearing very thick make-up and lots of lipstick. But it was stale – dirty. It smelt dirty.'

However important all this was to this man, the real reason for her visit was to talk about the progress Cornero had made with Dodo's case – she saw the urgency slipping away from her, and knew she was losing courage.

She leant forward and fixed him in the eye. 'Signore Scarlatti, I hope I may see Brigadiere Cornero soon.'

He threw her a sideways look glinting with humour. 'My name is Maresciallo Sacchetti,' he said.

Rose blushed.

'And I must tell you,' he went on more seriously, 'that Brigadiere Cornero married a lady from Montecalmo one month ago. We have a rule that because of this he cannot work here. He is living in another town.' He sat down and leant forward over his desk clasping his hands. 'I am now here to be of service to you, signora.'

She couldn't take it in. There must be some mistake. All the questions she had formed in her mind these past weeks were for Cornero: he alone had been there from the beginning; his links with the Reparto Informazioni e Sicurezza (RIS) from Siena were at first hand. Above all, he had actually known Dodo. Striving to grasp what his absence would mean for her, she covered her face with both hands to make a blank.

'Please, signora, don't be upset. I have the Pazzi file here,' he laid a hand on the computer already on the desk, 'and I will help you as much as I can.'

'He knew my husband,' she whispered, and trailed off.

There was an awkward silence, and she began again.

'Dodo liked Cornero. They … knew each other.'

'Of course, of course,' he nodded.

Betrayal. Betrayal of the cruellest, most deliberate kind. Cornero had betrayed Dodo by going away. She and Dodo had been dropped by the very man who had pledged to solve the case. And now this predator was sitting in his place. For some reason, she wanted to punish him. She struggled to clamp down her fury and felt her cheeks grow hot.

Raising her eyes no further than his folded hands on the desk she said, 'I am told that the killing of my husband Alfredo Pazzi was a mistake.' Now she looked him in the eye. 'Is this true?'

There was a silence as he stared at her.

'A mistake?'

'The bullet was meant for someone else.'

'May I ask where this rumour came from, signora?'

'Rumour? Isn't it common knowledge? His family know.'

'Where did they hear the information?'

'Why don't you ask them? Isn't that what's supposed to happen?'

'We have no information about that in our files. I have read every word myself. I miss nothing.'

'Well then, what *have* you discovered since I left three months ago, Signore …?' Her mind was a complete blank. What was his name?

'Sacchetti,' he quietly supplied.

She had lost her authority, she knew it, and with it, the clean line of questions she had carefully rehearsed. She cast about her wildly, but her mind was torn up and scattered all over the room.

She cried, '*Tell me why they killed him,*' and picked up the hem of her dress to dig into her eyes and cover her confusion. Oh, God, her self-respect had deserted her, she was gasping and hiccupping like a child. She hadn't meant to break down like this, she was begging him for information when he should have been offering it to her.

'I am very sorry to tell you, signora, that we know very little. It is difficult when we can find no motive.' He waited a while.

It was an age before she could trust herself to speak. 'You don't understand me. What I am saying is – there may have been a motive for killing someone *else!*'

'It is our business to treat rumour with, mmm …' he was tilting his hand like an aeroplane with a wing wobble. 'Well, let me say that there have been already many rumours spreading around. For the moment we are interested in only the evidence …'

She interrupted him, breathless with disbelief. 'Are you telling me you're not going to do anything about this? That my husband's family stand for nothing …?'

'You husband's family—'

'They want to know why this happened as much as I do—'

'Signora—'

'Let me tell you – because you're from Sicily so you may not know – the Pazzis are a respected family round here, they don't trade in rumours.'

'The Pazzi name is, of course, very …' Sacchetti's fingers flicked over the keyboard. He frowned at the screen, found what he wanted and leant back to fix her with a look.

He said, 'The Pazzi family know very well how important they are, and I am sure they would like to keep it like that …' He held up his hand and continued swiftly before Rose could interrupt him. 'Cornero himself … my predecessor, *Brigadiere Cornero*, has an entry here. I am sure you will like to hear it: "The fact that the Pazzi coat of arms includes a tusked boar in its heraldic composition is no secret. Although there is no evidence to suggest it has a bearing on this case, we cannot rule out a link between this and the circumstances of the killing."'

She searched for the hidden agenda he seemed to be hinting at. In the back of her mind she could hear the drone of black flies swarming round the crudely severed head, settling on its bristles matted with blood and grass.

'What are you saying? That my husband was … that they killed him because he was a Pazzi?'

'No, I am not saying that. But we have to consider that it would be very bad for the Pazzi family if other people believed this. It is better for them if their son … if people heard that he was mistaken for someone else. A tragic error, of course.'

'Oh …' She blinked, the penny was beginning to drop.

Sacchetti's shoulders lifted slowly and his palms opened.

'I am not saying it is a fact.'

Rose hung onto every ounce of concentration. Was he hinting that Tancredi and Augustina were spreading false information to protect the family name? It was unthinkable. She was about to lose her train of thought; Sacchetti's eyes were flashing up and down her body as if she'd accused him of the murder himself. She wanted to leave the heavy room and get out into the sun; the desire was almost impossible to fight. All this effort to make the appointment, to force herself up the hill and through the doors and up the stairs, and then to say it; and now, to have the meeting terminated, to have her information dismissed with a wave of the hand, her credibility wiped out. She had barely begun, barely arrived. If he thought the interview was over, she must say something to make him understand how serious it was because she had no more ideas to carry her forward, no more strength. She only wanted to escape this stifling room in order to think. Rose stood up, her heart thumping.

'I want you to reopen the investigation, Maresciallo Sacchetti, and the next time I come, I expect to find some answers.'

Sacchetti sat forward, his eyes burning.

'I assure you, Signora Pazzi, that this file has never been closed.'

Rose fled.

* * *

Sheep had nibbled the grass on the springy covering of the little hill and everywhere their droppings lay scattered. Rose lay on the turf with her eye on a solitary cloud. She moved her painting satchel to make a pillow and slumped back onto it. How else could she have behaved? His detachment was like a door slammed in her face; it was as if Dodo's case was already ancient history. He disapproved of her, she could feel it; she hadn't matched up to his expectations: a grieving widow, putty in his hands. But why did she attack him? She'd deliberately alienated him. After all, he was new here, he was only doing his best; how could she go back to him now? Oh God, she just felt so stupid and helpless, she might as well pack her stuff and go home. Pathetic, typical, and not even an option, so why think about it? She had a good look round her. Not far below, an ancient path of dusty white alabaster wound itself around the slope to the quarry on the other side of the hill, where, she remembered, the hewed stone had left a giant's bite. Nearby fields were invaded by clouds of meadow buttercup, and beyond them, an unbroken panorama of hills undulating around her stretched away to the distant Apennines; there wasn't a soul to be seen for miles.

She lay limply on the lea of the hill curled up as she would in bed, and allowed the meaning of Augustina's pointing finger to unravel. *What a child she once was.* If she'd had time during those frantic days to think about anyone else, she would have known it couldn't possibly be true that Augustina had loved her, they hadn't given her a chance, she and Dodo. And, really, why was Dodo in such a hurry? She was flattered: what other reason could there have been but that he loved her so much, he couldn't wait? – '*Pronto*, Rose, *pronto* we belong together, the world must know.' But now a fresh thought was forming: was he afraid that in the end he would crack under the family's disapproval – begin to share their point of view, even? There were certain English expressions Dodo liked to use: 'up to something' was one of them. 'Tancredi is up to something. Always he is up to something.' Did he suspect Tancredi would, given enough time, put a stop to their marriage? When he'd flown back the night before their wedding, it had plunged Dodo into a brooding sulk. But who else was there to comfort Augustina after her noisy breakdown in the front pew? Or to pacify the guests filing out behind them, all wide eyed, emerging from the family chapel? Only Tancredi. And now, who did Augustina have but Tancredi? Her only son was gone, and she was landed with her: the English girl, the upstart little foreigner. *Her only son.* Rose couldn't repeat it to herself without a tightness under her ribs as the sadness of that poor crumpled body pierced her chest.

A clunk of bells came and went on the breeze, and Rose sat up and reached for her satchel automatically. She turned her head to wait for the flock, quickly drying her cheeks with the flat of her hand. The skinny sheep – she knew them well – came up onto the brow of the hill grazing briskly, fanning out in their search for new grass. This was where an Etruscan helmet was found. She had kept some broken limpets and tiny chalk-white spindle shells they'd found near the dig, she and Dodo, she still had them. She slowly stroked the scratchy grass and felt all the dried bits and pieces pass under her fingers and collect in the damp dip of her palms. There had been a warm breeze as there was today, and his hands had smelt of earth from sifting the shells. She had a vivid picture of his head and smooth, shiny shoulders blocking the sun, and then when they rolled over and the sun was on her back for a change, the grass, she knew was pricking Dodo's back.

'*You are a professional painter? What do you paint?*'

That was the first time she'd been introduced to Augustina. In those first few moments she'd been forced to consider Augustina's overwhelming feelings for her son.

'Portraits, mainly. Well, it's how I earn my living – but, actually, I like landscape.'

'If Tancredi was here, you would see some good paintings.'

And Dodo had jumped to his feet and offered his hand to her. 'We don't have to wait for Tancredi, *I'll* take her to see them.'

'No, no, no,' Augustina was shaking her head and closing her eyes. 'Not without Tancredi; we must wait for him.'

'Mama, they're yours, they always have been; why must we wait for Tancredi to show us? It's always the same –' Dodo's hand came up to scoop the air, '"wait for Tancredi, he will know what to do."'

'*Basta, basta,*' she'd said in her lovely low voice. 'He is good to me, and, you know – I am not used to business.'

'This is not business. These paintings belonged to my father, they have been here for ever.'

'Oh, Dodo, Tancredi is your uncle, he is fond of you. Why can't you be a friend to him?'

'Why – when he hated my father?'

'No, Dodo, no.'

'He tried to tell me my father was no good. That the villa was falling to pieces because of him. It wasn't true. There was no money.'

Augustina was conciliatory.

'I know, I know. And that is why we need Tancredi. It means that the villa is beautiful again. Look around you.'

'I don't want to talk about Tancredi any more.'

Again that low caressing voice. 'Oh, Dodo, you are too harsh with him. He tells me—'

Brusquely he interrupted her. 'He hates me – because I am like my father.'

And then, without any warning: 'Mama, *I want to make Rose my wife.*'

Augustina's jaw dropped slightly. 'Your wife?' She turned her head to Rose for a split second, her eyes open wide as if seeing her for the first time. After that she remained fixed on Dodo, half beseeching, half fearful. But Dodo had been firm. He got up and walked towards Rose as she stood up to meet him, feeling his arm go round her as he said '*We love each other.*' And she saw the terrible bewilderment in Augustina's eyes – standing by while he left her side to go and put his arms around a girl she'd hardly met. All his love and loyalty crossing the room with him; they had watched it happen, she and Augustina, both of them helpless to stop it.

She felt the older woman's loss, even now. 'Oh, Dodo, you were careless with your mother, you were not gentle.' She spoke the words aloud, and wondered that if she hadn't loved him whether she would have liked him. The thought shocked her, and upset her, until she realised that the notion had never been far away since she had known him. It was a kind of brashness he had, a bravado – but this was part of him and she was charmed by it. She must have been because she melted whenever she saw him, she was melting even now at the thought of him. Their love for each other seemed to provide a certainty that overrode all opposition – Tancredi's, Augustina's, even her father's resistance to the hasty wedding. She thought of her father's sadness with a dull constriction in her throat. She'd tried to explain to him how right it was, and real – her and Dodo's love for each other. And all he would do was nod his head slightly and look sad. Oh God, what did it all mean, now? Well, she was alive for her father, that was one good thing. They had to tell themselves, *they* were the lucky ones, Augustina only had the horror of it all. Rose remembered her new mother-in-law fighting to restrain her feelings on the eve of their departure for England. Only two hours to go with suitcases almost packed, and Dodo had leaped into the front seat of his car with, 'Don't worry, I won't be late.'

Augustina was wringing her hands. 'A few more minutes to spend at home, and you must rush away like this for something crazy!'

'Not crazy, Mama. Tancredi tells me this place has the most fantastic views in Tuscany. I think I know it, it is a ruined village. I want to see it.'

'You will need permission to build on this plot. It will never happen. Wait, wait till you come back.'

'It will be too late. Tancredi knows about it, he says there are people who want it – very badly. It could be sold before it comes on the market. But if I like it he will do the deal for me. This *week*, he will do it.' The engine roared to life, and as always, he touched his foot on the throttle a few times for the joy of hearing it. 'Leave it to me. You will see, my wife will have the most beautiful house in Tuscany!'

But as he drove round the fountain preparing to head towards the big gates, Dodo stopped and jumped back out onto the gravel. He hit the bonnet with the flat of his hand and gestured towards the front wheel. 'Flat! *Cazzo!*' He called back. 'I have a flat tyre.'

Tancredi ran down the steps to speak to him, and the next thing they heard was a motorbike revving in the old stables. Augustina frantically picked her way down the steps after Tancredi. 'No, Dodo. No. You are not used to riding these things.'

'Mama, don't worry, I have had practice.' And he certainly looked at home sailing out on the motorbike with a huge smile for them under his helmet, slowly picking up speed, then quickly off and out of the big gates with a wave.

And that was the last time she saw Dodo alive.

Abruptly, she assembled her pastels and sketch book. The sheep were drifting fast and they'd soon be rounding the skirt of the hill and lost to sight. Now she must concentrate. Oh, immeasurably primitive and beautiful on the steeply slanting slope! She marked the thick paper with swiftly changing colour, rubbing it in with her finger to create mass or shape form, her head nodding from paper to sheep and then up to stunted olive, and it seemed no time at all before the last sheep was disappearing over the hill. She held her breath, leaning further and further forward – just as the last whisk of its tail told her she was done.

The picture looked good at arm's length. She was pleased, it was satisfactory. She lifted her head to catch the breeze in her nose and with a sigh, lay back onto the turf to bask in the wind's leisurely sound in the oaks below. She looked up and caught her breath – there was the hawk again! And it's seen me, she thought: a tiny figure in this vast landscape below, a girl lying on her back on a hillside looking up. The bird has it, she thought: the lightness I've lost.

Dodo's presence, which had been so strong a few minutes earlier, had drifted away leaving behind it a kind of peace. She packed away her paraphernalia, got to her feet and stretched. The white dress she had worn for Augustina billowed out as she searched for the little cloud, but it had disappeared without a blemish in the blue above. A crooked smile cracked slowly across her face as she half ran, half braked her way down the hillside, toes slipping out of sandals, arms flung wide for balance, painting satchel tossing up and then bumping back onto her rump with a clatter.

At the foot of the hill, she came across it again. The gleaming alabaster paving, exquisite in its pearly whiteness. She bent to touch it and marvel. Only here the paving of the old road was intact where it branched off from the bigger farm track. She wondered if the man whose helmet they had found had felt these cool blocks beneath his feet.

Rose stood up and swung her satchel across her body, and as she did so, heard a charging engine getting rapidly louder. To her right, a large motorbike roared round the corner making a beeline for her. She backed away, stepping wide into the grassy verge as the powerful machine slurred over the bumpy cobbles throwing its rider up from his saddle like a bucking bronco. As he shot past her, the young man glanced back through the visor, and seeing she was unscathed, rode on with a wave. Simultaneously, Rose had felt something wrap round her ankle with a hot, burning sensation. She looked down to see a snake thrashing frantically, trapped by her foot. She leaped back onto the path, and the snake had gone.

For a few moments Rose stared open mouthed at the two little holes in her leg. She knew she had been bitten by a poisonous snake, she had seen its tell-tale 'V'. Her instinct was to run, but where? She stood rooted to the spot drawing in deep draughts of air. Her mind went into limbo as she floated the possibilities, trying to take it step by step. She was miles from anywhere and time was critical. Either she should start walking down the farm track that eventually came to the road (it would take her about half an hour), or, should she head for the quarry? It was closer. Panting rapidly, she looked up at the old alabaster road after the motorbike. The quarry was definitely closer. Had he been on his way there? It was where the path ended. Her ankle was hot and throbbing, her breath coming from her in small squeaky cries. She made her decision. She would find him at the quarry.

Chapter 6

Rose made a dash up the old road shedding her satchel as she ran. Pelting up to where the path levelled out and the going was more even, she tried to steady her pace, but at the point at which it began its descent she skidded in her headlong rush. Her arms shot forward to break the fall and the palms of her hands dug into the stony surface, tearing the skin. Knees crashed down next, and she lurched sideways over onto the bank. Crushed vetch under the impact of her body threw up a small flurry of moths. As the breath was knocked out of her, she curled like a wood shaving. Her knees drew up towards her chin and bloodied palms were turned to the sun before the air rushed back into her lungs and pain took over.

She lay in the foetal position concentrating on the throb in her leg for a few seconds, maybe minutes. Grass crackled round her head and a trapped insect whirred in her ear. Blood smeared over the torn cotton of her dress as she tried to cover the burning bite with numb fingers. Half rolling, half levering herself till she was able to stagger into an upright position, she limped the remaining few yards onto the flat step of the quarry where she swayed to a stop. It spread out before her like the surface of the moon, cutting like a shelf into the hill. A dumper truck and generator with its lifeless engine lay close together a hundred yards off, and further on was the motorbike. Behind the machinery, in the distance, Rose caught sight of the rider sorting through a pile of whitish grey lumps of stone.

She cried, 'Help me,' but her voice was feeble. She tried again, but there was no projection. Rose limped towards the distant figure, testing her heavy limbs. Breathing painfully she negotiated the churned, stony earth in a dream. He seemed far away and intent on his task. She would wait until he was closer and try calling again.

He picked up a heavy chiselled stone and turned it over and over, this way and that, before at last he made his decision and started back to his bike cradling the stone against his belly. Rose paused and shouted with all her strength, cupping her hands to her mouth. He looked up and stopped. Wary of moving her rib cage again, she held herself in suspension. The man dropped his load and started to run towards her across the wide quarry floor.

'*Cosa e successo?*' he shouted as he approached, his eyes taking in the ripped dress and wounded hands. He stared intently at her swollen face.

'What happened? Did I hit you?' he spoke English.

'I've been bitten by a snake.'

Immediately he dropped his eyes to her leg and whistled. 'Your leg is very bad. Be still.' He pulled out the shirt from round his waist and peeled it off his torso in a single movement. Then, tearing at the seam, he managed to separate the front panel and rip it in two as he knelt on one knee. In fascination, she watched as he folded the cloth into a tourniquet, wrapping it swiftly round her lower calf. It was as if he'd been attending to snakebites all his life.

Rose felt a balloon filling out in her chest, pressing against her ribs. She cried out as he tightened the tourniquet, her chest about to burst.

'Too tight?' he asked looking up. 'Too much?'

'I don't know,' she whimpered.

'Is it comfortable?'

She put some pressure on her leg and drew up her skirt to look. The swelling had spread up from her ankle to the frayed cloth of his shirt.

'It's hot.'

'Wait here.' He wheeled away and ran towards his bike.

She knew him now, of course, he was the hunter who'd killed the boar.

For a second time the powerful motorbike approached her, cautiously this time till it drew alongside. He stopped with his feet touching the ground and indicated the pillion with a quick glance. 'At my house I have some serum.'

The sunburnt leather seat between her legs felt like a hot iron. Dizziness took hold as she hung her head, resting it between his shoulder blades. He twisted round carefully and asked her if she was well enough to travel. She groaned.

'Hold me. Tight. Don't let go.'

Slowly Rose's arms encircled his curved, cool body, and she laid her saturated cheek against his skin. The bike made gradual progress, inching forwards along the old road, every stone, every bump jolting her ribs. She allowed the cries to come freely as they picked up a little speed, riding back along the way she had come. Further down, they came across her satchel, and he slowed down to pick it up. She released her grip while he looped it round his neck so that it hung down in front. 'Hold me,' he instructed a second time, and once more she slipped her arms around him and they were off again down the wide farm track and up to the main road where the surface was smooth.

The next farm track was very bumpy although by this time her discomfort and pain had lost reality – she had entered a dream. The bike drew up on some rough ground at the side of a barn where three stone steps built against the wall led up to a door. An old cypress gave some shelter against the sun, and when the engine cut out there was a blessed silence. A single cicada rasped in the grass nearby. Rose stayed where she was in the dark shade of the cypress, her burning body slumped against his. She slackened her arms till they fell to her side but was unable to sit up on her own.

He turned. 'How are you feeling?'

Again she groaned.

'Please. Try very hard to get down.'

'I can't move.'

'I must park the bike.'

With painstaking slowness, she half slithered off the pillion seat and lurched against the scratchy cypress as with lightning speed he balanced the bike and grabbed her as she fell.

An hour after the serum injection Rose lay stretched out on sheepskin rugs piled onto a sofa under a window. She was in a big white room. Fighting off a curious state of tension, she tried to change her position, breathing with difficulty. The young Italian came in, pulling on the blue check shirt he was wearing when he'd shot the boar.

'Who are you?' she asked him.

'My name is Toni Vasari,' he replied.

She drifted off into a kind of sleep.

The tapestry was sumptuous and seemed to stretch up forever from the stone floor. It was a lively hunting scene and in precarious condition having a scattering of moth holes, a large one obliterating the back half of a doomed boar dashing through the woods. Rose lay with slit eyes trying to orientate herself. She felt like a diminutive Alice, in a room with walls stretching up to a faraway ceiling of beams and tiles. There was a cast-iron stove flanked by neat piles of logs, and beside them, two free-standing candle holders. At the foot of the tapestry opposite, a long, low sofa had been strewn with rugs and cushions.

In a kind of idle dream, and feeling almost relaxed, Rose wondered if a conversation would be possible with someone sitting on the sofa the other side of such a wide-open space. She spied a pile of books on a wooden chest against the wall.

If you wanted to read when it went dark, you'd have to sit in the uncomfortable high-backed chair next to the paraffin lamp like a monk in a cell. The lamp was placed on the chest, reflected by a mirror behind it, the only source of light apart from the candles. Who but a man would make do with this? Here on the sheepskins *she* would lie with her book.

Where had he gone, the person who lived here, the hunter on the motorbike? She had to let Patrick know she was safe. Rose tried to sit up and at once slumped back. Her head was a solid iron ball and her limbs, lead. She was cold. The springy softness of the wool was all she wanted. And yet her mind was clear, she needed to make a move. Where exactly was she? In Toni Vasari's house recovering from a snakebite, that much she knew. Toni Vasari who roamed the fields with a rifle. Why did he keep snake serum in the house? Was it possible she had stayed for so long pressed against the skin of someone who was not Dodo?

She turned over her hands and studied the lint bandages smelling of antiseptic and so neatly wound. She had remembered nothing of this. Had he done it himself, or was there a woman in the house? Where was this place? Slowly, very slowly, Rose dragged herself off the sofa and got to her feet.

He had taken off her sandals and the cold stone flags sent further shivers through the soles of her feet. She bent to pick up a shaggy skin to put round her shoulders invoking a cry of pain as her ribs twinged. Then, lifting her leg onto the sofa, she studied with fascination the raised red circle. In the centre was the snakebite itself: two neat punctures. The inflammation had localised and the leg seemed cooler.

The following moments were bleak in her snail-like progress to the window. Rose was convinced the experience had somehow turned her into a very old woman. This was what it felt like to be at the end of her life, each movement requiring superhuman effort. Once more the tears streamed down her face and she shivered violently under the strong-smelling skin. Self-pity overwhelmed her; she would never grow old naturally like other girls. From this moment on, she must prepare for a life of exhausted disability. She wished now she had been left to die on the alabaster path, freed from the horror of Dodo's death, spared the loneliness of living without him.

The land fell steeply away from where she stood at the high window and spread into the valley where there was a small lake; and to the right, long shadows from the woods were streaking over the fields. So it was late. Rose had no idea where she was. She stood framed in the open window shaking with cold and misery. She heard a car start up. So this wasn't so far from civilisation, then.

She could hear a cat. Or rather, she thought it was a cat: a piteous cry with a downward cadence. A fellow sufferer, instinctively she felt it. It was intermittent but insistent; she had to go to it. In the corner of the room, there was a low arch with another threadbare tapestry drawn across it. As she crossed the floor towards it, a movement caught her eye. It was Rose herself. She stared into the mirror at the hollow-eyed goat herd gazing out of it: a thin, chalk-white face framed by black matted hair.

Drawing aside the tapestry hanging, she saw below her a kitchen at the foot of three stone steps. She surveyed the primitive cavern with its cast-iron wood burner. The syringe had been left on the scrubbed table with a pile of empty packets torn open. It was dark. There was an iron grill across the high window, and the grassy bank outside was close enough to touch, but apart from half a dozen anonymous white cups and plates in a wooden rack above the stone sink, there were no belongings, no *things*. Except for a book lying open on a chair, she noticed. She stepped down into the kitchen on her way to read the title when she froze, checked by a smell of something imminent. She sniffed, hardly daring to lift her head, because the smell was attractive but dangerous. And she'd smelt it recently – in Augustina's private drawing room with the broken coffee cup on the tray. She could smell coffee, that was a part of it, and something else too; she was seeing the worn rug that lay flat on the tiles beneath Tancredi's polished shoe. Tancredi! It was his perfume. Almost blinded with a need to go back and hide, and at the same moment transfixed by a complete paralysis of her muscles, she found herself unable to go anywhere. The sheepskin slipped off her shoulders onto the floor and as she slowly, painfully bent to pick it up, a film of sweat cooled the surface of her skin and a sense of unreality – a sense of being somewhere else – made her hands shake uncontrollably. The tap which had been dripping since she came into the kitchen was now so loud it was drowning out the cat, and before she knew it, she had come back to earth. She crossed over to the sink and filled a cup – over-filled it so that it swelled up powerfully and streamed over her hand – desperate suddenly, to slake her thirst. The cool water spread out in threads inside her as she drank, filling the cup again and yet again until she'd had enough. There was just no way that Tancredi could have been here: her mind was playing tricks again.

The cat was almost certainly behind a door in the other corner, but the stove was irresistibly warm. She leaned gratefully over the blackened antique with its simmering pot, and opened the sheepskin to embrace the source of heat. And there she stayed until the shuddering lessened, and the danger seemed to pass. The cat was still crying behind the door but less often and more weakly as if it had lost heart.

'Puss, puss, puss,' she called, and the cry redoubled in vigour.

The iron ring seemed to lift a latch on the other side of the door, but the old door itself was stuck. She tried again with one of her bandaged hands and leaned her shoulder against it. Suddenly she realised it was locked.

'*Che fai?* What are you doing?' The voice expressed outrage.

'Your cat … Your cat …' Rose was too shocked to speak, she was choked with tears again and broke down helplessly.

He glanced at the sheepskin still clutched about her shoulders.

'You are cold. I will fetch a cover.' He bounded back up the steps into the other room and reappeared with a bright red rug. Taking off the skin and tossing it behind him, he wrapped the thick woollen rug securely round her shoulders.

'Come,' he said, trying to lead her back out of the kitchen; but by this time Rose was obstinate, hysterical, almost keening.

'Your cat's inside ... your cat, your cat ...' She was transported with grief.

He stepped back, regarding her in disbelief.

'You're not well, you must lie down,' he said brusquely and held out his hand for her. She shook her head and crumpled into a heap on the lower step weeping incoherently for the cat, knees drawn up under the blanket.

She heard him uttering oaths she'd never heard before while he sorted quickly through a heavy bunch of keys, and then he stepped over Rose to get to the door. She stood up behind him and waited for it to open.

The door swung open a little way and then was quickly closed and relocked as the cat made its escape, streaking through the kitchen and into the other room.

'So! The cat is free,' he announced turning to face her where she stood clutching her blanket, open mouthed. The momentary sight of the bright room behind him had been so unexpected, so astonishing, she was certain she was hallucinating.

But this time, she was warm when she lay on the pungent skins with the rug tucked around her. She had drunk a cup of strong camomile tea brought to her by Toni, and now the cat, a point-eared tabby, curled itself in the crook of her body, purring and stretching, luxuriating under the warmth of her fingers. She watched her host light the thick tallow candles and kneel to grasp a bundle of dry brush. The heavy doors of the burner groaned as he opened them to stuff inside the brittle branches. One match after another burnt down and scorched his fingers as a small flame lived and died on the branch. She heard more curses under his breath.

'Blow on it,' she said from where she lay.

He turned to look at her in surprise as if he had forgotten she was there, as if she were an impertinence. She didn't care; she hated his arrogance towards the cat.

'Blow on it,' she repeated, 'it's what I do,' and continued curling the cat's ear around her finger.

He stood up, his eyes directed at her but seeing beyond her. Then he crossed to the pile of books on the chest and selected one.

'Stop!' she called out, struggling to prop herself up as the cat jumped off the sofa and fled back to the kitchen. He was tearing pages out of an old book. 'What are you doing?'

Who would do this? He was a stranger to her. He frowned and shook his head as the crushed pages were tossed into the open doors of the stove. 'This one was not useful to me,' he said as the paper balls flared up.

She watched him add extra kindling to the fire, and once he'd closed the doors and opened the vents the combustion produced a palpitating roar. A strong whiff of rosemary reached her nostrils.

Toni stood up and brushed debris off his hands as he regarded Rose with a heavy frown. 'I advise some sleep. In one hour, maybe two, you will be well, and I will take you back.'

'Thank you,' she said, longing for the cat.

'I have some work to do in the kitchen.'

And as he passed by her on his way, she said, 'Toni, why don't you hang your paintings in here?'

He stopped. 'What are you saying?'

She was frightened by his tone and her voice could barely be heard. 'I thought these walls needed some pictures.'

His face cleared. 'You are saying "my house wants a woman's touch" – *Allora*, I like it like this.'

The cat trotted past him and jumped lightly back to its place on the rug, immediately starting to purr and knead its paws. Rose gave it an extravagant welcome, drawing it to her, burying her face in its soft ruff.

'Thank you for helping me,' she said to him, summoning a smile.

'It's nothing. Now you must rest,' he said, turning.

His detachment was unnatural, it made her uneasy. She needed to establish some kind of civilised relationship.

He said, 'I will call Il Centra D'Arte to say you are safe. What is your name?'

'Rose Pazzi.'

He stopped. And for a moment, before closing the tapestry hanging behind him, she could have sworn there was a change in him.

As if he knew me, she thought. Weird. He is secretive, he doesn't want me here, and he thinks I'm a hysteric. Well, maybe she was a hysteric, his indifference made her see red. How was she expected to ignore a crying cat? *His* cat, couldn't he see the creature was desperate? It wasn't a question of being sentimental even if her father teased her for it. She knew animals had souls, there was no doubt in her mind. Even the sheep that had inhabited this smelly skin. She thought of the time he'd heaved the dead boar about on the grass like the meat it undoubtedly was. Toni Vasari. Animals kept to their place in his world. Rose stroked the sleeping tabby now curled into a ball with its pink chin turned upwards. Now you're safe, she murmured in its ear. A flicker of something like fear took hold of her as she lay under the bright red rug staring at the fire. It had felt natural and easy to put her arms around Tony Vasari on the bike and this realisation disturbed her. The image of his smooth back had been with her since she first woke up. She was still unwell, surely it was this? Peculiar things were happening to her body, her mind. It was incredible to her that she should now be suffused with a longing to wrap herself around him again. He was attentive when she needed him, she acknowledged. She felt warm and looked-after in front of the fire. But towards animals he was hard. There was no knowing how long the cat might have been shut up. A picture of the half-glimpsed room where the cat had been trapped came back to her. Full of daylight, like a studio. Two Greek marbles, and on an easel, a small oil – the style was unmistakable yet the picture itself tantalisingly *un*familiar. Nevertheless, how could she mistake it? A Piero Della Francesca. Impossible. She sighed deeply, and, surprisingly, dropped instantly to sleep.

Chapter 7

'*Oh, don't move yet!*' The appeal was soundless.

Phoebe had mouthed it, screwing her face into a ball as Rose shifted her legs on the deckchair, still asleep. For twenty breathless minutes, the only movement on the terrace had been the shifting sun playing over her cotton dress – except for Phoebe's occasional and careful dips into her water jar followed by the brush's measured return to the palette. Rose's foot was now in a fiendish, head-on presentation, but she couldn't possibly alter it. Maybe she could leave it as it was – an unfinished portrait. It really was a rather attractive picture: a forest creature in innocent sleep.

She frowned at her own bound ankle, freshly dressed by Dill that morning, and there it was again, the farmer's face in his olive grove. Oh God, would it ever go away? Endlessly popping on and off like a neon light, the pendulous bottom lip, the moist brown eyes. She prayed to be released from the recurring spectacle.

This confinement to the terrace was getting her down. And oh, her ladder! She imagined all those highly proficient painters happening on her ladder before she could get to it. Her heart raced, it was almost too much. The ladder was hers. Didn't she break an ankle for it (strain a ligament, but just as painful)? And being stuck here, with this impossible landscape spread out on a plate for her, was upsetting her fragile state of mind. She had limped out onto the terrace after breakfast, gazed at the gentle folds and undulations of the hills and been reminded of the body of a woman lazing through clear water (at the time, her analogy had impressed her almost more than the landscape). And, did she eagerly assemble her painting gear? Prime her paintbrushes? No she did not. Phoebe stole a look behind her at the vast scape and snapped her eyes shut. Too much, just too much. Alright, she was a coward but she wasn't the only one. You weren't exactly jostling for space out here. She considered the two of them: she and Rose – a couple of cripples, and one of them dead to the world in a deckchair. All those healthy, strapping individuals were out there painting their quaint doorways with geranium pots. Dill had accepted a lift into San Gimignano with that character, Jim, who looked as if he might have been fighting Rommel in the Desert Rats. Jim had even taken his easel, so for him at least it was a serious expedition. Dill would be struggling, she knew. She was even more of a stranger to watercolour than she was herself. And without her elder sister there to keep an eye on things – her *practical* guardian angel if Dill only knew it – if Jim were to show the slightest chink in his armour, the merest whiff of vulnerability, she'd adopt him. They'd have him hanging around for days on end. It would be intolerable.

She looked at the sleeping urchin and marvelled at how utterly battered one could look after a day in the countryside. Just as well she was sleeping so much, poor little scrap. *Why* was she sleeping? It was, after all, only a snakebite. To look at her, you'd think she'd been grappling with a man-eating cobra.

'Ah, you're here!'

Patrick was emerging through the glass doors from the winter dining room.

'Very sensible to "stay put". May I have a look?'

Phoebe suddenly felt defensive about her picture. She hugged it to her and shot a panic-stricken look at Rose. 'Oh look, Rose has woken up!'

Rose opened her eyes. 'Was I asleep?'

'Best thing you could do,' said Patrick resting his hand on Rose's shoulder. 'Would you mind staying where you are for a minute because I think Phoebe is painting you. That right, Phoebe?'

'No, no, no. Well, yes, but I'm not sure it's in a fit state to look at just yet.'

Patrick smiled. 'Come on. Let's have your head on the block.'

Suddenly, Phoebe capitulated and released her portrait of Rose for this man who was, after all, her tutor.

Patrick bent over to look more closely. 'This has a spontaneous quality to it,' he said.

Phoebe's pulse raced. A spontaneous quality! And the way he said it! Did she detect surprise, admiration even? Her painting was validated, the course itself justified, her *raison d'être* established.

'Nice, relaxed weight in that body. But now, there are one or two things – this foot ...'

Phoebe shot forward. 'The foot's unfinished, she moved.'

For the next few minutes, Patrick gave Phoebe an unsolicited lesson in anatomy. Not that she wasn't expecting some teaching from him, of course she was, it was just that one naturally looked forward to a small list of accomplishments given his initial reaction. Metatarsus! What was he saying? She tried to relate his sketch to her painting and get her mind round the metatarsals but her disappointment had made her deaf. Her picture was a complete failure, obviously.

'It's not very good, is it?' she said.

'Not very good! It's a serious attempt to paint Rose asleep in a deckchair. It stands to be counted,' said Patrick who was now towering above her, and there was a hint of – oh, surely it wasn't exasperation? Phoebe was furious at her own naïvety.

'It's what you've learned, isn't it? That's your accomplishment this morning,' he said.

'Yes.'

'Apart from that, this is not a bad painting, not bad at all.'

Phoebe's face lit up briefly. 'Thanks.'

'May I see it?' Rose asked.

The request was polite enough, shy even, but Phoebe felt herself to be on the point of intimate exposure. What was the matter with her? She was a grown woman for God's sake, the cat was already out of the bag, everyone had the right to look at it, criticise it, *mock it* if they so wished. Phoebe passed over her portrait of Rose – to the subject herself – with the distinct feeling that she was peeling off her outer skin: pain mixed with a kind of itchy relief.

'It's really like me!' Rose said.

Phoebe observed her warmly. What an extraordinarily intelligent and beautiful girl.

Patrick said, 'There you are! And Rose is a highly regarded painter.'

A kind of euphoria lifted Phoebe comfortably into the shuddering heat on the terrace. Suspended in that first rush that comes usually only with wine, she welcomed, with a kind of excoriating pleasure, the blinding chinks of light that bore through the vine above her, searing her thighs.

'And dappled light is difficult and you've got it,' Rose said.

By this time, Phoebe was ready for anything. She wanted to gather them about her, clasp her new buddies in each arm and celebrate well into the afternoon. 'Let's go to the pub,' she said.

Patrick was unable to hide his amusement. 'I'm afraid I've got about three people to find before lunch, and they could be anywhere.' He waved his arm vaguely.

Rose looked genuinely disappointed. 'I'd really like to, but I can't move.'

Of course, her idea was impractical. Ungainly Red Cross scenarios sprang to mind; of course, it was ridiculous. Even so, that bar of Gianni's in the village looked reassuringly ordinary. She was determined to try it out as soon as this wretched ankle was better – preferably with Patrick.

'Another time, perhaps. Gianni's is a good place to go,' Patrick called, raising aloft his sketch book as he ducked back inside.

Phoebe beamed at the cosy prospect and stretched luxuriously. The whiff of a breeze swept upwards and lifted the trailing nasturtiums.

There was a cry as Rose tried to get up out of her deckchair. Tears rolled out and she slowly leant back.

'Oh, dear, can I help?' Phoebe was reluctant to move.

'It hurts if I don't keep still.'

'Your snakebite?'

'My rib. It's bruised. I fell over.' Her voice was shaky as a leaf.

Nasty maggots of irritation wriggled below the surface of Phoebe's skin. Minor accidents like this should be 'got on' with; after all, wasn't her own ankle killing her (huge eyes brimming, like a child's); what was she expected to do about it?

Rose ran fingers through her lavatory-brush hair. A lopsided smile split across her tear-streaked cheeks. She said, 'When I'm better, I want to invite you and your sister to meet my mother-in-law.' And then, as if her entire future rested on Phoebe's answer, she added, 'Maybe for tea?'

Phoebe was completely disarmed. How could it have slipped her mind? Rose was a widow, and here she was, barely out of childhood. 'Well, thank you, Rose. We'd like that very much.' She returned the smile, sank back into her chair and wondered suddenly how Dill was getting on without her. Even she had to admit it was unreasonable: to expect her sister to stay and keep her company with an offer like that. Everybody wanted to see San Gimignano. She wasn't sure about going with Jim though; she pictured him in the desert, thwacking his high boots with a cane as he reviewed a line of raw recruits.

'Feel like a cake?'

Jim drummed his fingers on the rickety table causing the coffee cups to wobble. A pigeon launched out from its niche in one of the towers and glided down to perch on the old well in the middle of the square.

'I won't, thanks, Jim, but why don't you have one?' Dill was not unaware of his impatience, but it was just so good to sit in the early morning sun before all the coach parties arrived.

'If you think there's time, then I think I will,' Jim said, standing up and plunging his hand in his pocket. Loose change rattled as he strode off into the café, too wound up to wait for the waiter.

He was not the most restful of companions, she had to admit, but he meant well. Was he really so anxious to make a start on their painting? There was so much to look at here in the piazza, to paint, even. Phoebe, she sensed, had been a little cross to hear she'd been offered a lift to San Gimignano in Jim's hired car. Truly, she'd no intention of leaving Phoebe stuck there at Il Centro with her poor ankle, and, of course, there was no question she would ever desert her, she had reassured her of that at the time. But when her sister had waved her away, saying that if she was going to tackle the landscape, the last thing she wanted was *people* breathing down her neck, it was then she decided she must take up Jim's offer. After all, how else might she have spent a day in this most beautiful of medieval cities had it not been for Jim's kindness?

Dill gazed at the barely populated square, fascinated at the sight of two elderly women, one of them really leaning into the other to make her point. She'd pushed her basket out of the way on her hip and was tugging unconsciously at her dainty little dog at the end of its lead. And the other one nodding back with tightly smiling mouth. If the truth be told, she was immensely happy to be here in Italy with Phoebe, even without Edward. His grumpy reminder that this was what his first wife had done, abandoned him to go off and do her own thing, was just not a proper comparison. As if she would ever abandon Edward! He was very dear to her, and her only sadness was that he and her other best beloved, Phoebe, didn't always hit it off as well as they might. She knew her sister to be rather forceful sometimes, but then Edward was not used to opposition, and, this time round, she confessed, he did seem to be a little unsympathetic to the idea of a painting holiday ('one of Phoebe's arty capers' he called it). Was it because he had been brought up with great paintings around him, as part of the wallpaper, so to speak? There was the business of the Stubbs. She knew he was attached to it, and she could see why. But, as she pointed out (as gently as she could), it wasn't an ancestor they were selling. She had never seen the point of having a Stubbs when you could look at the real thing any time you liked, and if the roof wasn't tackled soon, then they'd have to start with the Gainsborough of Great-Great-Grandfather. He'd been very stubborn. Poor darling, after all, he'd grown up with it. So that in the end, she'd taken him by the hand before breakfast one morning, down to the nursery paddock to look at Pearly Mist and her foal. Their breath was coming from their nostrils in puffs, with twice as many little puffs from the foal, and she could see there were tears in his eyes. 'Sell it. Sell the Stubbs,' he said. And she just knew that for him it was the most beautiful sight he'd ever seen, because it was for her too. It was plain for the whole world to understand: he'd watched a horse in motion. Not even a Stubbs could compete with that. That day she'd put a call through to Burlington's.

Dill sighed and felt her shoulders spread out in the sun. No, she didn't like leaving him behind, but Phoebe was right, she did tend to get a bit bogged down with the zoo and Edward's children and the rest of it, and forget there was another world out there. But now! Dill lifted her face to scan the walls of the *palazzo* surrounding the square – all covered randomly with windows and little holes – she was here! Sitting in the sun in the Piazza della Cisterna in San Gimignano drinking absolutely the best cappuccino she'd tasted ever. Had she been born lucky? It was a notion that came to her only recently, and Dill wondered now whether the deities had not perhaps piled too many riches on her, especially when she thought of Phoebe's struggle to keep body and soul together.

Two young backpackers, legs all askew, were sitting now on the steps that led up to the well. They pored over a guide book, their faces almost touching. But, just a minute – was it a well? Or was it a cistern, a water tank? Either way, it must have provided water for the city hundreds of years ago. The girl was getting up – how pretty she was! She joined the queue at the cash point set into the *palazzo* wall. There was already a man ahead of her in the queue; he was counting a wad of euros. Dill put down her coffee cup and craned forward to see him more clearly, just as the man turned round and bumped into the pretty girl behind him.

'Brought you one too, just in case you got hungry watching me.'

Dill looked up to see Jim standing over her juggling with two plates. She took them from him. 'Jim, over by the cash point, quickly! It's our Van Gogh expert, isn't it? The one with ...'

How extraordinary, he'd gone. Only the girl writing out a form. Dill ran her eye over a handful of people. Just disappeared! There was an arch with some steps near to the cash point. Was that where he'd gone? What a pity. You never know, he might have liked to join them. He did seem to be a loner, but then loners were often just waiting to be asked.

'Can't see him,' Jim said, forcing his head well back on his neck and drawing his brows together.

'Oh, Jim, is this for me? I am glad you got another one.'

'*Thought* you wanted one,' Jim nodded knowingly.

Dill sighed. 'And then, I suppose we really must rouse ourselves. Although I wouldn't mind settling on the piazza here.'

'Oh no. Couldn't possibly paint here. It'll be swarming with Japanese in five or ten minutes.'

There were certain disappointing aspects of Jim that ruffled her slightly. Dill wondered if he'd been in the Second World War, and then she realised he'd have to be about a hundred for that.

'Yes,' she said dubiously.

'When you're ready, we'll find a quiet spot further out.'

'Much more sensible, Jim.' She looked down at curlicues of chocolate powdered with cocoa, and steeled herself to take a bite of the cake.

Although supremely happy under an olive tree in its comfortable shade for the first forty minutes, after nearly two hours Dill was feeling hot and restless. Thank goodness, she had remembered to wear Edward's old shirt, so her arms were covered, although she did notice the backs of her hands were a worrying psychedelic pink. They were in the elevated public gardens in the old fortress. Jim had made a beeline for this airy spot – insofar as a beeline was possible given the circular medieval streets. From here there was a good view of the city with some nice clean shadows on the towers, and stretching around, the plain with its patchwork of vineyards. Dill lifted her white canvas hat and fanned her face before replacing it on her hair which was decidedly damp. It was heaven, but hot. She picked up her water bottle. Empty. Her picture had been really quite promising to start with, almost good enough to match up to one of Phoebe's, but in the last few minutes she had made some infuriating mistakes, and now there was nothing to be done about it.

'It's no good, Jim, I'm starting to flag,' Dill said, looking at the dark brown water in her jar (no wonder it was all going wrong). 'Do you think we deserve a beer?'

'Haven't quite finished this whaddya-call-it,' Jim called over, energetically. He was working in acrylic and had been bayoneting his palette with a coarse-bristled brush and jabbing away at his canvas with feverish intent. Every now and then he would thrust his head round the corner of the easel to glower at San Gimignano lying ahead of him, and then duck back to squint at his painting. Dill admired his staying power: he was in full sun by now, like her. His sinewy arms were the colour of a conker and his back tilted forward as straight as a rod. She couldn't see his painting.

She sighed and looked at young people perched in groups on the walls and grass swigging from bottles of water. Dill gazed at them longingly. It wasn't just that she was thirsty. Maybe if she went back to the café, they wouldn't mind if she used the *gabinetto*. No, much better if she had a quick orange juice and then used the *gabinetto*. And there must be a quicker route back than Jim's. From here she could see a street that seemed to go round the city ramparts. She could quite easily find her way to that, and from there, there were bound to be any number of archways leading into the Piazza della Cisterna.

Dill propped her watercolour against the stool, and as she stood up to stretch, she realised her need for the loo was actually quite urgent. The orange juice would have to wait. She went over to where Jim was sitting.

'May I see?' she said, coming to stand behind him.

'Wassat?' Jim muttered, hardly aware of her presence.

Dill blinked at the jagged representation of San Gimignano in hot colours.

'Oh. That is very powerful,' she said.

'Think so?' Jim said, pleased. 'I'm trying to get away from what I call Tuscan cliché.'

'Oh dear, I think that's what I'm trying to create,' Dill said, swaying sideways in faint embarrassment. 'Can I leave my stuff here for a while? I want to go back to the café. Nature calls!' She smiled back at Jim, already on her way.

As Dill ran down a flight of shallow steps at the end of a narrow street, she had the peculiar feeling she had come full circle. It wasn't that she didn't know where she was going, just that she hadn't realised she'd be going down before going up. She would ignore the steps leading up to the left because they were the steps she strongly suspected she'd taken a minute ago. She'd have to get up to the left eventually, that much was clear, so for the time being, it would be logical to continue down the path until some sort of opening – an arch would do, just as long as it took her in a general upward direction – an arch, steps, or even a bend in the street, so long as it took her up to the left. This hiccup in her plan was unfortunate because truly, she didn't know how much longer her poor bladder was going to hold out, and here she was, still going downhill. There was a niggling feeling that the shallow lot of steps were similar, if not identical to the first set of steps she'd taken soon after leaving the gardens. It may be sensible to go back the way she'd come and take the steps up to the left after all, because she did seem to be getting further away down here. And of course, she would have to remember that the steps would now be on her right. The double-back was now uphill which made the going slower, and Dill tried to remember if she had passed any rough ground on the way where she could at least empty her bladder.

She paused and dropped her head, aware of a painful contraction. Would she make it to the *gabinetto?* Here were the steps. Halfway up, she recognised a strong familiarity in the bits of vegetation pushing through the wall, and once out in the street at the top, her suspicion was confirmed that she had been this way once before, because – oh dear, what a noodle she was! She'd missed a small opening on her way round the first time. *This was the way!* A narrow entrance in the wall that at first glance had looked like a cul-de-sac turned out, now she could see it, to have a right-angled alley at the end of it.

It was the most promising sign so far. Dill turned left into the alley and was startled to see, facing her at the other end, a stuffed boar's head placed behind the glass window of a shop selling salami and olive oil. For a few moments, fascination dispelled sense of time and place as she approached, drawing near enough to see the complex arrangement of teeth and tusks. She wondered if the animal had had difficulty eating its food when it was rooting in the woods, and pictured its tusks tossing up clods of leaf mould in its search for truffles. In a daze, she turned right into a circular street. Then turning right again into a parallel street, Dill was puzzled to see an arch and though it, in the distance, open countryside. She realised she was on the upper ramparts of the city, the very spot she was originally aiming for – before heading back in for the Piazza della Cisterna. She turned to see if she could see Jim in the public gardens, but she must have come all the way round to the far side of the city because there were no public gardens, only more houses and streets below, and nothing but vineyards beyond. Here, the street was covered in tarmac instead of the usual stone paving, and there was nobody about. A bicycle was propped against the crumbling brick facade of a house, and a small car parked next to the low rampart. Further along, most of the shutters were closed for siesta and the washing hung still. Dill knew at once this was her moment of opportunity.

She looked around for a patch of grass. If she nipped down the road a couple of yards where the wall diminished to nothing before the street snaked round and continued back on itself, she might be able to jump down onto the narrow patch of grass in between. Even better, there were two young trees she could use for shelter. She scanned the streets and house facades. Nothing stirred. She could hear a radio playing far away somewhere in one of the shuttered houses, but otherwise, not a soul to be heard, not even the sound of swifts.

Dill let herself down no more than two feet onto the scrubby ground and picked her way over to one of the little trees. Standing close to its spindly trunk she lifted her skirt and quickly eased her pants down.

'Psssst!' The sibilant was forceful and might have come from anywhere.

Dill shot up and made a grab at sensible white cotton knickers down by her ankles. Her heart hammered and she almost keeled over in her haste to replace her clothes.

A low chuckle was coming from a window directly behind her, its shutters wide open. A low-browed woman leant comfortably on the window sill, her arms crossed to make a cradle for her bosom. She winked.

Dill's relief released her stricken muscles and she laughed as she swayed and dipped, clasping her hands together. 'Oh dear!' she gasped by way of a civilised rejoinder. But her stomach was not so quick to relax, and a painful cramp caused her to double over. She put her arm on the flimsy tree to prevent herself curling into a ball and her canvas hat fell off.

The woman said something and tossed her head sideways and up, and then raised her eyebrows twice in quick succession in a rather peculiar way.

'I'm afraid I'm English,' Dill called up. 'I don't understand what you're saying.'

She beckoned to Dill and nodded with an encouraging smile.

'Oh, how very kind of you, I'm so grateful.' It gushed out as half laugh, half gasp. The woman was offering her lavatory. It was an enormous piece of luck that she was spotted by a house owner rather than a passer-by.

Dill forced herself to straighten up against a pain that seemed to lock her intestines into a hard fist. She hobbled over the grass and waved up to the window. The woman stood up as she saw Dill scale the wall and approach the door directly below her. Suddenly her dark eyes widened and she disappeared from view.

The door swung open and Dill was immediately struck by the intensity of the woman's eyes which seemed almost to burn. She was as tall as Dill herself and looked her up and down. Dill dithered, uncertain if she was in fact invited in, when her wrist was tightly grasped and she was drawn inside and the door pushed behind her.

They were in a stone passage at the end of which was a dimly lit courtyard. She had to adjust to the sudden gloom, and stepped out blindly after the woman. As they reached the bottom of the steps at the end of the passage the woman slipped her hand round Dill's waist drawing her close. They mounted the steps in a kind of cosy sideways embrace which was a little too intimate for Dill, but her hostess must have felt she needed some support up the steps. The pain was gone but she felt strangely light headed as if she'd had too much sun. The door was ajar at the top of the steps, and the woman indicated she should go through. As she passed her by at the point of crossing the threshold of what must have been the living room, Dill received a blast of onioned breath combined with the equally strong odour of cheap cosmetics. Large vegetable dishes of cigarette stubs full to the brim were strewn around a plastic-covered sofa. A number of pictures – large canvases – were stacked, face to the wall, and a television was playing with the sound turned off.

It hit Dill that this was not a place in which she would like to spend very much more time. In fact, she suspected, there was something almost unwholesome about the atmosphere. On the other hand, the woman was kindly offering her lavatory; she must be careful not to offend her. She remembered Jim and turned to her hostess behind her. 'My friend is expecting me. He is in the public gardens.'

She was confronted with a distinct leer. The woman was standing far too close to her and pressed even closer to point to the door leading through to the next room. The voice was husky and low.

The room didn't look like a bathroom from where she was; on the other hand there were tiles on the floor; but then tiles were no special indication of a bathroom. Dill was starting to see fuzzy outlines, her mind was dislocated. She protested as she was being propelled towards the door. 'I don't think I will, after all, thank you. My friend is waiting in the public gardens.' She felt her waist gripped as she was half lifted along through the door into the other room. Although the shutters were closed, clearly to be seen standing up against the wall was an iron-framed bed strewn with filthy sheets. On the wall above, a gaudy Madonna cast down her eyes. The two of them ran across the room towards the bed glued together, Dill's feet barely touching the floor.

When they reached the bed, Dill felt her breath being crushed out of her as a tongue burst into her mouth thrusting deep into her throat. She felt nails being scraped across the skin of her chest as her shirt was torn aside and wrenched down over her shoulder. Teeth dug into her neck as her mouth was released. She screamed, 'No ...' And an extraordinary sound erupted from the corner of the room. A kind of compulsive retching, short and repetitive on an expiring cadence, ending with a series of small chuck-chuck-chucks ...

As the woman turned her head towards the tiny croaks, Dill ducked and ran for the door. She heard a shout behind her and made a dash for the next doorway leading out of the apartment. Stumbling down the steps in the gloom she found herself between the courtyard and the passage to the street. Here Dill hesitated, unable to see her way ahead. There was a rustle behind her. Her hair was grabbed and her head yanked back. She screamed and subsided backwards, partly on the stone step, and partly onto the body of the woman. A hand clapped over her mouth and she was trapped, pressed against a hard chest.

An angry question was shouted across the courtyard. Dill felt the woman stiffen and her hand tighten into a vice, blocking the air flow into her nostrils.

The whine of shutters being thrown open and a door banging provoked a short curse close to her ear, and in the next moment Dill was released. The woman was already racing back up the steps in stockinged feet. With the utmost concentration, Dill felt her way up the passage to the door outlined with light. Her fingers found the big key and fumbled uselessly with the intractable metal. She was aware that a wailing sound had pursued her and was all around her in the dark passage. She wanted to shout for help but the wailing was too loud. Finally she banged on the door with the flat of her hand and felt something warm and wet cover her inside legs and squelch into her sandals. The door was pushing against her, and she stepped back. It swung open as the wailing stopped.

Framed in the doorway in the sunshine stood the Van Gogh expert from Montecalmo.

'FFFuh – uh – ffffuh – Huh!' His eyes grew wider.

Dill lifted her arms around his neck and wept.

Chapter 8

Patrick had slipped into the refuge of his office to try and sort out the business of the new girl – at least to try and put his mind to it. Sandy hadn't mentioned the matter again, and he had to admit, he just hadn't the guts to approach her in her present mood. Better to leave it as long as he dared in the hope she'd have a change of heart, but catch it in time to apply to the agency if she was unable to come up with another girl. Wishful thinking: he barely had time to call the agency let alone hedge his bets. The whole thing had put him in a right old frazzle, and just when the season was under way.

Ah, but Margheretta had been pleased to see him. He saw her stretched out on the bed next to him, her arm tucked behind her head, her body tumbling down to her toes. The first time he'd caught sight of her armpits they'd knocked him sideways, he'd never seen so much hair. Now he loved to look at it curling in the middle and slightly damp, and when she dropped her arm, bushing out between the tender white cusp of her armpit. He could have done without the after-sex cigarette, he could always do without the after-sex cigarette, but then no woman was perfect and, after all, she was refreshingly beautiful, all female. All embracing, soft, pneumatic woman. Good God, he was getting another erection. He concentrated on the pencil holder on his desk. Taking out the clutch of pencils he laid them flat and covered them with his hand.

Did Sandy really mean what she said about finding a replacement? He'd be sunk if there was any kind of a hitch; the agency was risky, especially at short notice. On the other hand where else was he going to find a bilingual housekeeper-cum-bookkeeper? The effort of it all – seeing her through the first few weeks – it was enough to make him pack up altogether. Surely he was entitled to be angry about this? Wasn't he the injured party? He tried to imagine confronting Sandy, rattling his sabre a bit, but it went against the grain. She was the one who got angry. That episode in the kitchen. He felt guilty, of course he did, but he couldn't for the life of him fathom why he should. Cat shit started it. He pictured the little pile. Offensive, of course, especially in a kitchen, but that particular cat was always shitting. Really, women were quite prodigal with their emotions. No. It was a mystery the more he thought about it.

Well. Safety first. Patrick picked up the telephone and dialled the agency in England.

'Ah! Patrick Forster here. Yes, I believe I may be in a bit of a fix.' He dried up.

The small window ahead of him was at street level with the courtyard where a car had just drawn up blocking the view. He was watching legs climbing out, but there was something wrong, he was sure. It was two men and a woman, and the woman was moving slowly, too slowly. And one of the men was striding around hauling out luggage and slamming doors as if there was a war on.

'Um. Look. Uh …' Patrick opened and shut his mouth like a fish into the telephone. They were all shuffling towards the front door. 'Ring you back.' He put the receiver down.

As he opened his door into the hall he saw the three of them. Jim and Rankine seemed to be supporting one of the tall sisters who was hanging her head in a very odd way.

'Is everything alright?' Patrick asked.

'Raped by a lesbian,' Jim said, looking straight at Patrick.

'Oh, I wouldn't go as fuh … fuh … far as that,' Rankine protested.

'What else would you call it? Hm? What else would you call it?' Jim was on the way to bursting a blood vessel, a vein standing out like a drainpipe in his neck.

Patrick had an intimation of impending anarchy – that disorientation that comes with a sky full of lightning.

They all stopped. Dill withdrew her arms. 'I want to thank you both for being helpful, but I would like to go up to my room now.' Her voice was weak.

Patrick's reaction was automatic. 'I'll get someone to bring you a cup of tea.'

'Oh, yes.' Dill's relief was touching. She climbed the steps slowly towards her room.

Patrick strode through to the kitchen to fill the kettle. He couldn't dispel Jim's face from his mind. He hadn't encountered such ferocity for years. Those bushy eyebrows shooting up and down. The man was barking mad, he must be. Had he misheard him? His own father's hearing had gone early. Perhaps he'd said *ripped* by a lesbian, her shirt was certainly torn. But even that was an unlikely aberration, especially for San Gimignano. He was reminded of his premonition the evening he made his speech.

The kettle was ready. Where was the tea?

Sandy came in from the terrace and stood in the doorway with a basket of washing from the line. He tried to put a name to the colour of her hair which glowed sensationally.

She frowned at the kettle and said, 'I can do that.'

'It's for one of the sisters.'

'Who, Dill? Is she alright?'

'I'm not sure that she is.'

'What's happened to her?'

Patrick opened his mouth to speak, but for the life of him was unable to form a coherent answer.

She came into the kitchen skirting round him, tilting her head and eyeing him suspiciously, still carrying the washing. There was a tone in her hair that exactly matched the burnished rim of the copper cauldron above her head.

She said, 'Patrick. What has happened to Dill?'

'Look, Sandy. Can you go and have a word with her? It's girl stuff.'

There was a pause.

'She hasn't been raped?'

'I'm not sure.'

'What do you mean?'

'There's an element of doubt.'

Sandy's dark lips twitched slightly. 'It's a pity her sister isn't here. I'll take up her tea.'

A weight lifted from Patrick's chest. He *needed* Sandy here. Why was she leaving him? He watched her put down the basket and quickly assemble all the paraphernalia for tea, bang bang bang. Why couldn't he just give her a hug, get back to the business of teaching and forget this whole damn business of the new girl?

'Oh well. I suppose I must get through to the agency,' he said on his way out.

'Which agency?' Sandy asked sharply.

'Sandy, I can't hang around, I have to get a replacement for you.'

'I told you I'd *find* somebody.' She was furious. 'It's virtually *settled*. There's this friend of mine who's desperate to come. She's practical, she's good with money, she speaks Italian better than I do. She's just got to find someone to look after the *dog*, that's all.'

'Alright, alright, that's good, that's ...'

'And now you've gone and messed it all up. You *know* I wouldn't let you down.'

'Oh, Sandy.'

Her face rearranged itself into symmetrical marble.

'You think I've let you down?' she said.

'Well, yes, I do.'

She regarded him for a long stony moment.

'Actually, I'm doing you a favour, Caroline's perfect. You won't even miss me.'

'Who's Caroline?'

'This friend I've been talking about for the last five minutes.'

Patrick's shoulders dropped and he rubbed his forehead, blinking. Again he felt exhausted. It seemed there was an impenetrable wall around her.

He said, 'Alright. I'll leave it to you.'

She looked away as if she were about to cry. Could he ever say the right thing? As she crossed in front of him with the tray, her face was all sewn up. It was ridiculous. He was sure she was as depressed as he was.

The pool was really too small for serious swimming, but to have it to oneself was a luxury exceeding all else. Isolda glided through the water testing her crawl in short bursts. Vegetation disturbed the pencil beams of sunlight penetrating the wrought-iron gates at the end. They shafted uncertainly through the gloom before striking deep into the water from where darting scribbles of light reflected onto the grotto walls. Isolda touched her target, the marble toes of Leda. She assumed it was Leda. The wings of a swan brushed the statue's supine body as if the massive bird were drawing away from her. One look at the gaga expression on Leda's face confirmed her hunch. Well and truly shagged. Isolda dunked and came up. Then lifting her arms above her head, she drew away from the statue with the help of a small push, and in blissful solitude, allowed herself to float in the centre of the pool.

The fresco above her and all around was something else; incredibly well painted. Who could have done it? Surely not Patrick, not his style at all. These were almost Minoan in their delicacy, sensuality: animals and birds swooping through a forest of willowy branches and tall flowers arching overhead, almost meeting; three naked children played leap frog; another young boy swinging, trapeze-like, from trailing creepers. It was indeed an extraordinary thing to float below this dim, enchanted forest and feel her hot ears smacking in and out of the water. When was this pool finished, six or seven years ago? It was inconceivable that such time and dedication should go into an art centre for amateur lady watercolourists.

She reflected on the air of industry around her. It tired her just to look at them scurrying off with easels to get the best spots. To be on the outside of it was more disconcerting than she'd like to admit, she wasn't used to being on the 'outside' of anything. They were lucky to have a teacher with Patrick's dedication. He was for real: there wasn't a trace of condescension, he was impressive. And another thing, the enormous seriousness of these amateurs was not only surprising, it unsettled her. In the scheme of things, what they produced couldn't matter less, but to some of them it was life or death. By an aberrant quirk, might a painting of some quality result from this degree of zeal? Unthinkable! How could she even have toyed with the idea? (The moving reflections off the water gave the illusion of dappled light filtering through the frescoed forest. It was miraculous, an inspiration. Who had painted it?)

One thing was certain; flippancy was not understood in this ardent assembly of amateurs. Neither must she indulge in it, especially as there were certain areas where she was all too easily in danger of exposing herself for the fraud she was. For one thing, she couldn't draw for toffee. But then, drawing wasn't on the curriculum, thank God. As for painting – well yes, she should have given the painting more thought. (Directly overhead, a fresco monkey had launched itself from the branches of a tree, sailing from one side of the cavern to the other. It hung suspended between the arching branches, its pale underside open to inspection. Isolda looked up and marvelled.)

Back home in London a couple of weeks ago, her way forward had seemed simple enough. She would draw on her mental catalogue of abstract painters and merely rearrange the shapes and colours. Didn't she have a faultless memory for colour and form? It never failed her. Deciding which style she could acquire most easily without detection had seemed the most difficult decision at the time. It wouldn't have been too taxing to have passed herself off as a latter-day naïve of the St Ives school, for example, or even an abstract expressionist in the style of either a Hodgkin or a Heron, circa 1953. Now she was more than doubtful. There were obstacles: the painful events of that morning. She shuddered at the memory of her childish panic when on the point of imminent exposure.

Small ripples of water buffeted against the crown of her head and made her shiver afresh. There had to be a way out. But then, floating there in such utter comfort, sustained by the inspiration of the fresco all around her, Isolda allowed herself to consider the possibility of an authentic Isolda Seagram, her own work, in other words. The style would have to be up to date, of course, in line with today's avant-garde if she was going to be serious about it. The snag was that while it was indisputably in the vanguard – so new, in fact that public consciousness had yet to be fully informed of its future importance – Foetalism was hardly compatible with Tuscan landscape, especially the political variety currently favoured. Then she remembered she couldn't paint anyway and dismissed the idea with an irritable kick.

The antics of the morning came back to her with cruel clarity. Oh, this morning! She had been dabbing away at what she confidently perceived as a Fauve representation of a field of flowers when she spied Patrick approaching up the lane, and suddenly, blindingly, the picture had revealed itself as sub-kindergarten trash. She had dived into a hedge taking her picture with her but leaving her paints and stool behind. Not since 'hide and seek' as a child had she concealed herself from anyone. It was scandalous, and she must make sure it would never happen again. She simply hadn't the nerve, hadn't the steel to offer up her child's daub for serious criticism. She cared what he thought. It was a positive nuisance, especially as she was actually here on more important business, which, she now realised, was beginning to take second place. After her swim she'd get down to it. When she was cool and comfortable, she'd go to her room and apply some serious thought to ways and means of meeting him, the elusive collector, the man himself.

Isolda took a gulp of air and pinched her nose. Her rolling torso broke the surface: breasts, ribs, belly, thighs, knees, and finally toes trailing a few watery drops as she arched backwards under the water heading again for the grotto. She slipped from the pool and perched on the edge, twisting round to look up at the swan. The beak was open and its tongue visible. Webbed feet and mighty drumsticks straddled Leda's hips. What would it be like to be ravished by a swan? Isolda lay back against Leda and opened her mouth, rolling her eyes up at the fierce beak.

The electricity was switched on and light flooded the cavern. There was a mighty crack at the other end of the pool as a body hit the water broadside on. Isolda winced. The creature's arms were already flailing and its legs kicking up a foam as it headed towards her. She had to escape quickly. Too late. The swimmer had veered blindly towards the corner and it was Jim who hauled himself out. He was wearing the kind of swimming trunks her grandfather wore in those cavorting snaps in the South of France – knitted, with gaping spaces for the legs threatening to expose the hairy horrors of male genitalia. He began to throw himself into a series of physical jerks before bumping his head on the sloping side of the cavern. Isolda shouted with laughter, and for the first time Jim noticed he had an audience. He raised his arm in acknowledgement.

'You take your life in your hands if you go into San Gimignano, I tell you,' he said hoarsely.

'Really? Are they being attacked by the Goths?'

'Goths!' said Jim. 'It's lesbians you've got to keep an eye on.'

Isolda felt a prickle running up the nape of her neck and into her scalp. Was this real? The man must have run into a gay demo and taken against the shaved heads and fatigues. She had to watch her step here.

'Is this an aspect of San Gimignano I've been missing?'

'Ask Dill! She'll tell you!'

'What will she tell me?'

Jim's arms were akimbo and he was rocking on his heels. His eyebrows twitched suggestively.

Isolda prompted, 'That there is an invasion of lesbians in San Gimignano?'

She was not going to let this man get away with filthy winks and nudges. Jim's eyes bulged.

'She was attacked by one. *Carnally.*'

Isolda flushed with anger, she wasn't quite sure why. It was the man's bigotry. She wished she was anywhere, *anywhere* but here, because she felt she was about to say something rude to him, something cruel and searing he could never forget, thereby adding him to her growing list of lifelong enemies. Instead she recalled her vow of anonymity, but was unable to prevent her voice rising an octave.

'Is she injured?'

'Scratches all over her.'

'*Virgo intacta*, one trusts?' she squeaked.

'Well I ... I suppose she must be. But it was a pretty nasty business.'

'Well, ye-es. Poor poppet.' Isolda tipped her head sideways reassuringly.

She plopped back into the water and ploughed a dead straight furrow towards the iron gates.

Her feet left dark patches on the gritty stone and a spray of drops shot from her hair as she flicked back her head. Wrapping the towel round her hips, she resolved to come for a swim tomorrow at the same time; the pool had been promisingly deserted until that fool turned up. Panting with a heady mixture of exertion and outrage, Isolda decided that there was nothing like a swim, even if you had to endure stray lunatics.

On her way back to her room she had to pass through two small terraces to reach the house: leafy enclaves set aside as sculpture workshops. At this hour they were both deserted – obviously they were all in their rooms having a siesta, it was far too hot to be outside. She smelt smoke and stopped.

'You've discovered the pool, then?'

For a moment, the voice seemed to come from nowhere. Then she noticed a fresh billow of smoke, and saw Rankine tucked into a corner. He nodded and smiled, juggling with two brushes and a cigarette in his plump fingers.

This was *not* who she was expecting to come across. Easy now. Hold back. Be normal. There was no reason why he shouldn't legitimately be here on a painting holiday.

'Uh huh. *And* the fresco!' she said.

'Astonishing, isn't it?'

Rankine took a puff of his crumbling Gitane and blinked at his subject, a pitted little statue, a stone cherub supporting a scallop shell.

Isolda saw his picture and became still. Her skin crawled, her stomach clenched, she felt herself curl and wither into the bitter hag she suspected that underneath it all, she was. It was good. It was more than good. Damn you, Rankine, you're not supposed to be able to paint, it's why you *deal* in art. She wanted to whisk away the picture before anyone else saw it.

'So you're here to paint,' she said severely.

'Aren't you?' And she caught a knowing flicker from those china blue orbs.

'Of course.'

It was beyond belief: she'd laid a trap for herself and fallen straight into it. She was going to be rumbled, rumbled on two fronts. Not only by Patrick, but also by Rankine, she now realised.

There was a beautiful Rolex watch on his hairless wrist.

'Any idea who painted the fresco?' she asked.

'Fuf-fuf-fuf-raid not,' he replied, flattening the fag end beneath his canvas lace-up. His head was bowed, revealing an incipient pinky baldness through the downy hairs.

Isolda narrowed her eyes and bent forward to examine his picture.

'Mmmm … ye-es …' she murmured at length, watching him squirm from the corner of her eye. She straightened up and nodded towards his watch. 'Smart watch!' she said, and swung away, taking easy strides up the steps with a verve she could not feel.

Deep trouble. Rankine seemed to know why she was here, whereas, to judge from his painting ability, it was becoming increasingly clear to her that *his* presence in the group was perfectly innocent. Worse! There would be no mercy from these real painters, Patrick and Rankine. When the time came, she would be pilloried. Could she bear their inevitable show of tact when it came to assessing her portfolio (as yet non-existent)? She was seriously questioning why she had actually initiated this farce. Here she was, willingly squandering her skills and experience – not in the interests of Renaissance art, nor on behalf of Burlington's, but – was it possible? – to gorge her rapacious vanity. An expensive incursion into the ranks of all these dithering dabblers, *in her own time!* Well, inconceivably, it was so, and now pride was about to take a fall.

The gritty dust on the steps irritated the skin between her toes, her damp body felt dirty, and cavernous uncertainty seemed to lurk in these rooms that led one into another. She shivered.

Patrick was obviously not in his office, she'd knocked twice. But then why should he be? He'd be out in the fields and lanes with his more hardy students – looking for Isolda herself probably. She stood outside the door for a few seconds frowning down at her feet, the towel round her hips breaking the sinewy line of shiny black swimsuit and shiny black peg doll head.

'Hullo, can I help?'

It was Sandy, walking out from the kitchen drying her hands on a tea towel.

Isolda said, 'I need to send a fax. Urgently. Is that possible?'

'I don't see why not.' Sandy lobbed the tea towel onto her shoulder as she passed Isolda to open the office door. 'We charge for it,' she added.

Isolda got a whiff of shampoo as Sandy's copper mane passed her by, slightly wet. She was wearing a short tight skirt of faded denim and a loose singlet showing a disturbing amount of flesh. Isolda cast her eyes over the firm freckled skin and a covering of very fine, twenty-two-carat hair on her arm.

'Is it ready?' Sandy asked, standing by Patrick's desk in the gloom.

Isolda stared at her in a kind of fog. 'What?'

'The fax. Is it ready to go?'

'Ah! No. I have to write it.'

'Then you'll need paper.'

Sandy bent to open a drawer containing a box of plain copy-paper, and the singlet dipped and gaped, cradling breasts of amazing convexity. Who was she anyway, this goddess? Secretary? General factotum? Now she was placing a ballpoint pen on a single piece of paper on the desk.

'Know how to work it?' she asked briskly, lifting her eyes to Isolda, cold green marbles.

'Yes, I'm familiar with this one.'

'Going to England?'

'London.'

'You can pay me later if you like, but it'll be three euros.'

She was by the door now and Isolda tried to recall her name. A sharp anxiety gripped her. She had to keep her here, just for a minute or two longer – but what was her name? She called out just before she was lost to sight.

'Who painted the fresco in the swimming pool?'

Sandy turned and smiled. *She smiled! She was human.*

'I know! It's glorious, isn't it? Antonio Gozzoli painted that.'

'Gozzoli,' Isolda returned her smile. 'Benozzo Gozzoli better watch out, then.'

'If it was Benozzo Gozzoli we'd be charging twenty euros for a swim.'

'Who is Antonio?'

'He taught here once. But he lives in America now. Or it could be Rome, nobody quite knows.'

This was it, it was now or never: 'I believe the Villa Pazzi has some fine frescoes.' She held her breath.

Sandy's face darkened slightly. Her lips tightened.

'It's private, you can't see them. Tancredi Pazzi owns everything.'

Patience, don't rush in, she's going to say more. Suddenly, Isolda felt better: she was on course again. And by a stroke of spine-tingling luck, in the same darkening room as this Pre-Raphaelite angel.

'Not even Patrick has seen them. He's got some fantastic pictures apparently.'

'And the frescoes, did Antonio paint them?'

'*Antonio*! They're all Renaissance. But *actually* ... Antonio got his first big job restoring them. Tancredi Pazzi had heard about the swimming pool fresco and asked to see it. That's when it happened.' She gave the ghost of a smile. 'Patrick said he almost jumped out of his skin when he turned the light on.'

The phone rang on Patrick's desk. Sandy picked it up.

'Hi, Caroline ...' She put her hand over the receiver and mouthed. 'Don't go, won't be long.'

Isolda felt a delectable surge of complicity. It was the 'don't go', and the *inclusion* it implied. She immediately felt secure in the pecking order, one up on this crony Caroline on the other end of the line.

'What's wrong with kennels?' Sandy was saying with a deepening cleft between her eyebrows. She seemed incredulous, 'Eighty pounds a week! Shit! Well, what about your mum? She likes dogs, doesn't she?'

Sandy's green marbles were boring two holes into the desk top.

'Too old! She's fifty! Caroline, I'm sorry but you can't do this to me ... No, I'm sorry, but you can't put me in the shithouse like this ... You don't understand, I've booked the flight home on Thursday, *paid* for it. Two hundred and sixty-five fucking *euros* – shit, Caroline! Look, I can't talk now, I'll ring you back.' She replaced the receiver and pondered the telephone.

Isolda said, 'Can I help?'

Sandy turned slowly to face her, as if she were staring at a speck in the universe.

She tried again, 'Anything I can do?'

'I'm not staying. I can't stay,' Sandy said.

'Does this mean you're going?'

Sandy began to breathe deeply and noisily, her mouth tight shut. She was going to cry. Isolda had an overwhelming urge to put her arm round those freckled shoulders, but as usual, at the same count, the desire was checked.

'You can't! I mean please don't go, I've only just come.' What was she saying? She was losing her decorum.

Sandy wound the tea towel in both fists as if she were getting ready for a garrotting.

'You know what it's going to boil down to, don't you? It's going to boil down to *me* looking after that fucking dog.'

Isolda was unable to follow her train of thought, still less put it in context. All she knew was that she wanted it to stay like this for hours at a stretch, with the two of them in this dusky room so close they could reach out and touch. This earthly angel was now deep in thought, quite motionless – so still, she may have been the subject of an old photograph drained of colour except for her sepia hair and a few freckles on her nose.

Sandy slipped down from her perch and out of the office without looking back. Gone!

Gone.

A second stretched into an eternity of emptiness.

Ah, yes, now where was she? Isolda stared unseeingly at the fax machine.

This was not an unfamiliar thing, this sudden ineluctable plunge into love. It was rarely reciprocated, but that had nothing to do with it. It happened. It was a searing, tearing-to-pieces exposure to life. And eventually, she told herself, one day she would wake up, and be able to carry on without a blip.

Where was she? Fax. The fax to Diana.

S.O.S. Please dispatch 6 or 7 paintings in ones and twos – as and when paint dry. Your choice medium – watercolour, pastel, oil. General Tuscan landscape – distant mountains (maybe include San Gimignano), fretwork small vineyards, fields, olive groves, small farms, lines of cypress. Gorse in bloom. 32 x 41 cm or smaller. Secrecy essential. Will make it up to you. Izz.

Chapter 9

Bathed, dressed and still in turmoil half an hour later, Isolda lay on her bed and tried to direct her thoughts. Antonio Gozzoli. Was he a descendent of Benozzo Gozzoli? His Saint Augustine frescoes in San Gimignano were on her list of things she must visit. There had been no information on an Antonio Gozzoli; what were the other gaps in their information? And what *about* his fabulous fresco, its memory indelibly linked to the sensation of cool green water in her armpits and ears? Gratifying to know she wasn't the only one to recognise his amazing talent: Tancredi Pazzi had 'almost jumped out of his skin'. Yes, but she was already two days into the course and still no entrée to the Pazzi collection. How to get *in*? How to make the whole thing happen naturally?

Her old travelling clock ticked on as she began to muster her thoughts. So, Tancredi was known to them round here, but how exactly was he perceived – as difficult? Certainly elusive. Maybe invisible. On no account must she drop her guard if and when she came to meet him; as far as anyone knew she was here to paint: a student of art. To Harold, of course, the very idea of a major auction house lending its name to a clandestine investigation carried out by a member of its own staff was tantamount to perjury. She had a vision of Harold shaking his head gravely when she'd presented him with her big idea of coming to Montecalmo for a painting course. 'Unthinkable, unthinkable, Isolda, you don't *look* like an amateur painter. My instinct, anyway, is not to touch this consignment – any of it.' She remembered the euphoria of those heady weeks, and realised why she was so sure Harold would fall in with her plan. He was, after all, the cat that had the cream, all of it, and if they played their cards right, he would grow to be a very fat cat indeed. Even Harold could see that *they had to keep them coming*, and the only question that remained was, who held the key to this discrepancy that dare not speak its name? Tancredi Pazzi, or Sturt-Percy?

Her first sight of Sturt-Percy's dilapidated old house sprang to mind, grey and forgotten in that undulating Derbyshire wilderness. She had waited shivering on the steps, braced against the icy wind. Sturt-Percy had come to the door looking exactly as she imagined he would look from the telephone call: lank hair greased down, drooping bags under his eyes, and a charming smile revealing yellowing teeth. A threadbare tweed suit billowed a little at the knees. 'Oh, come in, come in,' he said in a voice resonating from upper sinuses. 'Weather fit to freeze your balls off.' Isolda recalled his watchful smile at her stunned response to his pictures. And all the brandy afterwards in front of the fire, with Sturt-Percy growing more indiscreet by the minute. His blurred eyes would hardly open in the end, and his tongue seemed too big for his mouth. 'Ever heard of Tancredi Pazzi? Grandson of old Paolo. Now *he* has some *astonishing* pictures. Bronzino, Castagno, Luini, Piero Della Francesca, couple more Paninis, absolutely astonishing. Strictly between the two of us – and I'm only saying this because you're an extremely exciting young woman – I think he's in the mood to sell.' She couldn't wait to get back to tell Harold.

Ah, but when Sturt-Percy's *first* batch arrived, that was a moment to remember! It was a feast. Superb, solid works of art, with a Pisanello drawing of two dogs she ached to possess (for which she was on the point of declaring herself bankrupt if the truth be known); an extraordinary collection ready to be unleashed onto the market, and all of it under Burlington's roof. A fortune was subsequently made, no question about that. 'We are the chosen,' Harold had said, 'the trusted haven for his treasures, his touch of Midas.'

And then there was the bombshell of the Panini in the second, much smaller batch. She voiced her suspicions only to him. 'I think it's a fake, Harold. And you know something? Remember when I went to see him? Well, Sturt-Percy said a *couple more* Paninis. Tancredi Pazzi had a *couple more Paninis* in his collection. Now why should he say that?'

Harold was confused. He said, 'What do you mean? That fake Paninis are being tossed off on a conveyor belt? The entire collection from Sturt-Percy was collected by his cousin at the turn of the century! It's been sitting in that rotting mansion for years! We have the provenance for every single picture.'

And then she'd rung Sturt-Percy to give him the merest hint of her suspicions, and he'd been very flaky indeed and demanded that the picture be sent back to him at once if they had doubts: 'And now look, I think I may have given you some very misleading information on Pazzi. I just – well, I got carried away by your estimates. It was sheer fantasy, and I hope you'll forget the whole idiotic episode.'

'So, you see Harold, he's hiding something.'

She had a nose for this. Hadn't she spotted a Victorian fake Panini only four years ago? She'd sent off the provenance to the MMPRD who'd confirmed her suspicions, and Burlington's had withdrawn it. There was apparently nothing fishy about the provenance for this one, but still she could smell something. Prolific Giovanni Paolo Panini with his architectural fragments wildly out of context, and so popular with tourists that forgeries were to be found far and wide. There was something that didn't quite fit with this one from Sturt-Percy, signed and dated 1739. Here was the Coliseum, there was an Arch of Titus, down here, the sarcophagus of Constantia, all perfectly unexceptional. But his figures! They were not only lively – that was always the case with Panini – but these were captivating, different, imbued with playfulness, *having fun.* And there was something else: she was familiar with his dogs, his horses, his birds, even his cows, but she'd never seen a monkey.

She begged him to forget the information she'd given him until she'd returned from the art course in Montecalmo. But Harold thought she was asking him to pass on a dodgy Panini. She had to be very firm, very persuasive: 'I'm not suggesting you put it in the auction, Harold! Just wait till I'm back from Italy in two weeks. No one need know: this is entirely off my own bat – I'm not asking for an official endorsement. Then, Harold, *then* you can decide, if you're going to wash your hands of the whole consignment … *or*, in the light of my new cosy relationship with Tancredi Pazzi – on my return – hang onto it!'

Isolda smiled up at the ceiling from her comfortable bed in Montecalmo. Greed had gained the upper hand, even with Harold. 'Look, Isolda, I'll hold fire for you. Alright, I know nothing about a fake Panini *yet*. But I absolutely want to make it clear that you're on your own.' Canny old Harold, he might even be thinking of her on his retirement in five years' time: Harold's replacement – at her age! She shivered. Complete fantasy – but then, hadn't she seen his eyes light up at her sheer cleverness? Mentally she ran her eye down the list of wet wicks in the Old Masters department. Drips, the lot of them. She couldn't think of one who would go out on a limb like this.

She fixed her eye on the cunning handmade light shade suspended above her head and could have sworn she smelt chocolate. The aroma steadily infiltrated her consciousness. In fact, she was finding it difficult to stick to her train of thought. Concentrate, Isolda, think. Struggling to dismiss the tantalising smell, she tried to bring herself back to the Pazzi collection, but it was difficult. The casual entrée was what she was after, but the possibilities were limited, and not only limited, but potentially hit-and-miss. The strongest link was this hopelessly neurotic little girl, Rose, the widow of a Pazzi son. Could she summon the necessary sympathy to win her trust and wheedle an invitation? She'd felt a kind of wary stand-offishness from the girl, but this was normal; most people were scared of her. Well, she'd have to try soon. In fact, if it weren't for this bizarre obstacle between them, she'd have got it over and done with sooner. How *did* one approach someone whose husband was the victim of a gruesome murder? Obviously, she mustn't give Rose the slightest hint that she knew about it. She shivered. The severed head of a boar. Tragic for the family, but so corny. Really, you'd think someone had put it there to implicate the Mafia.

Oh, why did Harold agree to let her go? She was hardly valued for her ability to melt into the background; in fact she had to be the least likely candidate for undercover work. She hadn't begun to imagine what this place would be like, she'd just dived in. Anyone else would have run a mile. With a dragging sensation in her chest, the revelation came to her: because they all had too much sense! Her colleagues, had they an inkling of what she had in mind, would have had the simple ordinary common-or-garden sense to see a course for amateur painters as the excruciating *mise-en-scène* she now so clearly recognised it was. What was she doing here? Isolda Seagram. The most formidable up-and-coming force at Burlington's, dreaded adversary in *any* debate! The urge to cut and run was almost overwhelming. She must go, and go quickly. Except. Except ... that Sandy was here. Here. Yards from where she lay on her bed.

She was on fire, and as always, it threatened to consume her. The picture of Sandy perched on the desk, she knew, would be destined to return to her again and again, her radiant immobility etched forever in her mind. Should she forget the whole thing and leave on the next available flight? Perhaps she should fork out 'two hundred and sixty-five fucking euros' and book a seat on Sandy's plane – assuming she was bound for London. What would that gain her? A few hours' blissful proximity. Then what? An empty lifetime without her. Why shouldn't she stay in this sun-drenched place and watch Sandy's freckles multiply, at least till Thursday. Why was this gloriously volatile and indispensable person leaving? There was something here in Montecalmo she wanted to avoid. Something that made her cry when she thought about it. Was it a person, a situation? And what about this dog? She longed to take the burden off those sweet shoulders.

Isolda turned to look at her clock by the bed. Five o'clock. It was a good time to visit the doolally sisters and check out that preposterous story.

Not even Jim's unlikely tale prepared her for the sober expressions and quietly folded hands confronting her in the second Van Gogh bedroom. Phoebe was giving her a distinctly hostile welcome. Rose, too, was there, mournfully gazing at Dill, who lay on the bed as pale as Millais' Ophelia. Isolda wondered if she could deal with this dirge-like display of solidarity.

'Dearie me!' she said, clasping her hands like everyone else.

Dill gave her the ghost of a smile from her pillow.

'We're not awfully good company, I'm afraid, but do come in.'

'Oh, Dill, you must rest, you know you must,' Phoebe said.

'It's alright, Phoebe, I'm really feeling much stronger.'

Isolda's legs were filling with lead. Was the story true? She felt horribly uncomfortable and wanted to escape. And yet, the need to stay around and have what must have been a gigantic misapprehension explained to her was uppermost.

'Are you ill?' she said. Her mouth was dry.

'Dill was attacked in San Gimignano,' Phoebe said quickly.

Rose said, 'By a woman.'

'Was she armed?' Isolda was icy calm.

'She wasn't armed, but she was terribly strong.' Dill's face crumbled momentarily. 'I was very stupid and went into her house to use the lavatory.'

'It was either that or doing it on the verge outside,' her sister said.

'Yes. And what did she do?'

'She kissed me.'

Isolda held her hands together more tightly to stop them shaking. She said, 'Yes?' She was waiting for more, but Dill was clearly struggling. 'I see. That must have been – very unpleasant.'

Dill nodded wordlessly.

'And after she had kissed you, what happened then?'

'I managed to escape,' Dill whispered.

'After you were kissed?'

Dill turned her face to the wall.

'I'm sorry, I thought you were *attacked*.'

Phoebe jumped to her feet, ablaze.

'Well, it wasn't a peck on the *cheek*!'

'Phoebe, please.' Dill succumbed to tears.

Phoebe went to her at once, 'I'm sorry, darling.'

Dill took her sister's hand, 'I want to forget it happened.' She turned beseeching eyes on Rose and Isolda. 'I really want to forget it happened.'

For the life of her, Isolda was unable to grasp what she'd been told. She tried to imagine herself passionately lusting after Dill in the street and forcing a kiss on her. It was a barrier one simply did not cross. There was clearly more to it, significantly more, but this was not the moment to find out. She was so angry she wanted to pack her bags and catch the next flight home. Instead, she forced her usual stab at conciliation and tilted her head.

'Of course. I'm so sorry. Do hope you feel better. See you at dinner.'

'Voila! Mesdames, 'sieur.'

Jason lowered the chocolate cake as if the slightest wobble would cause it to fracture. It sat centre table, wide and shallow and dark, decorated with paper-thin curls of a paler chocolate. In twos and threes they stopped what they were saying, and gasped. Jason caught Rose's eye and gave her a wink. She knew perfectly well he was from Essex because he'd told her about his father being made redundant at Dagenham; maybe he spoke French when he'd cooked something really special. She realised her mouth was watering.

'Bon appétit!' He made an elaborate bow as if he were a footman at the table of Louis XIV.

As Jason backed away from them he almost collided with Sandy passing by with two identical cakes for the other tables. She skilfully curved her body to avoid him, lifting the cakes aloft. 'I know this is good,' she called out, 'he let me lick the bowl.'

The cake sat there in the candlelight waiting to be devoured. Swifts were still cruising in the valleys and light was failing fast; yet along the trestle tables, lines of high complexions and clear eyes gleamed with colour. April, the American girl, nearest to Jason's confection, leant forward to savour the smell.

'Oh deep and dark. Bitter and sweet and deep and dark,' she said. She had been the first one to realise Patrick's point about Delacroix. 'Now, how do we do this?' she went on.

Picking up the knife, she looked round with a smile.

'Anyone noticed? There are nine of us. There is just no way I'm going to be able to cut this fairly. Anyone else like to do this?'

'You do it.' Rose responded with everyone else.

'Well, if you're all sure ...?'

'Go on. We trust you.'

April scored the surface of the cake in a series of bicycle spokes, and then she cut along the lines.

'Oh, this is almost a mousse, it's so light,' she said, licking a sliver attached to her finger. Her eyes opened wide and snapped shut in extravagant rapture. 'I'm right, I think I'm right! It's almost a mousse!'

'One slice is definitely bigger,' said a large man half out of his chair.

'Well, now!' April glinted. 'In that case ... Whoever feels most deprived and believes they've had the worst time – raise their hands first, and they can have the biggest piece.'

There was a pause.

'And then, those who feel the most secure can go last.'

She held absolute sway, the mantle of guru had been conferred upon her. Except that Isolda had something to say.

'If you put up your hand for the biggest piece, you're going to have an even worse time because you're going to be the most unpopular person at table.'

'Now that is a point,' April said.

'So the question is ...' Isolda went on, 'are you going to be more deprived by taking the biggest slice and making yourself the most unpopular person at table – or – by having a smaller slice and missing out on that extra mouthful?'

Rose was sure there was logic in this somewhere, but she was going almost deaf and blind thinking about the cake.

April's husband was sitting next to her. He lifted a finger and cleared his throat.

'I am a qualified psychiatrist. If he feels he needs it, I could offer my services free to the person who has the biggest slice.'

The man who had first noticed that there was a slice bigger than the rest stood up immediately and pushed back his chair so it crashed to the floor.

'I'm sorry but I'm suffering from pudding rage. I do hope nobody minds – I'm going to take the biggest slice.'

His huge chest towered over the table and in a trice, he'd removed the biggest slice of cake and whipped it up to his mouth.

Isolda turned to the psychiatrist.

'Is pudding rage a recognised syndrome, Doctor?'

'Well, now, I'm not too certain it would qualify as a case for treatment.'

'Now look!' The large man crammed almost the whole slice of cake into his mouth as he was simultaneously scrabbling at crumbly bits of chocolate that were dropping onto the table.

'Though, I think perhaps it should,' the psychiatrist added.

Half swallowing and half choking, the large man pointed at him and wagged his finger up and down. Then he struck the table with his fist, but was not yet able to speak without spitting out more cake.

Phoebe's voice came from the end of the table.

'Can we have our cake please?'

That did it. There was a crashing of china as everyone handed in their plates together. As the first spoonful met her tongue, Rose knew that she was somewhere close to tasting food for the gods. It was melting and elusive, sending delayed pinprick signals to separate parts of her mouth, while the aroma of chocolate itself hovered above and beyond her nostrils.

Phoebe said, 'Where's Jason? I want to ask him to marry me before anyone else gets in.'

'You're married already,' Isolda said.

'Don't tell him,' Phoebe said.

Rose basked. She melted like the chocolate in her mouth. The only missing element out here on the terrace was Dill who was upstairs having her supper on a tray. When Phoebe and Dill were together they merged into one rather overwhelming person: twice as forceful. Except that this afternoon, a miracle happened, Rose felt that she was automatically being included as the other sister. It was difficult to know why it had meant so much to her. She'd felt a kind of nostalgia, but it was a nostalgia for something she had never known, because after all how could she know what it was like to be a sister? She was an only child.

Rose heard Isolda, sitting on her right, explain to someone how to use a fax. She'd had a fright when Isolda had plonked herself down in the spare seat next to her and she just knew she was going to say something stupid and make a complete idiot of herself, but really, Isolda seemed to be making a big effort to be friendly to her. It was weird, too polite to be natural.

Rose looked out at the darkening valley and watched a big three-quarter moon inch its way up from behind a line of cypress on the hill. Very soon the halo of colour over the mountains would thicken into the dark velvet of night. Against her will, she thought of Toni Vasari. A dull ache in the pit of her stomach spread into her loins and she closed her eyes in confusion and a kind of dread. Her body divided into painful contesting parts: her ribs, her joints, her muscles, and now there was this. Please, dear God, let her think of Toni Vasari without wanting him. Tomorrow she would drag her pathetic body down to paint Lucia's house even if it killed her. She knew that if the painting went well, it would anaesthetise the pain. A lingering taste of chocolate clung to the folds under her tongue.

Sandy was wending her way between the tables towards them with a piece of paper in her hand. Rose heard Isolda break off what she was saying to her neighbour.

'Your fax!' Sandy waved the paper at Isolda.

Isolda became strangely animated and began to speak very fast.

'Oh, it's arrived! And in fact, I would have been very surprised if I hadn't heard back tonight. And, Sandy, how nice of you to bring it to me ...'

She took the rolled fax and swiftly unravelled it, smiling at Sandy. Her face dropped and the roll snapped shut. Rose saw the message, she couldn't help it – just a couple of words on a blank page.

Get stuffed. D.

Rose held her breath. Who would dare to tell this terrifying person to get stuffed? Isolda sat stiffly, her face a complete blank, until the big gold-capped cafetières were carried out to them and she announced '*Coffeeeee*!' in a loud voice. And when everyone turned to look at the loaded trays, she pushed the fax into her pocket.

Chapter 10

It nestled. For some reason, you couldn't say it perched, even though it had been built halfway down the valley on the brow of a hill. From Rose's painting position on a hillock looking down on Lucia's decrepit farmhouse, it seemed to be cradled in the centre of the landscape, closely cosseted by spring vegetation surrounded by a deep backdrop of mountains. Above them the sky was filled with the hurly-burly of thunder clouds, and dollops of cumulus raced above her head, so close that had she been a creature from another planet, she might have ducked. Brilliant periods of sun afforded her the distinction of shadow, but then the sun would vanish from Lucia's house and illuminate the valley behind. A noisy raindrop splashed onto her boater, another on her painting, and she wavered, half poised to take cover. But the clouds sped on, and the sky above shone hot and blue, good for another few minutes of work.

Through the grass down by Lucia's house a black cat stalked, while at the foot of a ladder a tabby sat twitching its tail waiting for the black one to get closer. Where the top of the ladder met the wall, in half a dozen holes below the eaves, feathery white tails bottomed up: Giovanni's doves busy tending their eggs. Directly above them on the mossy roof tiles, courting doves sunned themselves, stretching and puffing, dipping and twirling, constantly fluttering to the ground. There was a new tube of Chinese white in her box. Maybe, just *maybe*, she'd paint the doves in later. It was already a fairy-tale house … and with the doves? … *Non, nein, niente, ochi*! There was just no question about it; the doves would be too much. Her aches and pains were not so bad today; Toni Vasari was as thin air.

Giovanni and Lucia – where were they both? The house was not complete without Lucia perched on the step preparing vegetables, and Giovanni was forever hovering around.

Rose looked around her. It couldn't have been safer here: just outside the walls of Montecalmo, away from the road, unreachable by road, even; Patrick would be pleased with her. She was doing what he wanted: taking time off to paint. Her next task was to visit the castle back in the village to see if Kitty had picked up any rumours. Rumours were all she had to go on now until Sacchetti turned up with something fresh. She pictured Kitty's anxious little face leaning forward to catch every word. Would it be wise to tell her what her mother-in-law had said about what happened to Dodo – that it might have been 'a mistake'? Of course not! Kitty, of all people. No, this was far too tempting for Kitty to keep to herself.

At last! Here came Lucia – more hard and sinewy than Kitty, but no taller – in her apron clumping down the steps. Lifting her knees to support massive gumboots. Always in boots, winter and summer. Darting away, hacking the tumble of grasses with her small scythe around the dirt track. It seemed a funny way to tidy up: sudden, random dives at the weeds. Then she saw Rose and her face lit up. The scythe shot skywards in greeting and she called out something indistinguishable as she plodded up towards her. On her way, she made another swipe with the blade, this time scooping up the green stuff and lifting the pile to the side of her body. Rose waited for her with arms outstretched. Lucia dumped her bundle and Rose bent low to kiss her, suddenly consumed by the smell of aniseed.

'*Ciao*, Lucia! How are you? How's Giovanni?'

As if on cue, a thin, high cry of pain came from the house.

Lucia's cupped hand described circles in the air. 'Eh, Giovanni. He cries from the pain in here – *here.*' She put both sets of fingers to the centre of her bony chest as if to prise it apart. 'What can you say? He was ploughing yesterday.'

'Does he take medicine, Lucia?'

'He forgets. All the time, he forgets.' Lucia smiled suddenly and delved in her apron pocket. She brought out three elegant broad bean pods and pressed them in Rose's hand.

'*Benissimo!*' Rose exclaimed. She knew they'd be as sweet as honey.

Lucia stretched up and patted Rose's cheek. '*Che bella, bella.*'

She had the palest blue eyes Rose had ever seen, paler than aquamarine.

'Lucia, are you well?'

'Rosa, Rosa, how can I say I am well? Once I was a baby, then I was well. Then I was a beautiful girl like you and I was *more* than well. Ah, I was a juicy morsel in those far-off days for a good few *bei giovanotti*, I can tell you. When I was a mother, I was tired, so tired, and my children grew up to be strong. My beautiful children went off to Canada, all except one, just the one – the sweetest of all – and then …' she bent with a sigh to pick up her scythe and hobble in a semicircle around Rose using the scythe as a stick. 'Look at me now, I am old and nearly done.' She finished with a gleeful 'Heh …', brushing away her story with a flourish, and picked up her armful of greens.

'Eh, heh, heh. Now for the pig,' she said, and made for a narrow track that led up to the line of decrepit sties.

The broad bean pods were soft. Rose slid her thumb down the centre and picked out the sleeping beans. Juicy morsels, just as Lucia had been as a girl.

'Since when have peasants round here been quoting Dante?'

Rose had no idea where the question came from, but with a rush of disquiet she recognised the voice.

'Over here behind the fig!'

Isolda was standing behind a clump of brambles and a fig tree the other side of the hillock. She added, 'I've been here for an hour, I didn't know *you* were here. Who was she?'

'That was Lucia. I can only just make out what she says, her dialect is … OW!' Rose's ribs twinged as she collapsed onto her stool, desperate for more aspirin.

Isolda walked round from behind the brambles. She had on an outsize man's shirt worn as a smock over her clothes. It was laundry ironed and very clean, and here she was, striding up without even asking if Rose *wanted* to be interrupted. Lucky she felt so irritable; it gave her just enough strength to face the intruder.

'What is her dialect?' Isolda asked.

'Well, I don't think it's from round here. She is quite an actress: that was the story of her life,' Rose said. She was going to be quizzed; she could see it coming, so she wallowed in the pain and picked up her palette, frowning blindly at her painting.

Isolda smiled and turned to look at the house, her hands on her hips, her head tossed back in the wind.

'So this is where she lives, is it?'

There was another animal cry from inside.

'Dearie me,' said Isolda swinging round, her face questioning.

'That's Giovanni with his angina.'

Isolda was facing her directly now, her hands still bunched on her hips, bang in front of her view of the house. Rose cleaned her brush methodically and picked up a tube of Chinese white.

'You seem to know the family well!' Isolda said.

'For about two years, off and on.'

'Oh then you're practically a local yourself! Of course! You're part of the Pazzi family.'

Rose adjusted her painting nervously. Isolda was going to pursue this and she wasn't ready for it. She felt a prickle of anger and she was glad of it.

'Yes.' She tried to keep her eyes on her picture.

'I hear they have some marvellous paintings, I'd give anything to see them.'

Rose had squeezed some Chinese white onto her palette and was actually on the point of painting a dove. She blinked in disbelief.

'Kept under lock and key, they say. You must know it well – the collection, I mean. I believe it's quite important.'

'I don't quite know why I'm painting in this dove. I'd decided against it.'

'Why? If they're there, why not paint them in?'

'Aren't they a bit – you know, sentimental?'

'Of course they are. The entire cottage is over the top. That is what it is, sugar and spice and all things nice.'

Rose's hat, her arms, her shoulders were suddenly splattered with cold untidy drops of rain. Looking up into the blue, she saw a massive black cloud advancing on their flank. Isolda was galvanised. She grabbed Rose's painting and tried to cover it with her shirt while Rose bent to gather her materials. Together they set off back to the village in single file with a rumble of thunder in the west. The sun shone as bright as ever, but when Rose stopped suddenly, it went in.

'Where's your painting?' she asked, horrified at her selfishness.

Isolda almost bumped into her, 'Oh, you don't have to worry about that, I stuffed it under a bush.'

'It'll still get wet! You must go back for it.'

'It's perfectly safe.'

'You can't leave it there, you just can't! Give me my painting I'll carry it upside down.'

'Certainly not, it's far too risky.'

There was a crack of thunder and a shout. Lucia was leaping down the narrow trail towards them, elbows jutting. They stepped up into the grass to leave room for her as she passed them by on her way back to the house, waggling the scythe to acknowledge them, her voice breaking and burbling like a water bird.

Rose's panic was intensified by Isolda's presence behind her. 'It's really nice of you to look after my painting, but I can't let this happen, please go back for yours.'

'Let's just find some cover, shall we, and discuss this later.'

'*You* find some cover, Isolda, and I'll go back for it.'

'Look! How can I make you understand this? (A) I'm getting wet standing here in the pouring rain, and (B) I couldn't give a tinker's cuss about my fart-arsing painting!'

Rose's mouth fell open as she blinked at Isolda.

'No, really, what I'm trying to say is – you know – it's sweet of you to be so concerned, but actually my painting is absolutely watertight tucked under the blackberry bush.' Then Isolda lifted her head slowly, eyes widening. 'Look!'

A rainbow arched over the storm-dark valley. It sprang from the direction of Castiglioni in Chianti encompassing the now invisible San Gimignano, finally alighting on Torre del Cesi some distance behind Lucia's house, which was now in shadow.

'Come on,' Isolda said with a grin, and pushed in front of Rose to get ahead of her, still carefully protecting the painting. She looked behind her. 'Follow me, little one.'

Rose followed obediently, still smarting from Isolda's quite amazing snub. She had a sudden insight into the life of a dog. If it weren't such an agony to put one foot in front of the other, it might be quite nice to be taken for a walk, even in the rain. No decisions to be made, lots of smells to tickle your fancy. When she was better, she would abandon all struggle to be human and become Isolda's dog.

They passed the pigsties, most of them crumbling back into the grass, and the rain hit the wild fig trees smacking the flat leaves into a frenzy of movement. Isolda started to run, a long loping stride; Rose did her best to follow, gritting her teeth. She looked down to see the rain streaking across the landscape, pouring into olive orchards and vineyards, while further off, the sun glinted on a farmhouse roof. They forged up the trail till it rounded a corner, and here they emerged onto the path that led round the ramparts. Together they looked down into the valley.

People were scurrying up the paths and over the fields for shelter, some of them encumbered with stools and easels. Rose thought she saw Phoebe and Dill standing together looking back at the rainbow. Isolda laughed and renewed her pace, making for the road that led up into the town.

A car rounded the corner by the old tower that marked the East Gate. It crawled down the steep road towards them with its headlights on, the rain bouncing off the tarmac in front of it, a rusty wreck with rickety windscreen wipers that thumped and squeaked, sloshing aside copious streams of water. Rose and Isolda stepped up into a doorway for safety as the car rolled past, blinded by steamy windows.

'No use trying to get dry *now*. Come on!' Isolda said to Rose who had stepped back to lean against the door behind her.

How could she confess to this tall energetic person so full of life and certainty, and *expectancy*, that all she wanted to do was to lie down and be put out of pain, to be left alone and tucked up in bed? She stepped out onto the tarmac and immediately made her way back to the wall to sink against the wet boulder-like stones.

Isolda stopped and moved swiftly towards Rose.

'What is it? Your snakebite? You're feeling dizzy? Lean on my arm.'

She frowned and looked down the street. 'What's going on? They're coming back.'

The car that had driven past them no more than a minute earlier appeared from where they had last seen it leave the town, this time shooting uphill towards them in reverse, the engine's groan ascending to a scream. Unable to keep a straight line the driver rolled from one side of the road to the other while the car's body listed from left to right.

Isolda shouted, 'Keep in!' and threw her arm across Rose pinning her against the wall. The car, its white paintwork splattered with mud, suddenly lost momentum and drew alongside. The woman passenger lifted her white gloved hand to rub away the condensation. She lowered her sunglasses to observe Rose with certainty, her dark eyes widening as she met her stare. When the car began to free-wheel slowly forward, gathering momentum, the glasses were lifted back into position. And as they watched it disappearing through the East Gate, blinding sunshine flooded the town, beating off the tarmac, and Rose's constricted muscles relaxed. She slid slowly down the wall under Isolda's arm, and softly onto the road.

With her head tilting first to the left, then to the right, Kitty tried looking at them from several angles. These slippers were absolutely the last word in luxury: red satin with a dark sable pompom. They *titillated*, an essential quality in shoes at her age. Her daughter Twink was so clever to have found them! In Milan, she said, in a shop that still sold uncalled-for sizes. What a miraculous find after all those wasted years searching through Startrites for something sophisticated in size two. Glamour on tap in the evening of her life; really, she hadn't felt so pampered since she lived with Tiri in Budapest when he took her to those intoxicating musical comedies, dressed in Schiaparelli. She'd said as much to Twink just now on the telephone. She'd laughed, the darling girl, and said she'd look for the basket-work sandals in French blue.

A dreamy look lingered on Kitty's face, and with her hand still resting on the receiver, she craned forward on her precious chaise longue and gazed again at the slippers. A bandy leg was raised and a toe pointed. Not bad for seventy-five! Only herself to please now, of course, although she felt sure she had cut a dash at Patrick's the other night in the green slingbacks. Oh, she adored the start of the season, all those lively new faces – well, of course Patrick attracted the very best sort of person – and it was so characteristic of him to include her. Had she been indiscreet to let them know about Rose's tragedy? Patrick's Chianti always seemed to make her tongue run away with her, and then of course she was r*eady* to have a good old chatter after the long, lonely winter. She had to admit, the winters were not such fun here in Montecalmo. If she had the cash, come February, she'd be off to Morocco to stay with the Lafittes. As it was, after a trip to Milan for the family Christmas, her last few euros were simply gobbled up; prices nowadays took the breath away.

Kitty snuggled further into her Japanese bathrobe with its swirling chrysanthemum and blinked happily at the new slippers for the umpteenth time. To her joy, she'd found some nail varnish to match the scarlet satin. No, really, it was wicked to grumble when she was living here in the castle, courtesy of the old *Marchese*. Only the one room, it was true, but after she'd put behind her all those silly notions of 'coming down in the world', the idea of bedsitter life in a studio in Italy had grown on her. And surely it was deliciously avant-garde, was it not? Fitting, even, for her age and calling. The winters were busy in a different way for Patrick, he had so much work to do getting the place right for the next season, and then, he was never *not* working – grabbing his opportunity to go back to a picture when the sun came out. Of course, winter vegetables often made very attractive subjects for her, so you couldn't say she was idle. And look at the dozens of species of flowers that positively filled the fields in spring! Could she ever wish for a more abundant opportunity? And, if she was just a wee bitty lonely when the rainy days came, she had lovely hospitable Patrick to talk to. He was the heart and soul of this town as far as she was concerned, there was just no question about it, and if she hadn't been old enough to be his mother she'd have gone a bundle on him herself.

Nearly midnight, time to turn down the sheets. Kitty lifted a shiny chin (her face already carefully patted with cold cream) and gazed at the open window, a small square cut into the thick stone. If she'd chosen to climb onto a stool (which so far she hadn't even dared to think about) she would have been able to see out, and worse still, down. It was a sheer drop, the castle forming as it did a sizable corner of the ramparts of the town. She tilted her head slightly, and yes, she could still hear that nightingale. She remembered, once when there was a full moon and she was all tucked up for the night, a young barn owl had landed on the window ledge. He'd been dreadfully restless, half lifting his wings and rocking forward before launching himself off again. He never came back although she'd waited for him.

She frowned as she stretched up to reach the switch on the standard lamp, and then gave up, panting a little with the effort. It seemed to get more difficult each time. She really must get in an electrician to make a switch she could switch. She struggled for a few seconds in the light from the shade and then froze and turned her head towards the door.

It was a soft, rapid knocking followed by a pause. Her heart thumped with such force, it seemed to fill her ears. There it came again, but this time it was muffled by her heartbeats. As if to avoid another second of anticipation, Kitty made a dash for the door with the speed of a young robin crossing a newly mown lawn. She grappled with the big iron ring and pulled it towards her with all her might.

'*Antonio!*' Antonio Gozzoli. She took one look at the young man framed in the doorway and then Kitty knew she was going to faint.

A very wet, icy cold cloth was being pressed into her temples, and freezing water trickled down her neck, it was most uncomfortable. Where was she? Lying on her very own chaise longue covered by her Kashmir shawl, and water soaking her to the skin. Unbearable.

'No, no, please don't. Take it away.' She pushed away the arm tending her face.

'It's alright, it's me, Antonio. Kitty? Do you feel better?'

She saw his lean, worried face peering into hers.

'Yes, but I'm getting wet, quickly get a towel,' she said, close to outrage.

'I will dry your face.'

He discarded the wet cloth and used her precious Kashmir stole to dry her face and hair even though it was running down her neck. She would overlook his carelessness because in the first place, he was a man, and more especially because it was her darling Antonio come to visit her in the middle of the night. And down on his knee too, for all the world as if he were proposing.

'Is it really you?' she asked wonderingly of this amazingly romantic, broad-shouldered young man. 'Antonio, are you here? Everybody says you're in America. Or is it Rome?'

'And that is where I am. I am in America. Please don't say you have seen me.' He smiled and held her chin in his huge paw and gave it a tweak. 'Kitty, I am *happy* to see you.'

'It's a dream, I'm dreaming,' she was breathless.

'No, no, you are not dreaming, I am here to ask you something.'

Kitty lifted her arms and enfolded his dark head against the nape of her neck. His springing hair pressed against her chin, and it came to her with immense force that this bliss of holding a man in her arms after all these years, was the greatest bliss of all. She savoured the moment, breathing deeply to capture that musky smell that men have, but, alas, her nose was not as keen as it had been after all this time.

'Not before I've offered you a wee dram,' she said wagging an admonishing finger.

He smiled. 'Stay. I know where to look.'

It was miraculous, he'd not forgotten. She recalled his capability, all the odd jobs he'd put his hand to not so very long ago – how long was it actually – four, five years since he officially went away? If he weren't dashing off she might ask him to do the switch on the standard lamp.

Kitty sat up and took her glass from him. She turned a severe eye on the two tiny liqueur glasses. 'I see you've taken me at my word! Will it do the trick?' she said.

'Only this much, no more for you,' he said.

Oh dear, he *was* looking serious. And possibly older and sadder than when she last saw him. But for goodness sake, this was a cause for celebration surely. She must cheer him up. She moved her legs and made way for him, patting the seat.

'Welcome back, darling Antonio. We've all missed you so much,' Kitty said, raising her glass and downing the few drops which to her pleasant surprise seemed to give her an immediate kick. 'Although they tell me you sneak back sometimes when nobody's looking, naughty boy.'

'I come to see Nonno who is not very well—'

'D'ye mean Giovanni? Oh, I'm sorry to hear that.'

Antonio dropped his eyes. 'He is very ill. But, of course, I can't stay here.'

'Oh, dear boy, why? I've never understood why you left us all. *Why* can't you stay?' Antonio shook his head slightly. He wasn't going to tell her, she could see that. 'You've made your fame and fortune in America, haven't you?' She patted his hand.

He removed it. 'I am not a good person. It is best you know nothing.'

Kitty felt a shadow pass over her heart. What could he possibly mean? She found she had no words even to protest.

'I have some information about the execution of Alfredo Pazzi. I think that his wife would like to know it.'

About Dodo! That was dreadful; she was not expecting news of this sort. Her heart began to beat too fast again. She leant forward, and she must have looked frightened because he quickly took her hand again and stroked it.

'Kitty. I think it is not good for you, this.'

'Oh Antonio, I'm here to help. What can I do for you? Can I speak to Rose? Arrange for you to meet?'

'Yes. I must speak to her, but I have not much time.'

'But you know, Antonio, she is still very weak, she was bitten by a poisonous snake, poor wee mite.'

'In two days, I will call you to find out if she is strong enough to meet me.'

'You will telephone me? But when? I must be *here* for you, Antonio.'

A strange expression flickered across his face.

'I know when you are here, you turn on your light.'

'At night! You'll ring me at night. At night,' she repeated as if to calm herself, and noticed she was wringing her hands. 'Good heavens, Antonio darling, what on earth is going on? You were such a bonny, fresh-faced boy, and now, here you are—'

He interrupted. 'Forgive me, please forgive me, I am not the same.' He seemed nervous to be off like the young owl, and stood up. 'I hope you will not speak to Rose Pazzi until you have heard from me.' He bent to kiss her on the cheek.

'Oh, Antonio, this is too short a visit. Stay and have another whisky with me, just one?' she implored him.

He smiled and shook his head.

'There's so much to talk about,' she said, 'and … a hundred things to *fix*. The switch on the lamp!' she made it sound urgent, pointing to it.

'Can it wait?'

She sighed, 'Yes, I suppose it can wait.'

'Then, I will say goodbye. And remember, Antonio is in America.'

She nodded. The man was haunted, it was terrible.

She watched him walk over to the door already preoccupied with something else, and knew he wouldn't mind if he saw himself out, she just hadn't the strength to lift a finger.

He turned to look at her, and she did not know when she had been so moved by a person's sorrow.

He lingered at the door, hesitating. 'How is my fresco?'

'Your fresco is perfect, it's in perfect condition. Everybody remarks on it, everybody who comes. They love it, they just love it; it gives them so much pleasure.' *How* could she make him happy again? What could she do for him?

He nodded slightly and appeared satisfied. Then he cast his eye round the room seeming to relish certain objects before his face softened as they came to rest on her. He left without a sound.

Chapter 11

Isolda was observing a small group of Scandinavian tourists lingering over a fourteenth-century hunting scene: an especially lively fresco in the Sala di Dante. They moved round the room, dreamily drifting in each other's wake, and as each encountered *Virgin Enthroned*, Pinturicchio's huge painting (crudely restored, in Isolda's estimation), the visitor would step back several paces. Possibly finding themselves too close for comfort, they shuffled on into the next gallery.

She watched them disappear from the room, her hand on the plinth of Dante, a bust in silky black marble, and although her eyes returned to the inscription, in her mind she was cursing her abrasiveness – or whatever quality it was that turned people off. Would Rose, she wondered, have opened up about the Pazzi collection if she'd somehow handled their meeting in any other way? Was her desperation showing through? No, she'd kept it casual, she'd resisted the temptation to broach the question again after that bizarre episode when they'd almost been mown down by a car. Spread-eagled in the road, extraordinary. She'd even put the poor little mite to bed with an aspirin. She seemed contrite the next day, but somehow, so shaky, it didn't seem the right moment to tackle her. A passive hysteric, more than likely.

Her eyes narrowed as she traced Dante's fine profile. She followed the line of his forehead down to the tip of his aquiline nose and over the lips till she reached the jutting chin where she stopped to approve the model's sheer sensibility. This was a man she could give herself to.

The little waif was not all that she seemed. She certainly looked as if she might fall to pieces if you said an unkind word to her, but underneath she wondered if there may not be a will of steel. Was that collapse after the car episode a timely performance? A bid to wriggle out of more questions about the Pazzis, for example? Maddeningly unpredictable: she could not be sure of her. An accomplished watercolourist, clearly. Isolda released an irritable rush of breath. She was accustomed to a reciprocal deal from the people she respected. A sisterly welcome, or at least some friendly easing-up when a fellow student came up for a chat, surely that was normal? Look at the way she'd seized up the minute she'd appeared – before she'd *said* anything. Well, there was that remark about Dante, but it was small talk, wasn't it? Something anyone might throw out as a passing remark. Well, not really, not in this milieu. No, she might as well face up to it: the truth was, even an off-beat girl like Rose was as resistant to her charms as the rest of sub-bourgeois society. She stretched up, longing to place the palm of her hand against the hard contours of Dante's cheek but the bust was well out of reach. *This* man would have gauged her measure.

Outside the Museo Civico, the sun dazzled. It cut pink squares into the elevated gallery running round the open courtyard and cast deep shadows of ultramarine on the other side. All bitterly noted by Isolda who knew she hadn't a hope of painting it. She paused in the vibrant shadow and looked down into the narrow alley below. Her eye travelled up the wall opposite to where two cosy elevated gardens snuggled side by side, both of them tiny and imbued with stillness in the midday sun. One was an orchard, the other put down to single rows of mixed vegetables. Under an orange tree, almost hidden in the deep grass of the orchard, a mother cat suckled four or five kittens. Isolda gazed at the rotating licking movement of the cat's head, and again she questioned her sanity in coming to Italy. And having got here, was she mad to set out on a quest for paintings in San Gimignano? Diana's fax had triggered the whole desperate bid. The brutal body blow of *Get stuffed* delivered so conspicuously in view of the entire table – including Sandy – was not an episode she cared to dwell on. And then, lying in bed in the small hours, the idea of buying some small paintings had hit her like a thunderbolt. And the decision, moments later, to act on it, was followed by the most wonderful uninterrupted night's sleep. But she hadn't reckoned on the wear and tear of persuading a taxi to get her here at a sane and sensible rate. Ten haggling minutes. Nor, having arrived, of discovering, not the watercolour landscapes she craved, but dinky little pictures in dinky little galleries in the Via San Giovanni at a price that would undoubtedly deter her from chucking them out with the rubbish when it was all over. Thanks to her good sense she hadn't parted with a penny yet and nothing would induce her to; after all, none of the pictures she looked at remotely hinted at landscape, Tuscan or otherwise. Patrick might even have recognised one of two of the pictures from his last visit here. Unbelievably, she hadn't thought it through. And now she was panicking. Oh God, what was she to do?

Isolda strode back into the arched doorway of the Civico waving her ticket at the man in the booth. She ran upstairs past the Sala di Dante and burst anxiously into a small room above, as if what she needed to see, what she had to lay exclusive claim to, if only for a few minutes, might have been whisked away. Lippo Memmi's *Madonna*. Still here. She feasted her eyes on the transparent complexion and carrot-coloured hair, and prayed for inspiration – praying naturally, as she had done as a child, her hands folded as her nanny had taught her. A small party of German tourists wandered in and out behind her unnoticed. Time passed. The Madonna's pink cheeks were as high as Sandy's when she'd heard the news about the dog, but her gentle expression was a million miles away from her own ineffable Sandy, who might have modelled for Botticelli, so composed was she, so remote, so unattainable. Oh, *Mama di Dio* with your two stern saints, I am captivated by your beauty but I can never represent you with my brush. Tell me what to do. I have no talent, and I'm dying of love.

Finally, as she was about to leave the room her eye returned to the two tiny figures in the lower right foreground of the picture: a monk retreating from a boar. In proportion to the three main figures they were like large black insects. She pondered. Emblematic, yes of course. Lust, that was it. The boar represented lust. Its diminutive size was there to reassure the general populace that in the presence of the Holy Virgin all that bristling volatile energy would be pricked and patted and slapped down to size – no bigger than it should be. Would she, Isolda, have been fooled by all that symbolism had she lived in Renaissance Italy? Probably. Well, she was here, wasn't she? Prevailing on the Holy Virgin to dampen her ardour.

Outside, the tiny courtyard of the Civico was exactly as she had left it. Again, the powerful light had altered remembered patterns of colour; and although she was blinded by the sun to details of stone and brick, there was a razor sharpness to form and contour. There was nobody about, the place was deserted. Her heart leaped; and for a few seconds, feeling the rough parapet as she walked slowly down the steps looking down into the little square, it was not difficult to imagine woven cotton enfolding her legs and thin leather slippers beneath the soles of her feet; or the constriction of a doublet round her rib cage and a pleated peplum bouncing against her buttocks. She was a fourteenth-century lad hurrying to meet his betrothed waiting for him in the Piazza del Duomo. And when his beloved saw him her cheeks would flush with anticipation. 'He's come,' she'd whisper to her old nurse standing by, and she'd open her arms to embrace him, her carrot-coloured hair cascading over her bodice.

Isolda swung round the balustrade, propelled into the courtyard at breathless speed. A man bestrewn with camera equipment ducked under the arch as he came into the courtyard. Isolda confronted him, aghast. For a second she thought she was going to smack his big stupefied face, anything to get him out of her way. Instead she smacked her forehead. 'So sorry, I thought you were someone else.' She dropped her head, and politely stepped aside for him to pass.

She was losing her grip, this place was sweeping her away. A fourteenth-century *boy*? She walked slowly through the arched passage that led into the piazza and cast her eyes over the crowds sitting on the Duomo steps. Well, well! A fourteenth-century boy. How interesting. For a moment she saw an image of Virginia Woolf with her limpid eyes and Cupid's bow mouth. Isolda stopped and looked at the two towers framed by the arch at the end of the passage. Throughout her life, she had accepted her womanhood wholeheartedly. Not even in her most wretched moments had she wished herself a man. Why then should she have cast herself as a boy? Maybe this had been no more than déjà vu: a glimpse into her other life as a Romeo of San Gimignano. Fanciful? Isolda smiled. If she allowed herself more flights of fancy she might get to know herself better. The sound of a flute drifted intermittently through the crowds and she stopped and held her breath. Early Italian music, she knew it well: it fitted her fantasy. Surely she was hearing things. Some people brushed past her talking loudly, and when they had gone, it drifted back again. Purposefully she stepped out from under the arch and up some steps into another open courtyard.

A young musician was sitting on a low wall in the corner with the sun flashing on the silver of his flute. Although he played robustly, the effect was melancholic. In fact, it was almost too much to bear, but bear it she must. If she stood hidden just round the corner so that she could still hear the flute, she could indulge in the luxury of thinking about Sandy for a few more moments. Isolda leant against a pillar and peered through the iron gate at the underside of the long cloister lit by reflected sun. With her eye puzzling over the clever packing of brick she felt her body suffuse with the most powerful yearning she had known, and within the following moments realised that this was a corner of San Gimignano that in years to come she would recall in its entirety.

There was a rustle of movement further along the step and a young black vagrant settled himself down dumping his leather donkey bag next to him. For a moment Isolda gazed at him unseeingly. Slowly it dawned on her that he was a most unusual sight in this exclusive tourist trap. He opened a filthy A4 folder, took out a handful of small paintings and propped them against the wall. The civic authorities would have something to say about this! Those bijou art galleries in the Via San Giovanni would be out of business in a day. Isolda's eyes widened. Watercolours and pastels, unmounted, freshly torn from the pad, appeared along the wall, one after the other.

She was transfixed. *Landscapes.* And one with a view of San Gimignano. Her eyes bore into them with a fierce scrutiny. Tuscany in May (wasn't that a dash of gorse?), they must have been freshly painted, and so deft and sure. And the pastel of the barn in the moonlight – not bad *at all!* And, just a minute, a pencil drawing of a dog basking in the sun. That was beautiful.

'How much?'

'Which one?'

'All of them.'

'*All?*'

'That's what I said.'

'Okay. One thousand euros.'

'WHAT?' Isolda took a step backwards, stunned by the boy's barefaced cheek. He was asking a thousand pounds in today's currency rate.

'But that's … nearly two hundred pounds each.'

'That's about it, lady,' the boy said. He was an American.

Isolda gave him a long speculative look-over. She had a tough one here. A college drop-out living in self-imposed poverty, it was brazenly obvious.

'If I were buying *one*, I would not expect to pay as much as two hundred pounds. Since I am proposing to buy all of them, I would naturally anticipate a sizable reduction.'

'Excuse me, lady, you're talking to the artist. I've lived with these pictures, they're my friends. I definitely wouldn't be setting myself up here if I didn't have to eat.'

Isolda wasn't in the least impressed. He had definitely not lived with them long, they'd been dashed off in minutes; that was their charm. The gall to make an Oliver Twist out of it! Her taxi would be here in half an hour to take her back to Montecalmo. Was she going to beat him down? *Could she afford not to?* They'd make the mother of a fuss at work if she claimed this on expenses. She looked at his lean face and half-closed eyes; the boy had a kind of authority.

She took out her card and cheque book with heavy disapproval. The boy merely rolled his eyes with the most unmannerly snicker.

Isolda exploded. 'You can't expect me to travel round with thousands of euros in my pocket.'

'You see, lady, I don't have a bank account.'

Once again she hadn't anticipated this most obvious of probabilities. She, of all people.

The boy looked at his watch. 'The bank closes in three minutes. Gimme cash and I'll let you off a coupla hundred bucks.'

'Done. Stay here.'

Isolda sailed down the steps into the Piazza del Duomo and out into the Piazza della Cisterna where – yes, the doors to the bank were still open; her spirits lifted. A woman stepped out just as the door was being closed behind her. Isolda gasped and dived towards the door to hold it open. The manager blocked her way and she pushed him aside, calling over her shoulder as she passed him, 'It's alright, I won't be long,'

Inside the lights were being turned off, and behind the last window the clerk was pulling down his blind. She ran across the marble floor and tapped sharply against the glass. The blind shot up and for a moment she was taken aback by the clerk's look of horror and slack-mouthed dread. Isolda threw back her head and laughed reassuringly. 'No, no, no, no, I just want some money – nine hundred euros.'

She scrabbled in her bag for her wallet just as the solid front door behind her shut with a resounding boom – at which more window blinds shot up as bank employees scrambled back to their places. Isolda turned round and her immediate instinct was to back up against the counter as the manager made a menacing advance across the marble. He was pointing a large walkie-talkie at her and shaking it. 'The bank is closed, you must leave at once.'

'This is ridiculous, I'm here. Nine hundred euros, it'll take three minutes.'

'There is a cash point outside.'

'I don't have an *arrangement* for such a big withdrawal.'

'That is not my problem, signora,' he snapped, 'you will leave at once or I will call security.'

'Alright, alright, alright!'

They walked smartly abreast to the door. The manager held open the door with a stony stare and Isolda swept past him – but then almost immediately broke into a run once outside.

There were two people outside the cash point, one of them completing her transaction as Isolda approached. The man took her place and Isolda subsided like a spent balloon behind him, her heart banging away like a typewriter, hands on knees. Like this she waited, heaving for breath as endless hundreds of euros were counted – or so it appeared to Isolda's mounting incredulity. Then as she straightened up, the man collecting the money turned round to reveal himself as Rankine.

'Good God, it's you.' Isolda's eyes were round with surprise. Then brushing past him, she dived towards the cash point in the wall.

The message came up: *Il bancomat non dispone al momento di banconote.* The ATM is not currently able to dispense cash.

'*WHAT?*' Isolda slammed her hand against the wall and shouted '*I need the money.*'

Rankine had frozen in the act of putting his money into his inner pocket. His right hand clutching a massive wad of euros was poised, suspended in front of him. As she turned, Isolda spotted it and slowly registered. Her clenched expression ironed itself out.

'Did you see that?' she said lightly. 'It's not dispensing cash!'

'Well, yes, I ... I ...' Rankine seemed at a loss for words.

'First of all that officious bastard in the bank refuses to give me some money, then slams the door on me and turfs me out on the street. I mean, I *told* him the cash point was useless for the amount of money I need.'

'Oh, d-dear, uh ...' Rankine suddenly remembered to tuck the money into his jacket.

Isolda approached him measuring her steps. 'Rankine,' she began.

'Ffffreddy,' he broached.

'Freddy?'

'Call me F-f-f—'

'Freddy, of *course*! And please, think of me as Izz. Freddy, since you were lucky enough to get to the cash point before me – and indeed, clearly authorised to withdraw a most *unusual* amount of money – enough, it now appears, to break the bank, even –' She paused to give way to a tinkling laugh before composing herself again. 'Yes well – I wonder if you would do me the hugest favour and lend me a thousand euros?'

The question hung on the air. Rankine's mouth opened slightly.

He said finally, 'I'm af-f-f-fraid not. Sorry, but I need it.'

Isolda came close to him and lowered her voice.

'But I am desperate for it, it's vital I have it. Now. I need it now.'

'Well, I'm awfully sorry, but I have an equally urgent need for it.'

'You can't need *all* of it? You can't need *all* of those millions of euros I saw you buying? Can't you spare a thousand? I can give you a cheque, I can give you a cheque this minute.' She scrabbled in her handbag.

'I'd like to be able to help out, but I'm af-f-f-f-f—'

'Freddy.'

Rankine half ducked as Isolda laid a hand on his shoulder claiming his exclusive attention.

'Freddy, I'm in a desperate situation. Probably the most desperate situation I shall ever experience in the whole of my life. I'm begging you. *Begging* you to give me the money.'

Trapped by her mesmerising intensity, Rankine cast about him unhappily.

'Well, would it help to give you some of it?'

'How much?'

'Um. Well, should we say … I might be able to spare – about a hundred?'

She made a rapid calculation. Not nearly enough even for one picture. 'How about four hundred?' she said.

'No,' said Rankine.

'Three hundred and fifty then? *Please.*' She needed those extra few euros to play around with, she could always add a bit.

Isolda's face was so close to Rankine's he flinched every time she breathed on him; his protruding eyes were fixed, trance-like, in their sockets.

'Alright, three hundred and fifty.'

She released her grip on his shoulder.

In a stroke, Rankine appeared to be utterly exhausted. In a kind of slow motion, he reached into his inside pocket and drew out the wad of money and counted a handful of notes into Isolda's hand which she transferred at once to her pocket. She wavered; should she reward him with a kiss? He leant backwards and both his shoulders shot up. She thought not.

'Thanks, Freddy.'

Isolda turned to sprint back towards the Piazza del Duomo. She heard Rankine's voice calling after her. 'Haven't you f-f-f-f-f…?'

She glanced back to see him standing in the middle of the Piazza della Cisterna with his hand half raised towards her. Christ, she'd forgotten the cheque. She cupped her hands to her mouth and yelled, 'I won't forget!' and then lost herself in the crowd.

The boy was sitting there exactly as she'd left him, loosely cross legged, with all five paintings plus the sketch of the dog propped against the wall. Isolda slowed down as she approached him attempting to recover her breath. This was going to be tricky. He saw her, and a slow smile spread across his face.

'The lady has returned.' (Damned cheek.)

'The bank was closed.'

'Uh huh. Too bad.'

He was dead cool but she had his measure, she'd play it straight whether he believed her or not.

'But I met a friend with a lot of money on him.'

'You did?'

'Yes, I did. I asked him to lend me a thousand euros. He gave me three fifty. It's all I have.'

Before he could insult her with another of his sniggers, she drew her card from her bag and said, 'This is what I propose ...' she handed him her visiting card printed with her name under the auspices of Burlington's in larger print. She was relieved to see a flicker of interest – he was as worldly as she thought he was.

Looking up, he said, 'So they're good, huh?'

'They're not bad. Some of them show promise.'

'You gonna sell them on? A thousand per cent profit?'

Isolda threw back her head and laughed. She was trailing, she was a sluggard, she was not on her toes. It was a perfectly logical assumption, and she Hadn't Seen It Coming.

'You delude yourself if you think they are of any worth whatsoever. No, I'm giving you my card as surety on my word. I propose to give you three hundred and fifty in return for one painting, and a deposit of fifty for the rest which I shall take with me. I will show you my passport, and will send you the balance to any address you ...'

The boy was holding up his forefinger as if he might collapse with the effort.

'Slow down, lady, oh pleeese slow down.'

'I don't have much time.'

'Oh ho, I think you got time.'

'Well, go on then, *go on*! *What?*'

'Well ... I don't think I got this straight. You saying, you take my art work? And I'm left with the *de*-posit? Oh ho ... oh ho ho ho ho—'

'Look!' she cut into his interminable, head-wagging innuendo. I'm leaving San Gimignano in ten minutes. Can I offer you more? I have a bank account, a fixed address, verification of my place of work. One of the most *respected* auction houses ...'

He was very slowly jabbing his finger at her. 'And *that's* what bugs me.'

The boy was on the point of asking some uncomfortable questions in spite of his semi-somnambulant state. She looked at her watch. In eight minutes' time the taxi would be at the Porta San Giovanni.

'You really do want them, don't you?' the boy said.

'Yes. And – against my will – I am prepared to pay the outrageous price you're asking, so don't you think you owe me something?' She'd met her match, it was appalling; she suspected she was on the point of hyperventilating.

The boy lifted his eyelids a fraction to look at her and the corners of his mouth quivered slightly. He spoke with insolent deliberation.

'Six pictures, lady. You want all six? And they're *not* going into auction? An "outrageous price" for five worthless paintings and a drawing? Let us not d'loood ourselves – of no worth *what-so-ever*? Well, now, I can't help wondering why.'

Isolda was doing her best to cope with an extraordinary amount of air in her chest coupled with a twitch in her legs. She had an image of the taxi driver drumming his fingers and looking at his watch. Stepping forward she spoke fast, snatching short breaths when she could.

'Look. How about if I send you the balance – *and* the pictures? Except for the dog, I'd like to keep the dog.'

'*What?*'

She wondered if he'd heard her. She was forming the words with her mouth but couldn't get the sound out. Isolda leant closer to the boy. 'The balance immediately, the pictures in two weeks time, except for the dog. Then you can ... sell them ... twice!' The muscles in her chest had gone into painful spasm.

'Is this real?'

'Take it or leave it, I've got to go.' She was able to spit *that* out. She straightened up gagging like fish out of water and reached into her pocket for the money, and in her bag for the diary and a pen but couldn't find the diary. She found an old receipt and thrust it forward with a pencil.

The boy took them slowly, eyeing her suspiciously. 'You okay?'

'Give me my card. I'll write you an I.O.U.'

Nothing on earth would persuade this boy to get a move on, he was studying the receipt.

'You're supposed to be giving me your address,' she said. 'If you have one.'

The boy narrowed his eyes and fixed on a spot in the universe. Isolda seriously doubted if she could make it to the taxi given her rocketing heartbeat. She looked at her watch yet again.

'And your name,' she added.

The boy looked up at her.

'Ber*nard*. Got it? You come down on the last syllable.'

'Okay-okay-okay.' She was going mad.

He was writing it down at last. He handed back the scrap of paper and tilted his head towards the paintings arrayed against the wall.

'All yours, lady.'

She gathered up the pictures and swooped through the streets with the stately panic of a fleeing springbok.

Chapter 12

Water vapour. There was too much of it. All this radiant encapsulated light surrounding her, how was she to begin? This was not a sun-baked rock in the Aegean with clear-cut shadows and primary colours, it was early morning in the high pastures of northern Italy, far harder to paint. And what medium was she to use? She'd plodded down to the orchard with all the separate paraphernalia. If the hazy light was created by water (this question-and-answer technique of getting down to a picture was good, it helped her feel less lonely), if this cloud she was sitting in was created by water, wasn't it natural to paint it with water? Her deduction *appeared* to be logical, but was it? Banish the thought: watercolour, of course. Was it even worth asking? And she'd do it in pastel tomorrow. Why not? It eliminated falling foul of all those rules other people seemed to know about. She must embrace this ridiculous mood of optimism and allow her spirit to soar into the firmament. She would recite homilies, it helped: it's never too late, each day is a fresh beginning. And here was her ladder, there it stood. Oh joy! Leaning against the olive tree at an entirely insouciant angle. To catch it, to catch it. She'd been gazing at it long enough, now was the time to begin. But there was a niggle; something threatened to distract her. It was her shoes and bandage, they were sodden from the dew. A mere trifle! You suffered for your art, and time waits for no man.

Phoebe took a last overall look at the orchard before she embarked on the painting. So utterly consumed was she by the delicacy of the trees and billowing suffusions of light beneath the branches, that now there seemed no obstacle to overcome because she had become a moving part of it. She was the medium by which this vision would be represented effortlessly on the empty page. It would pass through her. She opened her sketch book and calmly stroked water out of the brush against the rim of the jar. The brush hovered above her unwashed palette of yesterday covered with – *Hell*, the nasturtium colours of her last painting. Never mind, keep calm, wipe it off. A wash, now. Of what? Which colour? Was she going for the light which was opaque, or the grass *through* the light? The mist was bluey white but creamy yellow where it was densest, giving somehow an impression of an overall blush of rose. But the grass was green except where it was yellow where the sun shone through the shards. She'd ignore the pinpricks of light from the dew, not a watercolour option – unless of course, she left tiny spaces for the paper underneath to speak for itself! Thin cross currents of anxiety wove a web across her inner eye. *Paint what you see, it's simple.* Back to the wash. Begin at the beginning. More water, lots of water then you can let the colours merge. She had begun! Ahhhhhhhhh!

So, like this, she worked – on the brink. For the moment, she possessed the very eye of the whirlwind, which was solitude. Deeply she dipped into the crafting of her picture; on the brink of satisfaction, she surfaced. Hearing nothing, oblivious of cold or heat, amazed by colour. The longer you looked the more you discovered. And the colours you'd first noticed in your travels had become so intense you wondered if there was something mysterious to the process of looking. And beneath the intensity of those impressions, more were lurking. Depths shot through with fathomless colour.

She had found a way. She had found a way of applying the paint to convey the light: this particular light, at this distance, under these conditions. The rush of adrenaline almost blinded her. *By accident.* Could she possibly repeat it tomorrow? No. It had happened, just happened. She was only halfway through her picture, and the enormity of what she had achieved appeared to be an accident. How could she go on? Another lick of paint and she might lose it. Half the picture to go, and this pitiless thing had happened. Clear the mind. Look at it. What else was to be done? The olive trees were vaguely painted in, and most of the ladder. Why shouldn't they stay like *that?* Phoebe was aware that she was breathing as if she had just emerged into the world: down to the depths of her soul. Her cheeks burned. *It was all there.*

The bedroom door crashed open and Dill swung round all crumpled and amazed.

'Let's go out and paint. Now!' Phoebe's paraphernalia slid to the floor except for her picture.

'But what about breakfast?' Dill clutched the top of her pyjamas together; she had been on the point of drawing aside the little curtain and had almost torn it off its rod in her fright.

'I just want to paint – all day, every single second of the day.'

'What's happened? I know! You've been painting your ladder!'

'Yes. And now I want to paint everything, *everything*. I've seen a million things.'

'Let me see, let me see!' Dill stretched out her arms.

Phoebe gave her the painting and her sister took it to the light. Her face said it all. It may have been a flash in the pan, her ladder picture, but one look at Dill's expression and she felt a moment of perfect confirmation.

'Oh, Phoebe!' was all Dill said, and beamed her china blue eyes full on.

At last, the old Dill! Her serenity, that radiant aura of comfort she had so badly missed in the last couple of days, had returned. She was better. Phoebe walked straight over and hugged her.

'Alright, we'll have breakfast, but no messing about.'

'Shh. What's that?' Dill stopped in front of her, her cotton skirt flecked with cuckoo spit from the fennel overhanging the path.

They had wandered off the beaten track, moving slowly with their stools and painting materials along what must have been an animal trail. The sound was very close, an intimate grunt of aqueous enjoyment coming from some crumbling stone sties. Phoebe said, 'It's a very big pig, and it thinks it's about to have its breakfast.'

'Oh, how perfectly *lovely*! I'm sure nobody would mind if we had a look at it.'

'We haven't got the time. Unless we're going to paint it.'

'We can't paint it, poor thing, it's all shut up in that tiny hut.'

Phoebe hoped she wasn't about to lose her new-found energy. She had, after all, been up since before six o'clock. And here they were, faffing about at ten, and still not started.

'Exactly,' she said, 'and we've come to paint, not look at pigs.'

'Darling we're not going to stop having fun, are we?'

'*Having fun?*'

'Well, yes. We're not going to stop having a good time together now, are we? Because of the painting, I mean?'

'Dill …' For a few seconds Phoebe was lost for words. 'I just can't believe you are ready to abandon tools and spend the major part of the morning wasting time with a pig.' Her sister was looking at her with a quizzical expression which made her frantic. 'We've just got to find a painting spot, Dill, the morning is half over.'

Dill said, 'Of course. And I can always come back another time and make sure the poor thing's comfortable.'

The pig grunted again, plainly in its seventh heaven. *Comfortable!* Oh God, oh God. The moment was leaking away: sun not too hot, shadows good, vegetation fresh, there wasn't even a second to lose.

At last Dill was on the move again and about to round a bend when she stopped to gaze at the view, her tall figure poised on the brink of a hilly void. *This* would make a picture! A human pillar etched against the landscape, hair lit up like oat grass. Too late, she'd moved on. What a place! The valley plunging down on their right, the hillside opposite soaring up again, so close you could almost touch it. She must get here early tomorrow. But for now she wanted something to anchor her picture: a tree, a building. Something to emphasise the compressed dynamic of these hills.

'Oh, what a dear little cottage! And look at the doves!'

She bumped into Dill who had stopped suddenly. They were both now looking down onto a farmhouse a few yards further down the path. This was it! She'd found her frame.

'Perfect. Let's park ourselves here.'

Phoebe sat down on a flat tree stump on a hillock some way above the house, and started unpacking her stuff. Dill began to criss-cross in front of her, walking backwards with her head tilted, considering the house, first through one eye then through the other. Finally she set down her stool close by. It crossed Phoebe's mind: rather too close for comfort. Was it possible that she herself was becoming an obsessive? She felt possessive of her time, almost churlish. Up to this moment in her life nothing would have made her happier than to sit close to Dill. She busied herself about her palette.

It was no use, she was going to have to use a pencil. This was a house, not endlessly malleable landscape. (What freedom that had given her! She hadn't realised how much.) The bulging little house had been built hundreds of years ago with the bare hands of the farmer who was going to live in it, most likely. And instead of reducing in scale with distance, it seemed to expand. She was really on the spot now with this wonky house. And she had only chosen it to illustrate the incredible dynamic of these hills. This was just about the biggest mountain of an obstacle. She could see the picture of the hills was going to be all about the house, just as the picture of the ladder was about the light.

Ah, but look at it! The cast of the roof almost touching the ground, tiles sagging. Two rusty iron tubes poking up to carry away the smoke on chilly evenings – why not? Didn't somebody say it snowed up here in winter? And deep, deep cuts for doorway and window. And the steps. Steep steps with sharp shadows leading up to a door under the eaves. Phoebe devoured the contours of the Tuscan farmhouse and made a note of where the light was coming from. Just a minute, was she really about to fill half the paper with a house? Had she lost her reason? It was the landscape that mattered. These hills had to be the first thing to hit you in the eye. Supposing she was to scale it down, make the house half the size, or even less? But she was too close for that, practically on top of it, and there was no way she could move further back. What was the answer? A big leap. An illicit action. She would break the rules and *widen her line of vision*. She remembered Patrick frowning slightly at her unwieldy landscape with everything in it as far as the eye could see, north, south, east and west. He held his pencil at arm's length and said, 'Keep within your line of vision.'

Phoebe felt suddenly that she wasn't solving her problem so much as playing unimaginable tricks with space. Her mind was soaring off the spectrum altogether. It wasn't right. Nothing was right. She was going bananas. The headway she'd made in the morning had done her in. Oh, to hell with it, why not just crash about like a child and paint a picture. No pencil outline, straight on with the brush. Wonky house, big hills – but at the last minute, restraint, don't forget it or you're lost. She heard herself groan like a trombone tuning up.

'Darling! What's the matter?' Dill half stood up and had to catch her stool before it fell over.

'Sorry, Dill, I'd forgotten you were there. I'll be alright once I've started.'

'Oh, thank goodness! You sounded in agony. I thought it might be appendicitis.'

Her sister was an angel, whereas Phoebe herself was as selfish as hell. That time when they were girls with plaits and she had refused to bring Dill a drink of water when she was in bed with flu, was one of those memories she had tried to forget. She'd actually told Dill to get it herself when she was too ill to move. It had been just one damn drink of water too many. When she went in to check up on Dill half an hour later, she was still lying there limply, except that tears were streaming down her cheeks. A careless groan from her, she noticed, and it was appendicitis.

Phoebe concentrated her attention once more on the house. She looked at the steps with the iron handrail on one side entwined with a rambling rose that was forcing itself up into a wisteria that covered part of the wall. The light was perfect, except that every time her eye went back to the old door at the top of the steps, the shadow had altered slightly. An optical absurdity, perhaps. She applied a wash for the sky.

Her eyes were not, after all, playing tricks, the door was very slowly pushing open. A tiny scarecrow wearing a trilby shuffled out. He closed the door behind him and carefully descended the steps.

Phoebe's voice was almost a whisper, as she tried not to move her head.

'Dill. Look!'

'I'm looking.'

'What is he?'

'He's a ... Has he been shut up?'

'There's a screw missing,' Phoebe said.

'Unless he's very, very old.'

'Uh-uh! He's seen us!'

'You're right. He's on his way up.'

The creature called something and swirled his hand in the air. He began his ascent towards them which after all was not very steep. Every now and again he'd stop and bow his head and a strange feral sound came from him.

Dill stood up in consternation. 'Phoebe, what are we going to do? I'm sure he is in pain.'

'We can't do anything. Sit down.'

Dill obediently sat and they both waited. Phoebe couldn't make out what he was telling them, but she guessed it was laced with bravado. He'd round it all off with a flirtatious chuckle which tapered off into one of his cries. As thin as a starling, the old man wheezed and squeaked up the slope towards Phoebe, rambling incoherently until he caught sight of her palette. It caught him by surprise. He came up close and fell silent, staring deeply into it with a kind of amazement, quite oblivious to her presence. She watched his sharp nose getting closer to it as if he were staring into the jaws of death. His mouth fell open and fine skin stretched tight across his cheeks. A rough cloth patch was held in place on the back of his jacket with child's stitches, and his shallow trilby with its tide marks of salty sweat had faded to neutral. She had never in her life observed a stranger at such close quarters. And it felt natural. Here she was, close enough to be his wife, or his dog, and yet he was unconscious of her. There was a distinct smell of rotting hay about him, not unpleasant. Phoebe held her breath and stole a look at Dill who was poised for action, her expression a question mark.

'Would you like to watch me painting?' Phoebe asked him, and drew her brush over the paper leaving a second wash of cerulean at the top.

It broke his ferocious concentration and he took two steps sideways and looked at her as if she had appeared fully packaged at that precise moment: a painter on her stool surrounded by bags, brushes and palette. Then he turned away and frowned, drawn into another landscape of the mind. His bird's claw of a hand lifted to point beyond the house, where he held it shakily as he talked, his voice fading to a plaintive whisper. He is telling me something terribly sad, Phoebe thought, poor old man.

She nodded and sighed and then said finally, 'But have you looked around you? Have you noticed these hills? Aren't they the most beautiful hills you've ever seen?'

'We've come to paint them,' said Dill.

At this, the old man swung round and noticed Dill behind him. His face lit up, and the remnants of a rakish grin made a ghostly appearance. He approached her with a kind of arthritic nonchalance, tilting his hat at an outlandish angle. In a wavering treble he made her what could only have been a proposition.

Dill stood up with one of her ravishing smiles and held out her hand. 'How do you do,' she said. The old man looked up at her in astonishment, dwarfed by her monumental presence. It seemed to silence him, and he looked round at Phoebe as if for confirmation.

'She won't eat you, I promise,' she said, at which the old man took heart and chuckled. Relieved, the two sisters chuckled with him.

He was invigorated. He attempted a few poses resembling, uncannily, a twenties Bathing Belle: one hand held behind his head with a knee bent in curtsey and thighs squeezed together; first one side then the other.

'Is he doing a tango?' Dill asked, half laughing. 'Ought we to clap?'

'But do we want to encourage him?' Phoebe said.

The old man snatched off his hat and with an effort, threw it up in the air with an 'Ehhh …!' And then, ignoring his trilby that had landed in the grass, he motioned to Phoebe to get up off her tree stump.

'I think he's going to ask me to boogie, Dill, what do I do?'

'You must boogie, of course,' said Dill.

Phoebe rose from her tree stump hoping he would notice her bandaged ankle. To her surprise, the old man was bent on sitting down. He slowly lowered himself on to the stump, landing with a bump and another of his painful whimpers. And then with elaborate ceremony, resting his elbow on one knee, he made his hand into a fist and turned it to face him. Very slowly he lowered his forehead onto his buckled fingers and held it there.

'Bravo! Bravo!' Dill said, clapping her hands for the old man. 'Oh, Phoebe, isn't that extraordinary? It's Rodin's *Thinker*. He wants us to paint him. We can't let him down.' She walked over to him laughing. 'Rodin,

signor! Rodin, Rodino. *Bravo! Si, si*, we would definitely like to paint you.'
She was nodding her head, there was no mistaking her message.

The old fellow looked up at her as if he were seeing a vision. He lifted his arms to her, with an incredulous smile.

Phoebe said, 'Dill, cool down, he's got the wrong end of the stick.'

'Oh, no, he knows we want to paint him, don't you, signore?'

'Dill, I swear he thinks you're an angel.'

'He wants us to paint him, don't worry, Phoebe.'

Dill stopped. The old man dropped loosely onto one knee and made the sign of the cross. He prayed rapidly in a kind of asthmatic whine, his uncovered head exposed to the sun, all pink and mottled.

Dill was held in a state of suspended animation, her mouth slightly open. A dove flew overhead towards the house and a cuckoo called three times in the valley.

Phoebe said, 'Go on then.'

'What?' Dill whispered.

'Do something!'

'What shall I do?'

'I don't know, waft him up to heaven.'

Dill was resolute now. She went up to the old man and laid her hand on his sharp skull. She bent over him. 'It's alright, signore, we're here to help you. Give me your hand.' She held out her hand and he placed his little claw into her palm. She covered it with her other hand and said, 'Let's go home, shall we? *Casa. Casa.*' The old man looked up at Dill as if he were holding his breath, and allowed himself to be helped up and led round to point down the hill.

'Giovanni!' A tiny figure with white hair and a stern face the colour of a conker had just stepped out of a side door of the house. She beckoned sharply to the old man, and a shrill tongue-lashing reached them in staccato bursts, although only Giovanni himself knew what she was saying. He frowned and turned away, muttering. Dill laid a hand on his shoulder and said, 'Stay, Giovanni.'

For a moment no one moved, then the old woman turned back to speak to someone inside the house, still grumbling and throwing her arms up at Giovanni on the hillock. A young man dipped to come out of the low doorway into the sun. He looked up at them, and Phoebe's heart flipped. Even from this distance, she was bowled over with his actorish good looks. In fact, he was the embodiment of Hamlet, or how she had always fancied Hamlet to be, with a lock of dark hair falling over a puckered forehead. She might even flatter him by asking if he were, in fact, an actor, were she to be introduced. But while the little granny was striding up the grassy hill towards them wagging a finger at Giovanni, Hamlet melted into thin air, and now she would never know. To her surprise she felt cheated of a rare opportunity. And then, for the tenth time since she had arrived, the realisation hit her. How could she have forgotten the biggest obstacle of all? Language! Oh, her wings were cruelly clipped.

Dill stepped cheerfully towards the old lady with her arm linked in the little scarecrow's as best she could. '*Buongiorno, signora*! We have very much enjoyed Giovanni's company.'

The old lady was caught short, transfixed in her squat gum boots. She scanned Dill's great height, her reprimands growing more uncertain. Then she caught Dill's eye and smiled and made her greetings.

Dill responded. 'Yes, you see, he went for a short walk, but now he's ready to come home. Is that right, Giovanni?' Dill held Giovanni's hand as she led him forwards, stopping to see how he was taking it.

Giovanni muttered at the ground and began to wheeze rapidly as his little wife came towards him, her voice cajoling in soft cadences. She nodded at Dill and put an arm round his waist and together she and Giovanni stumbled down the hill, proceeding in small rushes. Every now and again they paused for him to gather his breath. When they reached the house, they stopped.

Dill said, 'She's trying to make him wave. Oh, my goodness.'

The little couple had a short tussle, with Giovanni shrugging off his wife's hands.

'He's not a child, she must stop,' Phoebe said, agitated beyond proportion.

Finally the two turned to go inside.

'The hat!' Dill said.

'Oh my God, the hat!'

Phoebe grabbed Giovanni's trilby and holding it high in the air ran down the hill.

She had to duck to stand in the doorway of their kitchen holding out the greasy felt. 'You forgot this.'

Giovanni was already collapsed onto a rickety chair where his wife had put him. Empty cardboard boxes stacked against the walls almost reached the ceiling. The only other furniture apart from the bare wooden table and three chairs was a big American-style fridge. On top of it, a television rested. Two thick liqueur glasses stood next to a bottle of something on the table.

Giovanni's wife threw up her hands at the sight of Phoebe with the hat and began to cluck and crow in confusion. She took the trilby and put it back where it belonged on Giovanni's head and then went over to the sink. She took a handful of something in the corner although it was too dark to see what it was, and, still crooning away like an old hen, handed it to Phoebe. The sun pouring through the door lit up a small bouquet of fluted yellow flowers. When she took it and felt the fat prickly stems, Phoebe realised she was holding a bunch of young courgettes. Giovanni's lunch, she just knew it. It was no use protesting, she'd have to accept them.

'*Grazie, signora! Zucchini,* how delicious. Goodbye, Giovanni, *arrivederci.*'

At the sound of his name a tremor took hold of the old man and he turned to stare at her as if he'd never seen a woman in his life.

Phoebe picked her way round towards the back of the house holding her sprouting vegetables. It was interesting that when she was about to paint the house, she had mentally blocked out the wrecked car seat dumped against the wall, and if, afterwards, had she been quizzed, she may well have denied its existence. There was a whirring above her head and she was surrounded by doves descending all around her; they landed at her feet and pecked the stony earth. She caught a whiff of coconut as the wind blew through the branches of an old stump of gorse. There was nobody about, not even a feeling that somebody had walked this way recently although this was where she had seen him – her Hamlet with the lock of hair. She must check with Dill that she hadn't seen a ghost. A tabby cat padded round the corner and the doves took off, creating a draught on her face.

Chapter 13

It was the bony girl again. In all his teaching life he hadn't met anyone quite like this. Every day a fresh challenge. Now what was her name again? He plucked a handful of operas to mind: *Acis and Galatea*? *Dido and Aeneas*? Not quite, not quite. *Tristan and Isolde*. That was it.

'I've often asked myself this question, Isolda. What makes a painting last the test of time? Surprise, perhaps? If, every time you come back to it, it still holds the power to catch you out, well, there's got to be something extraordinary about it. I'm not saying that this automatically makes it a work of art, but surprise would be one of the elements.'

Isolda was not finished. 'Do you think that in the case of contemporary art, one might exchange the word surprise for shock? The perpetual quality of shock?'

'Well, that's an interesting thought, except that I think most of us are "unshockable" nowadays, aren't we?'

'Unless perhaps we can, in one way, define the durability of a work of art by its power to surprise us by shocking us every time we see it afresh!'

A lively stir of interest disturbed the rather respectful reception he'd so far received this morning. He'd always felt somewhat out of his depth with art theory; certainly he was out of touch with the art scene in London, tucked away here. For all he knew, she was raising the tone of the class. Look at the way they'd pricked up their ears. She was playing with him, that much was clear, the baggage. The question remained, racing round his head till his eyesight blurred. Was he up to it?

'But that would anyway support your theory of surprise!' Isolda finished with a flourish, unfolding a single massive hand for his continual fascination.

This was better. She could get up to all the mischief she wanted as long as she realised there was a class to run, and he was running it. And just a minute, wasn't it Isolda who'd produced that remarkable pastel, the old barn in a full moon? It certainly rivalled Cotman in atmosphere.

As he recalled Isolda's pastel, Patrick's consciousness was jarred slightly with an emerging fragment of memory. The old barn, of course! That's where he'd seen the man who'd come asking for Antonio Gozzoli. He'd skulked past him with all his dogs, a very dubious character. What did he want with Antonio? Antonio hadn't been around for years.

'What would Ruskin have made of modern art, Patrick?' It was Rose. It amazed him. She was still turning up for his lectures when she quite clearly must know them backwards. And here she was, giving him a nudge, knowing full well Ruskin was on the agenda today. What a girl! He turned hastily to his original mentor.

'I imagine he would be looking round him in despair, but certainly not in surprise,' he said, flashing a half smile at Isolda. 'The world has mostly gone the way he predicted, I'm afraid. Is it any wonder our artists are producing work some of us are not quite sure we want to look at? They are surrounded by unbeautiful things whichever way they turn.' He was throwing himself into the arena, he knew it. Isolda was going to come back at him. She was blinking rapidly. He could see it coming.

'Not if they come here.' It was the girl with the gammy ankle. 'Montecalmo is beautiful.'

Bless her! And a diligent student; he could do with more of this calibre. And now, thank God, he could get back on course without making too big a break. He flung his arms wide. 'Beautiful Montecalmo! Everybody wants to paint it. And most of us here want to know how.' Again he noticed a perceptible 'leaning forward', a kind of avidness. Did they really think he was actually going to provide the answer? Back to Ruskin, quick.

'Let's look at chiaroscuro, light and dark. Now, when you all go out there and look – I mean, really look – you will discover, with Ruskin, that "it is an absolute fact that shadows are as much colours as light is".'

That nice girl again: she was bursting to say something. One of the sisters – now which one was it, the duchess or the commoner? The commoner. Persephone? Psyche? Come on, come on, horses, man, horses. He'd played Juliet at school, for Pete's sake, still remembered every line: 'Gallop apace, you fiery footed steeds, towards Phoebus' lodging' – *Phoebe*!

'It's true, it's true,' Phoebe herself was saying. 'That's what I did, I looked. I mean, *I really looked*, and ... well, Ruskin's right!'

How marvellous! Girls still blushed; she was covered in confusion.

He beamed at her. 'Well, it looks as if Phoebe has shown us how to do it. She's gone out into the field and discovered it for herself. First thing this morning, I was hoping to send you all out to make your discoveries, but I'm afraid the weather is not promising.'

There was a pause here as Patrick glanced out of the window at the dark clouds rolling in from the west. There was no escaping it, there'd be rain and wind all day. Ah well, life drawing, then. Sandy's job. His heart sank to his boots. How? How on earth, in her present mood could he possibly expect her to do it? Not on the spur of the moment anyway even if she was hard up, not without some gob-smacking scene. Oh God he was depressed; not least because of the uncertainty of the new girl. What was he supposed to do about *that*? His hands were tied behind his back.

Uneasily, Patrick continued. 'Not to worry, we certainly won't waste our time. We may use today doing some life drawing.'

There was a crash that made everyone jump. Isolda bent to pick up a parcel of books she'd had on her knee. Her powerful voice filled the room: 'Oh what luck! I've *always* wanted to model. I do hope you're going to allow me to sit for you. Clothed or unclothed, I really don't mind.' She ducked to catch a sliding paperback.

'Well, that's very good of you. As it's "life" drawing it would be unclothed I'm afraid, but—'

'Unclothed! Fine, absolutely fine. Hasn't anyone noticed? I'm a shameful exhibitionist.'

'Oh!' Patrick raised his eyebrows, pleased to hear an isolated chuckle. 'Well, it's very kind of you. We do have a regular model here, it's Sandy, actually, you've all met her I think, but – and there is a but – it may be too short notice for her. In which case, Isolda, we'd all be very grateful to you.'

Patrick nodded round at everybody to encourage approval, and, to their credit, most of them looked quite happy about it. What an extraordinary piece of luck! It took the heat out of asking Sandy to do it. He would mention casually that Isolda had offered, and while he was at it, he might be able to touch on the subject of the new girl – offer to meet her off the plane or ... He found that while his eye was resting casually on Isolda in the corner, she seemed to be metamorphosing. Her eyes had doubled in size and – was this the beginnings of an epidemic? She'd flushed the most amazing colour. He felt a sudden concern for her. Was she in pain? There was something not quite reliable about the way she was staring into space. He decided to steer clear of her unless absolutely necessary. If she was anything like Sandy, she could lash out at any minute.

'Is there a danger of using too much colour?' It was Phoebe again with an anxious frown.

'I'm not sure I like the word "danger", it might inhibit you from having a go. A picture may have *too many* colours in it. But you'll know when that happens, it won't satisfy you, it won't match up to what you originally wanted to say.' It crossed Patrick's mind he'd better get back to some practical hints before they all started yawning. 'It's good discipline if you can occasionally limit your colours. If the weather's good tomorrow, I'd like to send you out into the town with only two colours in your palette – burnt sienna and ultramarine. You'll be surprised at what you can achieve.' He grinned at them. Poor hapless beggars, they thought they were going out to look at shadows. Oh well, keep them on their toes. He looked at his watch. Christ, time had crept up on him. And there came the rain!

'Half an hour for coffee; then, in studio two for life class.'

'But that's my job!' Sandy had just dumped a cardboard box of fruit on the marble top. She straightened up to confront Patrick. 'Who is this anyway?'

'Isolda. She's—'

'I know who she is, she sent a fax.'

'Yes, well, it was only an offer to—'

'Didn't you tell her I do it? I've always done it. I don't understand why you took her up on it.'

'No, no, she knows it's your job, and she knows that if you're keen to do it—'

'*Keen to do it*! What does it matter if I'm keen or not? It's my job. I depend on it as a matter of fact.'

'Of course you do, of *course* you do …' It was absolutely extraordinary the way she got the wrong end of the stick. He felt like a criminal.

'You're bored with me, aren't you? You want a change. Well, I'll be gone next week; you'll be able to have all the pretty women you like.'

Pretty women! God help them both, she was serious, her voice had dropped into her boots. What a thundering fool he was, what a thundering fool to think she'd be pleased.

'Sandy, you are the best model we've had. You know that.' And he meant it, she was a natural.

'No. I'm getting old.'

He burst out laughing, he couldn't help it. Really, the situation was running out of control. She was twenty-seven, he'd seen her passport – and what did age have to do with it in the first place? He looked at his watch. They were going to be late for class and there was no time now to mention the new girl.

He touched her arm. 'I'm glad you're doing it. Now come on, we're going to have to get a move on, and, well, it doesn't take a minute to change out of that lot, does it?' he said, indicating her shorts and T-shirt.

She hung her head and untied her apron, the stuffing knocked out of her. He was appalled. This was more disconcerting than the pyrotechnics he'd got used to. Patrick was suddenly as cast down as she was. Somehow he hadn't quite managed to make amends.

As Sandy left the kitchen, eyes averted, head bowed, he saw, beyond her on the terrace, Isolda gulping down her coffee. She wasn't looking normal even now. Turning towards the nasturtiums, then pivoting round to peer out at the landscape, to her left, to her right, as if she were a mechanical toy. True, she'd lost that dangerous colour, but wasn't it a bit abnormal that she was now so pale? Not knowing quite how she'd take it, Patrick walked out onto the terrace to inform her that Sandy was indeed doing her job.

The sarong, liberally splashed in tropical flowers and blue parakeets, slipped off her body and was thrown across the room. In the same movement she turned her back to them, legs apart, head twisted in profile.

'Three minutes,' Patrick called, and immediately they applied themselves, with the thick silence of heavy breathing and squeak of charcoal gathering force.

Isolda sat transfixed in their midst with a stick of charcoal between her thumb and forefinger. She was positioned centrally, directly behind Sandy whose back and buttock clefts made dark gashes in the spotlights. Her hair, caught up and taken back, continued the line of her jaw.

'Time's up,' Patrick interrupted. And Sandy turned, jumping a few millimetres off the floor, landing in position to face them – left arm tucked loosely behind, shoulders back, breasts thrust out, one leg slightly crossed over the other like a dancer.

'Three minutes.'

Isolda's head was gripped inside a maelstrom of a sort of 'rushing', a swirling of time, while she herself was caught by a hook in its path. In spite of this, her ears were functioning because there were sounds she could hear: the snap of charcoal breaking, for example. Then Patrick's footsteps, a long exhalation as if somebody could no longer hold in his breath. She was clearly aware of these sounds, but unable to register them.

'Time's up.'

Sandy turned sideways on. Left hand on hip, weight tipped back on left leg, right foot propped up against left ankle, head dropped.

'Two minutes.'

Sandy was almost within touching distance, naked and defenceless, and she, Isolda, was now cut loose from all she knew and hurled outwards at terrible speed. She, a living organism, was being swept out into space where matter and energy sliced round her in their sterile spheres. Unable to feel a connection, she could *see* clearly: a moist curl of pubic hair straying out onto the thigh, the point of the breasts in the act of wrinkling into a firm nipple, the vulnerable flesh of the tummy beneath the navel. Each detail of Sandy's anatomy was noted by Isolda with a degree of accuracy that only the eye of a lover, or a genius, was capable of.

Patrick was a dark shape weaving his way around them.

'Time's up. Two minutes.'

A swish of paper and general adjustment took place on the borders of consciousness.

Sandy had stepped forward, bending her knee, leaving the other leg stretched out behind. She brought her weight down onto both hands gripping her thigh.

'Are you alright?' The whisper was close to Isolda's right ear.

Isolda looked up into the face of an intruder. It was Patrick: unwanted, too close, and smelling of a man.

'What do you mean?'

There was an uncomfortable stir from the class, she must have spoken loudly.

Patrick lifted up an apologetic hand. 'Alright,' he whispered, and nodded as he moved on.

The blundering old fogy, what did he *say* to Sandy? What was going on in the kitchen before all this started? He'd laughed at her, shoulders heaving up and down, cruelly laughed. Her poor darling glorious girl had been crushed, standing there in her apron. She had longed to go to her, yearned to tell her she was loved, protected against the world; that she must stop putting her trust in Patrick, that it was she, Isolda, who would look after her. But she was stuck out there on the terrace unable to move; hating him, loathing him for being a man and making Sandy feel so much; knowing there was nothing she, Isolda, could do that would make the slightest difference; because she loved him. Sandy loved *him*.

Isolda's senses were on fire, it was an overwhelming burden to be part of her body again. She looked at the piece of charcoal in her fingers and down at the blank sheet of paper and felt her legs go weak. What had she been doing?

'Stop, everybody! Small break now, while Sandy has a rest. Alright, Sandy? Patrick raised his eyebrows in Sandy's direction. She moved swiftly over to her sarong and wound it expertly round her breasts. Isolda watched her tie the corners together and reach for a glass of water. People were stretching. Isolda's pulse thumped against her chest. This was Sandy with her hair up, an altogether new person. She was enjoying it, she took a pride in it, she got a kick out of it. She was a superb model.

Isolda noticed Patrick in the shadows stealing a look in her direction. He'd noticed the blank paper. In her mind's eye she erected a gamut of feasible excuses. She could say she was feeling sick! A stomach bug had completely paralysed her, prevented her from both drawing *and* leaving the room. On the other hand, if she was ill, it would be logical to leave the room leaning on Patrick's arm. She shuddered. Better to be seen making an initial effort to draw Sandy in spite of her gastric trouble, but to suffer a gradual disability as the bug began to take its toll. Two things were certain: firstly, she was going to stay put, wild horses would not budge her off her chair; secondly, she was not going to risk losing her reputation as a brilliant producer of pastels. Patrick's admiration over that picture of the barn was an overwhelming relief. What did it matter who'd done it? A good picture was justification of her presence on the course, and – she had to remind herself – far more important than Patrick's approbation. She tingled as the sarong slipped off. Sandy was climbing onto an old cabin trunk covered in rugs. She wriggled backwards until she was comfortably supported by the cushions piled against the wall, and then sank back into them.

'Forty minutes!'

The curtain was up. Isolda was on stage with Sandy. The resulting sense of exposure left her breathless. Caught unawares, she was locked into a tragedy for which nobody had given her the lines, and playing a role she didn't recognise, a role furthermore which was destined to dominate the play until the final curtain.

She sat immobilised in reflected light from Sandy's body, and before she knew what she was going to do, or even how she felt, disbelief crept over her. She had not been in the presence of such beauty, ever. There was some elusive charge under the lights, some delicate thing. The thought behind Sandy's expression imbued her limbs with a kind of yielding, a limpness, a radiance of molten gold. Her reclining body offered a glimpse of happiness that Isolda spontaneously claimed as belonging to her because she felt it too, and a corresponding warmth surged from her womb and reached the surface of her skin. To have this moment linger was the extent of all she wanted.

The door to Patrick's office was slightly ajar. Isolda could see him at his desk in the shadows with his hand resting heavily on the telephone. For a moment she paused to wonder at his lumbering male bulk. Sandy loved him, this crumbling monolith. What could he possibly offer her, except a shoulder to lean on?

It was almost lunchtime: she couldn't afford to linger. She knocked.

'Patrick, I'd like a word with you.'

He was on his feet in a trice.

'Isolda, please come in. Sit down, please.' He grabbed a chair for her as if she were about to collapse.

'There's something you have to know,' she said.

'Not serious, I hope?'

'Oh, I think you can say it's serious, Patrick.'

His face was a mass of wrinkles and furrows. 'I *wondered* if you weren't well. In fact, I was surprised to see you in class at all, you were even too weak to work. We have an excellent doctor in the village. The hospital is, oh – five minutes by car.'

Was it possible that anyone could be so blinkered?

'Sandy loves you.'

He leaned forward and inclined his ear slightly. 'I'm sorry, I didn't quite catch what you—'

'Deaf as well as blind?' she said.

He was attentive now.

'I think you said …' He looked her in the eye.

She was patient.

'Sandy loves you.'

Patrick subsided slowly into his chair, a mountain bear lodged with a fatal bullet. She could see him searching his memory for confirmation, his eyes roving over his desk, his breathing uneven. The message had gone home. Well, thank God you can feel, Isolda thought. He was grappling with something, she could see that. After an age, he spoke, and his voice was cracked.

'She is a child.'

Isolda almost choked on a rush of exasperation and despair.

'You speak like the old man you are.' Tears welled up and she was unable to stop them flooding down her face. 'She is a woman. She is the most beautiful woman on earth and I love her.' She collapsed onto the chair that Patrick had put out for her.

She felt her hands being taken. She withdrew and clenched them into fists, and he took one of them back and opened it out, turning it over, and all the time she was bawling like a baby.

The door opened. Sandy stood there, eyes as round as saucers, mouth open. She turned to go. Patrick was halfway out of his chair. They both called her name together, but she had gone.

Chapter 14

Kitty bent to inspect her left big toe which she knew very well she had to keep an eye on; it had always been that wee bit longer than the other one. Scuffed while she was climbing these devilish steps, but no blood, thank the good Lord. Why on earth she chose the toeless snakeskins this morning of all mornings, she just couldn't say, especially when she was half witless with worry.

'*Buongiorno.*'

It was Francesca Vitti's old mother on her way down with a lettuce in her basket – oh, she had never seen such perfection in a lettuce – but she had no time to stop and admire it. The old girl had a new stomach ailment and with a whiff of encouragement she'd be off, and once she was away, well, you could kiss goodbye to your personal schedule.

She acknowledged her with a wave.

'Hullo there, Signora Vitti dear! That is a very nice fresh lettuce! Don't tell me! It came from the *alimentari,* which just suits me fine because I'm on my way there this very minute for a piece of *Parmigiano.*' She leaned over and patted the old lady on the arm. 'It's good to see you looking so bonny, dear. That rain didn't do our old bones a scrap of good, did it? But now look at it! Beautiful!'

She glanced quickly up the flight of steps, and hitching up her skirt, launched out. Taking high strides, she placed her unsteady shoes on flat areas of stone till she reached the top. The church bell began to toll as she paused to catch her breath. She was going to be one or two minutes late, but then she didn't want to be caught waiting for them as they all came out for coffee, far too conspicuous. No, this was about right, but she wouldn't have to hang about. Kitty pulled her skirt up a further half-inch, the better to aid her progress up the main street, and almost broke into a canter past the *gelataria*. She must have been dreaming this morning when she'd decided on this skirt; she could always rely on it standing around at a cocktail party, but as for getting you somewhere in a hurry! And now look, she'd been spotted by the two old crows. Dear me, you'd think their mouths were sewn together. Oh, tut, why should she care, they weren't worth a fig. She nodded brightly at two elderly women standing in a doorway near to the *alimentari*. Ah, but here were the lettuces. Arranged like precious blooms in the sun. Oh, frill upon frill, and freshly plucked from the earth. She would paint one. When she'd seen Rose, she would go home and paint one before it lost its bloom. Three left. She saw the price. *2.50 Euros*! Did they think they were Fortnum and Mason's? She clicked her tongue and shook her head. Tourism had too much to answer for.

Kitty peered into the gloom of the shop and hovered. There was no question about the *Parmigiano*, she had to have it, it was life's necessity. She held her breath and blinked. What was she thinking? She'd be able to afford a dozen lettuces if she sold the painting. Oh, perfect logic! She made a swift choice and hurried into the delicatessen. Lifting the lettuce slowly above her head as if she were crowning a queen, Kitty passed it over the counter.

'Cecilia, *cara*! Keep this beautiful lettuce aside for me in a nice dark place, and I'll be back in half an hour. Oh, yes, and my usual lump of *Parmigiano*. You're the apple of my eye, Cecilia. *Ciao*!'

She darted out into the sunshine and made a beeline up the street towards the church. The Fantini brothers were in their usual spot on the bench. Now who was that they were chatting to? Surely it wasn't their nephew up from Florence? She believed it was. Oh, but what a bonny lad he'd grown into. And the head of hair on him, like a starling's wing. There wasn't a moment to spare. She waved. '*Buongiorno, signori*,' she called. She was treated to a robust response. The old rogues, it was heart warming. Oh, she'd chosen the right skirt after all! She was beginning to feel better, and only one more flight of steps. She hoped she'd see that dear wee dog who lived in the garden behind the gate. Anything – anything to keep her spirits up, she was positively dreading what was to come. Supposing she got the message wrong? So much depended on her.

Kitty glanced inside the open door of the church where the glow from the candles was just discernible. They'd be preparing for Vittoria's wedding next week. What a real old knees-up that was going to be with half the family coming over from Siena. She winced as she felt a muscle pull round her ankle, and stopped to give it rub, and as she did so, her heart fluttered as she noticed a family outside the *pizzeria* ordering lunch. Lunch already? She looked at her watch and gasped, she must have been dawdling. Whatever happened, she mustn't be too late.

This time she was on her way *down* the steps. Not such an effort, but every bit as hazardous. She clung grimly to the high stone wall, hand over hand, and reached the bottom without mishap. If her ankle gave her a twinge, she barely noticed. The little dog stuck its nose through the wrought iron gate in the lane, and wagged its tail as she flashed by.

'Hulloo there, doggy. I'll be back later to give you a cuddle.' The sound of her tapping shoes ricocheted round the old walls on either side. A cat hared along in front of her, its tail standing up like a bottle brush, and vanished up a covered alley. Now, why would a mangy tom get in such a panic at the mere sight of her? Kitty jumped violently and almost tripped over. The car horn had sounded only three or four feet behind her. Had they gone mad driving down here? There was barely enough room for two *people* abreast! She trotted quickly ahead of the advancing vehicle and manoeuvred herself into the covered alley, her heart thumping, and a trifle dizzy. The battered car drove past, its spongy suspension causing the front passenger to bounce around. Kitty's eyes widened. White gloves, no less, and fashionable sunglasses. Like royalty. Oh, but who was her hairdresser? Perfect permanent waves, not a curl out of place. Now what was the point of dressing up to be taken for a drive in a beat-up car like that? Exhaust fumes poured from the clattering pipe and spread into the alley. She covered her mouth and stepped back a few paces. When she emerged into the lane the car was edging out onto the street that took them away from the village. Really, they had no right to keep a filthy wreck like that on the road. And to bang on their horn just as they reached her! She burst into tears in the middle of the lane. She couldn't help it; it was pure shock, of course. What a nuisance. Oh, she felt so *disagreeable*. She'd have to find her mirror and check her mascara. For pity's sake, as long as her hair stayed up, she'd be fine. Where was her hanky? A nice long sniff of eau-de-cologne. That was it! Now then, you're alright, so just stop beating about the bush and get on with it.

Kitty paused outside the open door of Il Centro, and when she was sure she had a nice smile on her face, she negotiated the deep step, and once inside, eased down her skirt. Here she was, and not a minute too soon. Oh! The minute she set eyes on Patrick, she'd feel as right as rain.

'Kitty! This is an honour; you've come to join us! Let me get you a coffee.'

Patrick crossed the terrace and bent to give her a kiss on the cheek, and as he came close, she noticed that something had surely changed in him. Oh dear, oh dear, if she weren't in such a muddle herself, she wouldn't find it so disconcerting. Whatever happened, she must not let slip that Antonio was around. She patted in a wisp of hair that had escaped from her ribbon when Patrick had kissed her. Where on earth was Rose? All of them out here with their coffee and biscuits, and not a sign of that poor wee girl. Oh, and now the other side! Her hair was just not behaving itself this morning. She jumped as Patrick appeared with her coffee.

'Patrick dear, it's good to see you! Have you taken a walk down by the *alimentari* today and seen the lettuces? Oh, they've got some real beauties. Far too good to eat. Fit to paint, though. They've put one aside for me.'

'In that case, I'll wait to see the painting.'

Was he not going to give her a smile? This was not a Patrick she recognised. His mind was definitely somewhere else. She felt herself flounder, and decided she'd better get on with what she'd come for.

'As a matter of fact, I came to see how Rose was faring. That wee scrap of a girl. You don't recover overnight from the bite of a venomous snake.'

'Rose is recovering well. But if you want to see her, I think you're going to be unlucky. She wasn't in class this morning, I think she's out painting somewhere, I'm not sure where.'

Kitty's legs felt weak and her heart raced. She'd come all this way, and Rose wasn't here. She must keep her head.

'I'm awfully keen to see her, Patrick. Maybe if I took a walk, I may bump into her. She can't be too far away, can she?'

Patrick raised his eyebrow at her.

'Don't look at me, Patrick dear, I'm the wreck of the Hesperus this morning.'

'You're magnificent, Kitty,' he said, and actually smiled. 'No, it's just that I'm not sure that your very splendid shoes would survive the terrain out there.'

She glowed. He'd noticed her shoes; and what's more, he was looking a lot livelier for it.

'Tell you what,' he said, 'why don't I ask Rose to call on you when she gets back?'

Kitty hesitated. She had given herself till lunchtime to find Rose and be ready with her answer for Antonio. She was not sure she could risk the wait.

'Now that is a very sensible idea,' she said hoping he hadn't noticed what a turmoil she was in. 'So, I tell you what I'm going to do. I'll take a wee stroll around and about, and if I don't run across her, I'll expect to see her at home.'

Oh, *Mama di Dio*, she was so tired. Was she ever going to make the hill? It was a relief to hear that Sacchetti was away, even though she'd prepared herself properly this time. She wanted to feel strong before she faced him again. Rose side-stepped a bramble that stretched out over the track, and then lifted her head to look. A very small person was lurching down the hill towards her. She stopped to wave when she saw Rose, and then toppled sideways into the vegetation.

Kitty!

Rose dropped her satchel and stool, and ran up the track on a surge of energy. Kitty's hair was all over her face when she reached her, and she lay halfway into a bush. A shoe was missing.

'Rose, dear. Rose! I've been searching, searching for you. Where have you been?' She stretched out her hand. 'I've got myself caught in a prickly bush here.'

As Rose bent to disentangle her, Kitty went on talking.

'He wants you to meet him, dear. On the path to the old barn. *What about snakes?* I said to him, she's already half dead with a venomous snakebite. She knows what to do, he said, she'll wear *stivali.*'

Rose put her hands under Kitty's armpits and hauled her upright. She had been lying on her other shoe.

'Look at me, Rose dear, I'm a haystack! Can you see my ribbon? I cannot appear looking like this, we've got to find it.'

The ribbon was caught in amongst the rose thorns. Rose picked it off and untied it.

'Oh *there* it is! Now that's it. Gather up the hair on top – you can see how fine it is – and tidy me up, dear. It's like a furnace down here, I feel quite unwell.' She gave up trying to put on her shoe, and put her hand up to cover her eyes.

'Oh, Kitty, you must wear this!' Rose snatched off her hat and put it on the tiny head. She scanned the track for shade but the nearest tree was way up the track. Next to them were two thick bushes of wild rose. This would do. They pressed themselves between them into the shadow, sitting side by side on scratchy grass. Rose's straw boater enveloped Kitty's head entirely.

'No, dear, it won't do, I can't see a thing.'

Rose removed the boater and transferred it to a tuft of grass. She knew she had to hold back. Kitty must be given a moment to recover herself.

In the lull that followed they heard something clattering down from the top of the track. She'd only seen tractors on this path. It wasn't a tractor. A car. There was no time to look. The car's tyres wobbled over the rough stones pulverising the softer pebbles, and when the chassis hit the raised ground there was a sickening sound of compressing metal. Rose turned her back to the path and picked up the boater to cover Kitty's face. The car limped past leaving behind it a rolling column of fine chalk threatening to choke them. Dust spread into the vegetation, gathering into a white cloud that was now snaking down into the valley.

Rose blinked, grit scraping her eyes.

'Kitty?' Her heart was thumping.

Kitty lowered the boater coughing. She gasped.

'Yes, dear.'

'Who wants to see me?'

'Why, Antonio! Antonio Gozzoli.'

* * *

Well, she was here, where was he? Goose bumps flashed across the surface of her skin. Where exactly did Antonio Gozzoli expect to find her? On the path that led to the old barn. But she'd almost reached the fork where half of it tapered off into the track that led through the wood. Did he want her to take that and go all the way to the barn, or continue on the main track? There was no sign of him. Should she stay where she was?

Rose hesitated and looked at her watch. This was about the right time, a little before. She looked out over the fields towards the wood and strained to listen to distant music in a minor key – medieval perhaps. Sheep bells? She stopped and looked back up the track. What should she do? For some reason she was a bit dizzy. She decided to take the path that led directly to the barn.

It was strange about the bells, she had never seen sheep in these fields; she tried to imagine them grazing in the meadow around the barn the other side of the wood. This was the wood where she'd seen the sow and her piglets. She slowed down almost to a standstill. If she disappeared from sight in the trees, they might miss each other. But then Kitty had said he was very strict about not being seen so maybe this was where he wanted to meet her. The afternoon was overcast and a wind gusted through the leaves. Much cooler. She entered the wood.

The puddle in the path was down to a wet stain, and there were no blue butterflies. In fact it was very still, there was a deep silence.

Except for that sound. It came again. She stopped. Discordant bursts of music: rough, medieval sounds, made to come and go on a hollow pipe, and then, over it all, a continuous melancholy note. She shivered and began to move again, worried in case she was walking too fast, checking the path behind her. She tried to recall her father's voice, but her mind was too jumbled.

Dogs! *That* was it! Hunting! There was a hunt out there. She froze, and then walked cautiously round the bend towards the opening that led out onto the field.

And there was the barn, stranded in the middle of a sea of grass. The strange cacophony of sound was advancing but it was impossible to tell from where. Rose felt her scalp move. I'm going back, she thought, there's something wrong. Then, from the field she saw the backs of three men rise from the grass onto one knee, raise guns to shoulder height, and point them at the wood opposite. A large black boar crashed out of the trees into the field, heading towards the guns at tremendous speed with its tail pointing straight up like a stick. It saw the men and veered round, running parallel to them. There were three shots, and the boar fell just as the dogs burst out of the thicket. Rose turned and ran.

She ran back over the track, jumping clefts and gullies with sudden strength, deaf to every sound behind her, eyes stretched wide, the better to see the path below her feet. And then, with the opening through the trees in her sights, she stopped dead as she saw them. Pigs. They came in single file, crossing the path in front of her: first, a big tusked boar, then three more males, a line of yearlings, a sow and, following her, breaking into repeated little gallops, one after the other, the young ones. It was not as before: no crashing and breaking of twigs or rushing of leaves. There wasn't a sound as they crossed the path. The last piglet struggled up the bank and vanished into the thicket on her left leaving the path empty. Had she actually seen them? There wasn't a squeak out of them, all those pigs, crossing the path as if nothing was going to stop them. She waited for the guns. There were none. The air smelt dry and earthy as it rushed into her lungs. Safe! All of them, every single one of them, *safe!*

Suddenly convinced that the hounds had found a fresh scent closer to her she ran wildly, progressing in short darts till she reached the field. A motorbike started up with an accelerating roar somewhere out of sight, drowning out the shouts and barks behind her. And then it appeared, shooting out along the main track towards Montecalmo, thudding and skidding over the rough surface. It slid into the vegetation and revved in high squeals to haul itself back up again. In seconds it was up and over the top in swirls of chalky dust. She could hear it pelting along the main road until the whining petered out to a whimper, and finally, at long last, to nothing. And hearing the cicadas from the field gradually beginning to fill the silence that followed, Rose realised she could no longer hear the dogs either. She knew she had to sit down for a minute. Her legs gave way and she subsided onto the prickly grass.

Chapter 15

Isolda stood with the telephone in her hand listening for signs of life. Once more she put it down, and again she picked it up. As far as she could tell, there seemed to be nobody about, even in the kitchen. Il Centro appeared to be empty. She bowed her head. The sheer weight of her investment in this enterprise had taken the fun out of it. It had all got too serious. Hours of research she'd put into it. The Italian art information network had yielded absolutely nothing. If they knew anything of Pazzi's fabulous collection of late Renaissance art, they were keeping quiet about it. She'd strained her ingenuity to breaking point and got nowhere. Alright, the vital number was suddenly available at the press of a button, but even that episode had taken it out of her. Patrick had left her alone in the office to go out and speak to the plumber about the generator, when she realised she was gazing at the student file up on the screen with Rose Pazzi and her contact telephone number on the list. It was a small miracle. And yet now that she had the number in her hand and the moment had finally arrived, she could not shake off a feeling of failure. Rose had not come up with the friendly invitation to the villa that she'd tried so hard to winkle out of her, which meant that she would have to expose herself to a full frontal with Tancredi Pazzi – the very approach she wanted to avoid. If he turned her down, that would be it. She'd be flying home with her tail between her legs. How could she bear it?

Oh, come on, Isolda, just do it.

Quickly she dialled.

'I'd like to speak to Signore Tancredi Pazzi, please. My name is Isolda Seagram.' Passably fluent Italian, as far as she could hear her own voice over the sudden swirling in her ears.

'One moment, please.'

A female voice, she tried to gauge the level of authority. Signora Pazzi? A member of the household? All this scuffling! What did it mean? Ah, she hadn't finished.

'Excuse me, signora. Please, are you from England?'

Isolda had worked hard on her brisk opening.

'Well, yes, I am actually,' she said in English, somewhat mortified.

The retainer, probably. Suspicious old biddy.

'Ah ... aha, yes!'

What was *going on*? The phone was quietly set aside; she heard footsteps receding, and then silence. Was it possible, she wondered, to hear a heartbeat over the phone? She could barely hear herself think. Everything, as she well knew, depended on a mixture of confidence and charm. She was prepared, of course; probably over-rehearsed even: she had a friend who was interested in Roman antiquity – sculpture, perhaps, or even painting. Without even mentioning Panini, this would awaken his curiosity, stir his acquisitive streak, and even, with any luck, his enthusiastic response to at least one of the two contacts she had up her sleeve. Either a celebrated private collector living in California, or a dealer from the more nebulous regions of the art market. Pazzi himself could decide where he stood (which would be fascinating in itself), and if he wanted to sell, he'd have to allow her in. Once inside – well, that was up to her. The prospect of being admitted to the near impregnable Pazzi stronghold, she had to admit, unsettled her horribly. But she'd done it. She was on her way. Abruptly, the line was picked up.

'Ah, good afternoon. I am Tancredi Pazzi.'

Charm itself, and in perfect English.

'Good afternoon, Signore Pazzi. I am a friend of Rose ...'

He broke in, 'Yes, of course, we are to meet you this afternoon.'

She began to speak and then floundered, her face burned.

'We look forward to your company. I hope you can still come.'

'Oh! *Yes*, Signore Pazzi!'

There was a short pause.

'You are from La Centra D'Arte?'

'I am indeed. I am *indeed* from Il Centra D'Arte, and I want to thank you so much for your invitation.'

'*Prego.* There is a problem?'

'None at all.'

'Then we will see you this afternoon. Goodbye.'

'Signore Pazzi!'

'Yes?'

The receiver slipped, her hands were wet.

'I just want to know one thing …'

'Yes?'

'Can you remind me what time you are expecting me?'

'In forty-five minutes. The car will come for you shortly.'

Isolda was in suspense. She tried to form the simple sentence in her mind: 'the car … the car will come …' but words tumbled around scattering her wits. A few specks of dust filtered through a fugitive shaft of sunlight in an otherwise lifeless world. She stared through and beyond the wandering particles to focus on a Latin inscription on the stone step. Somebody, she was not aware of who it was, came in through the front door, clattered across the flags with noisy sandals and clambered the steps to their room. When the door slammed shut, reality settled into place like a thump on the back, and she drew breath.

Was it possible that she had accomplished, in the space of less than a minute, a victory of such breathtaking appositeness? The casual entrée she'd been searching for? *Without asking?*

Isolda's long legs scissored up the staircase two at a time. She entered her room and made straight for the window. The square outside was bright and empty, not a car in sight. She looked at the few clothes she'd brought with her lying neatly folded in the drawer, scooped them up and threw them onto the bed. The dressy pants she'd packed for just this occasion were at the cleaners, she realised, having paint spots removed. She swung open the wardrobe and stared at her three shirts and the one dress she'd packed for the final evening – an inappropriate scarlet. She stood there for a minute, her head turning from the wardrobe to the bed, from the bed to the wardrobe, and then made a second dash for the window. The square was exactly as before: empty in the afternoon sun. A snap decision now was vital. It would have to be the pants she'd travelled in – with a clean shirt. No, she'd be underdressed. The linen jacket then – more than slightly crumpled.

She paused in her chosen outfit before the big looking glass long enough only to dismiss it. Undistinguished. Worse still, unfresh. Unless ... She watched her eyes enlarge in the mirror. Inspiration! The still life that Patrick had set up yesterday in Studio One. Wasn't there an old silk fringed shawl draped over a jug? Would it still be there? She returned to the window and stuck her head out. A man in a formal black jacket was climbing out of a polished limousine parked outside the door beneath. Isolda picked up her panama hat and placed it on her head, and stopped. Who was Pazzi expecting in forty-five minutes? The question evaporated in her rush to reach the studio.

The still life was intact. The shawl gushed from the humble brown jug, and swirled across the table, a cascade of iridescent colour. Isolda's eyes fixed on the streaming silk as she crossed the room. Then she noticed Jim by the window mixing paint on his palette and paused, but only fractionally. Briskly she leant forward, picked up a corner of the shawl and threw it over her left shoulder. Jim looked up, his face registering horror.

She called out, 'Hello, Jim, I didn't see you!' as she strode from the room.

She ran.

Framed in the limousine's door, one dainty haunch swathed in floral print followed another into the back seat. As the chauffeur closed the door and took his place in front, Isolda nipped round to the other side and slid into the front seat beside him as the engine started up.

'Made it!' She broadcast a wide smile to the back-seat passengers: not one, but three of them, the two sisters, with Rose between them. Look at them! she thought, so pretty and disconcerted in their frocks. She nodded to the chauffeur to indicate that now she was here, he could get going.

Rose sat forward, her mouth open, dark rings under her eyes.

'I don't understand ...' She clutched a posy of wild flowers.

Isolda said, 'I'm sorry there wasn't time to warn you, Rose, but Signore Pazzi suggested that I should come with you. And since I have a meeting with him anyway, it did seem to be sensible.'

She turned to the chauffeur who appeared to be strangely passive. 'Thank you, driver, I think it is time to go. *Va avanti!*'

The chauffeur turned to Rose, his bushy eyebrows raised, and it was then that Isolda knew she was powerless. However inadequate the little waif, Rose was her undisputed hostess.

'Thank you, Iacopo,' Rose nodded to him, crestfallen. Rudely so in Isolda's opinion. Unwanted, yet again. Did she care? She did not.

In fact, so pressing was the speed of events, Isolda was half winded with exhilaration. And when she saw Jim run out of Il Centro in his painting apron she had to suppress a gust of laughter. As they pulled away she watched him duck to squint into the limousine windows: dusky glass, she noted with glee. He looked uncannily like a chimp, baring his teeth, his upper body swaying from left to right. Was she required to feel guilty about removing the scarf? She had to confess to feeling an odd twang. Isolda looked at him jigging in the blazing square, and remembered his bigotry in the swimming pool. She reduced him to a splat.

The bonnet edged forwards down a striped avenue of cypress at the end of which the villa was partly visible. They emerged into a circular forecourt in glittering sunshine and made a steady curve around a central fountain, drawing to a stop in front of the steps to the house.

As Iacopo opened her door for her Isolda stepped out in a kind of trance bathed in reflected colour from the facade of the house. It reminded her of rust, and, according to the play of light, it radiated warmth in every variation of the metal itself. Here was a villa of mid-Renaissance design, so elegant, so utterly buoyant in scale that in the presence of such perfection her throat constricted with emotion. As if to emphasise its gaiety, swallows flew above it in circumscribed arcs, and, to the right, a cedar of Lebanon spread its inky branches into the blue. Isolda revolved slowly, completing her inspection.

Iacopo was getting back into the car, and Rose, the little waif with a posy of flowers, had grown in stature; was transformed, furthermore, by the spirit of proprietorship. She was already leading the way up the staircase sharing a joke with the two sisters, regular girlie gossip. Isolda watched them. Was this what she wanted? She knew she yearned for it. Rose turned back and offered her an outstretched hand. 'Well, don't get left behind!' she said, positively sparkling with good humour. Isolda bounded up the steps towards them.

'Who did the frieze up there?' she asked, not daring to believe her eyes.

They all looked up to the arch above the portico. Rose looked back, her eyes gleamed.

'Della Robbia.'

'Della Robbia!' Isolda said simultaneously, childish in her triumph.

'Are you the fount of *all* knowledge?' Phoebe said.

Ignorant chit of a girl. Surely it was a normal, civilised observation? After all, here they all were in Italy, living near Florence. Just the same, it reminded her she was being careless; she hadn't yet decided how to play her part. Was she an art historian, or a wide-eyed amateur painter? A thousand curses, she hadn't prepared her ground plan. How was she to know she'd have to be the same person to Pazzi *and* to the crowd from Il Centro? She tilted her panama hat to shut out the villa as if to shade her eyes from the sinking sun. Merge into the background, she breathed, not for the first time. No need for a decision, she wasn't yet at the crossroads.

Above the frieze, the coat of arms caught her eye. She paused to look at it. It was divided by a diagonal line. The upper half enclosed a small castellated tower, and below the diagonal, a boar's head was clearly discernible.

The doors were already open to the entrance hall. Phoebe and Dill wandered inside slowly, oohing and aahing like babes in a vast gilded wood, their heads tilted towards a huge barrel-vaulted ceiling. No wonder, Isolda thought: nothing had quite prepared them for this. She suppressed her excitement. Who was the architect, the painter of the frescoes, and the dates? The effort to contain her curiosity was almost painful. She tried to relax her stiffened muscles.

Rose called out in a voice hardly loud enough to summon a mouse, 'Giselli ...' And here she comes, Isolda breathed: the retainer, if she wasn't mistaken. A little old crone appeared making a beeline for Rose, her arms outstretched. Isolda recognised her innocent ally who had almost certainly helped to put her on the guest list.

'This is my old friend, Giselli,' Rose turned to them with her arm around the old woman's shoulder. Giselli bowed in an agony of smiles and wringing of hands until Rose drew her aside to ask her a question, and they continued to discuss something urgently in a disjointed Italian, so low that Isolda found it difficult to catch: and all through, the old woman was nodding and patting Rose's hand.

As the muted voices continued, the two of them were moving steadily towards some glass doors leading onto a balcony which in turn opened wide to a view of the wooded hillside. And as the others walked through ahead of her, Isolda stole a last quick look behind her at the allegorical frescoes covering the walls. Of course! These must be the frescoes Antonio Gozzoli was commissioned to restore. Lucky man. She cast her eyes up to the crescent-shaped vault above the entrance and held her breath. The *lunette* was as fresh and playful as any Renaissance fresco she had seen. What need had Pazzi for pictures when he had these?

The balcony turned out to be a long loggia stretching the length of the villa, where a small party of people lounged in basket chairs. There were lemons, she noticed, growing in big pots all the way down to the end; and before she could take it all in, a movement caught her eye: a parrot, perched on the shoulder of a woman with blonde hair.

A man in a grey silk suit, faultlessly cut, detached himself from the others and came towards them. 'Rose, you have arrived with your friends!'

To Isolda's surprise, Rose swept past him with a brief 'Hello Tancredi' and went straight to a gaunt woman with greying hair sitting slightly apart. She bent towards her, placing the posy in her lap and kissed her cheek. 'I want to introduce you to my friends, Mama.'

Isolda realised, as Rose turned back to them, that the poor girl was stiff with nerves. She introduced Dill and Phoebe to Signora Pazzi with a fixed smile and unseeing eyes, quite forgetting to include Isolda herself. Behaving as she would in any other situation, Isolda walked forward with a smile, her hand outstretched towards the older woman, and announced her name firmly. A limp hand was lifted a few inches from Signora Pazzi's lap, and dulled eyes turned up towards her. The top of Isolda's head prickled as she took the icy fingers. She could almost see strings lifting the right arm and inclining the head. Would this puppet have been aware even that Rose was her daughter-in-law? The posy in her lap lay untouched. Quickly Isolda turned to the others to find herself, unexpectedly, the sole object of attention.

She laughed without humour, and said, 'What a treat it is to find a frieze by Della Robbia, especially when you're not looking for it!'

Pazzi's face brightened.

'We are very fortunate,' he said, animated suddenly. 'And we must show you the garden. We have some Venetian figures in our little theatre that will interest you, I think.'

Before he dealt with the remaining introductions, her host shot her a look she was unable to interpret. He took special care to include her, almost as if she were a guest of honour. And as they all found empty chairs, Isolda was aware of his continuing interest. Is he testing me? He knows I'm the unseen guest he spoke to on the phone just now. Oh God, I've been rumbled. She found she was taking in deep, noisy draughts of air. The basket chair creaked as she eased herself into it while she turned to listen to the woman next to her talking about her parrot. Her name, she gathered, was Sylvia, and she spoke in a strangulated Americanised drawl.

'He is a good boy, he like to take a wok. Every morning he take a wok.'

'Wouldn't he prefer to take a fly?' Isolda found herself saying in spite of herself.

'Yeah, he would prefer to take a fly, but when I cut his wing, he can't take a fly. Instead he take a wok.'

She was enunciating the words with nasal elaboration. Isolda felt herself heading for mental paralysis, and yet the need to keep the conversation going at this point was essential.

'Fascinating! Does he like to have his breakfast before he sets out?'

'Yeah, he like to have his breakfast. A little fruit, a rusk.'

Isolda found herself wishing the parrot would get off for its much vaunted walk without delay, taking its brain-dead owner with it preferably; but no, Sylvia was warming to her subject.

'Sometimes I don't know what he prefer. Sometimes he say to me, "*Pronto.*" Breakfast? I ask him. "*Pronto!*" he squeak.'

Isolda glanced at Pazzi brushing at his sleeve in irritation, and, for a second or two, was able to allow her attention to linger on him, covertly observing his fussy hands and prominent signet ring. He is sharp, she observed, as a razor. Sharper, even, than the young painter who got the better of her in San Gimignano. She closed her eyes remembering with distaste the American's sniggering laugh. A long draught of jasmine-scented air rushed through her nostrils. Relax, the time has not yet come.

Dill came over to say hello to the parrot and at last Isolda could sit back and look at the other two guests.

She guessed that the one gazing blankly at the balustrade facing him was possibly a business partner, whereas the other was a mystery, a real bruiser. He sat with his burly arms folded across bulging pectorals that strained his buttoned jacket to tearing point. Inscrutable, both of them, but then perhaps neither of them spoke English. She was going to have to grapple with the social discrepancies in a quiet moment later on. Then, to her surprise Rose went over to have a word with the Burly One. What did she call him, Rodolfo? She bent over to speak quietly to him while he shifted uncomfortably and chuckled nervously. She said something about the circus leaving town, and he repeated her words – circus left town. Was he part of a circus?

Dill and the parrot had floated off to their own encapsulated world. Dill leant closer.

'I think you already know you are a handsome boy,' she was saying. 'I wonder where you come from.'

Sylvia melted with pleasure, and acquired a kind of professional glamour suddenly, tossing her hair and lifting her face as if to the sun. 'He come from Patagonia, don't you, *caro*?'

The bird's feathers were a startling green, and every time it edged its way along Sylvia's shoulders and half lifted its clipped wings, it revealed flashes of red and blue.

'This is my Papageno,' Sylvia said, attempting to rub her cheek against its wing with lips parted like fifties Hollywood.

'Papageno!' Dill was clearly enchanted. 'And so, you play the flute?' she asked the parrot, whose journeys up and down his mistress's shoulder were growing ever more restless. Sylvia was puzzled, she shook her head.

'No, he don't play the flute.'

'*Dill!*' Phoebe's face had gone pink. '*Please*, Dill!'

But Dill leaned even closer to embark on a jolly Motzartian aria, her shapely mouth only inches away from Papageno's beak.

'Pa pa pa pa, papapapapapa …'

A piercing shriek from the parrot knocked them back into their chairs and propelled Tancredi to his feet. Papageno appeared to be venting a sudden rage on Sylvia, sidling round to the back of her neck and jabbing into her head, finishing up with a beak full of hair which it used, like a knotted sheet, to let itself down her back, step by step, in a flurry of feathers.

Tancredi lifted both arms above Sylvia's cowering body and brought them down onto the parrot, lifting it aloft as he turned and walked back to the edge of the balustrade where he hurled the bird into the void. It fell like a stone into the gardens below.

Sylvia stood up, her hair awry, in an agony of confusion. She stared beyond Tancredi to where the parrot had last been seen descending, and then looked at him with her mouth forming and reforming a series of soundless words. Then moaning in a soft sing-song, *non ... non ... non ... non ...* with every shake of her head, she crept over to the balcony to peer over. As everyone prepared themselves for action, she gasped and jack-knifed over the balustrade, both arms stretched out. Tancredi moved to grab her hips and she reared backwards wailing '*Papageno!*' before rushing to the steps at the end of the loggia. Dill and Rose swayed, drawn into Sylvia's wake as if attached to her, running down the steps and following her out into the garden. Hearing slowly approaching footsteps, Isolda and Signora Pazzi looked towards the house.

Giselli walked cautiously through the doors and out onto the loggia with a loaded trolley of tea and cucumber sandwiches. She looked round at the depleted gathering.

Isolda held her breath. Was nobody going to speak? She turned to Tancredi. He was frozen, arrested in the act of covertly glancing into the garden.

After a moment's uncertainty Giselli picked up the silver tea pot and smiled at the guests.

The smell of cucumber seemed to trigger Tancredi's two male guests into a kind of delirium. Restless scuffling sounds came from them. The business partner began to clear his throat several times in quick succession. His lizard eyes swivelled up and down the loggia, and he raised his hand repeatedly to smooth his hair into place, peering round his fingers as if he expected the three women to rush back up again.

The Burly One was suddenly dying to put his little hat on. His stubby fingers would close on the trilby which he'd scoop up till it was almost in place poised above his head, at which point he would freeze before replacing it on his knee. After repeating the attempt three times, he joined in all the noisy throat-clearing and scraping and stamping of feet before stopping abruptly when he saw Giselli approaching him. Now he cast his eyes down and furrowed his brows, a chastised child as he listened to the few quiet words she had with him.

There was an imperious gesture towards the tea trolley and they heard a curt '*Per favore*'. Tancredi had taken control, and whatever restraining effect Giselli had hoped for, it was too late. At a stroke, the two jittery Italians began to stuff themselves with cucumber sandwiches. Their ravenous hunger, whetted by a dainty measure of tea, was so powerful that Isolda panicked in case they demolished the entire plateful before she could get at them; she had to restrain herself from joining in the frenzy, and looked at Phoebe.

Phoebe said, 'What lovely sandwiches,' and managed a tight little smile.

Tancredi squared his shoulders and dabbed his lips with a linen napkin.

'Ah yes, of course – The Importance of Being a Cucumber Sandwich!' he said.

Isolda laughed. The ice had been broken.

Taking heart from the relaxed atmosphere, the Burly One took the last sandwich, opened his mouth and pushed it in, slapping his thighs to clear the crumbs. When he turned to them, still munching, and put on his hat, it seemed the signal to be off.

Tancredi looked round and stood up. 'If we are ready, I am sure you would like to see the garden.'

Signora Pazzi showed a small flicker of life as Tancredi approached her. He took her hand and raised it to his lips, speaking directly to her in a low voice. Then he looked towards Giselli and issued a short instruction. It was clear that Signora Pazzi would remain on the loggia with Giselli in attendance – wisely, it occurred to Isolda after a moment's thought: what if the puppet master forgot he was holding the strings and let her go? She spared a moment for the gruesome prospect of a pile of brittle limbs on the terrace. Were they now at last on the point of their collective escape into the garden? After all, they had the business of the parrot to attend to. Where was the parrot? In a far-off corner of the estate, she supposed, with the three of them nurturing the wretched bird back to life.

The burly guest jumped up, overtaking Tancredi to get to the end of the loggia first. He could hardly wait. His bow legs tilted him left and right down to the bottom of the loggia steps where he stopped to wait for everybody. He stuck his hands in his pockets and rocked from side to side and backwards and forwards, darting the odd look at Tancredi till his host caught up with him. It was extraordinary to see how much Tancredi tolerated him. Despite his visible restraint, and the occasional appearance of a fine fretwork of lines across his forehead, their host was scrupulously well mannered. In a way, it was part of his fascination, that and his meticulous attention to his appearance.

They followed Tancredi down a succession of interlocking balustraded steps linking the terraced gardens. Each one was superbly restored and maintained in high Renaissance style, Isolda noted. But couldn't the man slow down for a minute?

Phoebe was at her shoulder suddenly.

'I heard these gardens were practically a wilderness a few years ago,' she whispered.

'Who restored them?'

'Tancredi, after his brother died.'

Phoebe's attention was diverted to the burly guest, who seemed to be executing a jolly *cinquepace* to manoeuvre himself into a position by her side. Scandalously he started to ape Tancredi, strutting along smoothing his hair, pointing out a statue here, a sculpture there, and then pausing to flick a speck off his sleeve. He looked up into Phoebe's face and chuckled.

'My God,' Phoebe looked at Isolda. 'Over to you.' She quickened her pace to be up at the front with Tancredi. Even as Isolda hurried to catch up with her, she strived to imagine what role the Burly One would fill in a circus: did he take the tickets? One was forced to admit, one would not have marked him out as a natural choice to include in one's *belle soirée*. Concentrate. It was vital not to miss what their host had to say even though it was dawning on her with growing disappointment that Tancredi was on a treadmill. He seemed to be leading them on a brisk guided tour of the estate in order to finish as soon as possible and wash his hands of them. His haste, in this case, was barely within the bounds of courtesy. She could hardly take it in; they, his guests, were no more than sheep trotting after him, a faceless retinue baaing their awe and admiration.

This was not working. He'd forgotten her remark about the Della Robbia frieze; she felt her special status spiralling down to oblivion. She wanted to shout, 'Stop! I am someone to be reckoned with, don't you remember?'

A piece of sculpture brought her to a standstill. For a blessed moment, Isolda was impaled by its beauty: an eighteenth-century statue of a woman glancing back, drawing her robes around her as if she had been caught by prying eyes. And here she was on her pedestal fitting snugly into a clipped crevice in the hedge! Oh God – so much crying out for attention, couldn't they see?

She looked up to locate them. Almost out of sight. Unless they were sharp, all this would pass them by: the statuary, the fountains, the grotto, everything. It would whiz along without meaning to anyone. In fact it was a chore. Tancredi's role as a guide was a chore he had long ago perfected to a mechanical ritual that whenever necessary, he trotted out for undiscriminating guests. It was humiliating. It was making her acutely physically uncomfortable. Lumping her together with characters from the *Comedia dell'arte*! How could she bear it? Her breathing was running out of control, her armpits felt wet. She was on the point of screaming.

'A *perfect* watercolour!' Phoebe stretched out her hand like Boadicea summoning her troops.

They stopped in their tracks, blindly following the general direction of Phoebe's outstretched palm. The ridiculous girl seemed to be indicating a small fountain in a sunlit garden visible through an arch in the hedge.

Amazingly, Tancredi took her seriously.

'You are attracted to chiaroscuro,' he said, casting his eye over the dark yew hedge.

'I *am*!' said Phoebe.

'Then you must come and paint it!' he replied.

Isolda's mouth went dry. She tried to suppress a volatile panic that threatened to interfere with her vision. This was not supposed to happen.

She walked in a trance not even hearing what Phoebe and Tancredi were saying. The party were wending their way through a geometrical boxed parterre, the Burly One ahead of her. She focused on him with a kind of laser precision, while allowing her mind to empty. And, she noted, although he walked with a kind of rolling cowboy swagger with his hands in his trouser pockets, there was something self-conscious about it. Two or three times, he glanced back at her and then shrugged his right shoulder as if he wanted to disguise a nervous tick. How many guided tours of the garden had this rustic tagged along with, and why was he here? She marvelled at the accuracy of his aping of Tancredi. In a flash a crazy revelation seized her. Tancredi was mimicking the Burly One's parody of him! She was going mad, tipping over the edge. Make a plan. Something. Anything.

They arrived at a water garden, and even before they had clustered round, Tancredi was already rattling off the history of four seventeenth-century statues marking the corners of a pool. Looking at his watch, he drew their attention to the impression they gave of communicating to one another. Unlike their host, Isolda reflected grimly.

Without warning, a shout from the Burly One alerted them to something he'd spotted in the water and Tancredi's hand, which was resting on a jutting stone buttock, shot back as if it had been electrocuted. Pointing at what looked like a carp, the Burly One was positively galvanised with excitement. Then he laughed revealing a mouthful of rotten teeth. For once Tancredi lost his cool and snarled at him. It seemed to be the last straw. He was now in disarray. He pressed his middle finger between his brows as if a migraine were coming on and took some deep, measured breaths. This was it, proceedings were being wound up. She watched her last chance slipping away. He brushed his hands together.

'*Allora*! I hope you have enjoyed our beautiful garden ...'

Panic jolted her memory. The firm burgeoning flesh of that cupid – it was familiar. She narrowed her concentration on the bronze fountain in the central pond: a *putto* with its arms around a fat fish. For a split second, Isolda revelled in a vivid sense of time and place, and stepped airily into the middle of Tancredi's pronouncement.

'*Aha*! Now this is interesting! MMmmm…*yyyes*!'

Surprised, he turned to look at her. She felt the force of his attention, and held back for a couple of seconds.

'Very much in the style of Verrocchio …' She lingered on the word 'style', and then paused just long enough to create an impression of inner debate. 'But without the personality, perhaps. Has Baccio Bandinelli anything to do with this *putto*?'

Tancredi went through a delayed reaction.

There was a silence except for a small smacking sound coming from the stream of water spouting from the fish's mouth. It spread its concentric circles over the choppy surface till they lapped against the stone perimeter. Isolda's stolen silk scarf slid to the ground. She knelt slowly to pick it up, and even more slowly, replaced it on her left shoulder.

Tancredi opened the palms of his hands to her and held them wide. '*Allora*! We have had scholars here. Mostly they agree! Baccio Bandinelli! *Bravo*!'

Isolda's eyes met his with glowing gratification, goose pimples tightened over her skin. Bull's-eye!

There was a sharp gasp from Tancredi's business partner. His knuckle shot up to his mouth as he stared wide eyed at the fountain.

Tancredi beamed at him, nodding, 'Baccio Bandinelli! We are lucky to have him, you agree?'

The business partner pushed his jaw back into his neck, his eyes bulging while they waited for him to speak. His head began to poke in and out like a hen.

Isolda held her breath. He was concentrating hard, doubtful of her historical analysis yet perhaps more than a little mistrustful of his own. A butterfly fluttered in her chest as she prepared for his challenge. But then, an extended rumble in their midst suddenly released itself into a massive belch. Isolda stared as the business partner smiled, patting his chest and batting his eyelashes as he shrugged his shoulders helplessly. He was appealing for their indulgence. An almost uncontrollable urge to push the flatulent nitwit into the pond seized her. How could she have ascribed wit to this burping pillock? Her moment with Tancredi was in ruins.

But he trusted her. A slow thrill spread from a spot in the pit of Isolda's stomach, branched into her thighs and lodged in her knees. She couldn't say she was best buddies with him, but surely she was one step closer to his collection. They were following him through a long pergola entwined with wisteria, this time accompanied by a lively commentary. The grand tour appeared to be ongoing, the open-air theatre was back on the agenda, their host was in a good mood, and the Belcher, it appeared, had done no harm. She looked around her at leisure. At the little sun-baked bricks of the pillars stretching ahead, for instance: so worn, so rounded. With half closed eyes on the procession moving down the dappled tunnel ahead of her, and a woolly lightness in her limbs almost lifting her along, Isolda felt resolution ebbing away. She felt the tickle of that old familiar sensuality on its way. In spite of herself, she allowed it to permeate her pores. Piece by piece, troubling shards of memory peeled off into the mossy path behind her exposing an uncomplicated warmth towards her fellow beings. The Burly One, bless him, was nothing more than a knockabout court jester. She might even grow fond of him given time. He was directly ahead of her now, wearing his hat at a wildly rakish angle exposing the back of his head to the sun. Overdoing it as usual, of course, but then, how could he help it? He was an innocent, a natural. She had come to think of Tancredi as his mentor. And now that Tancredi had relaxed, the Burly One had begun to extend his God-given licence – nodding at them, eyes darting with merriment, blustering along ahead of her, half the size of anyone else. She noticed a licentious wink and, with it, a glimpse of teeth: striving to catch Phoebe's attention again.

There were two gardeners clipping a tall boundary hedge about twenty metres distant. She could see them through leafy spaces between the brick columns. Tancredi, she couldn't help noticing, maintained his villa and estate with the high degree of grooming that he lavished on himself; there must have been at least five or six workers weeding and clipping continuously to maintain this high standard, although she hadn't noticed them. She pictured Sandy by her side turning to her with a secret smile. She almost felt her hand as she reached out to touch her. This was quite simply the most beautiful garden she had seen, and it was entirely natural that the two of them should be walking down this enchanted tunnel together. Curled up on the grass at the foot of a dark hedge of yew a small greyhound lifted its head sharply to look at them – uncannily like the pencil drawing she had acquired, she decided. The thin gardener at the top of a ladder turned in their direction. He lowered his clippers and pushed back his baseball cap to wipe the sweat from his face. Her chest constricted and for few seconds she was blinded with panic. It was the American painter from San Gimignano. But then, a moment later he turned back to continue clipping. She'd been mistaken: from his profile, she could see it was someone else.

Although the hallucination had been momentary, its resonance was real enough. Supposing it had been him, that laid-back itinerant. And if *he* had seen *her* ... a burning agitation seized her. She must secure an invitation to view the collection without delay. If Tancredi gained an inkling, a mere whiff of her connection with Burlington's ... well, she didn't even have time to think it through. It was about time this damned meandering crowd of idiots got a move on: she wanted to be next to – *needed* to be next to – Tancredi. She had to stay by his side until she'd prised an invitation out of him. It shouldn't be too difficult. She pushed herself forward, unconsciously nudging the Belcher, who lurched towards the wisteria.

By the time she reached him, Tancredi had emerged from the pergola and was poised at the top of a flight of steps that led down to a sunken garden. The sun cut in to the darkly shadowed enclosure catching an alabaster statue on its pedestal. Isolda held her breath; it could have been Mozart himself. There were three more sculptures of the same period placed in a kind of semicircle on a grassy rostrum as if they were characters in an operetta; and at the top of a flight of steps at the back of the rostrum, two slim columns supported a pseudo-classical arch. She stopped, suddenly transfixed.

She said, 'It's the theatre!'

'Oh, *look at it!*' Phoebe's voice came from behind.

They both fixed on the grassy little theatre encircled by tall hedges, and already it seemed peopled with actors. Of course! These were the

Venetian figures Tancredi had talked about. A dramatic scene, one felt sure, was about to take place. She felt the beginnings of a laugh tickle in her chest. As she turned to Tancredi, she was pushed from behind and almost toppled off the step. Somebody took off at high speed. It was the Burly One. He rocked down the steps, shot across the lawn, leaped onto the stage, raised his hat to the statue and bowed to it. Tancredi and his guests were mute, trapped at the top of the steps while the Burly One pranced across the stage winking at them.

Isolda glanced around her for a reaction. Tancredi's expression was a surprise; he might have been watching a favoured child. He was *indulging* him. The Burly One was being given complete licence. He was strutting about the stage as if he owned it, inviting them to ridicule the statue, scoffing at it, as if it had spoken to him. He hunched his shoulders and mouthed its imagined dialogue lewdly behind his hand. Isolda gazed at him in disbelief. What was he actually saying? She heard Tancredi and the Belcher muttering to each other under their breath, but the Burly One was going from strength to strength: he seemed to be egging the statue on, aiming blows at the pedestal with his hat. He hollered something that amused him so much, he doubled up.

Phoebe laughed loudly. He heard her. There's no stopping him now, Isolda thought. He trotted up to them and from the edge of the stage, took off his hat and bowed. For one second Isolda thought he was going to topple off like Tweedle-Dum, but he straightened up slowly and then stopped. In the pause that followed, Isolda knew the situation was about to run out of control: he was looking up at Phoebe with his bushy eyebrows shooting up and down. Then he turned to the statue, shouted an insult, gave a final wink at Phoebe, and began to undo his fly buttons. This was too much for Tancredi. He held up his hand as he descended the steps, calling out.

They followed him, clattering down the steps, and as they did so, Phoebe called out, 'Bravo!' But the Burly One's head hung low, his hands stuffed into his pockets.

Between ticking him off, Tancredi swung away from him distractedly and plucked at the cuffs of his shirt, only to swing back as a fresh reprimand occurred to him.

Now is the time to divert him, Isolda thought, and swiftly crossed the grass towards him.

There was a commotion of female voices. Her heart sank.

Dill appeared between the two tall columns at the top of the steps leading to the back of the stage. Rose and Sylvia emerged to join her. Phoebe ran over and jumped up on stage to greet them, running up to the top of the steps where she turned to call to them. 'He is back in his cage. Papageno is back in his cage.'

Isolda went up to Tancredi and touched his arm.

'I want to thank you for showing us your theatre. It's beautiful,' she said quickly.

Tancredi bowed his head, 'We are proud of it.'

'Your Venetian figures are in a perfect setting.'

A flicker of a smile appeared at the corner of his mouth. She cringed inwardly. He thinks I'm crawling to him. I must get to the point.

He asked, 'And the entertainment?'

She succumbed to a blissful sense of relief, and laughed.

'What else is a theatre for?' she said.

Phoebe called out again, 'He's alive, he's alive and kicking!'

'Kiki!' The Burly One had pricked up his ears. A series of hoarse noises resounded from the stage as he muscled his way over to Phoebe. 'Kiki!' he chuckled, 'Kiki!'

Damn the Burly One. This was *her* moment, her ribs were bursting.

'And I hear you have a fine collection of paintings!'

But Tancredi's attention was being diverted. He glanced over to the Burly One, filigree lines collecting on his forehead. Tears pricked her eyes as she felt herself once more pushed to the margins. Never *mind* the bloody man – she almost screamed – look at *me*, listen to *me*.

'From the Florentine school, I believe!' it came out faintly.

A sharp reprimand from Tancredi caused the Burly One to check his advance up the steps towards Phoebe.

Loudly, Isolda said, 'Signore Pazzi!' and he turned to her.

'Forgive me,' he bowed. Then looking up at her, 'You like our *teatro*?' he said.

'Oh, I do!'

'On Thursday evening we have a concert here. Corelli, some Vivaldi. If you're still here, why don't you come?'

She stammered something silly and girlish that made him smile.

'We will be happy to see you,' he said.

And before she could speak he was already in conversation with the Belcher.

And that was that. She had been dismissed.

Isolda stood where she was, staring ahead of her, oblivious to the commotion.

Handed to her on a plate! Another chance.

Chapter 16

Kitty herself had no idea what on earth she was doing deep inside the dark cave of the *alimentari* with a perfectly ordinary lettuce in her hand. It had undoubtedly been plucked that morning, the root was still damp, but it wasn't a patch on yesterday's frilly green petticoat. And that, she realised, was why she was here: she just could not let go of that moment yesterday when her heart had soared into the blue sky above at the sight of such verdant loveliness. Well, she'd not got around to painting it and that was that; it wasn't a bit of good, all this dilly-dallying. Her frantic search for Rose yesterday came back to her now like a kind of nightmare. The whole episode had somehow become distilled into the wreckage of her shoes. She pictured them again, rough stones tearing at beautiful soft snakeskin; it made her weep. Frowning, she replaced the lettuce she'd selected, went back and paid for the cheese and bread. If she wasn't going to paint it, she certainly wasn't going to eat it at €2.30 apiece.

The *campanile's* bell was ringing as she re-emerged into the street. My, oh my, what a smart group of people milling outside the church. But not enough for a wedding, surely? And that was a rather plump wee girl cradling her bairn. Could it be her old friend Agnesi's granddaughter with her newborn? Of course it wasn't – she was growing dottier with every day that passed – and this must be the very day of the christening. Oh but she must go and acquaint herself with the bairn.

'Kitty! There you are.'

'Patrick! Oh, Patrick dear, you startled the living daylights out of me.' She held on to his arm to catch her breath. 'Are you on your way to the christening?'

His face was a blank sheet of paper.

She patted his hand. 'As if you had the time.'

'Kitty, can I invite myself for a cup of coffee?'

'Goodness me. Of course you can, *of course*. Goodness gracious me, you couldn't have chosen a better moment, Patrick dear.'

He took charge of the *Parmigiano* and the stick of bread, and held out his arm for her.

What pure joy it was to walk down the street with Patrick in the sunshine. She felt she had acquired an altogether new status. Oh, they were positively beaming approval at the sight of the two of them together. She felt tall: somebody very special with long legs. Let this moment last for a lifetime, she thought, lifting her face to Patrick at her side. But he wasn't looking at her. He was staring ahead of him like a man possessed. A stab of disappointment numbed her concern for him. But not for long.

'Patrick dear ...' she began. She wanted to ask him what in the world was making him so gloomy, but then decided against it. She tightened her grip on his arm and beamed at him. She'd wait till she'd got him in the house.

Now then, coffee: where had she put it? A wee drop of milk, it was all she had left. Those ginger nuts, would they still be fresh? If she'd known he was coming, she'd have topped up her biscuit tin just now in the village. Kitty peeped through the drape dividing the tiny kitchen from the living room. He was having a good long look at the pictures on the wall. Her heart thumped. Oh dear, oh dear, she was all of a 'mither'. Back to the coffee, quick, and grab the kettle while it's still hot, and careful down the step now, the tray weighs several hundredweights.

Kitty's eyes were bulging when she emerged from the kitchen. As always when a friend looked long and hard at a painting on her wall, especially if they had something definite to say, she found the rug from beneath her feet begin to slide – whether it was her own work or somebody else's, it didn't matter – she would never be able to look at the pictures through her own eyes again because there was a terrible danger they'd be sullied for life. She made it to the low table and collapsed onto the chaise longue. Oh, for pity's sake, Patrick, say something nice. He was pacing around the room peering at every single one of them.

She had to admit to being guilty of hanging her own work from time to time. Ringing the changes, of course, there was no point in having the same old picture to look at day in day out. But had she known he was going to be in here with his nose a mere inch or two away from them, she'd have hunted down her own two masterpieces, it might have added tone ...

Finally he turned around.

'I had forgotten how jolly they all were!'

She let out a little puff of relief. 'Jolly' was one of his favoured words.

'You had me on the edge of my seat there, Patrick. Come over and have your coffee while it's hot.'

His eyes travelled down to the coffee as if he'd noticed a large insect floating in it. Any minute now he was going to forget she was there at all. There was something he wanted to say, she was sure of that. She leant forward and called his name, softly so as not to startle him.

'Ah, yes, coffee.' He breezed over and picked up his cup. 'You know, this is awfully good of you to have me over on the spur of the moment, Kitty.' He began to gulp down his coffee as he talked. 'And I'm not going to take up your precious time any longer. I'll be off in a sec.'

'Don't be absurd, Patrick, sit yourself down and have a ginger nut. You can't go rushing off like this, you've just this minute got here. Now then.'

There was a knock on the door.

'*The electrics man*! Is it Thursday?'

'No, I think it's Tuesday.'

'Then who can this be?'

Patrick strode over to the door. She craned to see past him.

'Rose! Rose dear,' she called out, 'what a bundle of troubles you look today, come in, come in.'

Patrick ducked out of the arched doorway of the castle into the dazzling light and squared his shoulders. It was a mistake to think he could talk this over with anyone. He set off down the slope out of the town, across the main road, and up the shady road of cypresses to San Cristofero. All the same, how else was he going to sort himself out? I should be teaching, he told himself grimly, and stepped into the little nineteenth-century church with Romanesque arches. In an alcove, in the gloom, he found what he'd come to see.

To his relief the heavy side door was unlocked. It swung open with the usual groans and cracks, and blessed sunlight filtered in. And there it was still: *The Good Samaritan.* Bill's work. Lovely old Bill. Not everyone bequeathed his work to the church. And a good teacher, too; Il Centro had been lucky to have him. Nobody else he knew had Bill's ability to convey this immediacy of feeling in stone. It was tempting to link his art to his natural generosity, but Patrick had wrestled over this feeling before, he remembered, and decided the theory was unsound.

And here he was after all these years still coming to look at his old friend's sculpture, still trying to discover what it was exactly that made it so clearly what it represented. The Samaritan down on his knee, his broad back and shoulders at such an angle as to indicate a meticulous care in his task of lifting the emaciated figure off the ground. How did this lump of stone radiate compassion? There was barely a mark on the surface. He walked round the various counterpoints and tried to assess what it was that held the key: the angle of the skeletal arm draped round the Samaritan's head, for example; the distance between the helpless torso and the hastily folded knee of the Samaritan himself, perhaps. It never failed him, always absorbed him, and, invariably, after spending some time in this small enclave with Bill's sculpture, Patrick relocated a sense of his own reality.

The thick door thudded as he carefully replaced the latch and turned towards the hills, sniffing the warm air. Even after all these years he could still marvel at the sheer breadth of landscape before him. Did he love her? That day she'd stood beneath the copper saucepans in the kitchen, she looked magnificent. He pictured her body in life class and tried to sort out how he responded to it. He'd drawn her a dozen times and as always when it came to life class there was a significant part of himself he set aside: it had to be like this. That last forty-minute pose, he'd hardly had time to look at her, but he did remember being struck by a kind of aura she'd had lying back on those cushions; a lubriciousness combined with optimum health. It was extraordinarily potent now he came to think about it, and there was no question of it being a veneer; it was what she was, she *felt* it. Was it for him? If she loved him – and when

Isolda had put it to him point blank, he was afraid the truth of it had hit him like a cricket bat – then that radiant generosity was all for him. He felt strong stirrings, and with them a kind of panic. He was an old man, she was a young girl. What was he going to say to her?

A breeze rushed through the tall grasses at his feet and his eye was caught by shadows of clouds passing across the cradle of hills. For a few moments he closed his eyes to it. Loving Sandy. He didn't want to rush it; he'd test what it felt like bit by bit. It was a good thing to say it to himself a few times, face the possibility. That butcher's apron, she was never out of it; leaping off her perch on the stool to rescue a pan on the stove, wiping the sweat off her nose with the back of her hand. She already worried him silly working herself to the bone, that vibrant fiery-headed girl. He'd have to employ more help. The possibility of another pair of hands had already crossed his mind. He had a picture of the paring knife striking deep into the wooden table. He'd been on his way to see Margheretta! Of course! Why hadn't he understood?

Slowly he opened his eyes, and cautiously he gave himself measure: imagined lifting a strand of her hair to examine in the sun, getting close enough to check the *actual* colour of her eyes, feeling the breath from her mouth. It was no good, he was getting an erection again. Loving her: having her around for the rest of his life, *this* was what he was looking at. Could he get used to it? It was a concept he felt was almost within his grasp, but at the same time, a million miles from his reach. He had a clear picture of Isolda's monumental hand in his own during those terrible moments of tearing silence in his office. His heart went out to her: her bowed head, her tears shattering him. Who would have thought it? And what an agony for a woman to love a woman who could never love her back. She couldn't even tell her. How she must have hated *him*.

He flinched. A brace of swifts swooped by out of nowhere and raced out towards the hills.

For the first time the reality of Margheretta hit him and he was convulsed by a pre-emptive falling sensation. How could he have forgotten her, all those afternoons of mutual pleasure? It wasn't only that: he was fond of her, and he knew perfectly well she was more than fond of him. A brief scenario of an imploring Margheretta in his arms sprang to mind. It was unthinkable, he couldn't put her through all that: the suffering, the horrors of rejection. And then, to love Sandy, for him to plunge in *knowingly*. It was just not the sort of thing he did (especially someone as old and experienced as himself). Anyone could see it was fraught with hazards.

Even if Sandy loved him, it was a notion, a whim; she was young after all – young enough to put it behind her. She'd certainly find it easier to forget him now than if they'd been to bed with each other. (And that was another fantasy he couldn't allow himself to indulge in.) Much better not to start something that could end in misery for both of them. He was in a position of responsibility, for God's sake. Sandy would get over it. Of course she would.

And now he'd *finally* come to his senses he could think about his students. A brisk walk back to Il Centro to pick up his stuff, and then out to hunt them down.

Patrick took one look at the crowd outside the church and realised he should have gone round by the East Gate. It was a big wedding; they were all waiting for the bride to arrive. A local family he guessed, recently monied perhaps. A surprising number of dark glasses and spruced-up children. He recognised some of them. They'd backed off to form a circular space where a little girl in a white dress was practising her pirouettes. Rather charming but a nuisance, it was effectively blocking him off. How on earth was he going to fight his way through? It would be churlish anyway, he might as well wait for the bride like everyone else. He saw Rose on the other side of the crowd waving to catch his attention. He waved and shrugged cheerfully as if to say he was a bit stuck where he was. He couldn't believe how ill she looked, gaunt and hollow eyed. Nonsense to say she'd recovered from that snake episode, she plainly hadn't.

There was a commotion from the women surrounding the little girl, and as he turned to look at them, he had a lingering impression of a man standing close to Rose, watching her, although he couldn't be sure because the man was wearing sunglasses. When he turned back to check, the man wasn't there, and he wondered briefly why he'd caught his attention in the first place. It was the bullish shoulders and jutting neck; it awakened a memory of something somewhere that made him feel uncomfortable. The little girl had fallen over and there was a tremendous clucking and converging because she refused to be picked up, and lay in a heap with her frilly skirt sticking up like a flag.

A familiar car horn was announcing some sort of arrival and if he hadn't once owned a V.W. he wouldn't have known what to expect. Sure enough, here it was, edging its way through the crowd: a lime-green open-top Beetle polished to perfection and adorned with lilies and ribbons. As Patrick watched the bride step out he saw her look up at her father and he thought: he'll remember that look for the rest of his life, lucky fellow! She had so much froth and lace, it took some time to unhook it from the car door. Where was the little girl, wasn't she the bridesmaid? Apparently not. She appeared to be a guest like everyone else, being lifted high in her mother's arms to get a good view of the bride, her cheeks streaked with tears. But in fact the child wasn't looking at the bride; she was being distracted by a white gloved finger giving her a poke in the chest. She backed away from an admonishing wag; he wasn't surprised she didn't like it.

The bride and her father were walking slowly towards the church, passing between himself and the little girl, and Patrick could see that people were preparing themselves to follow the couple in. He decided to wait for a minute before he made a dash for it. Then he saw him again: the stocky man in dark glasses. This time he seemed to be staring for some seconds at the woman with gloves before he touched her arm and half turned to incline his head at something behind them. The woman turned to look, and at that moment Rose caught Patrick's eye again. She was trying to tell him something in sign language, he had no idea what it was. She finally laughed and waved both hands as if to dismiss her efforts to communicate, and turned to go. He was losing his touch, there was no doubt about it. A young person would have picked up what she was saying with no trouble at all. An unaccountable foreboding overcame him as his eyes returned to the odd couple. The man nudged the woman again and nodded his head to the back a second time. This time the woman slowly swivelled a full half-circle to see behind her and returned his nod. If the whole thing hadn't been so calculated, Patrick may not have noticed. As it was he didn't like it. What on earth was going on? The woman had left her post in the front row – the best view if she wanted to see the bride – and was now deliberately pushing her way to the back. And what made it strange was that the man was curiously *underplaying* his message: there were no words between them which might have been normal. Patrick searched for Rose. Where on earth had she gone? She was obviously on her way back to Il Centro, and of course, that's what she'd been trying to tell him.

Unable to see much more of what was going on and being fairly hemmed in, for several seconds Patrick folded his arms and sank into a limbo. He stood freewheeling through his memory with the sun beating down onto his shoulders, penetrating the thick cotton of his shirt. A man pushed past him with a large camera and excused himself. Then he asked him a question directly. Patrick looked at him unseeingly. Something was not quite right. He must get back. He must find Rose. The bride had just gone in and people were beginning to drift inside the church.

The green Beetle started its engine, preparing to drive off as the crowd fanned out. This was his chance. He strode through the guests and entered the lane behind them, moving quickly past the *pizzeria*.

'Eh, Patrick! *Come va*? Is Saturday still on?'

'I don't know, Franco, I'll call you.'

The waiter called after him with the score of the local team but Patrick had by now turned the corner and was halfway down a flight of steps. At the bottom he entered the lane in time to see a long shadow shrink into the square at the end. Some shutters above him swung open and a woman stuck her head out over a window box of geraniums. She called his name and Patrick lifted his hand in greeting but continued down the narrow street past a yapping poodle that threw itself into a frenzy as he passed. He reached the square and almost ran into Rankine who had at that split second put his hat on.

Patrick said, 'Where's Rose?'

Rankine turned blinking towards Il Centro behind him. 'She's inside, as f-f-f-f-ar as I know. I've just seen her.'

'See anyone else?'

'Anyone else?'

'Yes, a woman.'

Rankine stood in the sweltering square, an alarming shade of pink. He hesitated with his clutch of pencils and a sketch book.

'C-c-c-c-c-c—'

Patrick was already striding towards II Centro. He couldn't wait for an answer.

Once inside he called for Rose, and on hearing nothing crossed straight through the inner doors, past the kitchen, into the winter dining room and through into the printing studio, still calling her name. He found her in the main studio walking over to him, her eyes like saucers.

'*Patrick*! What's the matter? What's happened?'

He stood and looked at her. Everything was as it had always been. Nothing out of place, Rose standing in the middle of the studio, a lopsided grin about to streak across her face, as large as life. She said, 'You look as if you've seen a ghost!'

What a complete spectacle he'd made of himself! He let out a hearty laugh.

'Just checking up on my star student. How's the work going?'

'I was about to go out and have another go at the barn.'

Patrick said, 'Oh no, not down there.'

Rose looked at him with her head on one side.

'Patrick?'

'No, really, I mean it Rose, you've done a fine painting already, why not go on to something else?'

Was it her youth that gave her this insane invulnerability to danger? Had she really forgotten the white car episode so soon? No, of course not, look at her: she was only just hanging on to her sanity. He had to be a bit careful here.

'Look, Rose, I don't mind telling you, I'm not sure that you've recovered from this snakebite. You're not looking yourself, you know. Why don't you take it easy for a bit – put your feet up.' He had a brainwave. 'Tell you what, I'll make you a cup of tea.'

Rose chuckled quietly. How on earth was he going to get through to her?

'Come on, then,' he said, 'I'll buy you a drink.'

That did it. She gave him a somewhat penetrating look, but she was putting the masking tape back with her stuff.

'You sound like my father.'

'Well, you need looking after.'

'I only paint to forget, anyway.'

The poor girl, oh, the poor girl.

They walked past the kitchen and Patrick glanced in quickly. Only Jason with his hands in a bowl of flour. Sandy nowhere to be seen, thank God. They stepped out into the square.

He looked down at her and thought: what a wisp of a thing you are. Any minute you'll drift up and float over the town like Chagall's bride. Ah, but, of course, he was forgetting, Chagall's bride had a groom.

'Somebody asked me the other day where he could find Antonio Gozzoli,' Patrick said.

Rose stopped and looked at him. 'Who was it?'

'I don't know, I hadn't seen him before. Well, I might have done once.'

'What did you tell him?'

She sounded breathless and seemed rooted to the spot. He turned back to her.

'Rose, dear, are you sure you're well enough for this?'

'What did you tell him? Because he is in America, isn't he? I mean, we are talking about the man who painted the fresco, aren't we?'

'As far as I know. I told him he was wasting his time, he wasn't here.'

'What did this man look like?'

'Rather like a small bull about to charge.'

She was looking haggard again. Immediately he regretted mentioning the man. Say something jolly, man, cheer her up, he told himself. But he felt oppressed by the sun-baked afternoon beating down around him. Fuzzy seeds were lazily drifting here and there fastening onto his brain.

'What did you think of the little girl?'

'Which little girl?'

Was he losing his wits? Surely she'd seen her?

He took her elbow.

'Nothing, nothing. Let's get into the bar before it fills up,' he said.

Chapter 17

Jim's hair was lanky at the back and a film of perspiration covered his neck. Phoebe shifted closer to examine the reddish purple column of sinew and skin. Carmine with a touch of Prussian blue, she decided, if she happened to be painting it, which she wasn't. In fact she was casting about for something to think about, anything other than this tortuous journey. There was no question in her mind, Jim's dogged snail's pace was tantamount to provocation, and if he'd bothered to glance in his side mirror when they'd cornered, he'd have seen them: dozens of cars in a follow-my-leader behind them, hooting now in unison.

'Maniacs!' he muttered.

As he crawled round the cusp of yet another hairpin, Phoebe leant out to take a quick look at the curving queue of trapped humanity behind them. Two or three clenched fists shot out of the line of open windows. A moped, overtaking them all, was advancing rapidly. She withdrew her head. As it came alongside, the driver poked a single finger unpleasantly close to the open window causing the bike to wobble as he passed. He mouthed something incoherent, although all too explicit, if you added the obscene crook of the middle finger to the jutting upward movement.

Phoebe sat forward, feeling dangerously bottled up.

'Jim, I wonder if we should try and find a lay-by.'

'Call of nature?'

'Certainly not!'

Phoebe coloured. How could this man get it so wrong? She had a macabre vision of herself squatting by the roadside next to the hired Fiat while Jim airily whistled a tune.

'But it would be awfully nice to stop and look at the view,' Dill said.
Jim was mystified.

'Can't you look out of the window?'

'I just think we should let all this traffic get in front of us,' Phoebe
said rudely.

Her sister laid a restraining hand on her arm. She shrugged it off.

'Have you seen it, have you seen it? There's a five-mile tail back.
Half of Italy! *Look*!'

'Wassat?' Jim said.

Phoebe spoke clearly.

'I'm sorry, I just can't bear it. I would like to be *dropped off*.'

'Phoebe thought it would be more relaxing for you without all this
traffic behind you,' Dill said.

'Oh, ho, doesn't worry me. I'm used to road hogs here, you know.
All this mayhem – makes not the blindest difference to me.'

Phoebe clenched her teeth in silent mutiny. She would insist they stop
at the next village, wherever that was. Meanwhile they were committed
to their ghastly, heavy-footed Pied Piper journey all the way there. She
allowed herself a stealthy look at the woman in the Punto directly behind
them. Hunched shoulders, tight mouth, fingers gripping the wheel: it
wouldn't take much more of this to tip her over the edge. Phoebe put
herself in the woman's place, leaping whip-like out of the Punto, turfing
Jim out of his seat and across the bonnet of the Fiat. With a fistful
of safari jacket, she would tower over him, icy, rational and succinct.
Has it crossed your pea-pod of a mind, you self-satisfied prick, that
there may be 'other people' on the road apart from your geriatric self?
That they may have a train to catch? A pregnant woman! Have you
thought of that? On her way to hospital, you bastard, with her waters
breaking!

Dill shouted, 'Look out!'

Phoebe was thrown against her sister as Jim swerved to avoid a man
straying into the road in front of them. The man jumped out of the way
lurching back against the rocky cliff face.

'You bloody fool!' Jim shouted.

He spotted a lay-by on the opposite side, and with his eye riveted
on a parking space, he swerved across the road directly in front of an

oncoming lorry. The lorry braked and skidded but stayed on course, clunking and grinding down the hill as Jim drew into the lay-by.

The Fiat skidded to an abrupt halt while a continuous chorus of abuse streamed past them up the hill, and then was gone. The engine cut out, and the three of them sat slumped in silence, chastened by their brush with the lorry.

A bird sang, another trilled back. A hammer knocked miles away in the valley.

Phoebe climbed carefully out of the car with her eye on the sheer drop into the valley. Suddenly her body convulsed, and to her surprise she found she was watching a beige projectile of lumpy vomit shoot from her mouth and splash onto the stony ground.

Jim shouted, hoarse with excitement, 'Do you know something? That was bloody Rankine!' He had sprung from the car and was pacing about with his hands on his hips.

The man they'd almost killed themselves for, who indeed looked like Rankine, was now moving slowly up the road towards them keeping well into the cliff's slight overhang. He seemed to be holding his right hand close to his chest while with his left hand he gave little pushes away from the rock face to prevent himself stepping into the narrow gully. For once he was hatless. His scalp was a deep pink, visible through his hair, and as he got closer Phoebe noticed vertical lines of dirt streaked across his shirt and trousers. Two cars coming down the hill passed him by within an inch or two, their horns blaring. Rankine shrank cowering against the rock. They watched him step into the gully and flatten himself, and then slowly lift his left hand to search for some vegetation to cling to. Dill had already left the car and was running towards him.

'Dill. Come back.'

Phoebe's voice sounded thick and guttural, and she wondered if her legs were going to hold her up. Halfway across the lay-by, she had to lean for support against the car.

Dill was trying to pull Rankine's hand down from its grip round a wiry growth of scrub. Something small must have dislodged because Rankine ducked as if his head had been hit, and the two of them paused. It looked as though Dill were persuading him to follow her. The two of them were obscured for a few seconds by traffic passing in both directions before Dill could be seen hauling Rankine out of the gully to coax him up onto the side of the road.

Jim roared, 'I suppose you realise you damn near killed us!' His body was as tense as iron in his ancient safari shorts.

Dill guided Rankine towards them holding on to his hand. She fixed a deliberate eye on Jim as they entered the lay-by. 'Rankine needs our help,' she said steadily.

This is as close as Dill gets to anger, Phoebe thought. She stood swaying by the car.

Rankine stumbled and stopped.

'F-forgive me. I think I m-must have … I get suh-sunstroke easily.' He trailed off unhappily and bowed his head, breathing with difficulty. There was blood on his shirt front.

They heard a snort as Jim's hands fell from his hips and he turned to get back in the car. The door slammed behind him.

Dill said, 'Phoebe, can you get a hat out of the car? And then I think we must get Rankine to a doctor, he's been bitten by dogs.'

After all that had happened there wasn't the slimmest chance of even starting a picture, but with the sun already slanting into the square Phoebe dared herself to think the worst was over. She began to study the little tufts of vegetation dotting the tower of a *palazzo* set solidly against the sky. Would she include them in her painting, or might they detract from that crucial severity of line? This question of form had a habit of presenting itself frequently; in fact it had overtaken her endless ruminations on the pitfalls of colour. For years now, she had been aware that certain views caught her attention because they suggested particular paintings to her. Did she see bits of the world now only through other painters' eyes? Would she go to Venice and see it as a painting by Canaletto? Or even more bizarrely, to modern Cap Ferrat (she'd seen a disappointing photo of it recently) and long for the days of Dufy to make it more like Cap Ferrat? Not now, it seemed. Amazingly, her own style was getting to her first. She saw the potential of these *palazzi* framed as her own painting, potential flaws included. Did this mean she had become a proper practitioner? On the contrary, her pictures were growing more chaotic as she struggled with distance and perspective. No wonder she stuck to landscape; it disguised her clumsy craftsmanship. Even if her pictures bore no resemblance to what she was supposed to be painting, at least they still looked like places she'd like to visit. She wondered if Patrick had spotted this crippling deficiency. And if he had, come to think of it, why wasn't he telling her what to do? Briefly she imagined tackling Patrick on the subject, but suspected that in the end, she'd keep her guilty secret to herself. That being said, she could no more have painted a picture today than she might have eaten the pastry Rankine wanted them to have.

Phoebe took a long leisurely breath and released it slowly, feeling the tension in her shoulders go with it. She would never have to travel in Jim's car for the rest of her life. If he had decided to stay with them in San Gimignano, it wasn't hard to imagine them all being marshalled into separate reconnaissance parties to trot off and look for a doctor. As it was he'd driven off without a qualm, relieved to be out of it, leaving them all by the West Gate waving him off.

She wondered, idly, if Rankine realised how much he owed to Dill. He sat contentedly in her floppy sun hat in front of his teacup, his bitten hand bound in a bulbous covering of tight gauze. Judging from the sentimental smile he was lavishing on her sister, Phoebe had a hunch he might just be smitten. But then people were always smitten by Dill. Not that she blamed them, it was just that occasionally she honestly felt she deserved a little more attention; not only from other people, but from Dill herself. She'd actually been sick in the lay-by, for example. Her own sister hadn't noticed. And although she'd almost exploded with the effort, she'd managed to keep quiet about it. Dill would admire her for it when the time came to casually let it drop in passing.

'Only *one* dog, Rankine?' Dill was saying with the most bemused expression. 'I don't know why, I had thought it was a sort of ... pack. I can't think how I got that impression, especially as it's so unlikely.'

Her sister laughed as she waited for Rankine to speak.

Free of Jim for the rest of the day! Hours of strolling round the sights of this divine place without his abrasive presence. Meanwhile ... she closed her eyes and realised she was barely breathing ... meanwhile, they might go and have a look at the Gozzoli frescoes over in the church of ... now what was its name? Would Dill and Rankine notice if she had a short nap? Her legs were weak, she felt drained. She was drained. The will to pull herself together seemed to be seeping away from her. But she had to summon that last little bit of energy to formulate the question that had been buzzing round her head ever since she sat down: if the car had been travelling any faster, would they have run over Rankine? Killed him, perhaps? In other words, was their sloth-like progress the saving of Rankine? She groped for the threads she knew were there waiting to be connected before she sank into the oblivion she longed for. Ah, but if they'd been going any faster, they'd have been miles ahead, wouldn't they? Then Rankine may have been knocked over by someone else further down the line. Her head had only just dropped forward – or perhaps she imagined the two events occurring in quick succession – when she felt a hand closing round hers. She jumped into consciousness staring into Dill's wide-open eyes. She was repeating something over and over again. 'What's *that*, Phoebe? Phoebe, what's that noise?'

Phoebe glanced round, seeing everything but noticing nothing in particular. Rankine was sitting forward in concern, while the waiter continued his clearing of tables. She saw lazy afternoon tourists drifting past, somebody stepping away from the *cambio* stuffing a money belt, a woman crossing the square pushing a pram. Dill whimpered and brought her face closer to Phoebe's.

Phoebe turned to Rankine. 'What happened? Tell me what happened.'

Rankine was apparently grappling with some inner debate. He stammered in confusion.

Dill dug her fingernails deep into Phoebe's hand. 'Listen,' she insisted, her eyes staring. '*Listen!*'

Phoebe wondered briefly if she was in the middle of a dream. She closed her eyes to test reality. All went black and she was able to concentrate.

'I'm listening, Dill, I'm listening,' she said.

'Yes? *Yes?*'

'I can hear pigeons, some noise from the bar inside, boys shouting, a church bell, a baby crying, I think ...'

'A baby! A baby!'

Phoebe's eyes snapped open and she left her chair to put her arm around Dill's shoulders. Her sister was breathing in shuddering gasps as she stretched out her arm. She was pointing to a woman moving away from them down a sloping street, pushing a pram.

'It's in there,' she said.

They all turned to look at the disappearing pram.

Phoebe said, 'Darling, it's alright, it's just a baby. A newborn baby.'

As they looked, the woman stopped and turned to look back at them. As she did so, Rankine turned his back on her, fixing his eyes on his plate. The woman seemed to hesitate for a moment before she turned back to the pram. Within seconds she was lost in the crowd.

Dill said, 'Rankine, do you know that woman?'

Phoebe looked at her sister with the beginnings of astonishment; perhaps while she was sleeping strange events had taken place. Dill's pale eyes were studying Rankine with an unblinking insistence; her breathing had calmed. Rankine looked up slowly and returned her steady gaze.

'You were outside that house when I came out,' Dill said, and then her face softened. 'My knight in shining armour. Weren't you outside the house, Rankine?'

Rankine nodded. 'And the baby was inside.'

Dill took a sharp intake of breath. She studied him attentively.

'But how did you know?' Her eyes blinked rapidly now.

Phoebe slid slowly into her seat, allowing her hand to stay on Dill's shoulder. She felt obscurely that Rankine held the key to something that was about to hurt her sister, and that Dill knew it, but that in spite of this, she needed to know.

'I could hear there was a baby,' Rankine said. 'From the window.'

Dill leaned forward and searched gently into his face. She dropped her eyes and nodded as if to confirm something to herself.

'Alright,' she said softly.

Phoebe's arm fell to her side as a curious sensation of pins and needles ran over her scalp. Disbelief blurred her slow understanding of events taking place. The baby, of course, the baby in the room, the baby in the pram. The woman pushing the pram. The dumpy little woman pushing the pram.

Phoebe was breathless. 'My God! Was it her?'

Dill sat motionless with her eyes downcast. 'No.' She shook her head and then looked up, touching her lightly on the arm. 'It's alright, Phoebe. It was just the baby. It was the same baby.'

Phoebe addressed Rankine.

'Well, what are we waiting for? We must follow her. We must find out where she lives.'

Dill said, 'I don't think so. I think we must let her go.'

'Let her go!'

Rankine was shifting round in his chair.

'*Let her go*! When at last there's something we can do?'

Phoebe turned from one to the other. Both faces were wearing a kind of mask.

She said, 'We've talked about this. We've agreed. We've agreed that if only we could find the house, we could at least let the police know about it.'

Dill said, 'No, Phoebe, we didn't. I have never given you that impression, I have only wanted to forget it. It was you and Rose who wanted to take it further.'

Intimations of Phoebe's earlier nausea came and went. She was right, her sister was right; she and Rose had gone over it and over it. A sudden sweat lay on the surface of her skin, yet she was cold. They were on the brink of discovery. Was it possible that Dill was proposing they all sit here drinking tea while that woman pushed her pram out of sight and irrevocably out of reach?

She stood up.

'Just going for a stroll. Back soon.'

Rankine was galvanised into a plunging twist. His good arm crossed over his body as her arm was gripped. He stood up, still holding her arm.

'P-lease sit down,' Rankine was surprisingly strong.

'What are you doing? Let me go!' She wrenched away, but the grip was like iron.

'It m-might be another b-baby.' he said.

'Of *course* it's not another baby. You heard Dill – she was terrified. She *knows* it's that baby. Tell him, Dill. Tell him it's the same baby.'

191

Slowly Dill shook her head and dropped her eyes. Phoebe searched her face for an inkling of strength, a glimmer of support, but her sister's feelings were out of reach.

'You c-c-c-could never be sure.'

Transfixed by Rankine's full, moist lips as she might be by the mouth of a fish in a tank, Phoebe mulled over his words. To arrive at the house, not knowing for sure if it was the right one. It was a remote possibility, difficult to prove unless Dill was with her, and Dill wanted to forget the whole thing. Hopeless.

'You can let go of me now.' Her voice was expressionless.

As she slumped into her chair, her sister leant towards her; but even Dill seemed low in spirits.

'Thank you Phoebe. I know it was hard for you.'

The swifts were hotting up, the deckchair was comfortable, the day cooling but not too fast. Then why was her heart heavy? For a full fifteen minutes, she and Dill had been sitting side by side in silence, too exhausted to speak. They listened to Sandy setting the tables for dinner behind them, and gazed out at the sweeping convolutions of vineyards and fields in the late afternoon sun. The shadows are at their starting post, she thought, and I am a lump of lead.

Dill's deckchair creaked next to her.

'Oh, Phoebe, I'm so sorry,' she said at last.

The cat jumped up onto one of the trestle tables already set for dinner and sat washing itself. Phoebe tore up a nasturtium leaf and threw the bits over the balcony.

'It's not your fault.'

How could she blame Dill for this travesty of a day? It was Jim. Jim was answerable for all this. Phoebe sighed. But even that was beside the point. 'God is having his vengeance on me,' she said.

'God doesn't do that nowadays.'

'Yes he does.'

'Why would he?'

'For thinking I could paint a likeness of his beautiful world and spend a whole day without trying.'

Dill remained silent, she probably felt it was a rebuke. It wasn't of course, it made perfect sense: she had dared to imagine she was already a painter. Who but a dilettante would set out for a day's painting and limp back without putting brush to canvas? *This* was why she felt so restless. Not to have taken advantage of San Gimignano when they had their paints on them; to have taken a taxi straight back home after the episode with the baby. It was inexplicable, why had she agreed to it? They had all sat there in gloom. All three, unable to make a move in any other direction but this. Well, she had wasted a day; it was Jim's fault. There was no doubt the unspeakable man was only now toying with the idea of cleaning his brushes and packing up at some beauty spot or another.

Dill said, 'You see, Phoebe, you could hardly expect the police to take it seriously.'

Phoebe twisted round to face her sister.

'*I* did. Rankine did. What about Rose?'

'I think an Italian policeman would find it difficult to understand.'

'I'd *tell* him.' Phoebe realised she was almost shouting.

'But what would you tell him?'

'I'd tell him that you were kissed ... that you were kissed by a foul woman.'

Dill stretched out her hand to place on Phoebe's.

'Well, exactly.'

Phoebe heard a kind of chuckle coming from Dill's deckchair, and was gripped by instant mirth. Unable to convert a simultaneous sob to laughter, she was trapped like a wailing infant being tickled to the point of insanity. Her sister was almost as helpless: she spoke in a broken series of breathless sighs. 'And I can't think what the press would make of it.'

'Duchess with knickers down stumbles on sex ring.'

Dill took Phoebe's hand again, doubled up and completely winded.

Phoebe felt inspired. She began afresh. 'Suspected high-class hanky-panky in Sss ...' but was unable to continue. After several attempts to speak she gave up.

After some time, Dill said, 'There's something that puzzles me.' She seemed reluctant to continue.

Phoebe was on the point of exploding with fresh laughter.

'Go on then. What?'

'Well, you see, Rankine said he could hear the baby through the window.'

'Yes?'

'He was out on the street, but the baby was in the bedroom on the other side of the house, overlooking the courtyard.' Dill turned to her, full face. 'I don't see how he could have heard it.'

The cat jumped down from the table and ran inside.

'What's all this about a baby?' The voice behind them was unmistakably Isolda's. 'Look what I've got! Nicely chilled.' Isolda held up a bottle of white wine. 'Let's pinch some of these glasses.'

CHAPTER 18

She pitched her voice down into the valley.

'Giovanni, *basta*!'

He was in his underclothes making his way around the hillside with as much energy as he could muster. Thin bow legs carrying him forward, arms flailing against vegetation that got in his way, a body bowed towards his goal with terrible intent.

Rose called out again.

'Giovanni, Giovanni, *fermati*! *Fermati*!'

Doubting her chances of catching up with him from the top of the hill, she cupped her hands and gave him a last shout. But he was deaf to sound from the outside world, scuttling sideways as he lost his balance, and against all odds making swift headway. She picked her way down the hillside, dodging gorse and small trees, until the ground was level beneath her feet. The trail ahead dipped as it passed through a thin copse of oak on its way down the valley; that was where Giovanni would be. She marvelled at his speed.

'Giovanni! It's me, Rosa. It's me, Rosa, Giovanni.'

She had reached him and was walking alongside him now holding his arm, as thin and brittle as a stick. 'Slow down, Giovanni. It's alright now. It's alright; you don't have to go any further.'

High-pitched, whistling wheezes came with his breathing but at last he seemed to be aware of a restraining presence somewhere in the vicinity. He stopped and rocked unsteadily on the spot in his flannel long-johns with their single row of buttons from throat to crutch. One thin white leg rose out of its boot, shoelaces trailing, while the other boot had come off. Before she kneeled to tie the lace Rose lingered, fascinated by his bare, bird-like foot perched on the gravelly earth.

His eyes fastened on her, wild as a madman.

She smiled, her face very close to his.

'*Ciao*, Giovanni!'

He made a sound through his open mouth as he stared at her.

He doesn't recognise me, but I think he trusts me, Rose thought, unsettled by a long line of drool swinging from a gap in his teeth. Taking her time and nodding encouragement, she gathered up his fingers, powdery dry, and linked his arm through hers. 'Let's go for a walk!'

Gently she turned him round, and they began their spasmodic journey back towards the farmhouse.

A little way along, Giovanni stopped and lifted his free arm, vaguely encompassing the fields and vineyards in the valley below them. His squeaky voice seemed to come from a long way off.

'*Ottimo*! He doesn't want it.'

'Who doesn't want it, Giovanni?'

'*Ottimo...*! He started to wail, his rheumy eyes streamed.

Rose increased her grip on his arm and steered him forward – ruthlessly, she felt; he had started to limp. The frenzy that had sent him hurtling out of the house had dwindled with each trembling step, slowing him almost to a standstill. She raised her head, casting round for somebody, anybody, to come to her aid, but the hillside was deserted.

When Giovanni realised he was being taken back home, he resisted. Rose felt his arm slip away and had to grab it back. She thought: his energy has come back, he is like a child who doesn't want to go to school. Wordlessly, she appealed to Lucia to come to their rescue as she struggled with him, and then tightened her grip as the old man stumbled and stopped altogether when the familiar old farmhouse came into view. He was bawling openly now, and suddenly she wanted to join in with him. She whispered to him, 'Please don't, Giovanni, please don't cry.' But he was onto a treadmill now, in the last stages of misery. '*Ottimo*, Antonio, *Ottimo* ... Ayayayay ...'

At about twenty or thirty metres distance from the house, Rose noticed, in the open doorway, a figure in the slanting cut of shadow. She wondered if she had put him there to complete the composition:

the vital human element, the missing part of the landscape. Or was this figure of Dodo always going to be around, to catch her out at any given moment; passing in a crowd, sitting on a bus, as a huntsman in a tapestry? In disbelief she watched him recoil with snake-like speed and throw an instruction back into the house behind him. Within seconds he was sprinting up the path towards them.

Rose felt her strength ebb away. Toni Vasari was there in front of them panting like a hunted animal, and she knew that even if she'd had the breath to say anything, speech was irrelevant.

'Thank you, I will take him,' he said, and lifted the frail old man into his arms. She saw Lucia run out of the house and stop to shade her eyes from the sun. When the old lady saw Giovanni folded up and carried towards her at such an alarming pace, the automatic scolding and clucking must have died on her lips as her upper body buckled. She stumbled slowly round to stand in the doorway to usher them in.

It's over, Rose thought, they don't need me now. Good luck, Giovanni. She stood where her charge had been taken from her and suddenly needed to sit down. She sank onto the bank in amongst the fennel, hearing sobbing infusions of air racing into her lungs. Now at last she could cry with him, share it with him, his unhappiness, so big he didn't know what to do with it. It was a terrible disappointment, an overwhelming disappointment that had driven him out from his bed and down to his precious vineyards to wander the countryside; an old, old man who'd reached the end of his life only to be dealt a blow he could not support. Her heart was bursting with grief for him. And now she heard herself calling for Dodo over and over again. She told him she couldn't bear it without him, pleaded with him to come back, crying out that she needed him because she couldn't bear it any more. Maybe she wasn't crying for Giovanni in the first place, maybe he was an excuse; it was impossible to work it out, too exhausting to take in. She wanted to hide away and be left alone. She bowed her head and drew up her knees, trying to shut out the day.

When she looked up Toni Vasari was crouched in front of her on the path.

She looked away and wiped her face with her skirt.

He stretched out his arm and held her shoulder. 'Don't be sad,' he said.

He was too close. She was confused and tried to get up.

'Stay for a little. It's better for you.' Again she felt his hand restrain her. 'Thank you for bringing him home, he is very clever, he gets out, I don't know how.'

Rose saw his restless eyes glancing up and down the path, and thought: he really doesn't want to be here. Well then, why doesn't he go? But he seemed to be waiting for her to recover, head ducked down. He is staying because he wants to say something to me, and I think he doesn't know how to say it.

'I am Antonio Gozzoli.' It was a statement. He looked her full in the eye. 'I have something to tell you. Very soon, please.'

She stared at him.

'You are Toni Vasari.'

He nodded. 'Yes, I have two names.'

She felt foolish and began to stumble over her words.

He cut her short.

'It's true. Forgive me. I have to leave this place very soon. I must speak to you, but not here.'

'Where, then?' Rose said, her sense of control slipping. 'The barn? It's surrounded by huntsmen.'

'Tonight? They won't be there tonight.'

It was all moving too fast for her, she was unable to make decisions.

'Don't be scared. It will be dark, but safe for you.' He paused searching her face. 'I am asking you.'

'What time?'

There was a shout a little way back up the path; it was somebody from Il Centro.

The slats snapped shut over the face of Toni Vasari alias Antonio Gozzoli. He rose to his feet without a word and walked back to the farmhouse in no particular hurry but with abnormal speed.

Rose's courage was seeping away. She called out, 'I've come at the wrong time.'

It was plain to see that Kitty was in one of her tizzies, she'd rushed straight away to change out of some elaborate bedroom slippers. Rose got up from the chaise longue and hovered by the door. Was Kitty the right person to approach? Every time they'd talked about him recently she'd worked herself up into a fret.

She was calling from the bedroom. 'Rose dear, you will stop that nonsense this instant; you are one of the dearest people I most like to see.'

She came in again wearing some strappy shoes.

'Look at you, you poor wee bairn, leaping up and down. Come over here and sit yourself down.' Kitty patted the velvet alongside her. 'And leave your hair alone, my girl, or you'll wear it away.'

Rose sat obediently and clasped her hands together.

She plunged in. 'I'm meeting Antonio Gozzoli tonight at the barn.'

Kitty looked at Rose as if a precious belonging had been snatched from her. She shook her head, a little out of breath. 'No, no, not after dark, dear. You must be mistaken.'

Rose was surprised.

'I'm not scared of the dark; sometimes it makes me feel safer.'

'Even so, dear, it's not what a young girl should be expected to do. It beats me how a nice, well-brought-up boy like Antonio could have suggested it!' Kitty bounced upright. 'Have I taken leave of my senses? You must both meet here!' She was immediately deflated again. 'I'm losing my marbles, dear, I couldn't get in touch with him, even if I wanted to.'

How was she going to say it? She'd have to keep it light, keep it general; and not just yet awhile either, Kitty was an old lady. She checked a nervous impulse to laugh. A little girl's voice slipped out. 'Tell me about him, Kitty. You see, I don't really know who he is.'

Kitty looked doubtful. 'Uh huh.'

'He seems to be more than one person. Doesn't he? I mean, who is he – really?'

'You know, Rose dear, very few people know the answer to that question. I know just a wee bit. And I believe Patrick has some idea, but the lad himself is a closed book.'

'He burns books.'

'*Burns books*!' Kitty's eyes bulged.

'Once he did. To light a fire to keep me warm.'

'Well, dear, that was a lovely gesture.'

Why wasn't Kitty surprised to hear this about the book? When did she imagine Rose had even met Antonio Gozzoli? If she told Kitty she was scared of Antonio Gozzoli when he was Toni Vasari tearing up the book, would that surprise her? Dared she talk about this to Kitty? She remembered the wild distraction on her face when her ribbon caught in the bush.

'I think he knows Lucia and Giovanni very well,' Rose said.

'Well yes, dear, they brought him up. That much I do know. Those little people are his granny and grandfather.' She nodded weightily, then laid a tentative hand on Rose's arm. 'But, Rose, you know, I'm not at all sure I should have told you that.' She sat back, her face dazed. 'I just get so awfully confused these days. Dear me, I think I may have said too much.'

'But you said nothing that could hurt him, Kitty.'

Kitty began to talk fast and smack her lips as if there was no more spit left.

'Yes, well look, dear, nobody can persuade me it's a good idea to meet him at the dead of night, and I would urge you to be a sensible girl and wait till morning.'

Her cheeks burned. Granny and grandfather? Lucia and Giovanni! She could barely take it in. She decided to ask her now before it was too late.

'Can I just ask you one thing, Kitty? You see, I believe he is going to tell me something about Dodo. And I'm not sure …' She blurted it out. 'Is Antonio in trouble with the police?'

'Och! Gracious me, Rose dear!' Kitty was dreadfully out of breath. Her eyes scanned the room for inspiration, and then her face cleared and she leaned forward to lay a hand firmly on Rose's knee. 'One thing is certain. You can trust that man with your life.'

She remembered Tony Vasari tearing off his shirt and the way he bound her ankle.

'I already have.'

* * *

The field was ahead, its feathery grasses holding the half light under a sky densely packed with stars. She stopped at the edge of the wood and kept a wary eye on the moon inching up from behind the mountain to touch the perimeter of woods and hills. Where trees formed an arbour over her head as they did now, she was hidden, but to get to the barn she would have to cross the field, getting brighter now by the minute. The barn itself stood on a small mound about forty metres away from her, and a glowing pinkness in its brick walls made it seem homely, almost lived in. Fireflies clustered in its vicinity, thinning out into the field.

Rose hesitated, wondering if she should wait for a sign that he was there. An owl detached itself from the barn and glided over to the wood. Still she waited, listening to the scratching of cicadas.

In the canopy above her head, a nightingale began three long dying notes followed by an extended chuckle; so loud, so close that she was transfixed, pierced, convinced she was being mocked. A flame of shame and anger scrambled her brain. What was she doing here in the middle of the night, all because he refused to be seen in daylight? Shaking slightly, she looked behind her into the dim hole of the wood. It was too late, she couldn't turn back, but then, neither could she stay here in the wood. Her gorge rose in her throat. Now was the time to cross the field.

Knowing that she could be seen, even from a distance, Rose struck out in a straight line towards the barn in her borrowed boots. She trod quietly but swiftly through silent fireflies that winked so brightly that, for brief moments, those on the ground lit the stalks at her feet, turning them yellow.

The plane of the barn wall stretched up to a line of broken tiles jutting out beyond the eaves. Something moved up there. It alternately bulged or flicked out interrupting the jagged outline against the sky: a bird or a lizard? The door had rotted off its post and some fireflies had floated in.

Pale grass stretched all around her like a sea; she had never felt more visible. It was very still out there, and yet the air was not still, she was aware of something living that vanished when you looked. He, like her, would have to cross the field to get to the barn. She would see him coming, but only if she knew where to look. She decided she'd move slowly round the barn with her back to the wall and her eye on the boundary of the field so as not to miss him. Cobwebs and sprouting ferns stickied the palms of her hands as she felt her way around the walls, sliding stiff fingertips along the rough bricks until she reached the open doorway again. She had scanned the field's circumference in no more than one or two minutes; how long was she expected to hang around for him? She stayed close to the doorpost to wait for him. It was more than likely he wouldn't turn up. Shamed afresh, she decided she'd give him five minutes.

A cicada rasped loudly down by her foot and she wondered if she had trapped it. Then Rose saw him. He was standing by the other doorpost, completely motionless.

'It's me. Antonio.'

'*I didn't see you!*'

Her rising voice came as a shock to her. He moved forward quickly speaking in a whisper.

'Don't be afraid. Come inside.'

He moved inside the barn and held out his hand to her, but she had begun to tremble.

He said, 'Can you see the ladder?'

She nodded, there was a ladder in the centre of the floor.

'Please follow me up.'

'I can't.'

'You can. It's safe.'

'I can't because ...' She shuddered so violently she had to clamp her jaw.

His figure moved away from the ladder towards her.

'I can't because ... I'm ...' It was no good, each time she opened her mouth, her teeth chattered in volleys.

Suddenly she smelt him, and the next minute there was a rustling and his sweater was around her shoulders.

'I am going up. Follow me, please.'

She heard the ladder creak slightly as his dim form moved upwards, easier to see now in his shirt. When she saw his hand reach out to her from the top, she pushed her arms into the sleeves of his sweater and followed him up to a wooden platform below the beams of the roof.

She could see stars through gaps in the tiles as she felt her way towards him on hands and knees. The boards were rough with droppings, and dry stuff stuck to her sticky hands. She heard him say 'Stay there!' She stopped and hugged her knees to her chest, her jaw clamped shut.

Antonio slid over the boards till he was directly facing her and more visible. She turned to look behind her and understood why he'd stopped her exactly where she was. There was a gaping space in the wall through which he could see the field and wood below.

He began in a half whisper.

'Forgive me. It has to be like this. I can't show myself, it's not safe.'

Another convulsive shudder seized Rose's body.

He was silent.

Tell me what happened to Dodo, she thought.

He shifted slightly to peer through the gap behind her and then confronted her.

'Listen to me. You must leave at once. You must go home. You are in danger. There are men here who are paid money to kill. I must stay for a short time, but you – you must go. Already everyone here knows you have been to the *carabinieri*. It is not good to ask questions.'

'I've come here to ask questions! I can't go back not knowing who killed him.'

'Then look no further than me, Antonio. I am the cause of Alfredo's death. If you want the *carabinieri* to know, I am prepared for it, it would be justice.' He looked at her steadily. 'Do it. Then my life will be simple.'

Outlines were dissolving. Antonio and the shapes around him – the top of the ladder jutting up from the floor, a rotten rope hanging from a diagonal crossbeam, a pile of sacks, a battered petrol can – all started to disintegrate. What did he mean? Was he saying he killed Dodo? This was a dream, she was in danger. She must wake up. She was perching on a great height about to fall. She saw him lean across and touch her arm. She felt it, it steadied her. She wasn't in a dream. She breathed in some strong smells: hemp and oil and something dirty and organic and living. She was alert again. But what did he say? Something terrible.

'What do you mean?'

His shoulders sagged. He looked away, deflated.

'Because of what I do, some people make a lot of money. When it goes wrong, they can lose even more money. And that is what happened. When they lost money, they wanted revenge, they hired someone to kill me. But these men they hired were very stupid, because I was in Rome, and they didn't check. Your husband, Alfredo ... They killed your husband because they thought he was me.'

They crashed down on him like hammers, the arms that had gripped her knees. She raised herself up to get at him. He crooked his arms to defend himself. Arms flailing, she toppled. He fell back with her full weight on him. He gripped her wrists and forced her arms to unfold above his head and rolled her over onto her back. She bit him and heard him shout. Blood smothered her mouth; she felt it seep in under her tongue. His body rolled off her as she curled up in a shell. He said something. She couldn't hear it. She didn't want to, she was deaf and blind. It didn't matter; she wanted nothing more from him. He'd told her now. He was empty, she was empty. She had nothing to do any more, nowhere to go. She was coiling smaller and tighter, her cramped lungs pushing against her ribs till there was a gasp and she unclasped, coughing and crying together, choking on the blood in her throat.

And for a few minutes Rose lay on her side until gradually the smell of the floor became unbearable and she hauled herself up to arrange her limp legs into a sitting position, her head drooping slightly as she rested. Another covey of bats dropped from their moorings to flit out into the bright field.

Her mind was working slowly, but this was because something wouldn't fit.

'Why were you in Rome when they killed him?'

Antonio was hesitating, she sensed his reserve. 'It was necessary.'

'Necessary for your business?' She knew she was probing, but wasn't sure what she was looking for.

'Yes, I was asked to go. It was very quick.'

'Short notice.' She supplied the right words.

'Yes.' He touched her shoulder. 'You are trying to say it may not be me they wanted. You are trying to make me feel better. You are a good person. But I am not. It was me.'

He was still restless and seemed to be searching for the right words. 'Please. You understand, they are even more angry because they feel stupid – tricked, *double* tricked. They have made a mess of it. But – they haven't finished yet, no. The killing is not over.'

She heard the owl at close quarters, and felt a flicker of fear as time and place rushed back into focus. This barn was a mad place to hide. Antonio was holding his drenched shirt against his ear. Oh God, she had bitten him badly, the blood looked black.

Rose turned again to look through the gap behind her, flecked with bats. Her back was exposed to the field, she shifted to where she could see out more easily. When she looked for Antonio, he wasn't there.

'Come over here.' He had moved into the shadow.

She managed to crawl over slowly, the toes of her boots scraping along the floor.

He said quietly, 'Will you go home?'

She looked out at the moon suspended just above the range of mountains, then turned away. Her heart was so heavy she could hardly breathe without groaning.

'Maybe I will go home,' she said, wondering if she even had the strength to climb down the ladder.

She heard him release a long breath. He leaned forward slightly, still in shadow. 'I want to help you. I don't know how to do it.'

'There is something you can do,' she said finally.

'Of course.'

'Tell Giovanni you want his vineyards.'

'How did you know? How do you know about this?' He seemed astounded.

'He told me.'

'It is impossible. I have told him I cannot look after them. I have no choice, we must find someone else. He is very ill. Lucia called me, she thought he was going to die.'

She interrupted him, 'But he *can't* die until he knows what's going to happen to them. It's breaking his heart.'

There was another one of his silences, until at last he said, 'To be truthful, I thought he would not live so long. I came to say goodbye.' He nodded to himself, 'It's true, you are right, he is not a happy man.'

She burst out again, 'Well then, make him happy. Tell him you *want* his vineyards.'

'I will. I will tell him I want them.'

After a minute, she heard him slide towards her, but he said nothing.

She eased closer to the opening to look out, careless of her visibility now. Away from the moon the sky was a soft violet, and where humidity softened the earth, pale mountains blurred into purple woods.

Now her head was clear. Now she understood. She knew what she had been desperate to know for so long. And now that at last she knew why they'd killed Dodo, she felt a stirring of strength, an inkling that she was going to get better. She turned back to him.

'Thank you, Antonio, thank you for telling me. And – it's alright – I mean, you're free.'

She felt his hand on the back of her neck and the next moment he was kissing her. He was sucking her lips. Then he drew back and sat separately. 'Are you warm now?' he said.

'What?'

'Are you warm?'

'Yes.'

'I would like my sweater.'

'I don't understand.'

'If you are warm, take off the sweater.'

'Of course!'

She peeled of the sweater and handed it over, hardly believing what she was hearing. But then, why not? It was his sweater; she'd kept it for too long. *But he'd kissed her*! He was unwell.

'Are you cold?' she said.

'No, I am warm.'

'You are not cold?'

'I am very warm.'

'I see.'

His eyes never once left her face, and the sweater lay where she'd put it.

Now she considered him at her leisure.

'Take off your shirt,' she said.

At once, he undid the buttons on his shirt and peeled it off. He sat, attentive, one knee up. There was a small trickle of blood from his ear. The moon bleached all colour from his skin but missed the undulating hollows of his chest. Rose reached out her hand to smooth her palm in a slow swathe over the warm alabaster torso. She moved from one shoulder, down over the sharp nipples, and up to the other. Her fingers continued in and out of the dips at the base of his neck, and then up the swell of muscle on the side of his neck and on round to the back where his hair felt damp. She drew him towards her and kissed him exactly as he had kissed her, blood and salt combining. When she released him he laid his shirt flat beside him and his sweater over it. Reaching over and round her with both arms, he found the zip to loosen her dress. In one continuous movement it slipped off her shoulders as she felt one hand on the nape of her neck, the other against the small of her back cradling her down onto his sweater. On the brink of being tickled she took two sharp intakes of breath when he pressed her elbows against the floor above her head and in quick succession licked the dips just above her armpits. And when her breasts were taken and cupped in both hands she felt his mouth lift her nipple, and, as a fish leaps out of water and smacks the air, her back arched up from the floor.

Outside in the field and woods, the orchestration of animals and insects buzzed in preparation for the imminent battle, the sudden savagery to come. The hunter and the hunted, hidden but smelt, silent till caught. And above the dormant earth seething with life and its dispatch, the rocky planet hung low.

They must have heard her coming up the track; the dogs had begun their cacophony even before she could be seen. Up to now Rose had been deaf to sound, eyes fixed on the ground directly in front of her, knowing what she had to do. Her face in the shadow of her boater was flushed and wet.

As she rounded the corner she saw them rush the fence, leaping in the air to get at her, five of them, snarling and tearing at the wire netting. Up at a window set high under the eaves of the farmhouse in the middle distance, a low-browed woman appeared, and settled in for a long watch. She made no attempt to quieten the dogs. Instead, she kept her eyes on Rose who, as she passed by, sensed her vigilance like glue on her back. The commotion followed her until she reached the deserted village a little further up the track.

Here there was silence. There can't have been more than a handful of people living here all those years ago, two or three derelict farm buildings crumbling into the grass, nothing more. The little vineyards on the other hand were very well tended. Somebody had pruned and trained, and tended the grassy grids between them. Rose walked forward steadily, searching for the place. And then she stopped. It was here.

She raised her head, caught off guard by the return of her senses. Nostrils widened to the smell of wild mint; a green woodpecker chortled; small green nodules were forming into grapes. Twisted vine stumps planted in regiments filled the hillside with fresh growth and swept down to the woods that darkened the valley. Clods of grass beneath her feet sprouted untrodden, and a clump of mignonette sprang from the verge where it touched the track. The seed of this wild flower was lying dormant beneath the soil twelve weeks ago. Twelve weeks ago Cornero had found the motorbike overturned in a gully. He'd walked up the path past the gundogs and further still to this elevated place among the vineyards. On the spot where the mignonette now grew, he had found, like two residual carcases from a local abattoir, Dodo's body and, next to it, the boar's severed head.

The clump came out in a spray, intensely yellow. Rose stood for some time and looked at it, breathing but motionless. At night, they dumped him here on the stony earth and rolled out the sticky head – she'd seen the photograph. She removed her hat without taking her eyes off the spot where his broken body had lain, arm flung out – she'd come back to be shown exactly where.

Now, Rose lay down on the grassy verge and felt the tough stalks flatten beneath her as she covered, as accurately as she was able, the recorded imprint of Dodo's body. Stretching out in the sun with her head on the grass, she felt the welcome discomfort of sharp stones cutting into her arms and the smell of dust from the track that clogged her nose. This was where he had wanted to build his house for her; instead, it was where they'd killed him. Now she was as near to the ground as the nose of a dog. This was where she wanted to be for as long as she needed, to touch his fear and pain before she laid it to rest. The tears came in a faint, murmured, unending stream.

And, only when the sun had dipped, casting long shadows on the hillside, did the turmoil subside, allowing her to fall into a peaceful sleep.

Chapter 19

Isolda's mouth opened slightly. What was going on here? Rankine! Patrick and Rankine together! Had there been an accident? From her elevated position on the lower ramparts she had a bird's-eye view of the police station below from which she'd seen them both emerge with, if she wasn't too far off the mark, two plain-clothes police officers. She'd watched Patrick cross the road and slowly draw to a stop. He'd been about to return to the village, but evidently changed his mind and set off in the opposite direction down the hill leaving Rankine nodding and frowning with the two men. They'd walked over to a parked patrol car, climbed in, still talking, and driven off, leaving Isolda with an uncomfortable feeling that she was being excluded from a major conundrum for which, had they but known it, she would almost certainly have held the key. She sat on a nearby bench with a bump.

A gust of wind from the valley stirred an overhanging honeysuckle and half a dozen bees blew out and sailed off. She smelt the gorse on the other side of the road and to overcome a distressing lump in her throat took a long hungry draught of it. Unwanted. And now, of all life-diminishing shocks, this was the worst. Rankine was up to something. His presence on the course had always struck her as exceedingly odd. Even when she'd seen his watercolour of the *putto* – had actually caught him in the act of painting it – lingering suspicions refused to go away. The little scene she had witnessed just now confirmed everything; it gave him another dimension; revealed a side she would not have thought existed even. Whatever else you're here for, Rankine, she murmured, painting landscape is not it. Alright, my acquaintance with you is slight, but not so slight as to overlook this new-found authority you have mysteriously acquired. *That* was the difference: there wasn't a trace of his usual hesitation. He was talking fluently. And judging from the sharp way they were nodding to each other, it was something important, worldly, hardly a road accident. He was a dark horse, then. But so was she: it took one to know one. And by the same token therefore, was there a danger that he too had an inkling that she was also here under false pretences? Her telling remark after her swim, 'So you're here to paint, then!' was *not wise*. And then, that look in his eye when he said, 'Aren't you?' was doubly chilling. Oh well, she couldn't take it back. For better or for worse, it was writ in stone. Even so – and this was a notion slowly gathering pace, she noticed – could it be that their mutual connection to fine art held at least part of the answer to this disconcerting rapport with the police?

She watched an elderly woman limping up the hill with her stick, testing the pressure on her hip with each step.

The smallest clue was all she needed to put two and two together. She was tempted to approach the police directly. They would almost certainly be inclined to admit her into their confidence, once she'd explained her close relationship with Rankine and Patrick. They might very well be grateful to her. She had a brief image of the local chief inspector mesmerised by the application of her superior logic. But the scenario quickly irritated her with its absence of logic. Patrick was her most likely lead. She felt heat spreading through her body at the recollection of those moments in his office when she'd let herself down so badly: all that scandalous bawling while he'd hung on to her hand. And yet, she recognised that there had been a kind of solidarity between them; in fact if she were forced to be honest, those agonising moments in Patrick's office were one of the rare occasions when she had been accepted for who she was – she felt it.

'Patrick!'

Careful to make it a casual encounter, she waved to him, heading up for the little church.

He turned to view her with astonishment.

'I was just on my way up to look at the church!' she laughed, and then puckered her brow. 'Oh, Patrick, I happened to see you come

211

out of the police station, Rankine too. Has there been an accident ...?
I mean, you looked as if you'd had a bit of a shock. Can I help?'

'Ah, well. Good morning, Isolda, yes.' He was becoming ominously
hesitant and anxious.

'Oh, dear, am I prying?'

'Well, I don't see why you shouldn't know – as long as word doesn't
get around.'

'Of course not, of *course* not!'

'The police have picked up some sort of intelligence that there's
going to be a large-scale robbery somewhere in this area. They wanted
to know if I'd noticed any – oh, I don't know – unusual activity. The Art
Fraud Squad is following it up.'

The pit of Isolda's stomach contracted.

'Art Fraud?'

'Well, yes. I wondered about that myself. And to be frank, I have seen
a rather odd character around lately. I described him as well as I could.'
Patrick looked troubled, almost grim, his voice had dropped. 'Yes, they
wanted to hear more about him.'

'And Rankine?'

'Ah yes! Rankine! It seems I've been taken for a bit of a ride!' Patrick
had a momentary resurgence of energy, glancing briefly at Isolda with a
glint from the corner of his eye. 'Look, I'm really going to have to rely
on you, Isolda, to keep this under your hat. I'm afraid, if it gets out that
the police are onto it, the whole operation could go to the wall.'

'Patrick, I can assure you, this will go no further.'

'Good. I know I can rely on you.'

'Funnily enough, Patrick, I've always wondered what on earth
Rankine was doing on your course. I know him socially. He's a dealer.'

'Really!' Patrick said politely, pleasantly even. 'Is that what he is?'

'Oh, I'm not in a position to say – but I suspect he has quite
considerable talent.'

Now she'd really jumped the gun, blurting it all out. Why hadn't she
simply waited? But if Patrick was indiscreet in an unguarded moment,
he was not a natural gossip; he would not be drawn on the subject of
Rankine. 'I asked the police if I should be warning my students to lock
up their work!' he said.

Unable to laugh, Isolda grimaced. 'Except that I imagine there are one or two important fine art collections in this area.'

Patrick reacted robustly. 'Indeed there are. The Pazzis had a robbery recently. Quite serious, I'm told. They ran off with a couple of masterpieces, including I believe a Bronzino portrait.'

Isolda gasped. Why hadn't they heard about this important theft in London? Bronzino! You'd think information of this calibre would have flashed round the world. *And what was the Art Fraud Squad doing in Montecalmo?* She found she was struggling with another attack of sensory failure in her knees.

'What else does Pazzi have? A Michelangelo? A couple of Leonardos?'

Patrick seemed slightly abashed. 'I'm afraid I have never been invited up to see the collection. I think good old Tancredi likes to keep it to himself, although he's fairly amenable to showing off his very splendid garden.'

Isolda felt despondent, dulled. Even Patrick seemed resigned to being an outsider. How could she assume there was even a chance she'd get to see the collection?

She nodded, 'I've seen the garden. Actually, I've been invited to a concert on Thursday.'

Patrick raised his eyebrows and smiled at her with a mixture of curiosity and attentiveness. 'Have you now! Ah well, you must be one of the favoured few. He has one every year. Oh, musicians from Milan! And I assure you, people fight for an invitation.' He smiled again.

She'd taken on too much: all the futile wrangling to see the collection. What did it matter when all she wanted was to be with her beloved? Isolda sighed – her beloved, her beloved.

'I suppose I'll have to forget about wheedling an invitation for Sandy, then, if it's such a big deal,' she said, and then caught sight of Patrick's crumbling face, and burst out. 'She has an incredibly mundane life, she needs a break. She just needs to have some fun.'

His smile had vanished and a weariness infused his shoulders.

'I must remind you, Isolda, that Sandy does this job out of choice.' His voice was so low she could hardly hear it.

'A girl has to earn a living! This is not a proper job, she comes here because of you!'

This compulsive nagging of Patrick was intolerable for both of them; she'd be better off away from here where she wouldn't have to endure the burning glances Sandy flashed him. They almost brought tears to her eyes. What more could a girl do to set this man on fire?

They had reached the homely semi-circular area in front of the church, and here Patrick stopped.

'Isolda, I have thought about what you told me. Frankly, I haven't been able to think about much else, it really has turned my life upside down. And while I know it to be true … I seem to have reached a sort of stalemate.' He turned to face her. 'I am not for her, Isolda.'

Isolda's spirits leaped.

'Does she know?'

'I haven't spoken to her. Of course, I realise I'm going to have to say something before she goes, but … I just don't know what I …' He appealed to the immensity of landscape that lay before them. 'Sandy has a whole lifetime ahead of her.' And his arms dropped to his sides as if he were spent.

'Why don't you tell her what I said?' Isolda asked him.

'Betray your confidence?'

'It's the obvious answer.'

Patrick looked at her wonderingly, his lumbering understanding a few steps behind.

'You wouldn't mind her knowing?'

How could she make this *man* understand the agony of not being able to speak to Sandy? 'I would be willing to take the risk.'

'Thank you, Isolda, I believe you have shown me a way to do this.'

Patrick held out his hand to her in a clear expression of gratitude. 'Well, I must get on my way. Oh yes, and by the way, if you're visiting the church, the sculpture is worth a look. As a matter of fact it's by a friend of mine, Bill. He calls it *The Good Samaritan.*'

As he prepared to take himself off in the best mood she'd seen him in, he turned to indicate the swirling panorama strewn with sunshine and cloud-cast stretching around them, and said, 'You may think of having a go at doing a sketch here.'

She felt the constriction of fear in her groin, followed by a stab of anger. Surely it was his little joke? 'Have a go'! At this *infinity*?

Had he tried it himself? If so, she'd like to see the result. Even if he was speaking to someone who could actually draw – to be so glib about tackling such immensity.

'Sorry, Patrick, I'd rather jump off a cliff.' She was relieved to hear him laugh. He waved as he set off down the hill.

'Well, yes, there are less daunting subjects. See you at lunch.'

She gazed at two forms in marble, the one inclining towards the other. It was surprisingly moving. *The Good Samaritan*. Who was this man, Bill? Modern work of this calibre hidden away in a small, undistinguished church in Tuscany! First the swimming pool fresco, and now this. Did Patrick attract these extraordinary people around him? And another thing, why was he on his way up here in the first place? To commune with the Almighty? Whatever it was, she was glad of the introduction to this amazing lump of marble. Her gloom had lifted, she noted, she felt free of it and fired up for anything, except, she reminded herself sharply, for 'having a go'. She closed the church door behind her, resolving to come back for a second look.

And now here she was again, helplessly gazing at this view. The same landscape that Patrick had thought to link to Sandy's life, the life that stretched ahead of her. He was with her now, she was certain. Where would they go to be private? His office, that dark subterranean cave where the dusty light shafted onto the desk – his desk, the desk on which Sandy had perched, bare legs dangling, a pensive girl distilled forever in sepia.

How would he approach that Botticelli angel with her dark, unassailable lips? He'd lived so long without noticing her, bumbled about his business with Sandy under his nose for years, it would take no less than an earthquake to shake the veil from his eyes. It was going to be life or death for her when she knew he could never love her. But then when he told her that there was somebody who did, who adored her, would give her life for her ... Isolda wrapped her arms tightly around her shoulders with almost unbearable strength and dropped her head, screwing her eyes into the blackness of her skull. How could she bear it? She was allowing a licence to Patrick that only she, Isolda, had a right to. In a million years he would not be able to present her case fully. Only she could express her love to Sandy. And when Sandy heard her speak, could see her, feel her arms around her, something inside her would be stirred. Isolda released her grip and opened her eyes. The sun blinded her for a minute as she turned to the path of cypress Patrick had taken. Should she run back to the village? It may not be too late.

He knew he had to catch her while his resolve held sure, and thank God for Isolda's encouragement, he felt he was less likely to bungle it. Patrick strode off down the hill to find Sandy, refreshed suddenly at the sight of the young cypresses as they glided past him; he imagined them stacking up like pencils behind him. What a frank girl Isolda was, a straight talker. You could say anything to her and she'd take it on board, he felt sure of it. If only he'd known earlier that it wasn't going to bother her if he mentioned the episode in the office. The image of her sitting there in the semi-dark still evoked awe in him. How could such knowledge of love and pain belong in such a girl? How was it that he had seen none of what she'd told him? And here he was again, wondering if his increasing age was distancing him from the stuff of life. Well, he'd left her in the church with Bill's sculpture; it couldn't fail to inspire her.

He noticed the delivery van had stopped outside the entrance on the lower road which meant that Sandy would have to carry the groceries up the spiral steps to the kitchen. They knew perfectly well they were not supposed to deliver down here; he hoped this was a one-off. Sandy would be doubly harassed and very busy, and she'd be non-stop now till about three o'clock when she went off for her break. Well then, he'd wait till three, much better; it was madness to think of tackling this delicate matter here and now. In the meantime; he wasn't going to allow her to carry the boxes without help. Before he could get to it, the van pulled away.

Patrick bounded up the ramp to the big iron gates. Through the dull black fretwork he could see the boxes piled up at the bottom of the steps, about half a dozen. It simply wasn't on, he'd have to have a strong word with Simone. He picked up two five-litre cans of olive oil and mounted the steps.

Jason had his head in the dishwasher, clicking his tongue, when Patrick entered the kitchen. He withdrew his head sharply when he heard Patrick placing the cans under the sink.

'The extra virgin! Now we're in business.'

'Ah, Jason, where's Sandy, do you know?'

'Sandy went out about twenty minutes ago, she didn't say where.'

'Good. Well, for once it's a relief not to find her here, they've delivered the groceries downstairs. Would you be good enough to help me fetch them up before she gets back?'

'Anything for you, governor.'

'I don't want her humping heavy boxes.'

Jason looked at him askance as he headed for the steps. 'She's a big strapping girl, Patrick.' He said it quietly, even humorously, but it made Patrick mad.

'And that is precisely why we all expect her to do everything. It's about time we realised it. And now I'm going to call the *alimentari*, it's a scandal.' He went straight to the telephone in his office and let Jason get on with it.

Chapter 20

Isolda stood in the kitchen heavy with disappointment: 'Nah, Sandy's gone out.' She watched Jason bent double over a crate of chicken pieces. Il Centro was a bleak place without her; a pile of old stones, that was all. Jason blew a long breath from full cheeks then looked up suddenly, 'She could be fetching the Parmigiano.'

'Patrick in his office?'

Jason nodded. 'I wouldn't disturb him though, Isolda, he is not a happy bunny.'

There was nothing for it but to return to her room.

Once in her refuge with the bright little window and home-made lampshade, she forced herself to clear her mind and take stock of her surroundings; and her bedroom, as she now realised, was a haven of airy simplicity. An effort had been made to give it a touch of atmosphere: a white linen table cloth, a china jug. This was a room where she could think – *would* think. She kicked off her shoes and lay on the bed.

At once she was filled with an aching, all pervasive need. She heard herself groan, and rolled over onto her tummy, all good intentions no sooner invoked than forgotten. Here she went again. Every time she fell in love, she allowed herself to hope: found herself living the same words, the same kisses; felt herself melting with the same devouring need to demonstrate her love, that terrifying molten burden of the need to give. How could she have allowed herself to think this was going to be any different?

No good. It was no good, it wasn't going to happen; it was not going to happen. She swung her legs off the bed and perched on the edge, staring at the window. She couldn't *make* Sandy love her. Carefully she stood up, safely distanced from the fantasy of the bed, but trembling slightly.

Where was her painting shirt? She picked up her brush to run it through her hair, but the simple backwards action of bristle over scalp required more precision than her useless shaky hand was capable of. She was going down to the pool for a cool swim to loosen up and unravel, and then – you never know – perhaps the ga-ga Leda would turn her off. (Except that she might turn her on.) And after that, out with her newly acquired pastels and brand-new watercolours to find a quiet corner under a tree to slosh her palette around a bit, give it a used appearance. Should she happen to run across Patrick, she would present him with another picture from the selection she'd bought from the cheeky American in San Gimignano. She thought of him laboriously copying out his address for her. Where was that receipt? There was just no way it could be lost, she had not touched her bag since she'd paid the taxi back into Montecalmo.

She pounced on the large leather bag and shook the contents out onto the bed where they spilled out in a pile. Scrabbling among old boarding passes, museum fliers, brochures for Il Centra D'Arte, and finally half a dozen museum tickets sticking to an oozing sun block sampler, she discovered that two pockets within the bag were unzipped. Out came her wallet, her passport, all her make-up, three pens, a tampon, and a collection of visiting cards and receipts. She pounced. It was not among them. Her wallet! She searched every nook and cranny of her wallet. Not there. Isolda collapsed onto the edge of the bed and with a great effort shut her eyes to think herself back into San Gimignano. What normally happened to her change and receipts when she was in a hurry? The pocket of her pants! Her beige pants she'd worn on that frantic morning were hanging in the wardrobe and – she recalled the crackle now – there may have been something in the pocket. Yes!

A full two minutes later, Isolda was back sitting on the bed gazing blankly at the scrawled address. It was clearly written, there was no mistaking its legibility. Had Rose given it to her? No, here was his name:

Bernard Schiffano, c/o La Villa Pazzi, Siena, Toscana. Not some hick town in South Carolina then for this upstart hippy but the grandest villa in the area. Inexplicable.

Bernard Schiffano. She pictured his sleepy eyes and his 'Oh, ho hos' and his 'don't let's d'lood ourselves, lady', and then she froze. It was him. It had been him on top of the ladder in the Pazzis' garden. She had been right the first time. The gardener! For a long time Isolda remained where she was, staring at the table leg.

Rankine's rumpled leg came first as he eased himself out of a police car a little further up from the police station. The driver, a uniformed police officer, pulled the back door wide open to give him plenty of room.

The painting materials in Isolda's bag clattered as she strode down the hill towards the car, and Rankine, trapped on the pavement, saw Isolda approaching and blinked uncertainly.

'Oh. Huh … hullo, Isolda.'

'Rankine, if you haven't seen it, I must show you *The Good Samaritan*.'

'No, I—'

'You haven't! Good, then if you've got a minute, come with me, I'm on my way there.'

He was not altogether enthusiastic. And now that at last she'd got him halfway up the hill of cypress, she realised she was walking too fast for him, he was dabbing his face. She tried to steady them down to a pleasant but purposeful stroll while she talked at length about Patrick's well-kept secret. She could see he had his eye on a bench halfway up. She would suggest they sit and rest in a couple of minutes. Meanwhile, she judged, this was the precise moment to crack the carapace.

'Rankine, Patrick has told me why you and he were in the police station this morning. In confidence, of course.'

She was unprepared for his anger. He stopped and removed his glasses to look at her. 'Why?'

She was momentarily speechless. To her surprise she stammered slightly.

'I-I-I-I assure you, it will go no further.'

'But why did he tell you?' He had not taken his eyes off her.

'I asked him to, and I'm afraid he was caught off guard.' She felt uncomfortably guilty, as if she were betraying Patrick when in fact it was Patrick himself who had betrayed a confidence. It was clear now that Rankine was furious with him, and also with her.

He replaced his glasses and looked at his watch.

'I must get home.'

'No, Rankine, please.' She took his arm. 'Can we sit on the bench up there? I must speak to you.'

He was extremely reluctant to go any further.

She'd heard herself gulp in the middle of his name. Was it possible this man was exerting power over her?

'F-f-for a short time.'

'Oh, short. Very short. Look, just a few steps. Please … Freddy?' she wheedled.

He looked at her sternly, but seemed willing to be led to it.

She'd just noticed the bench itself was tilting backwards slightly so that the tips of the cypresses on the opposite side of the path were in their direct eye-line. She stole a glance at him to see if he was comfortable and couldn't help thinking they looked as if they were in bed together – which was all very well, but it had put them in an ultra leisurely position for her tricky opening gambit.

She said, 'I haven't come here to paint, Rankine.'

He turned his head to look at her with interest.

'You see, I can't. I can't draw either. I'm afraid my portfolio is full of somebody else's stuff, and Patrick thinks I'm quite good.'

He nodded seriously but said nothing. She had already determined to choose her words with candour, but it wasn't easy: she had banked everything on her hunch – that of his being a fellow conspirator.

'It's a cover. I'm here under my own steam, but in the hopes that whatever transpires, it will benefit Burlington's.'

'Have they uncovered a d-d-dicky consignment?'

He was onto it!

'Sort of. A fake Panini. We're not sure, so we're withdrawing it from the auction.'

'Your n-next Old M-masters'?'

He was getting closer.

'Well yes.'

'And you haven't infuh-formed your consignor?'

'Well, y-es. This is the tricky bit …' (It was, really tricky.) Was she going to give him the whole story? Their consignor's name? Above all, she needed reciprocal intelligence. This was her best way to get at it, but could she trust him not to spread foul rumour? Suspended above her like a burnished cross was Burlington's integrity.

She looked him in the eye. 'This is between you and me, Rankine.'

'U-nderstood.'

'Well, he doesn't like it, our consignor, and we're not pushing it because we don't want to rock the boat. Frankly, we want to keep it coming. He's still got some mouth-watering stuff up there. A distant cousin of his, an Edwardian collector, had hoarded it away. It's been sitting there for years.' Was Rankine going to poach their consignor? She noticed he'd started to blink frantically. She was slightly uneasy, he was a tad too eager.

'U-up where?'

She hesitated.

'Oh, up north. A massive tottering old house in the middle of nowhere – bits of stucco littering the steps, no wonder he's desperate for cash. He wasn't disappointed. We gave him good estimates, and in one or two cases, the bidding went through the roof.'

'And the various puh-puh-puh provenances?'

'Oh early. The inventory was drawn up on the death of Sturt-Percy's father in the war. Marvellous collection, predominately Renaissance. Incredible isn't it!'

'It-tit-tit-talian?'

Was Rankine onto it already? She felt herself losing breath slightly – *and* she'd mentioned Sturt-Percy. Oh well, put it behind her.

She nodded, raising her eyebrows to look at him. 'And guess whose name cropped up more than once: Paulo Pazzi, great-grandfather of Tancredi.'

Rankine smiled slightly as he mulled over what she'd just said.

They heard a slow tapping on the path. The old woman with the gammy hip she'd noticed earlier was edging her way up the hill towards them. She stopped to salute them with her stick, and as she struggled past on her way up to the church, she called out, 'As good as new, they said! And look at me.'

'Never trust a doctor, signora,' Rankine replied in fluent Italian.

'Ah, signore, you know them well. That's what my father said, and he was a doctor for thirty years!' She nodded approvingly as she waved her stick back at them.

Rankine turned sideways to look up at Isolda.

'If your last Old M-masters' sale was from the same consignor, I think you'll f-find your Panini f-fake is f-fairly recent.'

'*Recent*! The collection has been hidden away in England since 1911.'

'The cuc-cuc-collection was in Tancredi's possession until last year.'

Isolda was speechless. She stared at Rankine adjusting his glasses, quite unable to grasp what he was suggesting. If he was right, the ramifications for Burlington's were unthinkable.

Again she found herself stammering. 'Cuc-cu Burlington's acted in perfect faith.'

Rankine was nodding. 'I think you cuc-could make a good cuc-case for that.'

She was struggling with a rising desperation.

She said, 'How did Tancredi deal with the *sop-sop-soprigen* ...'

Rankine supplied the word: '*Soprintendenza*. He didn't. They were smuggled into Switzerland, we think. A consigning route we're getting to know a little bit about.'

'I-I-I-mean, h-how many more fakes do you think ...?'

'We suspect he has a very skilled forger.'

She raced to make the connection she knew was there. *Bernard Schiffano.*

'Uh-uh-um, could it be a black American?' she asked.

Rankine's puffy features acquired a sudden gravitas.

He said, 'Can you describe him?'

'Young, good-looking, and inek-*usably* cheeky.' She was floundering.

Rankine raised his eyebrows but said nothing.

'Now look, Rankine, I've told you all I know. I would expect sort of rescripination.'

Rankine folded his arms resolutely. 'Of course. Of course.' He turned to look at her, she thought almost kindly. She turned away from him, slowly colouring.

Rankine went on. 'Well, yes we wondered about Bernard Schiffano. Interesting to hear that he can paint. Very interesting indeed.'

She was startled. 'You mean, y-y-y-you know about him?'

'Only that he seems to be a sort of itinerant, and does odd jobs occasionally for Pazzi.'

'Tancredi.'

'Tancredi,' he affirmed.

In the midst of her unease, she glanced anxiously at Rankine who had his eye on some swallows skimming the tops of the cypresses. Together they observed them while she tried to analyse her verbal disintegration. Was this angle they were sitting at responsible for it? she wondered. She'd felt from the beginning there was something unsettling about the two of them tilting upwards, idly soaking up the sun. She crossed her arms, and then her legs, but felt that the forces of chaos, dangerously imminent, could snatch both arms and legs and splay them out to the wind.

Isolda took a deep, lengthy breath. 'Who are you, Rankine,' she said finally.

'Somewhat of a double agent,' he replied promptly. 'The Guardia di Finanza people have let it be known to various drug dealers – those who like to invest their millions in art – that I may be of service to them. Villains are sensitive to being bamboozled.'

A *double agent*. Another persona to grapple with. Revelations were coming thick and fast.

'Do you meet criminals – in-in…, you know – in person?'

'I do.'

'To authorise their pictures and so on?'

Rankine flashed her a look. '*Authenticate*, that's right, and occasionally, I suffer the consequences.'

'Do they, um, get violent?'

'They are unpredictable.'

There was no question about it, Rankine was an estimable person. Was the other, public persona, the timid one, an act? Because she was finding it all too easy to accept him as he was now – but it needed a commensurate adjustment in perception and she was lagging behind.

He said, 'One would not expect that you should send an immediate report back to Burlington's, naturally – about what has transpired between us.'

'Naturally. The last thing we want is an international alert.' Really, did he think she was a naïve idiot? 'And, I don't doubt they'll be doubling their surveillance on Vicar Fazzi.'

'Surveillance ...' he murmured under his breath. 'Oh, *trebling* it,' he confirmed robustly.

A sudden pain entered both Isolda's knees as her vision blurred.

He said, 'I think you may know, there has already been a killing in the Pazzi family. These same villains, we suspect, are in some way connected to it.' And, taking off his glasses for the second time that morning Rankine fixed her with his naked eye.

'We know that at some point soon there will be a crime in this area – but I don't know of anyone who is looking forward to it, Isolda.'

Chapter 21

Jason slithered across the kitchen floor in flip-flops with a box of tomatoes and red peppers, badly out of breath. He shed his load onto the work surface and leaned against it, hand on hip, filling his lungs before releasing a long breath. He saw Patrick emerge from his office and lifted his head.

'Oh, yeah, by the way, Patrick. We had a caller. Well, Sandy did.'

'A caller?'

Patrick became still.

'Yeah, this morning. A bloke asking for somebody. Now who did he want?' He pursed his lips and blew out his breath in short puffs, frowning at the ceiling.

Patrick barely opened his mouth to speak. 'Antonio Gozzoli?'

'That's it! Gozzoli!'

'What did he look like, this man who asked for him?'

'Well, a bit of a – you know.' Jason clenched his fists and nudged the air with his upper arms in subtle imitation of a boxer in the ring. 'A bit of a bruiser. Natty dresser, mind. Shades.'

'Shades? Shades of what?'

'Sunglasses, governor.'

'And a hat?'

'Nnnnn–o, no hat.'

'What did Sandy tell him?'

'She said this Gozzo person had been away for five years. But *he* said he'd been seen around only this week.' Jason shrugged his shoulders and opened his hands in casual take-your-pick mode.

All this must have been going on while he was with Isolda up at the church. The *carabinieri* had actually driven off while this man was here in Montecalmo. Why hadn't he been here to deal with the man? *Why hadn't he been here?*

He said, 'Where did you say Sandy had gone?'

'I didn't, she didn't say. Um. Have I said something ...?'

'Hold the fort, will you, Jason, I have a telephone call to make. If Sandy comes back in the meantime, don't hesitate to let me know.'

He returned to the office to ring the *carabinieri* without delay. There was no question, it was the same man. He picked up the telephone and started dialling before he remembered Sacchetti was going to be away till tomorrow. With his hand still holding the receiver he sat down slowly. Should he speak to a subordinate and warn him? The snag was that this whole business was supposed to be kept quiet. The receiver went back. For Chrissake, the Romanos were involved in this, why was he hesitating? And what were the Romanos doing up here – the most feared family in southern Italy? He clenched his hands together and put his elbows on the desk. Somehow, he knew it, he'd felt at the time that they hadn't heard the last of the murder of the Pazzi boy. A gruesome killing. It was a real mental effort to bring himself to think about it. They were certainly forced to examine it again this morning. And that was the surprise – Rankine. He knew as much about it as the *carabinieri*. There was undoubtedly more to him than mere art dealing; Sacchetti deferred to him, he had connections. He thought about the boxer type who'd called here this morning. Was it the same man he'd run into down by the old barn? There was something unpleasantly pushy about him, audacious almost, uncannily like the man at the wedding. *He'd* asked about Antonio. Why should they both want Antonio? The fact that Sacchetti had become so deadly serious when he'd described him had put the wind up him, he didn't mind admitting. Was he dangerous? It wouldn't surprise him in the least. Well, now it was confirmed: the suspected killers had been spotted here. But they were all supposed to keep it a secret! Sacchetti's insistence that nothing must cause these criminals to suspect that the *carabinieri* were onto them had left him feeling completely helpless. He felt the most awful prickling on the top of his head as he realised he should have warned Sandy about this. To hell with the bloody robbery when there were lives at stake; he was running an art school here with thirty-odd students under his protection – including Rose. His blood ran cold. He was going to do what he had to do.

Patrick dialled Kitty.

'Kitty dear, this is a quick call to ask if Sandy is with you, by any chance.'

'No Patrick, I've not seen a soul all morning.'

'Not to worry, I expect she's on her way back from the *alimentari*. Sorry to trouble you.'

'For goodness sake, Patrick, if you call this trouble, I'd welcome a good deal more of it.'

'May I call in again soon, Kitty?'

'I cannot think of anything nicer!'

Patrick looked at the answer-phone flashing. Business calls as usual. He decided to ignore it. He patted his pockets distractedly and left the office planning to liaise with Jason before setting out to look for Sandy, but when he reached the kitchen Jason was still coming up with boxes from downstairs. He left his load of groceries close to the fridge and slowly stretched upright with his hand on his back.

'My dear fellow,' Patrick called already heading for the steps. 'Let me do the rest.'

'No, no, that's the lot, governor.'

Patrick retraced his steps and spoke at speed.

'Jason, I'm going to see if Sandy is somewhere in the village. Can you think of anywhere she might be?'

'She might have remembered the *Parmigiano*, in which case it'll be the deli.'

'Look, I'll keep popping back in here to see if she's come back in the meantime.'

He was halfway out into the hall when Jason came after him.

'Have you got a mobile, Patrick?'

'Never felt the need for one.'

'You have now. Take mine.' He reached into his pocket and brought out a small cellphone. 'There you are, all ready to go.'

'What happens to it?'

'It'll vibrate in your pocket. That'll be me.'

'*Vibrate?*'

'Instead of ringing, it vibrates – go on, gives you a thrill if you're lucky.'

'I'm not sure I'm up to this, Jason.'

Jason was speaking to him emphatically. 'When Sandy gets back, I'll give you a buzz. You feel it. Take it out your pocket. And press this.' He pointed to a button.

'Jason, I'm very much in your debt.'

'Anytime, governor.'

Sandy's lodgings were on the other side, just off the piazza, fairly untrodden territory for him. The door was tucked into a recess in one of the narrower streets, and here he stopped. His eyes shot upwards as a peg dropped from above. Sandy's landlady was busy pegging out her washing outside a second-floor window. Her head appeared over the tea towels.

'*Ciao*, Patrick!'

'Ah, Felicia, *ciao*! I am looking for Sandy.'

'Come and look. Up the stairs, on the right.'

He picked up the peg and stepped inside. Felicia was already coming down the steps towards him nodding and pointing to the door.

'*Si, si, si,* Sandy.'

She took him straight up to it, and when she saw him hesitate, she knocked. When there was no reply, she walked in and beckoned to him, 'Come!'

Together they stood just inside Sandy's room. Through his discomfort he could not help but notice the effort to make of this sparse bedsit a home. The single bed against the wall covered with an Indian cloth, a string of candles on the window, and pinned up on the wall, a poster: a detail from *La Madonna del Magnificat*. He was riveted by it – the Madonna's face. Why did she now spring to life after all these years? Again he ran his eye over the modest arrangement, and was moved by it: the Indian cloth, a string of candles and the print. Yet he was ashamed to have so readily stepped into her room. He would have been content to have been told she was not there; instead when he was offered proof, his curiosity had got the better of him.

Halfway down the main street he spotted Rankine about to order from Gianni at an outside table. He hailed him.

'Rankine, I'm glad to have seen you. I'd like to offer you a beer if you have a minute. Make mine a coffee, Gianni. I'll be with you in a jiffy.' He almost broke into a run.

Inside the *alimentari* Simone interrupted her dealings with a customer when she saw him bound in.

'Oh, Patrick, I can explain. You were too quick. It was the boy. We have a new boy. Now I have told him what to do. He won't make the same mistake again.'

Oh Lord, he must have made an almighty fuss, he'd rarely seen Simone so agitated.

'That's perfectly alright, Simone. Have you seen Sandy?'

'Sandy? No.'

Where was she? Patrick came out in deep thought, frowning into the cobbles, forgetting entirely that he'd left Rankine sitting outside Gianni's. When he caught sight of him leaning into the light saluting him with a rolled up newspaper at once he felt better. Yes, of course! At last here was someone he could talk to freely. He drew out a chair just as Gianni delivered the coffee, and launched straight in.

'Rankine, the bloke I described to Sacchetti and the others was at Il Centro this morning. He quizzed Sandy about the whereabouts of Antonio Gozzoli.'

Rankine blinked and leaned towards him.

Patrick continued, 'Sacchetti is away till tomorrow. Are you in touch with him? I think he should know.'

And then he saw her. He saw Sandy with her back towards them crossing the piazza heading for Il Centro. Immediately he leaped to his feet and hurried to catch up. He heard Rankine saying something. 'Y-your coc-coc-coc-'

He called back. 'Sorry, Rankine, I'll settle up later.'

When he eventually drew alongside Sandy she turned to him in mild surprise, her face as calm as a millpond.

'Patrick! What's the matter? What's happened?'

He felt utterly ridiculous. It wasn't the first time he'd made a song and dance over that damn bloke.

'Sorry, Sandy, I wanted to warn you about that rather unpleasant character you talked to this morning. It really isn't a good idea – in any way – to fraternise with him.'

'*Fraternise?* I wouldn't. I didn't. What do you take me for?'

'No, no, no, of course not. It's just that you disappeared for a few minutes – as you are *perfectly entitled* to do … and …Well, what I mean is, I'm glad we've found you.'

'Actually, I was in the travel agents. Caroline's coming on Saturday. I leave on Sunday. It'll give me time to show her around.'

He'd forgotten. The fact that she was actually leaving had been pushed to the back of his mind. In fact it had completely slipped away altogether with all this business with the *carabinieri*. She was looking at him waiting for a reaction, but for once, he was speechless.

'I did tell you about this, Patrick. I did warn you. You've known for a long time.'

He felt a most peculiar sensation near his crutch and wondered fleetingly if he was going down with something, a sudden rash.

'They can all cope quite well without me, you know … Patrick? You've gone peculiar. Shall we go back to Il Centro?'

'It's alright, Sandy, it's just that I have a suspicion an insect has gone up my trouser leg. A bee probably.'

'Oh, my God. Quickly, open your flies.'

'I can't do that here. We're in the piazza.'

'Of course you can, you don't want a sting on your …' She was making an authoritative move on his trouser belt.

'No,no,no. Wait one minute.' He backed away a few steps and put an exploratory hand into his pocket. 'If I can just grab it and squeeze it before it does any damage.'

A smiling Father Sebastiano, lifting his hand in greeting as he crossed the piazza towards them, abruptly switched direction and passed them by with his eyes averted.

As he was half saluting Father Sebastiano with one hand, with his other he discovered a smooth hard object that seemed to have a life of its own. Tentatively, he brought it out to look at it.

Sandy said, 'Give it to me,' and grabbed Jason's mobile telephone from his hand.

She handed it back to him. 'It's for you.'

'Yes?' he held it to his ear, and heard Jason speaking to him.

'Look, Patrick, I really don't want to worry you, but I have a student here who said you were definitely going to give him some of your time this morning. Between ourselves, Patrick, he's on his way to being a tiny bit O.T.T.'

Patrick wasn't often rattled with students because he'd always done his best for them, and he had a feeling they recognised it. There had always been for him a dread of letting people down, and on this occasion, of course, he had unwittingly done just that. The man had been waiting for him outside the walls of Montecalmo, halfway through a painting of the castle, apparently unable to get to grips with the composition until he had included a tree. Jason had done his best to calm him down, but out had come a whole string of grievances stretching back for days; a still life vandalised while he was painting it, that was one of them (something Patrick found hard to visualise). You had to respect his fervour, and that was the point, the man was undoubtedly serious about his painting. But the feeling was that he unleashed an unstoppable fury onto his canvases. He thought of his picture of San Gimignano; had it been war-torn Berlin it would have been shockingly effective. What was he to do with Jim? He had no affinity with his vision or style, his juxtaposition of colour made him uncomfortably hot, and now here he was, being asked how to paint a tree.

'You see, I'm, alright with buildings. I can do walls, castles, that sort of thing. But I'm no good with trees. The way I do it, you couldn't say for sure it was a tree.' He sat with the sun directly behind him, the top of his head the colour of a mottled conker.

'Which tree were you thinking of?'

'I thought I'd move this one over here, closer to the castle.'

'An acacia. A nice gnarled shape …'

'That's why I thought of it. I thought, if I make it all gnarled, it'll look like a tree. The trouble is, you've got branches coming straight at you.'

'Ah, well now. You've identified the age-old problem of how to make it look as if the branch is growing towards you.'

Jim was beginning to bristle. 'Yes! That is exactly what I said. So how do I do it?'

'You look at it,' Patrick said quietly. 'You keep on looking. I'm sorry, Jim, there's no other way.' The poor bloke looked thunderstruck.

Rankine had just come into view further down the path and seemed to be hovering. He sat on a bench at the foot of the walls and opened his newspaper. Patrick's memory gave him an almost physical jolt. He called, 'I'll be right with you, Rankine.'

Jim swung round to glare at him. 'I thought you were supposed to be with me!'

Patrick put his hand on Jim's shoulder.

'And so I am, Jim, and so I am. I'd like you to make a start on this acacia. And I'll be back later to see if I can give you a few pointers.' He strode off at a smart pace before he could be nailed down on a time.

He was beginning to warm to Rankine, the amiable fellow; there was absolutely no reproach in him. He'd let him down over the drink at Gianni's and then not returned to make amends. Now here he was, actually pleased to see him.

'Rankine, I insist on following up on that drink. This evening, perhaps. After dinner.'

He was about to sit next to him on the bench when Rankine stood up and stuffed the rolled newspaper into his pocket. 'I thought we m-might take a walk.' He glanced over at Jim who was eyeing them both.

They walked away from Jim along the path that hugged the ramparts of the town, and as soon as they were out of view, Rankine produced a folded piece of paper which he handed to Patrick.

'S-acchetti's number. He'll w-want a description.'

Sandy stood by his desk, having pushed her hair away from her ear with the telephone receiver. She was describing the man, the boxer type, to Sacchetti, and, Patrick noted with a sinking sensation, in a voice strangely devoid of energy. He wiped away a film of itchy perspiration from his forehead. Sandy's face was lit by reflected light off the desk, eyes cast down, inscrutable, ethereal. He had no idea what she was feeling.

'I think that he thought I'd know where to find Antonio Gozzoli because I work here.'

A slight frown crossed her brow, and then cleared.

'Yes, I might have seen him before – I might have seen him at a wedding the other day outside the church. He was wearing a white suit and pointed shoes, if it was him. Last Saturday.'

She broke off briefly to look across at Patrick in a kind of dream before turning back to the telephone. 'That's alright, happy to help.'

She put the phone down and looked at him. 'What was all that about?'

'I'm absolutely sure there's nothing to worry about, my dear, it's just that the *carabinieri* have been sniffing around and have asked me to report on, well, you know, any suspicious types.'

'I see. Something's going on, is it?'

'They think a robbery has been planned. It depends on secrecy, of course, if they're going to catch them at it.' He picked up the Sellotape dispenser and shifted it three inches to the left. 'I've already said something about it to Isolda.'

'Oh, of course! She would be the first to know!'

She flounced to the door tossing her head, her chest heaving. Patrick was dumbfounded. What on earth was happening to her?

Dramatically, she stood by the door, her hand on the handle.

'I'm sorry if I interrupted something in here other day. It must have really put you off.'

'Sandy, what are you saying?' He spoke as quietly as he could; she was in danger of summoning the entire household.

'I can't believe you've got a "thing" for her, it's grotesque.'

He had a vivid picture of himself sitting here in the semi-darkness holding Isolda's hand.

'What did she do? Break down and sob her heart out for you?'

'Close the door and come over here.' Patrick undercut her with an authority he did not feel. She complied immediately, something akin to shame or fear colouring her face.

'Please sit down,' he said, having no idea of how he would proceed; but there was nowhere to sit, there being piles of paper on two chairs. He cleared one of them for her and she duly sat down while he picked up the sticky-tape dispenser again and weighed it in one hand before replacing it on the desk with careful deliberation.

'It isn't what you think,' he said.

Sandy had her eyes fixed firmly on the floor, her mouth tight.

Finally, he launched himself. 'Isolda came to tell me something I should have known already. You are going to have to forgive me, my dear, but I fear I've been out of touch with young people lately – what they feel.'

She appeared to be on the point of explosion, her eyes were flashing all round the room. 'What has Isolda to do with your feelings?'

'Please let me finish, my dear, I ...'

He checked himself, he couldn't let this pass.

'Isolda has deep feelings and extraordinary intuition about people. You are going to have to hear me out, Sandy.' Her face was twisting itself into knots, he'd have to look at something else. 'This may come as a shock to you, but it's the truth. She came to tell me that she loves you. She knew it was hopeless because she knew that you loved me.'

Sandy raised her eyes to him. 'Is that what she said?'

'She did. It explained a great deal to me. She said, in effect, I was blind to what was ... there for all to see.' He hoped against hope he'd said nothing to humiliate her.

Sandy dropped her face into her hands and lowered it onto her knees, remaining in a crouched position. Her shoulders came up to cover her ears and a muffled high-pitched wail escaped her. And then another.

He stepped forward fully intending to reassure her with a hug, but in the nick of time realised that an unconsidered gesture like this might provoke absolutely anything. He stopped in his tracks. Somehow she had to be told what he'd come to say.

'Please don't, my dear,' he said. Dear God, his impotence appalled him.

Her head shot up wildly. 'That's the fourth time you've called me "my dear". You pity me.'

'Oh, no.' He was emphatic, he had to show her. 'Oh, no, Sandy, I have never pitied you; you are one of the most remarkable people I know. But I have to face up to some difficult questions, and I ... I'm not finding it easy.'

Now his emotions were beginning to cloud his judgement. First, he had to remember it was a straight 'Sandy', if he was going to address her. Secondly, she simply had to understand it couldn't work; the two of them together. The extraordinary thing was, the fundamental reason for this was beginning to escape him. It was the sheer impossibility of it, but what exactly was it? The age gap. He was too old, that was it.

'You see, Sandy, I'm a bit too old for someone as young and, and ...'

'Sexually active?'

'No, of course not,' he murmured. This was taking him into deep waters. He had to press home to her that she had *her own life* ahead of her – a family to look forward to.

She looked him dangerously in the eye and said, 'Margheretta has no complaints, I imagine.'

'Margheretta and I have an understanding. You, Sandy, have your whole wonderful life ahead of you. To tie yourself to me at your age would be just about as disastrous as any decision you could make.'

She looked up at the window, her green eyes mournful, her dark lips relaxed.

'My whole wonderful life,' she repeated colourlessly. 'You are the only wonderful thing in my life. I don't care how old you say you are, you're the only one I want to spend the whole of my life loving. I've loved you for years and years. It hasn't changed.'

She turned away from the window to look at him, and something happened to him. He stepped towards her, his arms outstretched. She rose from the chair, her streaked face on the brink of bewilderment, and he kissed her.

Chapter 22

Phoebe looked at her watch. It was exactly the same time of morning as when she first arrived to paint the farmhouse. Beautifully judged. She couldn't wait. The sun would be on the steps that led up to the door with that fretwork of shadow on the wall from the climbing rose; the doves would be busy; and, of course – as if she could forget – there was the valley, that deep, plunging, problematical cleft behind the farmhouse. This time, she hoped, there'd be no Giovanni to divert her; she absolutely had to be left alone to get those dimensions into shape. Solitude was hard to come by here. And come to think of it, how did she think she could achieve anything worthwhile without it? But hadn't she *wanted* Dill to come with her? Of course. She'd worked her pants off to prise her from the steely clutches of Edward. But even so, Dill had never understood her seriousness. To take the fun out of going out for a day's painting was, for Dill, to miss the point, she'd said so. Truly exasperating. How could painting be fun? It was unadulterated frustration and hard work. Even when occasionally you got that little tickle of excitement when it seemed to be on the brink of working, you had no way of knowing that it had worked until it was finished. Her paintings were changing as she went along. In fact they might change direction altogether and become something else. *And this was what worried her.* Like the ladder painting in the orchard. When you looked at it, essentially, you saw light. The painting was about light.

She paused for a moment on the grassy path to conjure it in her mind's eye. A hazy morning under the olive trees with, faintly discernible, a ladder disappearing into the blur of foliage. Each day she took it out to view it with critical detachment, and so far it had not diminished in any way. But this was her one niggle: how could she be sure it wasn't an accident? Did it matter even? Wasn't it better to say she'd recognised when to let go and say she'd finished? This gave her a glimmer of confidence. Even so, she may put it to Patrick. If a satisfactory painting is a million miles away from what you thought you were going to finish up with, what is the point of starting another one? You couldn't say you were going to learn anything if this was the way you carried on. The whole thing was fraught with uncertainty.

She was brushing past all the giant stalks of broken fennel now, surrounding herself with its extraordinary smell. She broke off a flower spray and held it up to her nostrils. The smell flooded in: a dual bouquet reaching opposite ends of the spectrum. But as she moved closer to the farmhouse, something was wrong. When she scanned the pockets of vegetation dotting the valley searching for beauty, she saw only banality. She told herself to keep calm, this had happened before. Really, the idea that painting was anywhere near approaching fun was just laughable. If painting was fun, the whole world would be at it. Luckily, Dill had said she was going for a walk to visit a goat she'd spotted tethered by the wayside.

Who was it? *Who was it?* It was the worst thing that could have happened. Somebody had pinched her spot: the exact position on the hillock, a foot below the flat tree stump, the perfect position. Phoebe stopped, unsure of what to do. And then, as if she had a sixth sense that someone was behind her, Rose swivelled round on her stool, 'Phoebe! Oh, I know what's happened; I'm in your place!' she called.

Quelling the resentment already threatening to half choke her, Phoebe walked over to look at Rose's painting of the farmhouse. Slowly she put down her easel and the stool she carried. She was shocked. It shook her to see how alien someone else's vision could be. Was this the farmhouse she knew so well? Well, of course it was, it was just different.

'Rose, how do you do it? All that plunging space behind the house looking like space! I mean, it's not fair, it just isn't. What is the point of even beginning?'

Rose laid her palette and brush on the grass and stood up.

'I insist you sit down and begin *now*,' she said. 'I've finished, and I'm going to leave you here.' She started to pack away her paints and dismantle her painting and easel. 'Come on,' she said with a smile, 'get your stuff out.'

And then she became alert, slowly standing upright. 'Can you hear something? Dogs?'

'No, I don't hear dogs.'

Rose rested her canvas against the sawn tree but seemed preoccupied. She looked back at the farmhouse once or twice.

'There. Can you see them?'

Phoebe looked down into the valley expecting to see dogs. What she saw was about four or five men in single file walking along an animal trail that followed the contours of the hill they were standing on. They were heading down towards a wood and some carried rifles in their hands while others had one slung over their shoulder. She said, 'They look like huntsmen.'

Rose was breathing in little snatches, her eyes fixed on them. She glanced again at the farmhouse and then back to the moving line of men.

'Phoebe, I'm going to call on Lucia. I'll leave my painting here with you, if you don't mind, it's not dry. I'll be back in a minute.' She walked quickly down the slope towards the house.

There was an implacable sense of purpose about the men, a brusque, no-nonsense way they walked in a line. One of them looked up and noticed Phoebe. She felt exposed on the brow of the hill. Better settle her stool and screw her easel into position, safer to show them she was here to paint. She assembled the various tools of her trade around her and prepared herself to wrestle with the problem of space.

Phoebe looked out over the familiar scene. Everything was in place: the doves, the wisteria, the stunted acacia; the only difference being a wispy column of smoke coming from the chimney stack. She unscrewed her water bottle, dipped in her brush, picked up her palette, and during the next few seconds, wondered if she was going mad. Just behind her easel she thought she'd seen a pig tripping across the grass. She stood up slowly and caught sight of it again making a semicircle around her until it stopped the other side of the tree stump and looked at her. A large pink pig. For a horrified couple of seconds, she half expected a pursuing pack of dogs in its wake, and swung round to look back up the path.

'*Phoebe!*' Dill was rounding the corner by the fennel, waving and calling. She ran over the grass towards the pig, her long legs dangerously uncoordinated.

She'd done it, Dill had let the pig out.

'Head it off, Phoebe, and send it back up the path.'

The pig took fright and made an about turn followed by another small semicircle. Still clutching her paintbrush and palette, Phoebe tried to manoeuvre herself to a safe distance behind the animal, but it made a dash for her easel, knocking over her stool. When it saw Dill approaching it stopped, and its abrupt halt checked her sister in her tracks. She stood there taking long plunging breaths.

'It escaped, Phoebe. Honestly, it just couldn't wait. It's not happy in there.'

'Of course it's bloody happy, it's all it knows, that's its life!' Rage and exasperation were bringing Phoebe quickly to the point of tears.

'Oh ...' Dill's agonised eyes searched her sister's face. 'I suppose you may be right.'

'Of *course* I'm right! Why didn't you take the *goat* for a walk? That would have made everyone happy.'

Dill said in a small voice. 'The goat wasn't there.'

'This is a painting spot, Dill. It's where people come to paint.'

Her sister was wringing her hands looking so utterly miserable that Phoebe felt she ought to make amends. She spoke as kindly as she was able, but felt murderous. 'Why don't you go and fetch the old lady in the house while I keep the pig here?' Dill nodded and began walking cautiously down to the farmhouse, stealing looks over her shoulder every few seconds. Then she ran.

Curled up on the grass to the side of the pig Phoebe saw the strap she used to tie up her easel. It was a shortish strap but she might just be able to slip it over its neck.

The pig eyed Phoebe sharply. Was this wise? she wondered; the pig seemed to be reading her thoughts. She approached it steadily by degrees, drawing out from her pocket the fennel head she'd plucked. The pig switched its vigilance to the yellow spray of buds in her outstretched hand, bucking away in tiny, skittish darts. Holding out the fennel, crooning to it as Dill crooned to her foaling mares, Phoebe closed in on the pig. She put out her other hand. It instantly flinched, emitting three or four high panicky grunts and shot away at an angle. From there it turned round to look at her. She was astonished at its sensitivity. She had touched the hairs on its back – only the hairs on the tough pink hide of its back. She considered it wonderingly, with new respect.

There was a commotion down by the farmhouse. Dill was heading up the slope with Lucia, her long strides provoking Lucia into gigantic efforts to keep up with her, knees bent in heavy wellies, arms striking the air before her as if she were cross-country skiing. As they drew level with the brow, Lucia caught sight of the pig and released a rounded yowl of fury. It threw the pig into a frenzy of squealing and it cantered in a half circle before heading for Rose's painting at top speed.

Phoebe shouted, '*NO!*'

The oily canvas landed face down on the grass as the pig brushed past, and as Lucia approached the animal on its flank, her arms flailing, it reversed direction and trampled back over the underside of the fallen canvas.

Phoebe shouted, 'Stop it, Dill. I *beg* you to stop it.'

Dill was in extreme anguish. 'It's terrified, Phoebe, it needs to be calmed down.'

The pig gave Lucia a look, and took off at top speed down the path leading to its sty. Lucia waded after it, her arm sawing the air in time to her threats. She turned back and screeched something, her voice almost giving out.

'I think she wants me to go and help,' Dill said.

'Go on then.'

Dill looked beseechingly at her for a split second, and then left her to join Lucia.

Phoebe's legs were lead. The upturned canvas had dents crossing the blank underside and a small split. On turning it over, she saw the damage was irreversible: the paint was smeared, grass and dusty debris stuck to the sticky surface. There was nothing she could do.

A noise, was it dogs? Instinctively she looked towards the farmhouse. It might have been dogs, but it had faded away. There it came again, it was familiar – a weird sort of wailing. Something bad was happening inside the house, her mouth went dry. The door at the top of the steps swung open and Rose appeared. She looked round then shouted at the top of her voice.

'*Lucia!*'

Phoebe half held up her hand to attract Rose's attention. The painting was back against the tree stump, where Rose had left it, but there was no escape, she had to tell her. It was the pig! It was entirely the pig. It escaped from its sty and went berserk. She began to run down the slope towards Rose with her announcement.

Rose interrupted her, calling, 'Where is she? Where's Lucia? Have you seen her? There she is!' Rose raced past her down the steps.

As soon as Lucia could take in what she was saying, she allowed Rose to support her down the hillock towards the house where Rose virtually carried her up the steps towards the open door. She called quietly down to Phoebe standing at the bottom.

'Giovanni is very ill.'

Phoebe thought of the frail little skeleton that was Giovanni. 'Shall I call for a doctor, an ambulance?'

'*No!*' Rose's eyes were restless. She looked relieved when she saw that Dill was on her way. She whispered, 'Phoebe, can you both come in with us, please?'

The four of them shuffled into the black space that lay behind the door where it glittered with pinpricks of light like a night sky. A clapping of wings startled Phoebe into covering her ears as she ducked. A bird flew out of the dark into the daylight.

Rose turned to the two sisters and whispered, 'Close the door, please.'

Dill pushed the door to, behind them.

They were standing on the wide untreated boards of a barn. Disconcerting streaks of light shone up through the gaps from the room below, although the bright green hillside seen through a tiny triangular window close to floor level opposite shone like an emerald in the semi-darkness. Phoebe was becoming aware of a bed in the centre of the floor in the almost empty room. On the further side of the bed she saw a dark shape – something piled up, perhaps. Or even a figure crouching. Was this Giovanni's bedroom?

The window was blocked by Lucia holding up a blanket to cover the bed as she moved across it. She spread the covering over a shallow bump and then searched for her crucifix beneath her shirt. They heard a faint whining protestation endlessly repeated under Lucia's breath as if she were having a bad dream.

Phoebe felt Dill's hand creep into hers as they both stood a short distance from the foot of the bed. Her sister's hand tightened suddenly as the door to the hillock swung open slowly with a passing breeze, and light flooded over her. Giovanni rose bolt upright from his bed with his full attention on Dill, brightly illuminated. Keeping his eyes on her, he prepared to climb out of bed. Lucia put her hands on his shoulders to push him back but it was a struggle until Rose wrapped her arms around his thin torso to hold him in place.

Phoebe turned to whisper to Dill.

'Stay in the light. He thinks you're the Holy Virgin.'

Rose released Giovanni cautiously. He dropped his head to cross himself. Raising his eyes again to the light, he looked at Dill, his face an ecstatic mask of taut skin: two empty holes for his eyes, a bigger one for his mouth.

He was murmuring.

'*Ave Maria, gratia plena ... Dominus tecum ... Benedicta tu in ...*'

And then Dill smiled at him, and the tight skin across his cheeks lifted and stretched while speech failed him altogether.

Her sister broke away slightly from Phoebe, still smiling, and held out both the palms of her hands in welcome to Giovanni.

'Peace, Giovanni. *Pace!... Pace!* ...'

Giovanni's extraordinary strength failed him suddenly and he keeled sideways.

A young man's arm came out to catch him. The figure had risen from his crouching position at the side of the bed, and both he and Rose supported him back onto the pillows.

Phoebe caught her breath.

Lucia wailed, '*O, Dio mio.*'

Two wrenching sobs came from the pillow as the young man pressed his face into it. Rose touched his shoulder and he turned away from the pillow towards her, transferring his face to the crook of her neck. His aborted cries were released in an agony of reversal. Phoebe felt her throat swell. Who was he? Was he her Hamlet? They knew each other so well, he and Rose, they clung to each other. She watched him until he slowly curled in and withdrew from her. She felt tearful and jealous, and then ashamed of herself.

Dill reached out to close Giovanni's eyes, and laid a hand on Lucia who had crumpled onto the bed.

The door to the hillside was swinging on its hinges. It framed a figure with a rifle standing in the grass, a little way off. Phoebe caught sight of him frowning at the house, focusing on the door as if he were trying to see something more clearly. Before she could warn anyone a man's voice called out a sudden question from the room below. They all heard it.

Lucia sat up abruptly. She looked quickly at the young man, who had already made a silent dive for the small triangular window. He put out his head to look down, and then leant further out to look up. Phoebe pressed her hands to her ears as his body completely filled the space. It was simply not possible for a grown man to squeeze out of this window. She heard his breath catching in faint sharp cries before a chink of light became bigger. By degrees the window was back to being a complete triangle. With her mouth in a tight line, Rose thumped across the floor to the open trap at the head of a wooden stair, and clattered down to the bottom.

Phoebe closed the swinging door carefully to shut the huntsman out, and as she turned back to the dark room a stream of subdued fury from Rose was clearly to be heard through the gaps in the floor. The man's voice dropped, then rose harshly as he obviously prepared to mount the stairs.

Almost immediately, his head appeared through the trap. A dark moustache hung down either side of his lower lip and the barrel of his rifle pointed to the rafters. He paused with his head at floor level squinting round at the bed. Lucia flew towards him screeching like a peacock, pointing at Giovanni. Then she lost impetus and stepped backwards, colliding with Dill as the man continued his ascent. Dill stood her ground, preventing Lucia from retreating further.

The huntsman came to stand in front of them, his legs apart, looking them up and down silently before glancing round. The triangular window took his attention. He frowned and hesitated. His body had brought with it into the room an unpleasantly sour, sweet smell, alleviated partly by fresh tobacco smoke, especially strong when he moved. Giovanni's upturned face held his brief attention on his way over to the triangle of light where he bent on one knee preparing to look out.

Abruptly Lucia threw herself back onto her knees by the bedside moaning and rocking. Phoebe felt herself blush: she was play-acting, it wouldn't convince anyone. But Lucia only increased her lamentation, stoking up her panic.

The hunter swung round as Rose ran up the wooden steps from downstairs and shot up through the trap, almost alight with the verbal onslaught that streamed from the very pit of her stomach. The word *carabinieri* was repeated at least three times, and it was enough to gain his attention.

They heard the kick-start of a motorbike outside, and Rose was immobilised. Her eyes and mouth opened wide, her hair stood out in spikes. The bike's engine revved prematurely and rumbled up the scale into a scream; there was a shout followed by – no more than a few metres from the house – the shot from a rifle, and Rose crumpled to the floor.

For a moment nothing moved.

Lucia crouched, intimidated, engulfed by the bed. The hunter was galvanised. He pushed his head out through the little window, and then withdrew, walking swiftly towards them away from the window and straight over to the doorway that led onto the hillock. He swung open the door and was gone, leaving it slowly swinging on its hinges.

Phoebe could still hear the motorbike. It was getting fainter.

She said, 'Wake up, Rose, he got away.'

Rose opened her glazed eyes and fixed them on Phoebe's. Then as if Phoebe were transformed into a train coming towards her, she took a deep draught of air and cried out 'Antonio,' as she tried to get up.

Dill held onto her. 'Rose, can you hear us? Antonio is safe. Antonio got away.'

Chapter 23

When she pushed with her shoulder against the heavy old door, it felt extraordinarily light. Rose almost fell inside, her hair standing on end.

She was confronted by Kitty arrested in mid-flight on her way to her kitchen; she stood stricken in the centre of the floor staring at Rose. 'He's just been on the phone.'

'Is he alright?' Rose shouted.

Kitty was looking at her strangely; she was unable to tell what she was thinking.

'Now, just wait a wee while, dear ...'

'He is hurt isn't he? *Kitty? Tell me.*'

'See me to the couch dear, I have to sit down.'

'Yes, yes. Oh, Kitty, I can't bear it, tell me if he's hurt.'

Rose led Kitty over to the chaise longue, where she lowered her slowly onto the seat. 'In the kitchen, dear, on the shelf above the kettle. There's a half bottle of Glenmorangie. Bring a glass.'

Rose raced blindly to the kitchen; her eyes flashed round. There was a bottle of whisky but no glasses anywhere. She saw an upturned coffee cup on the draining board and grabbed it.

'Is this alright, Kitty? It's a cup.'

She was reminded of Kitty's age suddenly at the sight of her ashen face, but Kitty had a gritty look about the mouth, and took the brimming cup as if she were in a trance and raised it to her lips.

After a few moments, she said, 'He wants you to take him painkillers, and ...'

'*He is hurt. Oh, God.*'

Whisky splashed out of the bottle onto Rose's dress and the cap wouldn't screw back on again. It slipped out of her hand and bounced away across the floor.

'Oh, I'm sorry, I'm sorry. Please go on.'

Kitty was silenced. She sat very still. Every very few seconds she paused to take another sip from her cup. She may have been cross about the spilled whisky, or maybe her interruption had offended her, Rose had no way of knowing; it was just a question now of keeping still till she was ready. She spotted the screw cap under a chair, and retrieved it quietly before creeping back to sit down.

There seemed to be very little breath left for Kitty to speak, and when the words came they were formed slowly and carefully.

She leant the bicycle against the old cypress, and out of the corner of her eye noticed Antonio's motorbike hidden in the overhanging branches of a holm oak nearby. Rose wheeled her bike over to push it into the deep green cover next to it. Picking up the hem of her dress she wiped the perspiration from her face, and raised her head to listen as she scanned the empty valley: only a green woodpecker and that same noisy cicada in the scrubby grass under the cypress. Antonio's house seemed undisturbed, as isolated as ever. But he'd said she mustn't loiter near to the house however deserted it might seem. Her instructions were to remain out of sight and to listen until all the insects and birds were in full voice. To alert him to her presence, she mimicked the call of a cuckoo three times in quick succession; and stood pressed into the big cypress out of the sun. Her thoughts were with him, buried in the cavernous quiet of the house, quieter by far than it was out here.

Together with her terrible anxiety for him was a longing to see him again, to touch him. She wanted to quieten his haunted eyes and kiss him. So that when she saw him slumped at the kitchen table with the back of his shirt soaked in blood, she was cut short with an irresistible weakness in her legs. She collapsed into the other chair.

He said, 'Have you seen Kitty?'

She dragged her satchel up onto her knee and one by one laid out the few things Kitty had asked her to bring: painkillers, alcohol, a packet of razor blades, sterile dressings, eyebrow tweezers. Lucia had given her a small grubby package for him earlier; she held it up for him to see. 'From Lucia!' she said and set it apart on a corner of the table. His eyes devoured the small collection before finally he nodded and looked up at her.

'I have a bullet in my shoulder.'

His face altered, and she saw such need for her in his expression that Rose left her chair to kneel by him. She wrapped her arms around his waist and laid her head against him.

'I know what to do,' she said, almost overwhelmed by the smell of blood. 'I'm good at treating animals too, Antonio. They trust me.'

She tried to smile and stood up, already knowing almost to the last detail what would be required of her.

It was true that people brought their pets for her to treat when they were worried about them: she had set tiny legs in splints and massaged joints back into place. And once when out on a trek, she had successfully cut a fish hook from the pad of her cousin's thumb without losing her nerve. It was the memory of this that gave her the confidence to see her through the operation to remove the bullet, although nothing had prepared her for so much blood.

She worked in silence, using his various cries as guidelines to the amount of invasive damage she was inflicting with her razor and tweezers. The blood poured out the instant she had swabbed the wound, and when the swabs were saturated it ran down the side of his back till she snatched a fresh one.

Antonio had no strength to lift his left arm; she had to rest it on the table till she found the bullet. It had gone in fairly close to the armpit, catching the edge of the shoulder blade but missing the ribs, penetrating just below the shoulder joint. The sight of the bullet stuck within the torn muscle was a shock, an evil metal malevolence. It was the only moment when her concentration left her; but it slid out easily. She laid the bullet on top of the fleshy debris on the saucer before immediately applying pressure on the wound and binding it tightly with surgical tape; then she washed her hands and came back to the table to sit with him in a state of elation. It was over, they had both come through it.

Antonio took the rolled towel from between his teeth leaving his face blotched and haggard with exhaustion, and still to her surprise, she couldn't help smiling.

He said, 'You are brave. And you care for people ... and animals.' He flashed her a look.

She felt strong, as if she'd achieved something, and wondered if now was the time to say it – to ask him directly. It was something she had to know; the question had been burning into her and only Antonio could answer it. But how could she bring herself to do it? She looked at him sitting there and a kind of dread filled her; he was at his weakest, surely, it was unfair. Suddenly her mouth went dry.

'Antonio.' Rose leaned forward to look him in the eyes. 'On the day when Dodo was killed, why did you go to Rome?'

'Tancredi asked me to go.'

'At short notice?'

'It was important I leave at once.'

'Did he say why?'

'To meet a client. But actually there was no client. Afterwards, Tancredi told me that my life was in danger here – that they wanted to punish him by killing me. He drove me to Pisa for an early flight.'

'And did he come here to collect you?' The prick of needles spread lightly over her scalp. 'Or did you ride over to the villa?'

'I rode over and left my bike at the villa.'

Rose forced herself to breathe. There was one more thing, another question.

'You said "tricked. They felt stupid, tricked". Tricked because the paintings they'd bought were forged. But why *doubly* tricked, Antonio?'

'Oh ... yes.' His hand came up slowly to rub his forehead, his eyelids closed halfway. He'd had enough, she must stop these questions. But although he seemed exhausted Antonio continued in a weaker voice. 'I heard Tancredi on the telephone. He said ...' There was a pause while he took a few moments to concentrate. He continued, 'He said, "*You think I sent him?* My brother's son! Are you mad? I did nothing, it was your mistake. You can't do this to me."'

The leaden chill of fear spread over her flesh. He'd told her what she wanted to know. Something she had never even dared suspect. But now that Antonio had said it, she wondered if the knowledge was too shocking to bear. How could she deal with this? She subsided slowly and shuddered. Not now. She must push it aside and think about it later.

'And now, Antonio,' she touched him on his arm and forced a smile, 'you must see a doctor. I will ask him to come and see you here, and I'll tell him to keep it secret.'

'Never. Don't even think about it.'

'You are in danger from infection—'

'You have done an excellent job. I will rest, and in one or two days' time, I will be ready to go to Roma. If I need to, I will find a hospital.'

The shock of hearing he would be going to Rome silenced her. It stunned her with disbelief that he could turn his back on her so carelessly. Leaden darkness was rushing, directionless, waiting to envelop her. She knew that in his mind he had already gone. She was losing him, it had started to happen. His blurred image was shifting and changing shape through tears that had filled her eyes. Who was he? She didn't know him, only that he'd touched her and made her feel blissful, but that was for a couple of hours on a single night; and even though he must have known how it was for her, his love-making might have been one of those spontaneous things that happened whenever he felt like it. So why should she mean any more to him than any other girl? He hadn't talked to her much except to say that she was a beautiful person, which sounded too spiritual for her liking, like a priest; it was what he had said with his kisses and his hands and the warmth of his body that she preferred to think of, his beautiful body – his poor, damaged body. The image of his curved white back and its perfection before the bullet was too much to bear because she was losing all of him, body and soul. A thin faraway whining came and went and the darkness came down. Her hands came up to shield her face from him and misery rolled in like the grey English sea.

Then at a certain point, she wasn't sure when, Rose felt her hand being touched by his and this time his fingers were icy cold which shocked her into common sense. She wiped her eyes, and saw such sadness in his expression that she had to put up her hands to hide her face all over again.

At last, he said, 'Rosa,' and just looked at her.

And then he said, 'Do you like me kissing you?'

'I love it, I love you kissing me.' She was unable to move.

'*Carissima.*' His face became vacant, he was almost asleep, but his red-rimmed eyes continued to look into hers.

'Come to Roma with me.'

Rose sat at the table in the cramped, familiar kitchen. She fixed her eyes on Lucia's back in the darkness over by the sink, her spindly legs disappearing into a pair of large sheepskin slippers. Antonio would be lying across his own sheepskins striving to keep his eyes open, trying to keep alert. She saw his rifle in her mind's eye propped against the crook of his arm, and she thought: you can't make it on your own, Antonio.

Lucia was assembling glasses and a bottle of something. A candle had been placed in the centre of the table, and outside, the sinking sun had left a clear patch of vermilion behind the hillock.

Although she couldn't see it from where she sat in the farmhouse kitchen, Rose knew that from the terrace of Il Centro the strata of rose pink lying beneath the green would be showing now behind the hills. They will have finished their evening meal, and the bats will be hunting, she thought. Only Patrick knew she was with Lucia.

Should she insist on staying the night with her? Lucia came over to the table carrying a round tray with small tumblers and a thick dark green bottle with a darkly mottled cork. There were two blue china saucers, one displaying some bobbly biscuits, the other holding a spoonful of Giovanni's slim green olives. Lucia's sinews dilated in her sunburnt stick of an arm as she grasped the cork and twisted. It slid out with a hollow pop and when she poured, it was a tawny colour and clung to the glass like oil.

Rose lifted her glass in a toast. 'Giovanni had a good long life.'

Lucia pushed out her lips to meet the liquor before it left the glass, and held it in her mouth before smacking her lips with satisfaction. For a few moments afterwards, she sat and gazed at Rose, her eyes brightly liquid in the candlelight. She seemed to be on the brink of a question, but the question never came.

Rose put down the glass and leant forward to lay her hand on Lucia's. 'And he knew that Antonio would take care of his olives. He died happy.'

Immediately, Lucia withdrew her hand and waved it in front of her face, shaking her head from side to side. 'Olives, olives, always his olives. Who will have my olive trees? Antonio, he wanted to paint his pictures, but we kept him at home. Ay, ay, we kept him at home.'

Lucia looked down at her glass, nodding and making her ay, ay noises of regret. And then she looked Rose full in the face as if for emphasis. 'We kept him at home.'

'But, Lucia, where else could he go?'

Lucia's eyes were moving obsessively around the perimeter of the floor. She took a biscuit and replaced it again, murmuring something to herself. Suddenly she got up from her chair and went quickly into the adjoining room. Seconds later she was back with something folded in yellowing tissue paper which she unwrapped, handing to Rose a tiny pair of baby shoes with satin ribbons to tie. 'Antonio's,' she said.

Rose took them in the palm of her hand and thought of Antonio's unimaginably small feet inside them; and then she looked at Lucia who'd kept them all these years and was surprised because Lucia was not sentimental.

'For you and Antonio. For your son,' Lucia said.

Air rushed into Rose's lungs. '*Oh!*'

Lucia leant forward and patted her cheek, 'Call him Giovanni.'

Rose was speechless. She was being claimed as a member of the family and was expected to fall in with it, naturally, without a word. For a while nothing was spoken. She felt numb, paralysed, stupid, as if she were receiving a proposal from the wrong person before she was ready. And that her time was running out, because here was Lucia waiting for her response with her blue eyes fixed on her, breathing hard and leaning forward slightly. Could she see that this was what Rose wanted before she knew it herself? And that she must bequeath her Antonio's baby shoes, because, naturally, having babies was the point of it all? With the dawning of a belief that everything seemed to be falling into place, she looked up and met Lucia's eyes.

Encouraged, Lucia leant back in her chair and nodded.

'Galia bought them. *Si, si,* even before he was born,' she said.

'Antonio's mother?'

Lucia nodded.

'His mother, my Galia. Antonio was five days. Only five days when she died.'

Lucia began to fidget with the position of the saucers and then swept some traces of biscuit off the table. She had begun to breathe noisily again.

'And she gave to me – to her mother – a letter for him, for the baby. But Giovanni saw it, and he took it. And he opened it.' Lucia took a long unsteady breath. 'Father Tomaso knew what was in it, only Father Tomaso and Giovanni. I found the letter and I hid it. *Si*. I hid the letter inside the floor where Giovanni could not find it. And Giovanni beat me, he beat me, but I would not say where it was hidden. Because it was Antonio's letter. Antonio's letter from his mother. He has never seen it.'

'Why, Lucia? Why has Antonio not seen his letter?'

'Giovanni didn't want it. Giovanni would have killed me.'

'And, Giovanni, did he tell you what was in the letter?' She guessed that neither she nor Giovanni could read.

Lucia grabbed a biscuit uncertainly, but then put it back again. She seemed uncomfortable and looked away. 'Giovanni didn't tell me.'

'I gave your parcel to Antonio. Was that the letter?'

Lucia nodded. 'The letter. And …' Her hand came up and described a circle around her neck.

'A necklace?'

'*Si*. Galia's pearls.'

'I will see that Antonio reads his mother's letter.'

Lucia's fine face screwed itself into a walnut shell.

Rose leaned towards her. 'Don't be afraid, Lucia. It'll be alright.'

Tomorrow morning, very early, before anyone woke up, she'd go to him (and search for the cat till she found it).

It invaded her nostrils: that heavy odour of crushed pine that always caused a tightening in the pit of her stomach – but she hadn't reached Antonio's barn just yet, although she must be close to it. Too early for tourists on the road – no wonder the air was so keen and pure; and now this was her chance to freewheel: the main road was dipping quite steeply ahead of her and the breeze passing through her hair. Had his painkillers been strong enough? A fresh film of perspiration spread from her back into her hair as she visualised his agonising pain. Amateur surgery. She had no idea how his body would withstand it; no idea what to expect. Rose put furious pressure now on the pedals; it would take her four or five minutes to get there. A car coming up fast behind her suddenly skidded down to a crawl in front of her. What was happening? Slowly it began to pick up. White. The white car.

Panic numbed her hands. Her hearing went; shock clouded her vision. She squeezed on her brakes and thought she would faint. It was the same white car – she'd seen a white glove as they shot past. Confusion seized her, but she kept control, changed gear and pedalled quickly but kept the bike moving slowly. There was a bend in the road ahead. 'Go on,' she hissed, 'go on!' She willed the car to keep moving, to get round the bend. 'Slowly,' she instructed herself as her pedals whizzed round quickly but slackly, 'slowly as you can.' If she could maintain this low speed, the white car would be lost to sight before she closed in on it. '*Oh, God, I think it's going to stop.*' She cast about her, left and right. Nowhere to go.

Coming up, there was a farm track to her left; to her right, the steep scrubby hillside. Now. She had to decide now. Back up the hill? Or the farm track? Which? She squeezed her brakes and prepared to dismount – just as the car, slowly but surely, was inching round the bend.

It wouldn't carry on, it wouldn't continue on its journey, it would be there – waiting for her. It would sit tight and wait for her to catch them up. But supposing they came back to find her? She made a lightning decision to ignore the track on her left, it was too obvious (they'd read her mind and follow her). She dismounted and ran back uphill, pushing the bike in front of her. A low bush at the roadside growing in a shallow ditch at the foot of the hill was the only cover. Pulling aside thick prickly branches she pushed and squeezed the front wheel and handlebars a little way into the bush, but it was big enough to conceal only half the bike: there was a branch in the centre of the bush that blocked the handlebars; the back wheel stuck out the other side, easily visible to traffic travelling down the hill. She'd made the wrong decision, but now it was too late. The whine of a car in reverse started up and became quickly louder. There was only one thing to do: snap off a clutch of small branches for camouflage and crouch as close to

her bike as she could get. She held the leaves in front of her body and
kept still.

It emerged round the bend weaving from left to right, dangerously
veering towards the bare hill face before righting itself violently. When
it reached the farm track, instead of stopping, it reversed straight past it
heading for Rose.

She ducked and shrank as a thudding vibration of sound on the
tarmac behind her approached with a tearing and a swishing she had
never heard before. The noise was upon her now: a party of cyclists
in racing helmets inches from her crouching form, flashing by at
incredible speed. They saw the white car reversing up their side of the
road towards them and began shouting. The car stopped dead and the
cyclists swerved to avoid it, giving it a wide berth but unable to check the
insane speed they'd built up. Their furious oaths were snatched by the
wind as they approached the corner and vanished in ones and twos as if
sucked round by an invisible force.

Now the white car seemed to be hesitating. Rose waited. They'd
seen her in the rear view mirror; they'd caught sight of her white T-shirt
through her camouflage. She fought an instinct to flinch, to drop her
branches and run, to scramble up the hillside. Without moving her head
she glanced at the hill above her. Impossible: there was an overhang.
Then, to her disbelief, she watched the white car begin to slide silently
downhill. Slowly it began to pick up speed before clattering into life as
the engine kicked in. When it reached the path to the farm, it swerved
to its left across the road and turned in. A familiar cloud of dust traced
its progress down the track.

Antonio lay across the sheepskins with his rifle alongside him.
He barely stirred when she slipped in. She knew something was wrong.
He murmured something to her, and she half started towards him to
catch what he was saying until she realised he wanted her to lock the
door behind her. There were at least three locks on the door and she
had taken only one key. It had been a fight to persuade him to leave the
others unlocked, but now she firmly secured all three locks to the door
and moved swiftly over to him.

His face was flushed and his eyes glassy and only half open. She dropped her satchel packed with food, and felt his forehead. It was frighteningly hot, but she had to tell him, 'Antonio, the white car! It passed me on the road. I hid, but I think it's still looking for me.'

He opened his eyes wide and looked at her.

'Who was inside?'

'I saw the white gloves.'

'We can't stay here.' His breathing was laboured.

'Antonio, you have a high temperature. I'm going to ask Patrick what to do. Don't try to stop me, it's the only way.'

She looked around for his cell-phone, and even though she knew he was convinced that someone somewhere might be able to trace his calls, this was an emergency. She went to search for it in the kitchen where she had last seen it. The phone was not there, but she saw that the letter had been taken out of the wrapping. She reached out and gathered up the letter with the polythene package to take it back for him.

'Antonio, have you read the letter?'

He nodded. 'Read it,' he said in a far away voice.

The envelope was small. In careful, curly writing was the name 'Antonio Tura'. It had been torn open – by Giovanni, she supposed – and was covered in blotches. Inside there were two stained pages of lined paper filled with faded ink and smelling of earth. With difficulty, she read:

> To my darling baby Antonio, my own. From the time that I knew I had a baby inside me, I have wanted you. You are the best thing that has happened to me in my life from the very beginning to the end. When you were born you opened your eyes to look at me. I like to think you will remember me from that long look, because soon I shall not be here to take care of you, my darling baby. When you are eighteen years old you will read this letter, and you will know that your father is Tancredi Pazzi. I am writing this now for the very first time. I have never said his name to anyone, even Tancredi. If he sees the pearls, he will remember. Now I look at your fingers and toes and I think you are a gift from God. I am blessed with

great happiness, and also great sadness. Your loving mother watches over you. From Galia Tura.

The wrapping paper inside had turned to dust and fluttered down with the necklace as it slid out. It was hard to tell that they were pearls: greyish, yellowish beads, like tiny pebbles on an English beach.

Patrick had come out before breakfast to give himself time to think. It was the best time of the morning out here, and for once, nobody about but a couple of collared doves for company. A choice of sun or shade on the terrace, San Cristofero and the cypresses just pushing through the mist still lying thick along the valley, and a moment's solitude in store. It was fresh, nippy even, with a slight wind so that the bowl of his coffee mug warmed his hands very well indeed. He was an extraordinarily lucky man, filled, at this moment, with a huge amount of gratitude and nowhere immediately to put it. The natural thing for him now was to thank God for this wonderful girl. He wanted to leave his votive offering at the feet of his deity and feel better for it. Was it realistic at his age to worry himself silly over the big question still? He'd listened to the scepticism around him; yet over the years of living so close to great works of art he had been persuaded of at least the possibility of the existence of God. Art transcended reason, after all, and so – he thought with a fresh pang – did love. He pictured a sturdy terracotta sculpture he'd seen in Rome recently, and remembered the striding, smiling figure with his long braided hair – Apollo, the Etruscan god of light. In spirit, he'd always thought of himself as Etruscan: glad to be alive. Apollo then! – didn't he owe his very life and livelihood to him?

He had left Sandy asleep still, hair all over the pillow. Her love for him was a mystery. How did he deserve it? He was the chosen recipient of her miraculous female bounty, over and above anyone else. He couldn't deny it. It was ineluctably so. There it was, he could only marvel and return it. Had he ever been loved like this? He had not been aware of it. Had his own loving ever produced such rapture? In his remembrance of all his most treasured moments of love-making, he could honestly say it had not. And the astonishing revelation was that this volatile girl whom he knew perfectly well, whom he drove to regular paroxysms of rage, could turn into a melting pot of tenderness and passion such as he had never known. Since he first kissed her, he had not once been reminded of his age. In fact he hadn't felt like this since he was about sixteen . . . Ah! Now alarm bells were clanging. Were these late pangs of youth part and parcel of the ignominious cavortings of an old letch?

The sun had just come round, touching the tiles of the old washhouse in front of him. Who would have thought there were so many tones in clay: every conceivable subtlety of colour to be found in old terracotta? He was close enough to see the crusting of grey-blue lichen, and mercury shadows that came with a slanting sun; and as his eyes rested on the tiles he thought, although I am prepared to face up to reality and see myself as a doting old fool, in my heart I do not believe it. This wonderful thing that has happened to me has changed me, but whatever it has made me, it is for the good. It has allowed me to understand the world better, to see young people more clearly. I am in touch again. After five wasted years, this marvellous girl, this Botticelli Madonna and termagant spitting hellfire all in one, has at last given me what she has always wanted to; and I find I am able to give her in measure what she wants from me.

He heard the telephone ringing inside the house and roused himself to answer it.

Chapter 24

I was a grand occasion, alright: the Villa Pazzi resplendent against the setting sun. The frisson it produced for Isolda this evening was almost too much for her pulse, unreliable at the best of times. Party guests were queuing in their cars, slowly waiting their turn to ascend the curving staircase, but for Isolda cooped up in her taxi, that hoped-for intimate moment with Tancredi before the guests arrived had long since vanished, and all the irresistible charm and guile she'd rehearsed for him was wasted. She was as tense as a cat. If she only felt free to lay her hands on the taxi driver and throttle him she might then be able to unclench her jaw: he had been late to collect her at Il Centro, and her Italian was not so fluent as to give the man the hammering he deserved. Isolda watched a limo in front of them pause in front of the central horseshoe staircase to allow a couple in evening dress slowly to gather themselves together before ascending the steps.

Would it do – her short scarlet dress? The tasselled shawl had certainly tempered the shock of so much red; she remembered that moment of serendipity when she'd noticed the same scarlet in tiny flowers appearing within the pattern and had promptly flung the glowing silk to its best dramatic effect across her shoulders. She was bad, very bad, a thief, and what was worse, unrepentant; but at the moment, with her memory of Jim refreshed, she began to feel a notch more humorous. The cab driver was suddenly treated to a brilliant smile, wholly undeserved in the light of his tardiness, but who cared, she felt like it. Now she was in the swing.

The glorious warmth of the villa's facade was dimmed, set as it was in the path of the sun sinking behind the building. It cut through the Great Hall with its barrel-vaulted ceiling, straight through the villa and out of the windows at the front, turning them a dazzling gold. Within the dark recesses of the portico behind the six columns, tall torches were in place on either side of the main door, ready to be lit at the onset of dusk. She looked up at a line of windows under the eaves and noticed they were all unshuttered. Where are they, Tancredi? Where do you keep your Bronzino, your Castagno, your Piero Della Francesca? And especially, *especially* those two dodgy Paninis? The chatter from the crowd in the Great Hall seemed to form a buffer round him and his agents of privacy. A tremor went through her. She mounted the steps.

For a few seconds Isolda was blinded as she walked in. She decided to infiltrate the guests and turn her back on the sun, the better to see the frescoes. And here they were. Every swirling body in its flying robe illuminated by the golden light pouring in – striding, posturing, dancing, luxuriating – just as, on a lower level, Tancredi's guests, chiselled in the light, flamboyantly broadcast their social superiority. Who was she going to talk to? To which of these cast-iron cliques would she announce herself? A young liveried footman smiled and dropped his eyes to a silver tray he carried from which reflections of the sun ricocheted round the ceiling like an escaping genie from a bottle. She selected a glass and felt the dry champagne tickle and enlarge the roof of her mouth. This time she had the luxury of time to linger on the lunette, to stay with it and examine her first response. She marvelled afresh and felt the familiar spread of well-being; the beginnings of 'letting go', that insidious enemy of intent she knew of old.

'Hello, Isolda.'

Sandy stood not two feet away from her, in a green dress.

Isolda was suspended in a moment of incandescent disbelief. Tears pricked her eyes. She wasn't sure that if she laughed, she would not cry.

'Patrick and I were invited at the last minute,' Sandy said, and hesitated slightly. 'I wanted to say something first. Shall we get some air?' She indicated the back loggia.

This shimmering creature all done up in green was at the moment suggesting that she alone was to join her on the loggia. This 'other person' held out her freckled arm to lead the way through open glass doors. Outside there were just as many people, but it was quieter. Sandy weaved her way between them. Isolda followed blindly.

Between the pillars next to a lemon pot the green sylph stopped and rested her hand on the wall.

'I'm here with Patrick. I mean … we're together.' She looked at her.

Following the shock of being looked full in the eye, Isolda understood nothing. What were Sandy's eyes saying? Sandy seemed to be half smiling. A shy smile. Was there hope in it? Was Sandy expecting a response from her? She echoed the smile and wondered if this palpably alive presence was moving towards her. Yes, she was shyly smiling and was moving to embrace her. She felt herself losing the strength to stand.

Sandy said softly, 'I want to thank you for bringing me and Patrick together, Isolda.'

Isolda's knees partially gave way as she stretched out to the balustrade to steady herself. Her glass smashed and hit the tiled floor, and now the moment had vanished. There was confusion: people milling about: Sandy picking up the broken glass, a maid bustling towards them.

She stood by the column and felt a gossamer weight on her feet. Her shawl had slipped off. As Sandy came over to pick it up the nearness of her hand caused goose pimples to spread up from her foot; and when she handed the shawl to her, she saw again the light carapace of red gold hairs on her arm. Too close, she was too close. How did she dare stand so close and not touch?

'You see, Patrick told me how you felt about me.'

She smelt warm patchouli.

'And I want to say, I think you are a truly amazing person.' Her pounding proximity quickened.

'And somebody is going to be lucky to have someone like you loving them. But not me though. Sorry.'

She touched her, then. Lightly on the arm; and peered at her uncertainly through a few strands of Pre-Raphaelite hair. Her head turned quickly. 'Oh look!' she said, and beckoned to a nearby footman. 'Over here! *Portaloqui, per favore!*' and reached out to take a fresh glass of champagne.

The glass was offered to Isolda. She took it.

'Anyway …' Sandy paused. 'We're sure to bump into each other,' she concluded.

And she was gone. Gone. It was goodbye. Finally, she'd grasped what it was all about. She'd been dismissed. Brushed aside. And that was that.

She alone was responsible for this. She had handed Patrick over on a plate; engineered every move in fact; worst of all, made evident her own irrelevance.

And she was left behind. Living, breathing, panicking, having to live her life.

The champagne tasted metallic. She laid down the glass and turned towards the garden.

Unseeing as a ghost she moved away from the loggia and followed the remembered path of Tancredi's tour. Invisible fountains, sculptures, water garden passed her by. The mazed parterres were a vaguely perceived hindrance she avoided; and it wasn't until she saw its domed roof that she was drawn to the grotto.

Inside, votive candles had been placed within small recesses and somebody had provided two folding chairs. She sat down. It was private here, and dark, out of the sun. A carved satyr grinned and his nymphs peered through the stone leaves of the grotto's walls. Apart from them she was alone listening to a trickle of water.

'*Pronto!*'

It was the cracked voice of a witch!

She scanned the nooks and crannies around her and saw a movement up near the ceiling next to a stone scallop shell. A parrot was sharpening its beak on the corroded stone. He sailed down to perch on the marble head of Juno lifting her arm heavenwards, and rocked backwards and forwards as he tried to find his balance.

One of the open arches to the garden dimmed as a tall figure filled the space. The parrot took off with a screech, flying round the circular upper walls of the grotto until he found his niche again near the scallop shell. Here he tucked himself.

The figure muttered as its walking stick probed the shadowy interior of the grotto.

Isolda stiffened. This woman was old and unsteady on her feet, half blind, most likely. She must announce her presence before she gave her the fright of her life. She spoke Italian.

'Good evening, signora. Please come and join me. I am over here.'
The old lady stood swaying on her feet.

'Papageno?' she called. The voice was low and musically enunciated.
It was the puppet!

Isolda leaped up.

'Good evening, Signora Pazzi. I am Rose's friend, Isolda. Do you remember, we met?'

Signora Pazzi's sentences were as slow-moving as the sea bed. 'I knew he would be here. The woman has gone back without him.'

'Ah, that would be Sylvia! I'd say he is a wise old bird.'

An extraordinarily soft, subtle chucking sound began in the old lady's throat which, as it rose in scale, turned into a rapid cackle before it cut off abruptly.

She was mad. The puppet was mad.

'Do sit down, Signora Pazzi. There's a chair over here.'

'Lead me to it, I can't see.'

Isolda took her broom handle of an arm and guided her to her own chair. She herself took the other chair which creaked slightly making Papageno shuffle on his perch. She kept a sharp eye on the bird. And then she took a closer look at Signora Pazzi. She wasn't old. Anorexic, rickety, but not old.

She said, boisterously, 'I'm looking forward to the concert.'

Once more the cackling giggle soared up the scale and cut out at its height.

'Tancredi gave me a smoke to liven me up,' droned Signora Pazzi.

So that was it! Tancredi had fed her a spliff. She was stoned.

Papageno was shuffling about again up near the scallop shell; Isolda didn't like it, he was getting restless. What was she doing here? She was sandwiched. Paralysed between two mad creatures! She stole a look at Signora Pazzi. Silent tears streamed down her cheeks, her mouth open. A single Aaaaah was released with gathering anguish.

Oh God, this was different. This was grief. Unmistakable, inescapable. Isolda felt the weight inside her own chest and let it go. It was noisy but over in seconds. The relief took longer, seeping through her; and she wanted to hold onto it, to savour every bit of it. Signora Pazzi turned to her and Isolda put her arms around the fragile shoulders and held her close. And here to two women stayed for as long as they wanted, clutched in mutual catharsis; until at long last, a drowsy comfort spread between them and they drew apart. And when Isolda opened her eyes and looked around them, nymphs and shepherds had come out of the stony wood, frozen in everlasting play, while Juno, in her bounty, saluted them.

Papageno took off and sailed out of the open arch into the garden.

Isolda stood at the top of the steps where she was able to take a quick look at the theatre before the audience was summoned. Rows of folding chairs had been arranged on the lawn of the auditorium, and on stage a solitary young man tuned a harpsichord surrounded by empty music stands. Forming a fast-receding backcloth the tips of cypress and umbrella pine were catching the last of the sinking sun. Suddenly they dimmed as the sun vanished. Somebody turned on the electricity hidden behind the line of tiny bushes shielding the footlights, and the theatre was revealed in dynamic form. With the scene lit, dark banks of clipped yew hedges emerged to take their proper place as the wings of the stage.

She remembered the Burly One's amazing performance when they'd first been shown the theatre, followed by Tancredi's consternation when he realised he was about to open his fly buttons and reveal his appendage. Was it any wonder? The copious bulge beneath the Burly One's trousers was enough to alert even the least observant. She took her imagination one step further, and then wished she hadn't. A delayed shudder caught up with her.

The lights went out and an electrician came on with a bulb in his hand. He ducked behind a marble shepherdess on her plinth to replace the dead spotlight, and as he walked back to his place in the wings, another man appeared from a little further upstage. He climbed the steps towards the central Doric arch and slipped round the side. The lights came on, and for a few moments Isolda grappled with a sense of disbelief. It was Rankine.

Was it Rankine? The lights had been out. What was he doing here? She needed a drink. The whole Signora Pazzi episode had left her light headed, especially after dealing with Giselli's consternation when she'd handed her over. And where was Tancredi? He was her host, she deserved better. She turned and headed towards the nucleus of chatter nearby. Here there would be more to drink for certain.

She was right. There was a trestle table covered by a damask tablecloth in the corner of the water garden, darkened now by overhanging trees. She whisked a *bruschetta* from a small feast of goodies and crammed it, unyielding, into her mouth. It wouldn't go down, her mouth was dry. But never mind, the space beneath the table was gratifyingly filled with perspiring ice buckets.

She cast her eye around. Groups of people had gathered in clusters round the fountain. Abstractly she watched the footman's grave acquiescence behind the table as he filled her glass for the third time in quick succession. She was drinking this stuff like water, but sadly, still a bystander. Just as well, she had too much to think about. What were you doing behind the scenes, Rankine? What am I missing? Rankine, I need to be in the picture. If this is routine security, there must be more of you, where are you all? She looked around at the impeccable grooming, the expensive hair, the aging diamonds, and realised Tancredi's guests all knew each other. They'd spot a policeman at once, and so would she. She felt an unwelcome stab of disappointment. He'd left her in the dark, damn him to hell.

Two women sat on the stone wall and bent over to graze their fingers and drooping bracelets over the surface of the pool. Baccio Bandinelli's fish spewed its fine jet of water upwards while Isolda frowned at the choppy water scattering a million reflected flames from the torches. It was I who identified the sculptor of this *putto* and his fish for you, Tancredi, remember? It was my triumph on the day of the cucumber sandwiches – the *vanishing* cucumber sandwiches – I am waiting for a few words of welcome. She felt distinctly combative, a familiar mood from which a residual breeze passed through her mind disturbing a string of tiny alarm bells. Oh, who cared what social misdemeanours she might be tempted to commit? She might as well be invisible for all the attention she'd had. Not a single dowager had acknowledged her presence, let alone a solitary lounge lizard. She glanced down at the shawl atop her scarlet dress and decided she looked frowsy. She was bored with this combination, she'd spent too long looking at it. Why shouldn't she tie the shawl around her head as a turban with a long tasselled tail falling over her ear? The effect would be electrifying – haute couture at a single stroke. She removed her shawl with a flourish – and then fell still. Her host was approaching.

Her hands turned wet. She cursed the third glass of champagne. It was difficult to know if Tancredi was making an attempt to cross the water garden specifically to speak to her, hampered as he was by sallies from the crowd. She watched dowagers cravenly plucking at his sleeve. It was unseemly, *she* wanted to speak to him. There were certain unfrivolous things to talk about: questions; a veiled warning certainly. She was on the point of latching herself onto his entourage when she stopped; she was right: he was on his way over to her. He looked up twice and met her eye with what seemed to be the light of recognition. With difficulty she stayed at her post near the fountain and watched him making his royal progress, gracefully acknowledging his courtiers from left to right.

'Good evening, I hope you are enjoying yourself.'

He stood, she thought, rather close to her as if he were about to deliver a confidence, in addition to which there was a tantalising scent about him that made her want to get closer.

'Oh, your garden at night is, is …' she threw out her hands and clapped them together. (She was actually embarrassing herself, she must have downed half a bottle.)

Tancredi nodded as if compliments were his due to be paid and dispensed with as rapidly as possible.

And then she detected a warmth, an intimacy almost.

'My sister-in-law tells me that you have been very kind to her. I hope that you will join us this evening for a light supper after the concert.' He shrugged by way of dismissing the importance of his invitation. 'Small. Informal. The family.'

The stage was set, the audience more or less settled, the musicians anticipated. Dazed and unable to concentrate on anything but Tancredi's 'small, informal family supper' and especially the opportunities arising from this small, informal family supper, Isolda was yet sufficiently unsure of her mental acuity, should the moment arrive, to deal with anything that was not directly concerned with this small, informal family supper, and so had deliberately chosen to sit at the end of the back row as far from Sandy as possible. She needed some detachment from the audience while she pretended to listen to the concert in order to prepare herself, and by sheer dint of concentration, get herself sober.

A cloudless evening sky arched over them, opalescent still, while torches, placed to light up steps and mark boundaries, assured them of vital guidelines for the sudden dark when it fell. A rapid lull impressed itself on the one or two stragglers who immediately subsided into their chairs. In a few moments of ensuing silence, distant sighing and chucking of nightingales could be heard from the ilex woods, and a smell of cut grass hung over the sunken auditorium.

Swiftly, Tancredi appeared from the wings and as he did so, an instant rush of applause greeted him. He walked down stage centre to bow to them, lifting his arms as if in benediction. '*Buona sera, amici*! I welcome you back to our beautiful theatre once again, to hear the music of our country played to you by international musicians from ...'

Isolda couldn't imagine why she should feel so drunk: a mere three glasses? Nevertheless if she was going to keel over in a stupor, best not to fall against her next-door neighbour. She took a quick look at the man sitting next to her: not unlike the Belcher.

The opening bars of a Vivaldi violin concerto burst with unexpected vigour from the chamber group on the platform. Far from being able to relegate the programme to background music, Isolda found herself locked in to every note. Fast and explosive, brilliantly played. In one powerful stroke it answered a hunger she hadn't known was in her, and at once, she felt the performance galvanise her fighting spirit, the impulse she was losing sight of. For the first time on this tumultuous evening, she was surfing the wave that would carry her through it.

And then came the concerto's slow movement, and with it, instant capitulation. She gasped and held her breath, but it was too late, her next-door neighbour glanced at her twice in quick succession: she was causing a disturbance. A stream of tears ran down her face. What was happening? What was this music doing to her? She rose from her seat and slipped round the back between a double wall of yew hedges encircling the theatre. There was nowhere to go. How could this happen again within an hour of her breakdown in the grotto? It was ridiculous. She fell sideways. The scratchy hedge caved in comfortably to her weight and the shawl covered her face. Loss. Infinite loss. She had lost all hope of loving her, her creamy, beautiful girl. What should she do to escape this pain? Where could she hide? She searched for somewhere to put herself in amongst the dense hedging surrounding her but there was not the smallest enclave to be seen. But why shouldn't she stay where she was? It was as private as anywhere. She would stay. She would welcome the music, embrace it, allow it to run its course. The hedge was harsh, but a refuge, it muffled embarrassing noises. It would shelter her until she was released from these devastating chords. Never again would she allow herself the indulgence of love. She would be on guard now for the rest of her life, and soon she would be untouchable.

A slight movement caught her eye, further down the grassy path between the hedges. Something grey, something lean and hairy hugging the hedge, hurrying towards her. It was the small greyhound. She caught her breath and squatted down in its path in order to waylay it; she needed to touch it, she yearned for the comfort of its warm body and doggy smell, the moist lick of its tongue in her ear, its generous breath. But it avoided her outstretched arms and slipped by her, glancing up, catching her eye as it passed. She watched it trotting away from her with its head dead level, neither too slow nor too fast, measuring its speed to avoid attention, blind to distraction, intent on its goal, down the grassy passage, It was the first time a dog had not stopped to greet her. Where was it going? It was unnatural. She felt doubly unsettled, and took some deep exploratory breaths.

The last movement had brought with it a dramatic change in mood. She noticed a discreet hand-painted signpost opposite pointing to the *gabinetto* down the path from where she had seen the dog approaching. The *gabinetto* would provide privacy.

Isolda stopped. There was a small grunt as somebody burst through an arch cut into the hedge, brushing her aside. A muscular body pelted away from her down the path ahead. He dived through another opening, and then before she could draw breath he appeared again, having taken a wrong turn, and cut directly across her field of vision into the arch opposite, tough little legs running full tilt. He was an identical build to the Burly One.

She could already see the corner of the *gabinetto*, the portable lavatory at the end of the path, and made a dash for it, desperate for invisibility. As she passed the arch through which the man had disappeared she caught sight of something untidy: a violent convulsion. Isolda stopped and moved back a pace or two to look.

In the middle of a grassy space flanked by a couple of marble statues was the Burly One with another small squat man having a boxing match. Behind them was a small garden behind a low balustrade enclosed by a semicircle of joined arches. For a minute Isolda assumed she was looking at another little theatre with the two men, actors, rehearsing a scene. The bully was wheezing, the Burly One whining and squeaking, and when the bully thought of a new reprimand he would follow it up with a rapier clip round the ear. Isolda was uncertain. Were they rehearsing? Or was she called upon to put a rescue mission into operation?

The Burly One was suddenly caught by the scruff of his neck and almost throttled while the stronger one pointed in the direction of the stage with his free hand. His voice was obviously inhibited by the need to keep his voice down, it came out as a guttural instruction millimetres from his victim's face: '*Fallo pure. Ciò che ti dico!*' What was he saying? 'Do it. Just do what I say.' Isolda tensed, this was not a play. The Burly One kicked out and caught the bully on his shin and was instantly released. He made a rapid dive onto the grass to avoid a salvo of blows and somersaulted over and over till he reached the balustrade onto which he jumped, using it as a diving board to leap several feet into the garden on the other side. His clone followed, stronger but not so agile; he struggled to keep up with the Burly One who had found a path behind the semicircle of joined arches. Isolda saw him flashing past behind the pillars, each column of stone interrupting his movement for a second, like a camera shutter. Behind him, the bully followed, hampered by a limp.

Isolda froze. She'd lost sight of both of them and was blocking their nearest exit. She wavered. The wheezing and whimpering was faintly audible. She had no idea where it was coming from but it was coming closer accompanied by strenuous squeaks. She made a dash for the *gabinetto*.

A strong round of applause marked the end of the concerto just as Isolda entered one of the two doors of the Portakabin and closed it behind her.

It was stuffy and claustrophobic and almost impossible to breathe. She wouldn't be able to stay here long; neither could she leave just for the moment. The water from the steel wash basin inside the tiny closet was blessedly cold. She splashed her face and pulled down the cover of the lavatory to sit down.

She closed her eyes and then opened them wide and forced herself to breathe. It was vital to reclaim her rational self. Hallucinating at this stage was a disadvantage, but these extraordinary visions were always momentary after binge drinking. Common sense told her she wouldn't take long to dry out. There was a scuffle outside and a bang against the wall of the Portakabin.

The Burly Ones! They had pursued her to the *gabinetto*! They were going to break the door down and haul her out! They were going to punch her to a pulp! She hugged her knees and shrivelled, a grasshopper dehydrating in the sun.

She heard two women with English voices: snatched, rising almost to the point of hysteria yet contained in whispers.

'What's the matter? What's happened?'

'It was her. She looked at me. I can't, I can't … Oh God.'

'It's alright, darling, it's alright.'

'I've got to go, *quickly*!'

The door of the next-door closet slammed open with a heavy impact on metal and as the applause died down a strong jet of liquid hit the lavatory pan.

Phoebe and Dill! Here!

A harpsichord sonata began.

'I can't go back, I just … Oh God.'

'We'll stay here, darling. You're safe with me. Sh … sh …'

'But Phoebe …' a half sob caught Dill's throat and a meandering wail took over.

'Quiet, quiet, sh, sh …'

Isolda imagined Phoebe crouched on the floor of the closet wiping Dill's tears. The door would still be open behind her to allow room for both of them.

'She was a man.'

'What do you mean, she was a man?'

'She was a footman ... and she ...' there was a further pause and the sound of a winnowing vibrato, the sort a child makes as it tries to draw breath when it has gone beyond its tether.

'What? What did she do?'

'He *looked* at me, and ... he *knew* it was me. And ...'

'Yes?'

'I thought he was going to ... But he went away.'

Isolda's first impulse was to throw open her door and offer help: to find this androgynous villain and bring either him or her to justice. But something was inhibiting her – not least that she had eavesdropped, albeit unwittingly. More than that was her own confusion. If this was the woman who had forced a kiss on Dill in San Gimignano, something she was unable to imagine however hard she tried, the fact that she had not been a woman at all but a man would at last make sense of the whole mysterious episode. The Kisser was a man.

'Dill ... are you sure it was "her"?'

There was a sob.

'Phoebe, I just *know* it was her. I just ... I just ...'

'I believe you, darling, I *believe* you. Now look ...'

The harpsichord player was reaching spectacular levels of improvised virtuosity.

'When this has finished, we must go back to our seats, and if you see her – if you see him – you must point him out straight away.'

'*Go back?*'

'Yes, darling, we're going to get a grip on ourselves and go back and calmly sit down as if nothing has happened. Nothing *has* happened, don't forget. We'll be alright.'

There was a sharp and enthusiastic blast of applause that continued for a full half-minute. It almost drowned the rush of water from the cistern as a prolonged scuffling next door indicated to Isolda that the two sisters were leaving the closet. She put her head in her hands to think.

Thinking rationally was not within her grasp. She was in a vortex: one of the many bodies swirling towards the suction, hurtling higgledy-piggledy into the centre, quicker and quicker and round and round. Tancredi, the Kisser, the Burly Ones, dowagers, Dill, lounge lizards, Signora Pazzi, Phoebe, Rankine … *Rankine*!

Isolda sat straight up and looked ahead.

She must find him. He must be warned. Would he believe her? All three of them – the Kisser and two Burly Ones – roaming round the villa gardens on the very evening when to secure an invitation was a privilege accorded only to the few was – was – what was it? Was it beyond belief? To a rational person? Were both her eyes and ears peopled with fantastical figures? She felt the slimy tentacles of doubt constricting her lungs. The atmosphere in the cubicle was as thick as soup. She had to get out. When she opened the door, it was dark outside. Rankine was waiting for her. He lifted his finger shyly from where he stood by the hedge.

With a shaft of light from the stage slanting across his face he looked uncannily like Orson Wells in *The Third Man*, but with spectacles. She stopped and stared at him from the little iron steps of the Portakabin.

She would put his reality to the test. Going straight up to him, she said, 'How did you know I was here?'

'You were suh-suh-suh-seen.'

'Seen! Who saw me?'

'C-could you k-keep your voice d-down a b-b-b-…' He moved into shadow.

Isolda felt susceptible to the slightest criticism. Had she been shouting? She followed his example and stepped out of the light.

'Rankine, I-I-I …' She heard her voice shake although she knew she'd taken the level down to a near whisper.

'Please go on.' He was attentive.

'I think there's … something strange going on.' For one moment of grotesque embarrassment she thought she was going to cry.

'Yes?'

'Well … First of all, two small fat men are fighting each other, and secondly, the woman who kissed Dill in San Gimignano is here, but she seems to be a man.'

'The transvestite. Who saw him?'

She was suffused with relief. Miraculously Rankine was informed.

'He recognised Dill and frightened her to death. He is one of the footmen.'

'Is one of the small men an acrobat?'

'He could be!'

Rankine fumbled in his pocket and brought out a packet of Gitanes. He was about to put one in his mouth when he paused and held it out in front of him as an object of momentary contemplation. Eventually, still deep in thought, he slowly put the cigarette back into the packet and returned it to his pocket.

'It's going wrong for them. It's unfortunate in a way, we're ready for them.'

'Is this "the night"?'

'This is the night, but they're in disarray. We think there may be a crisis from the top.'

'Who are they, Rankine?'

'Afraid I'll have to disappear for a moment. So sorry.'

Isolda heard the door of the Portakabin open and swung round to look. It was a dowager gathering up her skirts to climb in. She closed the door behind her with difficulty.

When Isolda turned back, Rankine had vanished. He re-emerged after a few seconds, clearly disturbed by something she had said. He looked up at her with his myopic blue eyes and hesitated.

'If you see the black American, can you mention …'

A man in evening dress appeared but stopped when he saw Rankine and casually put his hands in his pockets and looked the other way. A policeman, she suspected.

For once Rankine's usually bland plump face was distorted. 'Just – stay by him, if you don't mind, Isolda. And – keep your distance from the transvestite.'

Isolda went back to take her seat, furiously pondering her instructions. Was she to believe that Bernard was here too? Was there anyone who was not here? There was one footman standing at the bottom of the steps at the back, and as far as she could see he was a pretty boy of about sixteen, hardly the Kisser; she could relax and think for a minute. She would leave before the end of the movement and look for Bernard. But why was she doing it? How would she explain herself to him when she found him? Oh hullo, Bernard! Mind if I hang around? No, I'm perfectly satisfied with your pictures, your pictures are more than satisfactory – really! You've got more to show me! Well, ye-es, I could be interested. *Just a minute, didn't she owe him money?* Oh no, no, it was vital she stay out of his way, and if it weren't for Rankine's sudden agitation ... That was a point, why had Rankine been so alarmed suddenly? Was it the mention of the Kisser? 'The transvestite' as he called him? It was true that the man had put the fear of death into Dill, but surely Rankine hardly imagined the Kisser would wreak his violent, male fantasies on her. Isolda? Because if he tried any kind of hanky-panky with her, he'd be crying out for mercy by the time she'd finished with him. Surely Rankine saw this instinctively. So perhaps he really was dangerous; not just a lewd opportunist cruising San Gimignano for gullible tourists, but vicious, a killer, even. And was he here to get Bernard? Was that why Rankine asked her to stay by him? To protect him? To be witness to an attack perhaps? The dog. Oh my God, *of course*, it was Bernard's dog. Why weren't they together? She prepared to slip away and make a quick reconnaissance; the concert was nearly over.

The last movement of the quintet finished with a flourish. The final chord sounded, and with impeccable timing, smack on the beat, a short figure in baggy trousers shot on stage from the wings. He took a flying leap and landed with both feet centre stage to propel himself high into the air into a double forward somersault. There were gasps and squeals and the musicians rose to their feet. The figure landed safely on his feet and swivelled to face the audience. He took a hat from his pocket, crammed the hat on his bright orange wig, clapped his hands and spread his arms wide as if to say, *Howzatt!* His face was painted white with a terrible red gash across his mouth.

There was consternation. Isolda was half aware of a shot from a gun. Tancredi leaped from his seat in the front row and jumped up on stage. The clown saw him and executed a comic double-take when he spotted Tancredi staggering to get to his feet in his haste to get at him, and quickly set off at a gallop heading for the central Doric arch, turning round constantly to check that Tancredi wasn't gaining on him.

Aware suddenly of a fatal loss of dignity, Tancredi slowed down and turning to the audience, twisted his face into the appearance of a rueful smile, opened his palms and raised his shoulders in a shrug. He held his arm out to the musicians to take their bow, at which point, the clown, beneath the Doric arch, grabbed his moment to synchronise his own bow with the orchestra's, sweeping the ground with his hat in a grand circular movement. The audience was of one voice in its immediate expression of surprise. It stood and clapped and stamped its approval while releasing a stream of chatter.

Isolda's heart hammered in her chest. Did she hear a shot? Was it from the villa? Had she fatally delayed Rankine's instruction to stay close to Bernard? She'd let him down. Something bad had happened. She'd heard a shot.

Half walking, half running, Isolda headed for the water garden. The footman who had served her earlier was drinking the remains of a bottle of champagne next to the fountain. His chin, tilting up, jerked down quickly when he saw her, and his mouthful sprayed out over the gravel, a small boy caught stealing apples. It was unbelievable but neither he nor the maid collecting stray glasses was aware that anything was amiss.

But rising up towards the villa in the ascending vegetation of the garden there was activity. Movement on the flights of steps where the torches flickered; swaying, whitish blobs winding upwards. The silvery white wigs of footmen running up towards the house.

Without hesitation Isolda removed her smart shoes and leaped up the first flight of steps, making the ascent to the top so fast that very soon some shouts from the villa surprised her with their proximity. She paused to lean against the sheer outer wall of the staircase leading down from the loggia, unable to maintain her speed.

The sound of footsteps half clattering, half scuttling down the steps above her took her by surprise. A tall footman rounded the corner, almost losing his balance in unfamiliar shoes. He stopped dead in his tracks when he saw her and she heard a sharp searing sound as he drew in his breath through his teeth. Both of them, she realised, were equally lit by the torch fixed at the bottom of the steps. For seconds they stood immobilised face to face, before he remembered himself and nodded in a manner befitting his subservient position. Except that he wasn't subservient at all, he was cold and curt, and his clothes were too tight, and laughably short in the sleeve. She watched him cross in front of her, almost sauntering along the gravel towards an adjacent part of the garden, leaving behind him the unmistakable sour male smell of fear. Footsteps running down the same set of steps caused her to flatten herself against the wall. Two men in evening dress shot out from the steps and continued on down the central staircase towards the lower parterre without seeing her. If they were chasing him they'd gone the wrong way. Should she have directed them? It had all happened so quickly.

Isolda looked up at the yellow glow of the arched loggia and watched a footman run out to the balustrade. He searched below the perpendicular face of the wall for several moments, then lifted his head to look out into the darkness of the garden before going back inside.

The loggia was deserted. From the head of the staircase Isolda began walking the length of its tiled floor. Moths of varying sizes circled the torches burning low on either side of the glass doors, and the glow from the hall shone dimly though the windows to illuminate two or three lemon trees in their pots. The doors were wide open. She looked through into the Great Hall. Empty, with an open front door opposite. There seemed to be a hastily abandoned quality to this desertion, a feeling that only seconds before she appeared people had been criss-crossing the floor and going about their business in several directions. From down below she heard a distant imbroglio of china and saucepans in the kitchens and was relieved that at least life was going on somewhere in the house.

Inside, with only four globes of light positioned in the corners of the Great Hall, the frescoes were given the warmth and proximity of a dying fire. Isolda felt a palpable thrill of intimacy with the half-naked figures. Comfortably enveloped in the vast empty space, wrapped in the companionability of paint and tempera, she watched the dangers to Bernard recede; she judged Rankine's fears for him – if he was fearful at all – to be fanciful, as improbable, very likely, as her hallucinations earlier in the evening. The wild-goose chase was over. There was no shot. She breathed easily and with pleasure as her eye moved over the folds of cloth, the swell of a cheek. Here she knew where she was, it was her place in the world, it was reality. There was a movement below her eye level, almost a shadow: a skulking dog: the greyhound, picking its way guiltily towards the door into the passage. She smelt blood and looked down. There was a dark pool of it at her feet.

An exchange of shouts from the drive coincided with an attack of paralysis. Should she turn and run, or go straight to the front door and out onto the portico shouting at the top of her voice to confront the threat outside? Suddenly she felt deprived of air. To avoid suffocating, she shot towards the front door. Down below in the drive two men were escorting the tall footman to a car as Isolda burst out onto the front portico. A driver was waiting for them next to the car with its doors already open. As the three of them approached the car the footman broke free from their grip, tearing his embroidered coat in the struggle. He staggered away across the drive with over-reaching strides before he tripped and fell, hampered by handcuffs. His escorts pounced on him together, hauled him up, and, as if they were glued together, the three of them half jostled, half shuffled into the back seat. The car's sudden momentum caused the doors to slam in quick succession as it drove off leaving behind dark furrows in the gravel.

Chapter 25

He had begun with a sense of foreboding at the start of this rather splendid occasion – and it didn't surprise him in the least when he thought about all that had happened this morning. On the other hand, now the concert was under way, sitting here with Vivaldi playing and Sandy so close to him – well, the heart absolutely soared. In fact, the concert, now it had begun, was a respite: a chair to sit down in at last, and time to sift through the rather terrifying events that had taken place in the last twenty-four hours. The point was this: that he felt personally responsible for any influence coming from Il Centro, bad and good. Montecalmo had always been a refuge from the horrors that afflicted the rest of the world, it was a place where people came to paint and find spiritual refreshment. Its people were in the very tiles and stones, and as far as he understood them, hard working and law abiding; but now, in an obscure way, he felt that the origins of this new dark element were to be found somewhere in Il Centro itself; that he, as a relative newcomer, had either introduced it, or had allowed it to slip through his fingers to roam unchecked. There was that first evening of the season, just before he made his speech out on the terrace, when he'd been hit with a sense of some uncontrollable energy being unleashed. It had vanished almost immediately but the force of it was actually quite alarming. What was it exactly? He cast his eye over to the right where Tancredi sat in the front row with old Signora Pazzi (except that she wasn't so old, he had to remind himself), and next to her, the two tall sisters and Rose. Yes, Rose. He was forced to admit, it was Rose's arrival here such a relatively short time ago, a few months, that had somehow sparked off this upheaval. It wasn't her doing, of that he was sure; she was definitely a force to be reckoned with, but underneath, a sweet, genuine girl – and surprisingly brave. She'd battled on incredibly well after Alfredo's death. And to perform surgery! For all that, her very presence seemed to have shaken Montecalmo to the core. Her telephone call on the terrace this morning had been a bolt from the blue. Worse, it had completely wiped out any chance of teaching for the day.

His first thought was to phone Sacchetti. If someone is out to kill you your first move is to get in the *carabinieri*. But no, Rose would have none of it. He was immediately embroiled in heavy cloak-and-dagger stuff. Antonio had to be concealed inside Il Centro because he needed to be kept out of harm's way while he came to a decision. He wouldn't mind betting the 'decision' had already been made by Rose, and that Antonio merely had to be persuaded that it was the right thing to do. The poor man was in terrible shape, dreadful pain, almost unrecognisable as the Michelangelo's *Adam* he had waved off to America five or six years ago. Of course, it could be that Rose's indomitable strength of mind was what he needed. She had certainly acquired invitations to the concert in double-quick time for himself and Sandy, not to mention the two tall sisters – it had left them all quite breathless. Briefly, he tried to imagine Rose negotiating her terms for extra invitations from Tancredi, but it was beyond him. He felt a stab of outrage. What she entirely failed to see was that he, and he alone, was responsible for all his students, every one of them. He absolutely *could not risk* allowing a convicted killer on the loose anywhere near Il Centro. And what's more, he'd said so – and a fat lot of good it had done him.

Well, that was the end of the Vivaldi, and an excellent performance it was! The two sisters in the front row shot up and seemed to be in a fearful hurry to get somewhere, the *gabinetto* he supposed. They looked different. It was something about the blonde one, her cowed shoulders and abject dependency on her sister, who looked so fierce and tight lipped, absolutely charging along holding her hand. He had a disturbing image of the blonde sister outside his office after her trip to San Gimignano. God knows what had happened to her there, he had never been able to work it out. There again, the incident seemed to be yet more evidence of the dark undercurrents dragging so many of them along with it, and he included himself.

Ah, a harpsichord sonata! Absolutely no chin, the fellow. Spectacularly good, though. Obviously one of those odd psychological compensations, triumph over adversity.

He couldn't forget Antonio's face lying back in the pillows, ravaged by pain, infinitely sad. Whatever it was that had happened to him in the intervening years, it must have been devastating. He'd had to tackle him, and quickly, and in the end he'd been brutally direct, there was no alternative; Rose's whimsical ideas of coming to a 'decision' simply had to be swept aside in the interests of safety. As he understood it, Antonio's life was in immediate danger. There was nothing to be gained by delaying a call to the *carabinieri*. Antonio's reply had absolutely knocked him sideways: 'I am wanted by the *carabinieri*.'

Why hadn't Sacchetti told him? He soon realised. They knew what crime they were chasing, but the identity of the criminal was in doubt.

So that was it, Antonio was wanted for forging Old Masters. Only a painter of unusual talent could do that and get away with it. But why? His amazing fresco in the swimming pool was enough to tell you the man was an original. Forgery. Was it a failure of nerve? Money? He could hardly catch what he'd been trying to say, his voice had been so weak. 'I am coming to the end. Tell them to take me away.' Sacchetti was there before you could say snap. Although, thinking back on what Antonio had said, he wondered if it wasn't a hospital he'd asked for. Rose had been unequivocal: *carabinieri*. She'd collared Sacchetti on the way out and seemed to be furiously bargaining with him.

Then to Patrick's surprise she'd turned on her heel and was advancing with deadly purpose in his direction. He tried to step out of her way but his wrist was grasped, and to make matters even more public, she'd made no effort to lower her voice.

'Patrick! Antonio is about to make a confession to Sacchetti, and it's incredible, but he's refusing to implicate Tancredi.' She was tight lipped. 'It's *because* of him he's in such a mess; and I think Tancredi's going to do a runner. Tonight. I want you there please. After the concert, stay near me, and don't go away.' *This* was a Rose he recognised, by God!

Well, here they all were, gathered together in the Pazzi dining room, and here he was, becoming more and more persuaded that this extraordinary evening was turning out to be a pleasant surprise, altogether refreshing, especially with such a startling acrobatic display thrown in with the concert. It had the kind of improvised quality that had you holding your breath till it was over. Although, he had to admit, there was a lingering doubt in his mind as to whether Tancredi was not actually trying to put a stop to it. On the other hand, maybe the man had always had a yen for burlesque, and was only now revealing himself in his true colours – all that fulsome satisfaction after his double act with the clown was enough to persuade you of it, compliments showering in. He looked at him sitting firmly in his place at the head of the table – not, apparently, poised for flight.

He had to remember his brief for this evening: to stay by Rose and keep a strict eye on their host. And he knew it was going to be difficult – he could barely keep his eyes off the fresco covering every inch of the wall and ceiling. He had an idle shot at identifying the painter, but he couldn't be absolutely sure: eighteenth century, on all counts. And even if it was only lit by candles and the single candelabra above the dining table, you could see its hunting party very clearly, more like a jolly ballet in the open air. Imagine having a dining room like this! It conjured fantastic scenarios, gave you licence to invent yourself, no strings attached. And if it hadn't been for the fear that Tancredi might disappear at any moment, you'd think dinner was going with a terrific swing thanks to the present company; not least Rose herself, who was possessed by a kind of, dare he say, demonic energy. He was fascinated by the transformation in her. Gone was all that panic-stricken haste of the morning. Somehow she'd managed to calm herself down and gather up all his leading lights from Il Centro, and bring them here for dinner. It was unheard of, quite an extraordinary occasion. Somehow, he felt they were all in capable hands, and that she was going to be able to cope without him. Sandy, bless her, was doing her best with poor Signora Pazzi. She was a sad woman, not strong. Ah! She was actually nibbling an amaretto biscuit.

He'd missed the joke, he must concentrate; they were all laughing. But not Tancredi, he noticed. One felt that he was keeping his counsel. Had he any idea of what Rose saw ahead for him? Had anyone?

Rose was about to speak. There was a twinkle in her eye, or was it a determined glint?

'Isolda!' Rose said. 'Tell us about your adventure.'

Isolda was thrown into confusion.

'Dill would like to hear it,' Rose went on. She looked round. 'We all would. It's important.' She smiled and nodded encouragement to Isolda.

It was extraordinary how this girl was in command. Isolda, on the other hand seemed reluctant to speak. She kept looking at Tancredi.

She said, 'I wouldn't call it an adventure, but if Signore Pazzi wouldn't mind …'

Rose broke in, 'Oh, Tancredi doesn't mind, do you, Tancredi, because from now on there are going to be no more secrets.'

You could have heard a pin drop.

There was an almighty pause before Tancredi finally acceded with a disdainful bow of the head.

'Isolda?' Rose was inviting her to begin.

With half an eye on Tancredi, Isolda began slowly to tell them.

'Well, during the concert I heard a shot. And before I could get up to the villa – just below the loggia – I almost bumped into one of the footmen running down the steps. He was very tall and his clothes were too small for him.'

There was a gasp from one of the sisters, Dill, the blonde one. She buried her face in her hands with a strange sound. Phoebe put her arm around her and then swung round to face Isolda with what looked to Patrick very like venom. 'What did he look like?' she asked.

'Oh, hollow cheeked. And hard eyes.'

Phoebe said, 'That's him!'

Patrick was trying hard to grapple with the train of events, he was completely lost. He'd have to ask someone in a minute. Too late, Isolda was about to start the next part of the story.

'Inside the hall there was no one to be seen, but on the floor, I noticed a pool of blood.'

The two sisters and Sandy gasped. He absolutely dreaded what was coming next, all his worries were coming back.

'Then someone shouted from the drive, and I went to see what was happening. The footman was being taken to a car that was waiting to take him away. Police, I think.'

Dill whispered, hardly audible, 'Whose blood was it?'

Isolda shook her head. 'I don't know.'

'Thank you, Isolda,' Rose said.

Patrick looked over to Sandy. There was no doubt she was as much in the dark as he was. He directed his question at Rose. 'Who was the footman?'

They all spoke at once.

Rose said, 'A contract killer. There's a big prison near here. He escaped from it last year.'

'Dill was attacked by him in San Gimignano when he was disguised as a woman,' Phoebe said.

'I knew he wasn't a transvestite, not a real one,' Isolda was the last to be heard.

Tancredi stood up.

'Would you excuse me?' he prepared to leave the table.

Rose was on her feet immediately.

'Not yet, Tancredi. Please sit down, I haven't finished.'

'I have finished. I have heard enough.'

'Not everything.'

'I am sure our guests will be happy to have coffee on the loggia where, of course, I will join them later.'

Patrick tensed his legs, preparing himself for action. He looked at Rose. She was bright pink, absolutely on fire, but in control.

'The police are outside,' she said.

'Then they will know where to find me.'

'They have wanted you for questioning all day.' Rose nodded to the footman standing by the door and he slipped out. 'But, they've agreed to wait.'

Signora Pazzi whimpered and her hands began to shake.

Rose was clearly fighting her own distress. 'It's alright, Mama. Don't be afraid.'

Patrick relaxed back into his chair and Isolda got up quickly and asked Sandy to give up her chair next to Signora Pazzi. She took Sandy's place and held the old lady's hands in hers. Meanwhile, Sandy came to sit by Patrick in Isolda's chair. He caught her eye and took her hand.

Tancredi looked as white as a sheet and sat down slowly.

The door opened and Antonio walked in with his arm in a sling.

Tancredi gasped as he leaped to his feet again, his face shockingly undone.

'*Cos'è successo?*'

'*Una pallottola, ma non è niente.*'

Tancredi's eyes bulged '*A bullet*! Where? Where did it happen?'

'Outside the village – but I am better.' Antonio passed it off lightly.

Rose crossed the room to take Antonio by the hand and lead him to her place at the table. Clearly observing Tancredi's near emotional collapse at the sight of Antonio she had paused for a few seconds to allow them to speak. She continued, 'This is Antonio Gozzoli, otherwise known as Toni Vasari or Antonio Tura,' she announced, and then went on to introduce the two sisters and Isolda to Antonio.

Interestingly, his face had lost all its tension, a perfectly empty canvas.

There was a short pause before Rose said, 'Antonio has something to say to Tancredi.'

Now there was confusion. Patrick half rose from his chair together with Sandy and the two sisters, until Rose stopped them all. 'Oh, please stay!' she called out. 'I want you to be here, everybody.'

They all settled back in their seats.

Antonio turned to Rose and murmured something.

She replied quietly, 'I know, but they are my friends, Antonio. I need them to be here.' She was all strength. 'It's different now. It's alright. You can say anything you want.'

Antonio raised his eyes to Tancredi, who seemed to have had the breath knocked from his body.

'I decided to give myself up to the *carabinieri*. I have told them only that I counterfeit paintings. When they ask me about you, I remain silent.'

Tancredi subsided into his chair, incomprehension clouding his features.

'Why? Why have you done this?' He glanced at Rose and nodded to himself. 'It is the girl. She made you do this.'

'No.' Antonio shook his head emphatically. 'It isn't Rose, I want to live a better life.'

Tancredi erupted, his strength rekindled. 'A better life! Are you mad? You could have lived in *luxury*! Built up a collection of your own! I paid you fantastic money. You chose to live like a peasant, a peasant …'

Antonio's shoulders were beginning to shake and his head fell back a little as he winced. Patrick realised he had started to laugh until he was caught with the pain from his shoulder.

'I am a peasant,' he said, 'and peasants do not build collections.'

This was too much for Tancredi, he was almost apoplectic – on the point of tears almost. 'What are you talking about? You know more about fine art than any historian in the Uffizi you care to name!'

All traces of irony left Antonio's face. 'Do you forget? You have forgotten. Because of us, Alfredo was killed. And again it has happened. Again. Because they couldn't find *me*—' he struck his chest with an open hand, '— they killed Bernard.' He diminished like a pricked balloon.

'Bernard!' Isolda leant forward. 'Not Bernard?'

Antonio looked at her. 'You knew him? He was my friend. He taught me about jazz.'

'He was a tramp!' Tancredi was close to outrage.

'He gave you beautiful drawings. And what did Bernard get from you? Nothing, peanuts.'

'What was the point? He spent it on drugs!' Tancredi's voice had soared up the scale to break beyond its natural pitch into the accidental squeak of a stringed instrument.

'Yes,' Antonio nodded, 'and now he is dead.'

Tancredi released an inaudible expletive and batted the air with the back of his hand as if to dismiss the company around him.

'I have endured this nonsense for too long. I cannot stay here.' He swung away from the table.

Patrick leaped up as Rose cried out to Tancredi, 'Stop! I have something to say.'

Tancredi noticed Patrick move towards him and was taken aback; his confusion stopped him for a moment. He turned from Rose and back to Patrick, and, noting their collusion, returned stonily to his place. He waited to hear what Rose had to say, but was casting his eyes around the room in an insolent manner.

She spoke urgently. 'Is that right, Tancredi? Was the bullet that killed Dodo meant for Antonio? Was Dodo killed by mistake – by the Romano family – your very good customers you cheated? Oh yes, they were out for revenge, they were going to kill for it. The question was, who?'

'What are you saying? You know nothing!' Tancredi was apoplectic, but she had his attention.

'You ran Antonio to Pisa, to catch an early morning flight for Rome. But Dodo was persuaded – *persuaded*, Tancredi – to get in his car and drive up to the deserted village to look at a plot of land to build his house. "A dream location", you said.'

Tancredi looked as if he might hit her, but Rose was unstoppable.

'I was *there*, Tancredi – I heard you say that. And the killer lived in that village. I know because I've seen him there. He wears a wig and dresses like a woman.'

Dill stifled a cry.

'Well it didn't take much to persuade Dodo. He was all ready to go. But then something happened. The car had a flat tyre ...' She waited and looked at Tancredi long and hard. Augustina clapped a hand over her mouth, a knife clattered on a plate. Rose continued, 'But that was alright, because he could use Antonio's motorbike, he'd left it behind with you when you drove him to Pisa.' She paused again. Tancredi's face was cold and inscrutable, but he was listening.

'So, of course, Dodo was – well – an unexpected ride on a big motorbike!' She took a minute to control her emotions before she went on. 'The killer would have seen Dodo ride up, because, you see, every time the dogs barked he came to the window to have a look, I've seen him.'

Her voice was beginning to shudder slightly. Patrick was on the point of intervening.

'Well, Dodo was a sitting target, riding slowly up that steep hill. So easy, and ... then, how simple to find a boar's head, they throw plenty to the dogs ... and there are plenty of dogs ... behind the netting.' Her voice was beginning to falter, she flashed an appeal to Antonio. He immediately moved to stand close to her.

'Did you know already, Tancredi?' she asked him, straight out, her eyes level with his.

'What are you saying? Of course not. I knew none of this – *none* of it.' All this time he had been obsessively stretching his arms and plucking at his shirt cuffs, only pausing to frown at his lapels before flicking away specks of dust.

'You didn't know that Antonio was your son?'

He stopped all movement and swung his head round to look at everybody in the room. It was quite clear the man was thunderstruck, floundering. They were all of them at sea.

Antonio's hand came up to wipe perspiration from his brow. He took a grubby packet from his pocket. 'I read a letter from my mother yesterday,' he said. He walked over to Tancredi and laid the packet in front of him. 'She sent these pearls for you to look at.'

'For *me*?' It was as if a gadfly had landed on his nose. Tancredi picked up the rather foul disintegrating polythene, and something slid onto the table. He picked it up and looked at it dangling down between his thumb and forefinger. It appeared to be a necklace.

Slowly, Tancredi's whole demeanour began to fragment and then collect itself. He simply stayed where he was, not moving. 'Galia!' he said.

'Galia was my mother,' Antonio said. 'She died. After I was born.'

The necklace broke, releasing the small yellowish grey beads onto the dining table, bouncing and rolling everywhere over the polished wood. Arms came out from right and left to pick them up, and hands cupped to catch them as they dropped towards the floor.

Tancredi was looking at Antonio as if for the first time. His lips parted slowly while he tried to deal with the news. He seemed to be trying to grasp at speech, but without the breath to carry it. When it came it was no more than a whisper: 'My son.' He nipped his lips together and whipped a handkerchief from his pocket to press into his face. He took a deep breath, but made no sound. The man was rigid.

They all heard it: a hollow groan that appeared to be dragged up from somewhere very deep. Patrick felt Sandy take his hand and move closer to him. She was transfixed on Tancredi; but, the sound did not come from Tancredi.

Augustina was slowly rising to her feet, every part of her body as stiff as her brother-in-law's. Patrick was aware of a very high degree of anger, tightly contained. It was pure, not twisted in any way. Somehow, it held authority. You could trust it.

Her eyes were like gimlets as she leaned towards Tancredi, not the flicker of a muscle in her face. And there she waited, sheer willpower forcing him to look at her. Finally, Tancredi exposed his face. She remained in her place, invincible.

'You *betrayed* our family.'

'Augustina.' Tancredi's voice had softened. 'Augustina, I was young, I was a young man.'

'Pah! Of course!' she exploded sharply with a dismissive gesture of her hand. Maintaining her eye level, she leaned further towards him. 'When Dodo didn't come back, I telephoned Cornero. I asked him, "Who owns this plot of land?" And he said, "We think it is the Romanos. They want to build a holiday complex. It will cover the hill."' Nodding slightly, she stood back to survey his mesmerised face. And now she began to breathe in snatches as her memory sharpened. 'I was afraid. I knew it could be dangerous. I said to you, Alfredo is not back. Please. Go. Find him.' She had moved towards him again as if reliving her entreaty.

Tancredi threw out his arms. 'He wanted a house. I was doing him a favour!'

'*Your hands were black that morning.*' It came out like gunshot. She took a step back. There was no mistaking her message. 'Black. You sent him to be killed, so the villa could be yours!'

Augustina turned aside to reveal her profile to him and closed her eyes. 'And now you have a son.'

She began to lose control; her features cracked open into ugly distortion. Isolda reached out to her but Augustina focused on something outside herself suddenly. Her features abruptly re-formed in a fresh mould: quickly she described the cross; hastily she tilted her face up to the candelabra on an undercurrent of prayer. Then, with eyes shut and hands pressed together, Augustina sank onto her chair in prayer.

Tancredi stared at her for several seconds. He released an involuntary shout followed by a convulsion of the shoulders that locked him into a suspended intake of breath. Holding his free arm out as if to fend off further communication, his hand clamped over his mouth he moved quickly towards the wall opposite the double doors. Here the fresco had been extended over a narrow door, to include it in the picture. This door had a small pewter handle. Patrick had been facing it all evening, but hadn't noticed it. The door opened for Tancredi and he stepped through it as if through thin air.

They were all immobilised, eyes fixed on the closed door.

Rose whipped her head round to stare at him, wild eyed. '*Patrick!*'

He was galvanised as everyone stepped aside for him. As he arrived at the door he reached for the handle and froze as he heard Rose's voice call out 'Stop!' He turned to her.

She was a picture of indecision: pitched towards him, yet rooted to the floor, her hands reaching towards him, as if sleep-walking. What did she want him to do?

'*Now!* Go!' she instructed.

He wrenched open the door and almost fell into a long narrow passage that finished in a flight of stairs. Quite empty. Where was he? These were servants' quarters, evidently, unpainted and under-lit, and might have connected to the kitchen. He called out 'Signore Pazzi!' and then ran the length of the passage to the top of the stairs. He paused for a moment before continuing down to the foot of the staircase where two doorless passages converged and stretched away into a murky distance. Here it was completely silent. There was no one to be seen. Furthermore there was no sense of anyone having been here. He made his way quickly up again.

They were all exactly as he left them, grouped round the table in frozen attitudes of shock.

'He's not there. It's deserted,' he said to Rose.

'There's a concealed door.' She spoke so quietly, he had to crane forward to hear her.

The footman standing by the double doors left the room. Within seconds, half a dozen men were inside the dining room with them. They fanned round the table – police – all in plain clothes.

'Where is Sacchetti?' Rose asked one of them.

'Sacchetti is not here,' came the curt reply.

'I have a guarantee from Sacchetti—'

The footman pushed past, leading the way to the small door that Patrick had left ajar. He and a policeman both plunged through. Rose stood directly in front of Antonio to prevent two *carabinieri* putting him in handcuffs.

Antonio adroitly walked round her and offered his healthy arm to them. He spoke to her softly. 'Rosa. We have broken the bargain, Tancredi has gone.'

Rose buried her face in her hands. Patrick looked at her helplessly; what was he supposed to have done? She looked up at Antonio, her eyes appealing to him. Antonio was escorted from the room in handcuffs, his head twisting round to look at Rose.

As he left, Rankine came in, very much out of breath. He made a quick appraisal of the room and relayed a rapid message to one of the men, then lifted his head to address them all.

'Sorry but may we cuh … clear the room?' He pushed the big double doors wide open.

'Yes, of course,' Rose said, back in control. 'I will take Mama up to her rooms and …' she included all of them '… there will be coffee on the loggia. Please – can you wait for me there?'

As Patrick led the way he turned to have one more look at Augustina, a diminutive figure in a dim pool of light from the candelabra, the low, insistent litany pushed out at the start of every diminishing cadence. When Rose touched her shoulder, slowly she turned as if waking from a dream, and lifted up her face to her daughter-in-law. And, in that moment, there came such a softening of her features that for a few seconds, Patrick was captivated. There was an element of wonder in her expression. Was it gratitude? She took Rose's hand and patted it. He felt he was witness to an extraordinary moment.

He walked through the double doors into the corridor outside and was immediately brought to a standstill. Two more *carabinieri*, one in evening dress, half rose from their chairs. When they recognised Patrick and his party from La Centra D'Arte, they nodded and ushered them through to the Great Hall at the end of the passage. He looked round at Sandy and his students. All very sober. They were looking at him to guide them.

They made their way to the Great Hall and out through the open French doors onto the loggia where it had turned quite cool, he noticed.

Chapter 26

They all sat in silence listening to nightingales and frogs. How could they do otherwise? Moths circled round the flames of the torches which were only just flickering now. Scorched corpses were scattered on the tiles like bits of fluff. If you stood up to look out over the balustrade, you could still see the low glimmer of a torch lighting a staircase down into the garden.

Patrick felt acutely that he'd let Rose down. He only half understood her ambivalence. She had fatally delayed him, yet moments later, spurred him on. Did she want the outcome to be left to chance? Well, he'd gone. Tancredi had escaped. The villa might be riddled with secret passages for all anyone knew. Did Rose know of them?

Patrick couldn't help wondering if irreparable damage had been done: although how and to whom, he couldn't say. Enormous violence had been unleashed, they'd all felt the lash of it; yet, in some way he was beginning to feel a sense of release. He felt calm. Something had happened in that room to make it cleaner.

Yet here they were in a kind of limbo – his little party from Il Centro. He looked at Sandy and she smiled at him, caught in a shaft of light from the hall, bless her. She looked exhausted, overwhelmed, they all did. There was too much to take in. Antonio, a brilliant but directionless lad, and impeccable Tancredi with his eye for business; they could not have been further apart – and yet they were father and son. Look at the fury unleashed in Augustina to hear the news of Antonio. Why? Was it proprietorship? The Villa Pazzi was always going to be Dodo's. And now some woman had borne Tancredi a son: another son to the family, born out of wedlock, but – and here Patrick was guessing – with rights of kin that on Dodo's death would call into question his right of succession in the ancestral line. Supplant his memory, even. The very idea to Augustina would be an outrage. Was this the root of her fury? It was a strong reason. He couldn't forget that ice-cold resolve, it seemed to *release* something in her. In that moment, she became a younger woman almost, she shed a burden – the burden of not knowing, perhaps.

Ah yes, it was common to all of them: the insupportable burden of suspecting but not knowing about Tancredi's crime. For months she had kept quiet about her suspicions. And tonight – *it was out*! She'd been right. She realised she had been through all this – *all this* – she had suffered on behalf of Tancredi who was not only guilty but had gone even further, he'd destroyed the Pazzi lineage. No wonder she used the word 'betrayed'. It all made sense. First, Rose herself – the conveyor of truth from which the unthinkable had emerged to stun them all; and then Augustina – holding the last piece in the jigsaw, ah yes, the flat tyre and the extraordinary spectacle of Tancredi's dirty hands. And as far as Patrick could see, the circumstantial evidence, at least, was irrefutable: Tancredi had sent Dodo into Romano territory on Antonio's motorbike knowing the likely consequences. A heinous sin for Augustina. She was now in deepest prayer. He felt sure she was praying for the strength to forgive him. He would like to think so. There was already a change in her. Look at the way her face relaxed when she saw it was Rose who'd touched her shoulder! She was resilient. More than he would have imagined, there was hope for the poor woman. Yes, he believed there was a chance she would begin to heal.

There was a rattle of china behind them. Patrick rose up as if from a deep dream to take a laden tray from a small comfortable-looking woman standing in the doorway. She nodded and smiled and went to position a table on which to rest the tray before she motioned to him to sit down while she served the coffee.

The coffee was strong and steaming hot. It seemed to revive them all.

At last, surprisingly, it was Dill who broke the silence.

'Oh dear, I'm not sure I understand. Surely Tancredi couldn't possibly have …' She trailed off as she ran a distracted hand through her hair. 'I mean, I really don't think Tancredi has it in him to *kill* somebody.'

'Only Tancredi could tell you that.'

It was Rose who spoke. She stood behind them in the doorway, pinched and drained of colour. Her shoulders were drawn together as if she were cold. Patrick stood up and led her to a chair. He poured a coffee for her, took off his jacket to put round her shoulders and went back to his chair.

There was simply nothing he could think of to say. Neither was it clear precisely how Rose judged this extraordinary landslide. He looked at her – coffee beside her forgotten – huge eyes searching her conscience. When he thought of her authority over the dinner table, her command over Tancredi – astonishing! What made a woman behave in this decisive way? Love? Grief? Injustice? It was all of them. Overnight she had turned into a headstrong evangelist bent on exposing the truth. She could see that there was a need for a final reckoning in this family; she knew that it had to be done and that she could do it.

Patrick decided to take his courage in both hands and ask Rose why she had prevented him from laying his hands on Tancredi at the crucial moment.

'Why did you stop me, Rose?' he asked her as gently as he could.

She spoke in a low voice. 'Tancredi is Antonio's father.'

He realised now she'd got more than she'd bargained for, poor girl. It had been a dangerous quest, this hunt for the truth. Suddenly she was in a position of power over Tancredi's fate. And now, a new and very volatile question threatened to undermine her peace of mind. Should she keep quiet about Tancredi, or tell the *carabinieri* what she knew?

One thing had been worrying him. In fact the very idea that Rose had been in that lonely spot with the very killer that had tried to abduct her made his blood run cold.

'Rose, this woman in the window – the killer, I mean. What on earth did you do when you saw her?'

'I didn't recognise her. She looked different. It was the wig – she'd put it on in a hurry, it came down over her forehead. She was still adjusting it when she first came to the window – which is why I had time to hide my face under my hat before she saw me.'

Dill was leaning forward. 'That's exactly how she looked at the window in San Gimignano.'

'I realised afterwards who she was,' Rose said.

'Who *he* was,' Phoebe corrected her.

'The Kisser!' Isolda said. 'The Kisser who killed Bernard.' She took a sip of coffee to hide her distress.

Patrick knew now that the home of that dark genie had been here in the Villa Pazzi. Had it finally been laid to rest? There was a fifty-fifty chance, he thought. Il Centro was merely an art centre, nothing more nor less. It stood there unoffending, as it had remained for centuries, a peaceful refuge from the embattled world.

Isolda shifted uncomfortably in her chair. She cleared her throat and glanced at Patrick.

'Since Rose has said there will be no more secrets, I would like to confess mine – if nobody minds.'

She wrapped a Victorian shawl defensively round her shoulders as if to shield herself from the onslaught to come. Before Patrick could take a second look at the shawl, which struck him as oddly familiar, she looked him in the eye. His heart absolutely sank. Could he cope with this?

'All my work has been painted by Bernard, I'm afraid, Patrick – the watercolours, the pastel of the barn by moonlight. There are still two to come. You see, I can't paint for toffee.'

What was this? Isolda, who of all people was the most critical of her fellow students' work, was cheating. Strangely, certain things were falling into place. Her odd habit of striding into the hedge when he was on his way to see her was just one example. He was seized with a most immoderate laugh that may well have been heard inside the villa. It was appalling, he just let all the mirth roll out unchecked. Sandy flashed him an extremely powerful warning shot but it didn't make any difference.

'Oh, Isolda, my dear girl, my dear girl. I'm so sorry. If it weren't for this poor man … it doesn't matter a scrap, it really doesn't.' He looked at them all. Scandalised expressions wherever he turned; quickly he pulled himself together and hoped he was forgiven.

Rose said to Isolda, 'How did you come to know Bernard?'

'He was selling his pictures on the step in San Gimignano. What am I to do? I still owed him money. Oh God.'

'Antonio would like the pastel of the barn!' Rose said suddenly. 'I know he would. And if Patrick agrees, you could donate the watercolours to II Centro.'

'Of *course*! Yes of course. I'll get them framed.' She looked at Rose with something approaching admiration. 'And before I leave tomorrow, I—'

There was a chorus of opposition from Sandy and the two sisters.

Isolda was firm. 'How can I stay for another day's painting when I don't paint? Or for the end-of-term show when I've got nothing to show? I'm going to treat myself to a day in Florence. That is—' She hesitated before turning her full attention on Rose. 'Would you mind if I called on Signora Pazzi before I go, Rose? Not just to say goodbye, there is something I want to ask her.'

'Of course,' Rose answered. 'Come tomorrow after her morning prayers.' She sat huddled in Patrick's jacket.

Sandy said, 'But this doesn't mean you have to miss the end-of-term show?'

Isolda stood up.

'I'm a disreputable coward, Sandy! How can I stay here now? Even though I'd rather be here than anywhere else on earth.' She moved restlessly to the balustrade and fell still, her eyes averted.

There was a murmur of voices in the Great Hall and footsteps walked swiftly to and fro over the floor. A shadow blocked the light coming through the French doors and fell over the loggia tiles.

'*Rankine!*' Rose leaped from her chair. 'Have you found him?'

'Signore Pazzi has offered his suh-services to the *carabinieri*.'

Rose gasped. She half laughed, half cried her relief to everybody.

Rankine smiled. 'He has given a package to S-Sacchetti to give to his lawyer.'

There was a shout from the garden.

'*Avanti*! The front! The back is covered.'

A powerful searchlight blinded them suddenly before plunging them back into darkness again.

Rankine said, 'Ah! I think I m-might be needed.'

He made for the steps quickly with the beam sweeping from left to right. Before disappearing from sight, he turned back to them. 'G-gardens out of bounds, s-sorry. I'd like you all to s-stay where you are.'

They sat back in their seats a little tensely and listened to isolated shouts and the sudden illumination of branches and leaves. Footsteps running along the lower perimeter of the loggia continued up the steps towards them. Panting noisily, a man in evening dress mounted the last few steps and staggered slightly as he negotiated the lemon pots on his way to the French doors. 'Stay here,' was his terse instruction to them as he passed through into the Great Hall and out of the doors at the front. He was wearing a gun holster strapped diagonally across his shirt front.

Isolda leaned towards Rose. 'Rose, I don't care what he says, I've got to have a pee, sorry.'

'Can't you hang on?' Rose whispered. 'Then I can show you where to go.'

'No, no, no, no, I know where to go, don't worry.' Isolda was already out of her seat and moving swiftly towards the open French doors, hugging the door post and sidling round the wall of the Great Hall on the other side.

Patrick shot up and made a dive to prevent her.

Isolda hissed at him. 'No, no, don't stop me, I can't wait. Go back.'

Sandy was halfway out of her chair, 'Isolda knows what she's doing, Patrick. There's nothing you can do.'

They heard a roar of warning followed by a loud report from the front of the house, accompanied by more shouts coming from different directions.

They all rose from their chairs and looked at each other quickly.

'It's not Isolda,' Sandy said, 'She's inside.'

Footsteps ran along the gravel of the parterre below the loggia and seemed to pass round to the side of the house.

Patrick started to walk back to his chair. 'I think the rest of us must do as Rankine says and stay put.'

From the forecourt, there was a slamming of car doors and a car engine started up, followed by another. They heard Rankine call an instruction from the front portico on the other side of the Great Hall behind them.

A few seconds later, he appeared in the open French doors trying to catch his breath. A big smile spread over his face. 'We've guh-got him. Alive!'

Phoebe and Dill were almost radiant with curiosity. 'Who? Who is it? Who?'

'The tit-transvestite's driver.'

A slow suspicion was beginning to dawn on Patrick that this man was the nasty piece of work who'd been dogging his life for the past two weeks. He asked, 'Does this fellow look like a boxer and drive a clapped-out Fiat?'

'That's him.' Rankine's fleshy mouth pursed into a tight rosebud of distaste.

'And is he one of the huntsmen?' Rose asked

Rankine was heading for a chair. 'Yes, he is, and he doesn't only shoot buh-boar out there in the valley. Many a score has been settled this way, I'm afraid. By a-accident, of course.' He looked around for a chair as he was patting his pocket. 'We suspect he was responsible for the diversion created by the clown. It turned out to be an effective cover.'

Rose's hand shot up to cover her mouth. 'For the shot that killed Bernard?'

Rankine nodded. 'F-fraid so.'

'Well, Rankine,' Patrick said, 'it looks as if you have comprehensively wound it all up.'

'F-fraid not,' Rankine replied in his gentle voice. 'These two men we have are small fry, the bub-big fuh-fish are still out there.' He spotted a large basket chair and sank into it with a keen expectation of luxury.

'You look as if you need a drink, Rankine. Will coffee do you?' Patrick was already looking into the coffee pot.

'If there's any guh-going. And, um – w-would anyone m-mind if I …?' He brought out a battered packet of Gitanes from his pocket and offered them up.

'If anyone deserves a smoke, it's you, my friend.' Patrick smiled broadly at the girls. 'And, if nobody minds, I think I'll join you.' There was a moment's complicity between the two of them as a match was struck. 'But look, Rankine,' Patrick went on, 'Wasn't this going to be the night of the robbery? I mean – the big one?' He hadn't indulged in a cigarette for years, he felt a heady rush suddenly.

'That's what we all thought – Tancredi, everyone. It was a red herring. The Romano outfit knew they were going to land up with fuh-fakes because they'd been cheated by Tancredi before. Sadly, it was more effective to present the b-body of one of his fuh-forgers.'

'Are you going to catch them, Rankine – the Romanos? You've done extremely well so far.'

'I imagine the *carabinieri* are going to rely rather heavily on evidence from T-Tancredi and the tit-transvestite to put them away.'

In a flash, Patrick realised that Tancredi was going to slip out of it. To give any evidence on the Romanos would implicate him as a fraudster. And then, if the Romanos' backs were up against the wall, Tancredi's part in Dodo's death would almost certainly come to light – *if there was anything tangible there in the first place*! Patrick rubbed his forehead, he was in danger of losing sight of what had once seemed irrefutable. 'Yes, Rankine, but what about Tancredi himself?'

Rankine blinked at him in the semi-darkness and then noticed the girls stiff with tension as they bent towards him, avid for his next pronouncement.

'Ah! You see, this is a small community. People want a quiet life.' He paused and raised his eyebrows.

'What on earth do you *mean*, Rankine?' Phoebe burst out. 'I hope they're going to put him in jail.'

He thought for a few seconds before he smiled slightly. 'It's p-possible.'

'Is that all you can tell us?' Phoebe was indignant.

'Ah, well, you see, I guh-go home tomorrow. This c-case is in the hands of the *c-carabinieri.*'

Dill's round blue eyes had been resting on Rankine for some time. She leant towards him with a tentative air of incredulity. '*You're a dark horse*, Rankine.'

'Yes, we thought you were one of *us*!' Phoebe said.

Rankine acknowledged his new-found status with the vestige of a smile. He released a final puff from the stub of his Gitanes, and looked round the loggia. 'Wasn't Isolda here when I left?'

A sudden commotion: a panting, a gasping, an aborted explosion of laughter behind them caused them to swing round only to behold Isolda herself in the doorway with her arms flung high in the air.

She shouted, 'I've found the Paninis! *Both Paninis! They're both up there!*'

He usually rather enjoyed the show on the last day. There was an air of excitement and very often, when it came to hanging the work, the territorial impulse could bulge dangerously. Particularly when an especially prolific student, usually a man, insisted on hanging his every picture to take up half a studio wall. This was when he quietly slipped out here to Gianni's for a glass until the preparations were over and they'd sorted themselves out. The village was invited, of course, but very few villagers came, even though one or two tourists turned up. Kitty never missed, neither did Lucia and Giovanni. Ah yes, but they wouldn't see Giovanni this year. He'd miss old Giovanni. Mad as a hatter in his last couple of years, but then, it had been hard for him. He thought back over all those evenings when he'd shared a glass with them, hearing the same lament over and over again as one by one they'd watched their sons go off to America, quite helpless to stop them.

To be perfectly honest, he'd even miss Isolda, off on her day in Florence. The baggage! Turning up here posing as a student, already suspecting Tancredi was operating a racket; fresh from Burlington's of all places, and without a word! She had shamelessly used them, had actually arrived not having the faintest idea of how to hold a brush, nor even the slightest intention of finding out. And now, when it came to it, even she, even Isolda felt ambivalent about putting Tancredi behind bars. He found that extremely interesting. All very well if you were a member of the village community with Tancredi as the reigning Pazzi. To give evidence that would label him a criminal would give rise to all kinds of social turmoil; he could see Rankine's point. But, Isolda!

He was glad Rankine had given him a call from the airport. Surprisingly, he said he'd like to sign on there and then come back next year as a student! Tremendous! Patrick looked forward to it. He had an attractive, quirky quality to his work. Not a bad sleuth either, quietly closing in on Tancredi. His flight was being called, he realised; you could hear the traveller's panic in his voice, so Patrick plunged in quickly.

'Will it pay Tancredi to tell the *carabinieri* what he knows about the Romanos?'

'Ah. To win immunity from prosecution!'

'He'd have to watch his back, though.'

'Undoubtedly. Even with protection.'

'I'd say Tancredi has got himself into a right old fix.'

'I'd say he'll f-find a way round it, the old fuh-fox. S-see you next year!'

Was Rankine privy to Italian law? he wondered. It wouldn't surprise him, he seemed to know everything.

But now, Isolda seemed to be more preoccupied with how she was going to break the news to Burlington's. She'd been somewhat tense yesterday. 'Quite honestly, Patrick, I don't know how I'm going to present it to them. It's a bag of tricks, you realise. I mean, it's not just the Paninis, you know, this whole thing has the potential of *a major incident*! And it won't stop at Burlington's. This whole scandal is going to put the entire art establishment into free fall.' She was holding her furrowed brow in the cup of her hand before she shot up with a fresh revelation. 'And what about the investors who've spent millions on *fakes*? They are going to be baying for *blood*! Harold! Harold, what have I done? Poor Isolda, she was shaking her head, her eyes bulging. 'The most sensible thing I can do is to sell these Paninis and clear off to Argentina before it hits the headlines. Oh, Jesus.' She buried her head in her hands.

'Certainly not! Good God!' He had to be firm with her, she was getting herself into the most almighty muddle. 'Now look. There is no doubt that this is going to shake the very foundations of the art establishment. And, yes …' (he had to tread carefully) '… I know you belong to the high end of the art market which will always be there as long as we produce great art.' He had to rack his brains to find the right words to say what had to be said. 'But now look. If it gets us to re-evaluate this whole ethos of commerce in art, it might expose it as the venal poppycock it has become.' He was glad he'd got that off his chest. He went further. 'You have to ask yourself – is a beautiful painting any less beautiful because it's a forgery?'

'Probably not, if it was painted by Antonio Gozzoli.' She smiled guardedly.

'Exactly. Beauty speaks for itself!' He was firm on this. 'Yes, of course, there are going to be a few people who'll see this as a nest of hornets. They'd rather you'd left well alone, and they will undoubtedly be stung.' Isolda's eyes were closing to shut out the world. 'But on the other hand, we can't allow cheating. That is beyond question. I don't mind betting, Isolda, that when all this blows over, you will go down in art history as a shining emissary of the truth.'

'Gosh, Patrick! Is that what you think?' She was rapidly mulling it over.

'Oh, believe me, Isolda, I'm proud to know two such fearless women – you and Rose between you.'

He'd heard her visit to the Pazzi household had been complicated by some talk of adopting a dog; something, on reflection, he was absolutely not prepared to get embroiled in. He had twenty-six new students arriving on Saturday.

Now. To the business in hand.

Patrick stepped out of Gianni's, all mirrors and reflected light, and into the hot sunshine. The *campanile* was striking the quarter, almost time for proceedings to begin. Kitty's sudden dash towards him from the middle of the piazza somewhat shattered his inner calm in preparation for his speech. Especially as he had to reach out and catch her as she left the heel of her shoe in a crack.

'*Patrick*, dear! What about that extraordinary concert party! Rose has told me all about it. I've just delivered her over to Il Centro, but I couldn't find you so I came looking.'

'Good to see you, Kitty, we can walk over together.'

'Oh, that poor, wee girl, Patrick, she's madly in love with him – Antonio – the rascal! *What's he been up to?* Well, he's got about a year behind bars, but with good conduct, maybe a few months. Oh, she cried and cried, there was nothing I could do.'

'Your "poor, wee girl", Kitty, has turned into a very strong woman indeed. I have no doubt she will survive all this. But yes, I do believe she loves him.'

It was clear that Rose had not divulged the scandal of Tancredi's paternity. Wise girl.

Father Sebastiano was crossing the piazza towards them, his face wreathed in smiles.

'*Buona sera, Padre*! I trust you are well? Afraid we have to get back for the show, mustn't be late.' He waved energetically. 'Did you see the match?'

Kitty broke in. 'Now look, Patrick, is it true? Because as I am standing here, I could not believe a word of it.'

His heart missed a beat. Rose had told her. But how much? He had to tread carefully.

'Ah! Now. Are we talking about Antonio?'

Kitty remonstrated. 'We are talking about Antonio and *Tancredi*!'

'Father and son! Yes, Kitty, difficult to believe, but Tancredi seemed to accept it on the spot.'

'Well, I'll tell you something you may not have heard.' Kitty rested her hand on his arm with a dramatic air of conspiracy. They both paused soberly for a moment in front of the church to allow the significance to sink in. 'Rumour has it that Tancredi will persuade Signora Pazzi to make Antonio the beneficiary of the Pazzi estate. What do you think of that?'

'Sheer speculation, Kitty!' He wagged a reprimanding forefinger between them. 'You'll be hearing wedding bells next.'

This was encouraging! Just about everyone had surpassed themselves, there were pictures covering every conceivable inch of space. He spotted Lucia making a tour of inspection. At least half a dozen views of her house to compare as usual, and only what she'd come to expect over the years. It always charmed him to see what serious consideration she gave to every one of them.

Four small landscapes caught his eye, one of them a pastel of the barn by moonlight. Ah, yes, these were going to be passed off by Isolda as her own work. Did he say 'emissary of the truth'? Well, here they were: enchanting, all four of them; and at the very least he'd put a stop to her crazy idea of bolting off to Argentina. Mad girl! Now if *Tancredi* were to come up with the same proposal … Patrick stood stock still. The top of his scalp prickled. He was seized with a strong premonition, and with it a clear picture of the man himself, impassively examining his fingernails as he planned his immaculate disappearance. It was plausible. More than plausible, it was entirely reasonable. *That was it.* In a nutshell.

Feeling somewhat like the king of the castle, Patrick took a deep breath and reached out for an exploratory taste of wine laid out for the toast. It was sweet! Undrinkable! Unacceptable, surely? It wasn't from the consignment they'd pushed to the back of the cellar, was it, those five-litre bottles they hadn't dared show the light of day? He looked at Sandy and she winked at him. She'd decided to serve it! Thrift was laudable, but this was surely beyond the pale. They'd have to get together and decide on a line of demarcation. He had a quick look around; the wine was hardly touched. The two sisters standing near him had left their glasses on a window ledge.

'*Edward!*'

Dill threw out her arms and ran towards an uncomfortably tall man standing in the doorway looking as if he'd rather be anywhere but amid a motley crowd of students.

Dill brought him over.

'Patrick! Phoebe! Look who's arrived without telling anyone. This is my husband! Meet Edward!'

Well. This was a bit of an onslaught on the eve of his speech, however charming the fellow.

To his surprise Phoebe looked thunderous.

'Hullo, Edward, have you come to check up on Dill?'

'Not "check up",' he replied smoothly, 'scoop up. I've come to scoop her up and whisk her off to Florence where she can tell me all about art.'

'But this was supposed to be *our* holiday.'

Surely this was a bit blunt, the poor fellow had just arrived.

Dill said, 'Oh, but you're coming too, Phoebe!'

'*NO!*' Edward and Phoebe were both of one voice, in fact it was more of a shout.

Phoebe burst out, 'I can't believe this is happening. Why couldn't you stay at home and *wait* for Dill?' she was beseeching him. 'It was only another day!'

He was afraid Phoebe was going to leave the room overcome with despair. A full-scale family drama was threatening to engulf them, he could see it coming, and an unpleasant whiff of armpits was undermining his entire grip on the situation. Should he invite Edward to join in a toast with the sweet wine? Unwise.

'This is the first time – *the first time* – I've at last been able to do what I really want to do,' Phoebe was saying, 'and you've arrived in the middle of the most important day to ruin it.'

Out of the corner of his eye he saw Sandy on her way to offer Edward a glass of wine. He tried to distract her before she got to him. Too late. Edward was now lifting the glass to his lips. He took a taste and caved in slightly as if he had a raw lemon in his mouth. He seemed to be stuck, unable to straighten up. Was it cramp? His mind raced. He hoped to God it wasn't a stroke. Curbing his panic he nodded to Sandy, and she took a spoon and knocked rapidly on the glass. Looking as if he were about to sneeze, Edward was slowly recovering his composure. Patrick's first student group of the season turned to face him and instantly, it settled him; he couldn't have hoped for a better bunch.

'Congratulations to everybody! This is a very gratifying moment for me, looking round these walls. I've followed your progress very closely, and I can see there has been a great deal of hard work and real tenacity, and in some cases, much improvement. Every so often, not frequently – about every five years or so – one of our students comes up with a picture that stands out. When this happens, we like to award a prize. Two weeks' free tuition on any one of our courses.' He had a look around to enjoy their surprise. 'Well! I'm, delighted to say, a painting has emerged in a really quite startling way – you may already have spotted it. We are presenting the award to Phoebe, for her splendid watercolour of a ladder in an olive orchard. I believe we all know the ladder and the orchard very well.'

He had rarely seen such blank astonishment in a girl. He held up his hand to stem a wave of exuberance beginning to gather force.

'Before we drink a toast, and you all go and have a look at it, I'd like to draw your attention to the economy in this watercolour. A minimum of paint for the maximum effect. A misty morning permeated with light, and not a shadow in sight. Not a subject many of us would attempt. And yet, in spite of her difficulties with "suffused light" at the beginning of this course, and, I would say, partly arising from her fascination with it – Phoebe had a go. And look at the result! A painting of light that,

I have to say, stopped me in my tracks. Yes, on a morning when most of us were still in bed she captured a moment and held it. And furthermore she knew when to stop.'

As old as Giovanni himself, but clearly with life enough for the task ahead, the three standard bearers in floppy peaked hats inched slowly, slowly, through the giant portal and out into the piazza. Rose watched the cortege sway out from the church into the dazzling sunlight, each step in perfect time, every forward movement revealing more velvet, more satin, more tassels. 'Misericordia di Montecalmo' it said, embroidered on their banners. Behind them followed Father Sebastiano staring fixedly into the middle distance, swinging the incense as he intoned: *Lord, now let your servant go in peace according to thy word, for mine eyes ...* His robes swirled rhythmically in time to his step. And next, barely heavier, it seemed, than a box of matches, piled high with flowers, came Giovanni's coffin. Pall bearers bore him gently out into the piazza and slid the wooden box lightly into the hearse.

This was the moment when Rose stepped into the shadow of the portal waiting to see Lucia as she followed the coffin. Patrick had urged her to slip out before the service was over to be sure to catch Antonio in case they took him away early. And now Lucia was visible positioned directly below the soaring arch of the church doorway, her slim cheeks burnt orange-red from the sun. Her two sons had arrived for the funeral in the nick of time, and although they were on either side of her now claiming an elbow apiece, Lucia seemed indifferent to them. She stands alone, Rose thought, she always has, even with Giovanni when she had him, and now without him; it makes no difference. The smallest widow in Montecalmo. She is vigilant, following the progress of the coffin holding the wasted body of the hard man she served and whose children she loved.

Rose drew closer to the portal waiting for the right moment. She had seen Antonio standing in shadow inside the church doorway, a few strands of hair on his bowed head catching the sun. The *carabiniere* turned to look at him, still almost glued to his side (surely they weren't handcuffed?). Elusive, secretive Antonio was about to join the procession through the town in broad daylight for all to see, and within an hour he would be back in prison. Everyone would know. How could he bear it? There was a collective movement from the cortege as it swung forward. Antonio was the first to be lit in the blaze of the piazza. His jacket hung off him in folds since he'd lost so much weight and his hair was slicked back to keep it in place. He was walking lightly with a kind of leashed energy.

She stepped out quickly. He saw her hurrying towards him and stopped.

Heads turned. His bodyguard was alarmed. She fell in beside Antonio for a minute, and as he bent a little towards her, so did the *carabiniere*. For the first time Antonio seemed uncertain, almost scared.

'Will you come and see me?' he asked her, his voice was hoarse.

'Every day. Twice if they'll let me,' she replied, responding to his sudden smile. '*Mio caro.*'

His bodyguard lifted a cautionary hand.

'*A domani,*' she waved.

Rose dropped back and watched the cortege break up and rearrange itself into the final pattern for the procession; and all this time Antonio kept twisting round to look at her, never once able to wipe the smile from his face.

When Patrick came out to join her, she hugged the breath from his body.

He looked at her, faintly amazed. 'What's this all about, Rose?'

The standard bearers, arthritic but upright, began their journey to the *cimitero* drawing the hearse and mourners in their wake. They tramped softly over the cobbles past the *gelateria* on their left and the *alimentari* a little further down on their right – its shutters closed this afternoon to enable Cecilia and her husband to pay their respects to Giovanni. And at the West Gate, its towering arch framing the procession, they passed through and out of town.

With the valley ahead and all eyes fixed on the little church of San Cristofero on the hill, the crocodile snaked down to the main road that makes a detour round Montecalmo. Here they stopped while traffic came to a halt. In groups of three and four the cortege straggled cautiously across the tarmac before pausing to muster their collective strength prior to tackling the avenue up to the church. Mindful of the very old among them, the dreaming column nudged slowly upwards through the pencil shadows of cypress, and upon reaching the airy patch of ground in front of San Cristofero – fanning, nodding, dabbing – the party gathered round. Then, as if startled by a sudden noise, with one accord, each face lifted to meet a gust of wind that rushed up from the valley.

Revived, and ready now to proceed, Giovanni's mourners turned to face the gates of the *cimitero* to the right of the church. And once inside the old familiar place, every eye among them searched and found his family's vault where sentinel lamps around the enclosing walls burned steadily.

Lucia, almost dwarfed by headstones, turned suddenly and searched between the groups of villagers behind her, whereupon Antonio swiftly left his post and went to stand at her side. Together at last, Rose thought. Lucia is satisfied. For her, the time has come: Giovanni is being safely delivered to his ancestors – lusty, canny Giovanni, her lord and master for the past fifty years. And as for Antonio, her grandson, he will be going to prison for long enough to think about who he is. And when he comes out, I think he will know, and I will be here to help him find out if he doesn't.

Rose looked up. Cruising swallows that had been flying so high she had strained to see them were descending as if by some unseen signal to meet the first insects of the evening rising now from under the warm stones and grasses.